SUNBURN

IMAGE COMICS, INC.

Robert Kirkman – Chief Operating Officer
Erik Larsen – Chief Financial Officer
Todd McFarlane – President
Marc Silvestri – Chief Executive Officer
Jim Valentino – Vice President

Eric Stephenson – Publisher / Chief Creative Officer
Nicole Lapalme – Vice President of Finance
Leanna Caunter – Accounting Analyst
Sue Korpela – Accounting & HR Manager
Matt Parkinson – Vice President of Sales & Publishing Planning
Lorelei Bunjes – Vice President of Digital Strategy
Dirk Wood – Vice President of International Sales & Licensing
Ryan Brewer – International Sales & Licensing Manager
Alex Cox – Director of Direct Market Sales
Chloe Ramos – Book Market & Library Sales Manager
Emilio Bautista – Digital Sales Coordinator
Jon Schlaffman – Specialty Sales Coordinator
Kat Salazar – Vice President of PR & Marketing
Deanna Phelps – Marketing Design Manager
Drew Fitzgerald – Marketing Content Associate
Heather Doornink – Vice President of Production
Drew Gill – Art Director
Hilary DiLoreto – Print Manager
Tricia Ramos – Traffic Manager
Melissa Gifford – Content Manager
Erika Schnatz – Senior Production Artist
Wesley Griffith – Production Artist
Rich Fowlks – Production Artist

IMAGECOMICS.COM

SUNBURN

ANDI WATSON

story

SIMON GANE

art

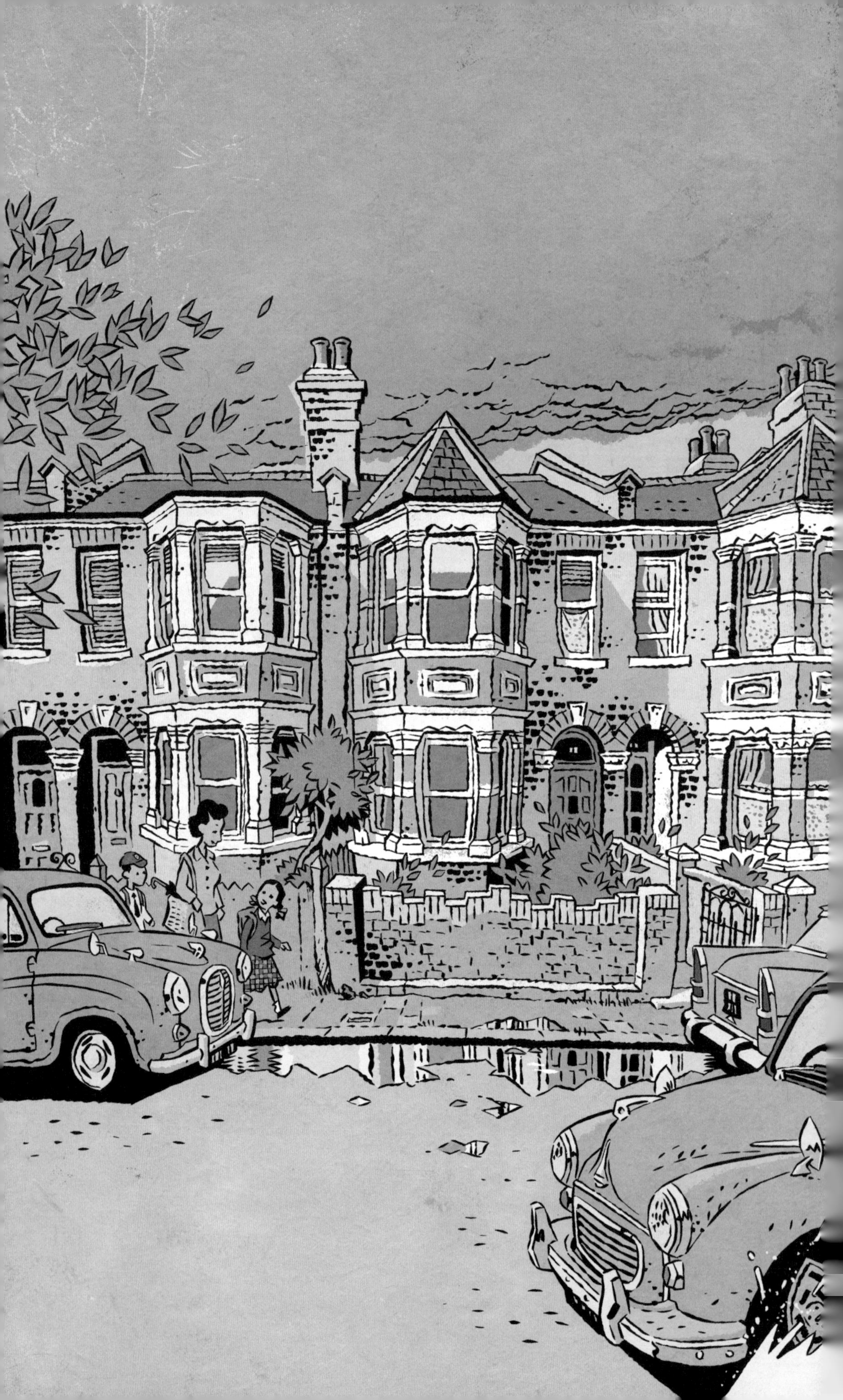

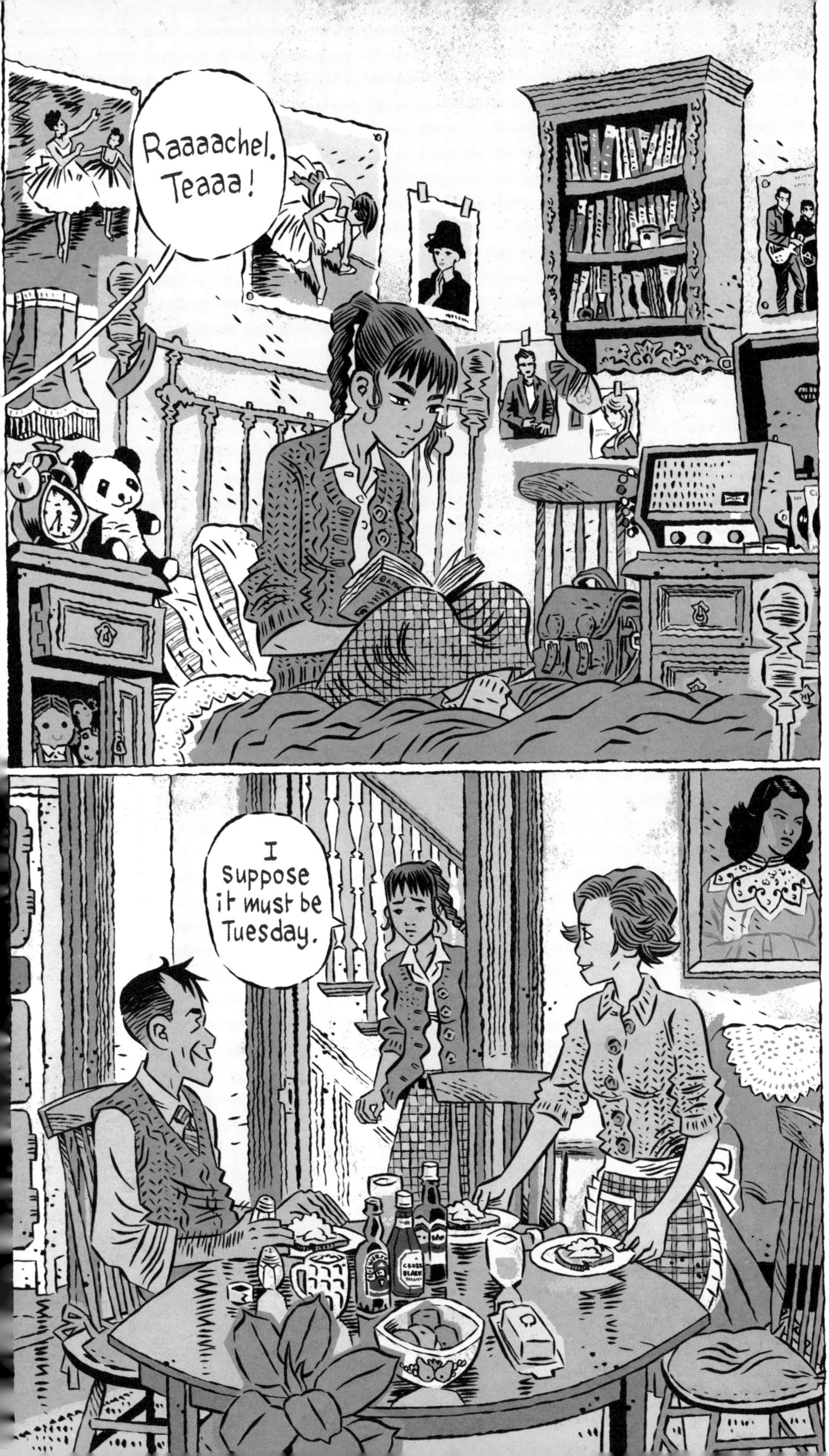
Raaaachel. Teaaa!
I suppose it must be Tuesday.

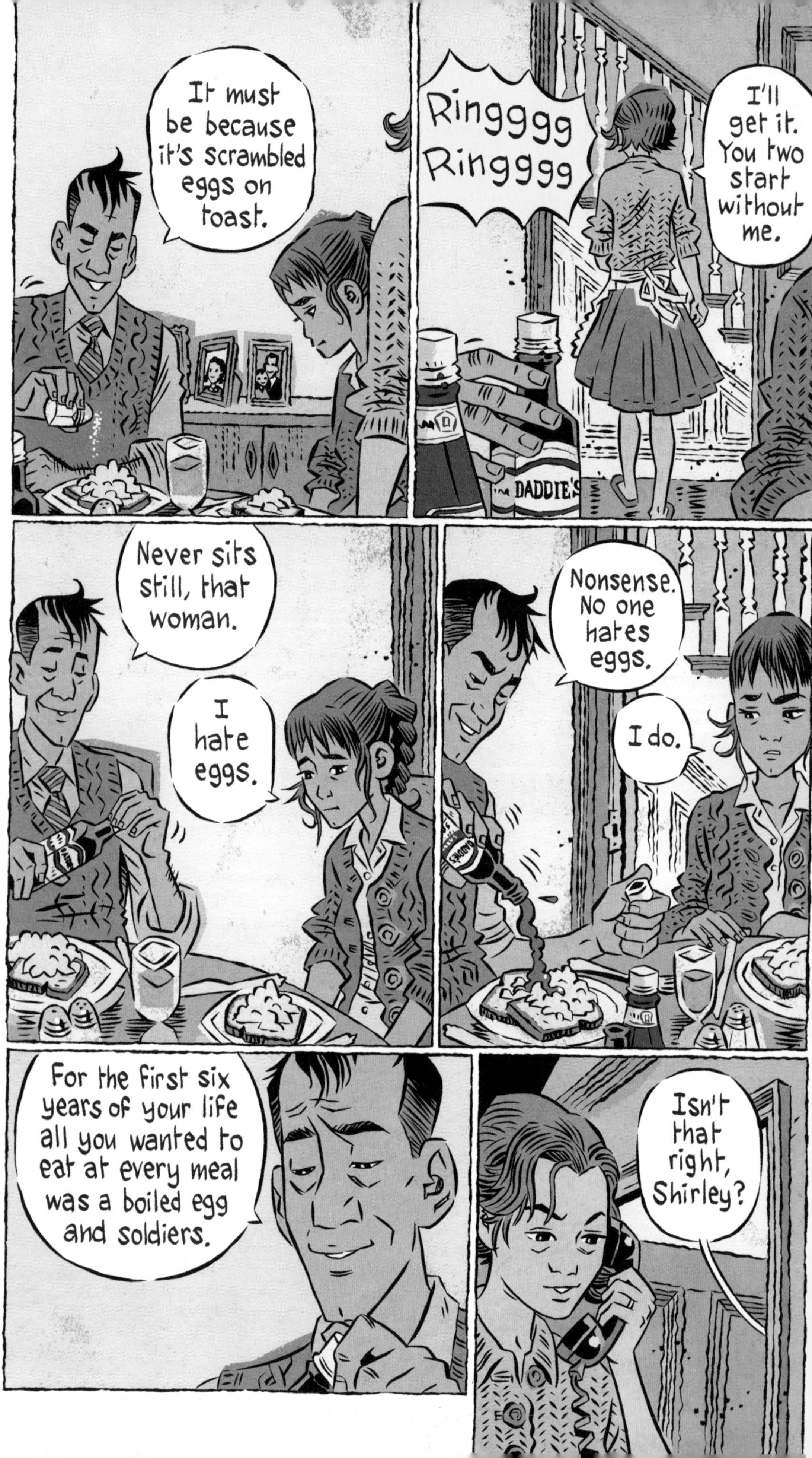
It must be because it's scrambled eggs on toast.
Ringgggg Ringgggg
I'll get it. You two start without me.
DADDIE'S
Never sits still, that woman.
I hate eggs.
Nonsense. No one hates eggs.
I do.
For the first six years of your life all you wanted to eat at every meal was a boiled egg and soldiers.
Isn't that right, Shirley?

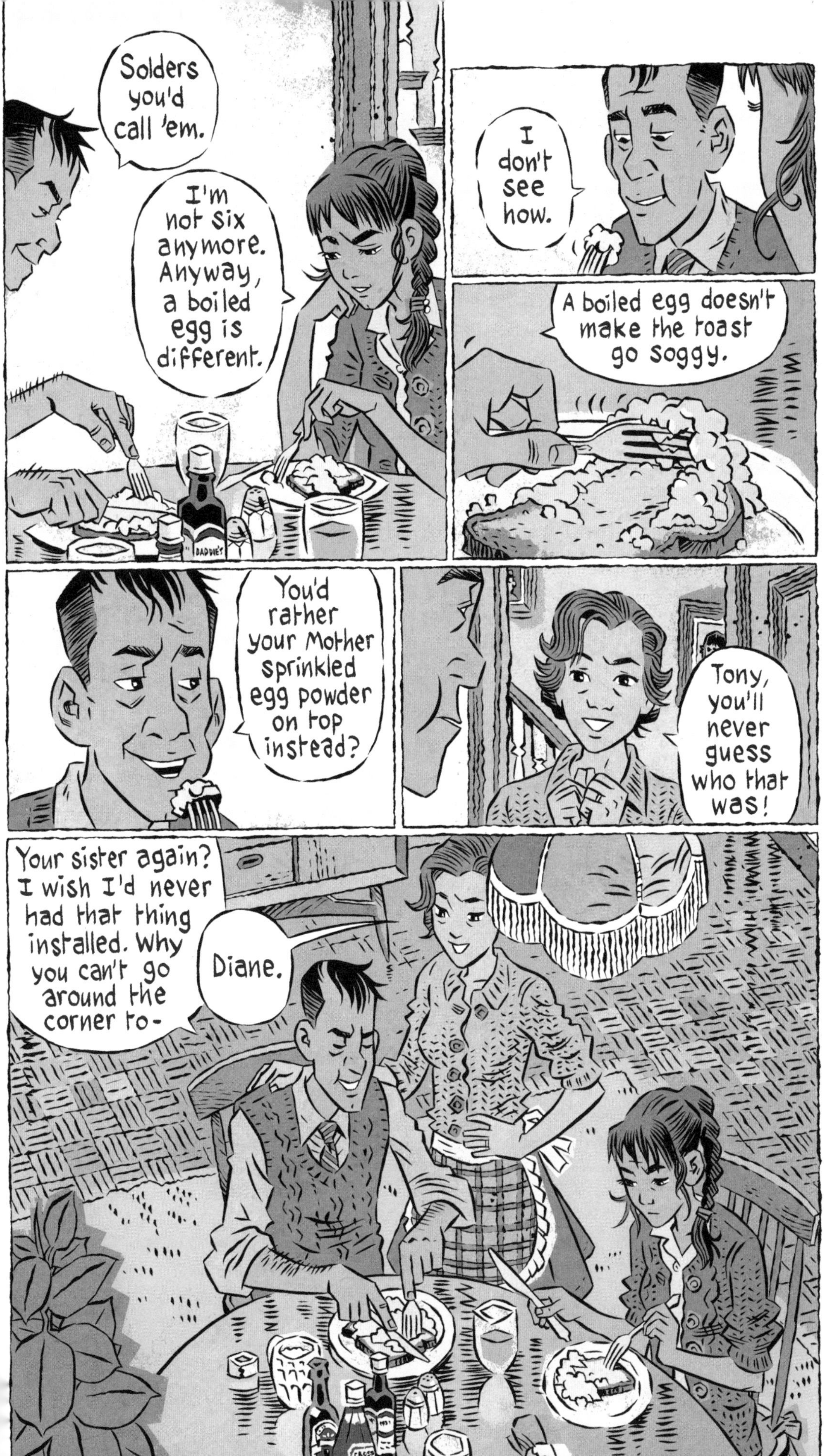
Solders you'd call 'em.
I'm not six anymore. Anyway, a boiled egg is different.
BADDIE'S
I don't see how.
A boiled egg doesn't make the toast go soggy.
You'd rather your Mother sprinkled egg powder on top instead?
Tony, you'll never guess who that was!
Your sister again? I wish I'd never had that thing installed. Why you can't go around the corner to-
Diane.

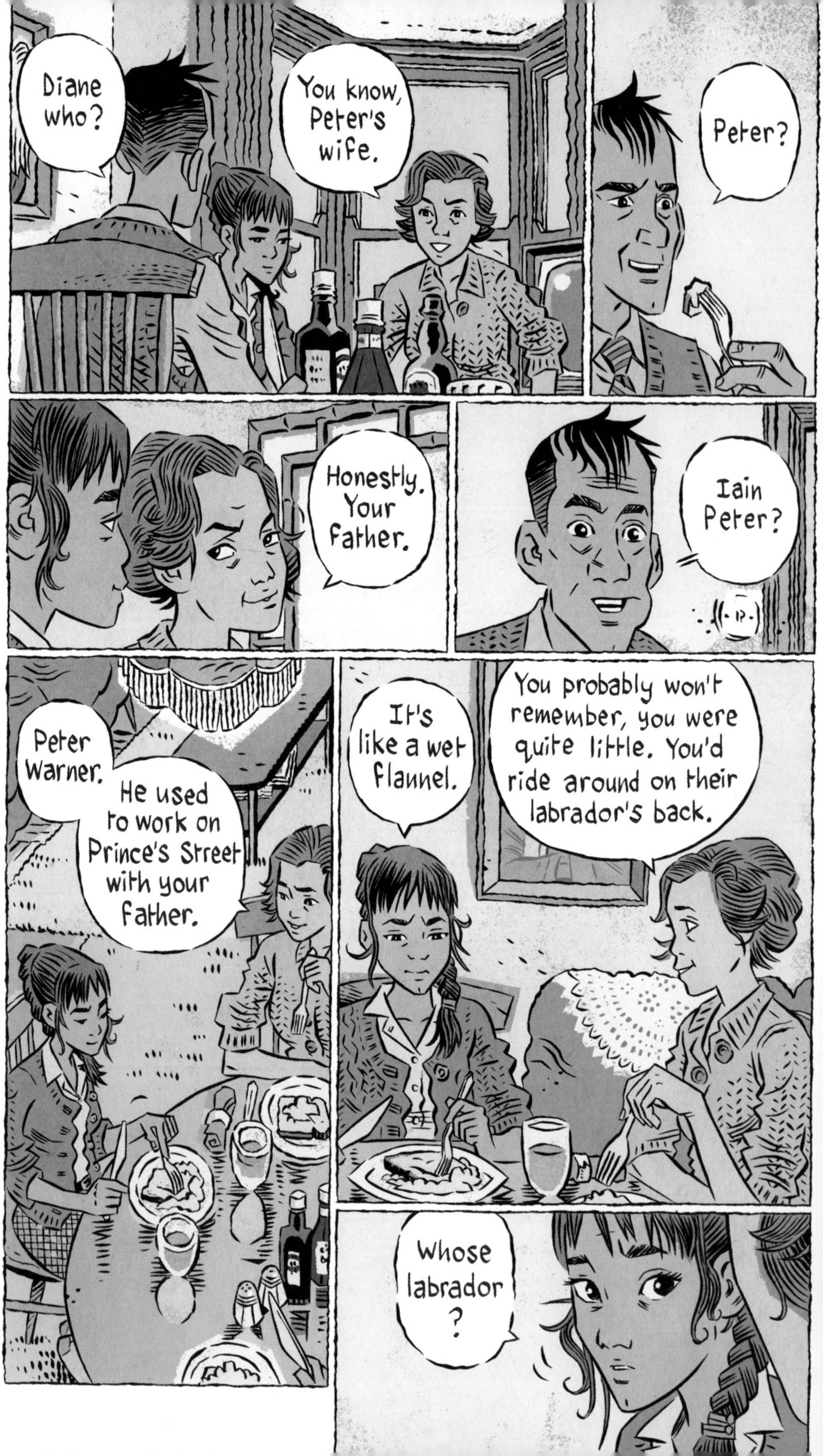
Diane who?
You know, Peter's wife.
Peter?
Honestly. Your father.
Iain Peter?
Peter Warner.
He used to work on Prince's Street with your father.
It's like a wet flannel.
You probably won't remember, you were quite little. You'd ride around on their labrador's back.
Whose labrador?

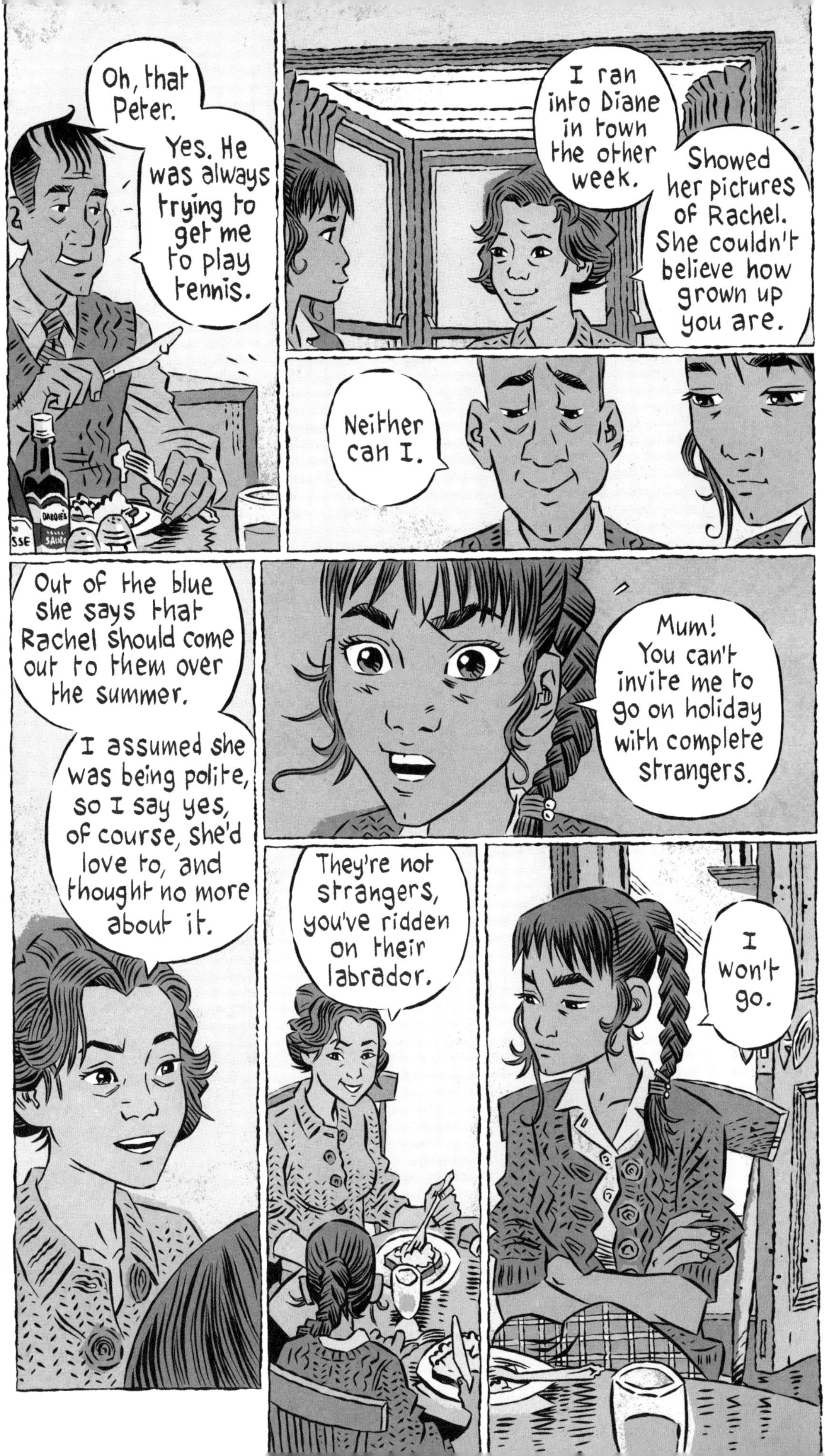
Oh, that Peter.
Yes. He was always trying to get me to play tennis.
DADDIE'S SAUCE
I ran into Diane in town the other week.
Showed her pictures of Rachel. She couldn't believe how grown up you are.
Neither can I.
Out of the blue she says that Rachel should come out to them over the summer.
I assumed she was being polite, so I say yes, of course, she'd love to, and thought no more about it.
Mum! You can't invite me to go on holiday with complete strangers.
They're not strangers, you've ridden on their labrador.
I won't go.

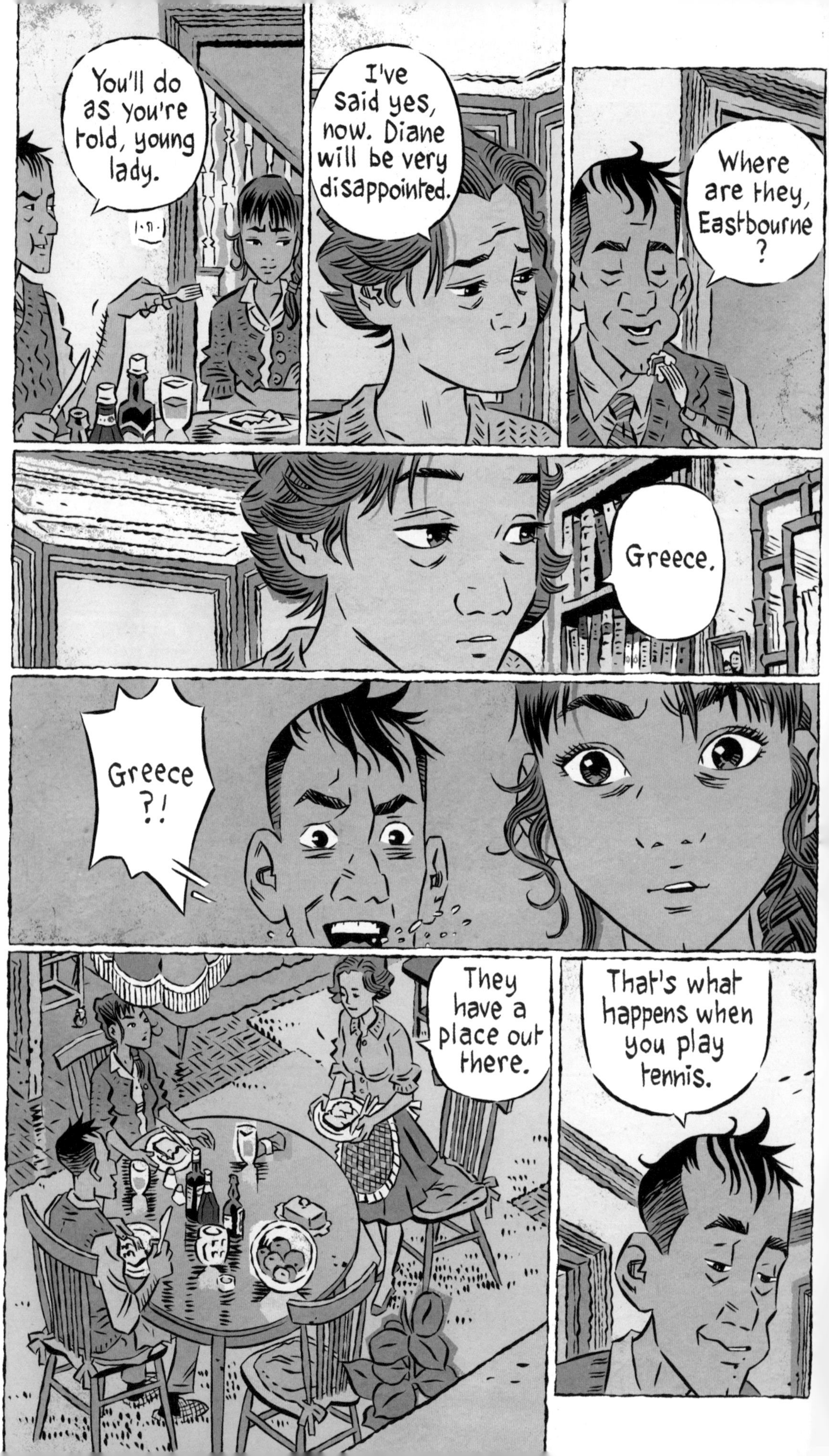
You'll do as you're told, young lady.
I've said yes, now. Diane will be very disappointed.
Where are they, Eastbourne?
Greece.
Greece?!
They have a place out there.
That's what happens when you play tennis.

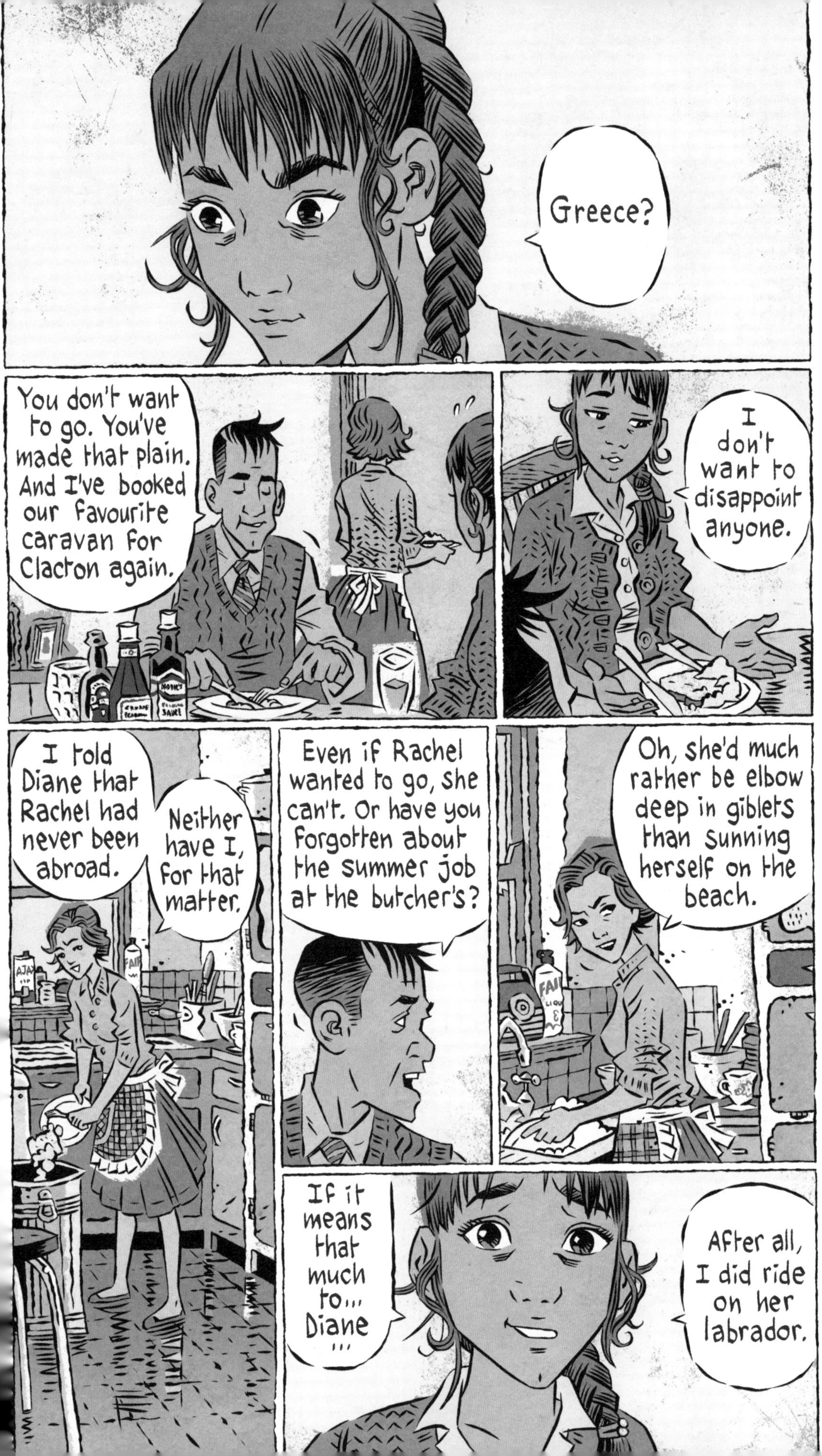
Greece?
You don't want to go. You've made that plain. And I've booked our favourite caravan for Clacton again.
I don't want to disappoint anyone.
I told Diane that Rachel had never been abroad.
Neither have I, for that matter.
Even if Rachel wanted to go, she can't. Or have you forgotten about the summer job at the butcher's?
Oh, she'd much rather be elbow deep in giblets than sunning herself on the beach.
If it means that much to... Diane ...
After all, I did ride on her labrador.

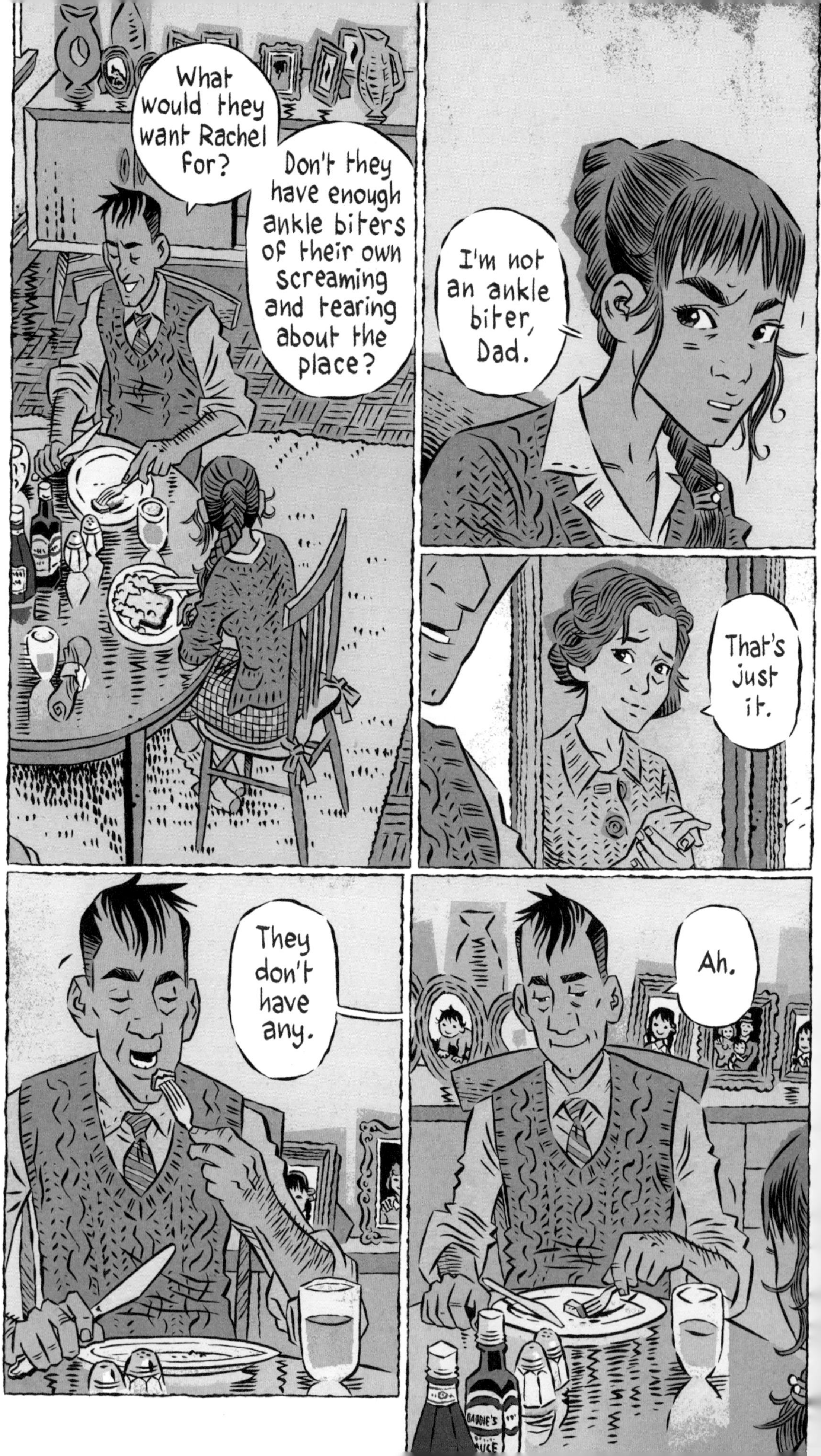
What would they want Rachel for?
Don't they have enough ankle biters of their own screaming and tearing about the place?
I'm not an ankle biter, Dad.
That's just it.
They don't have any.
Ah.

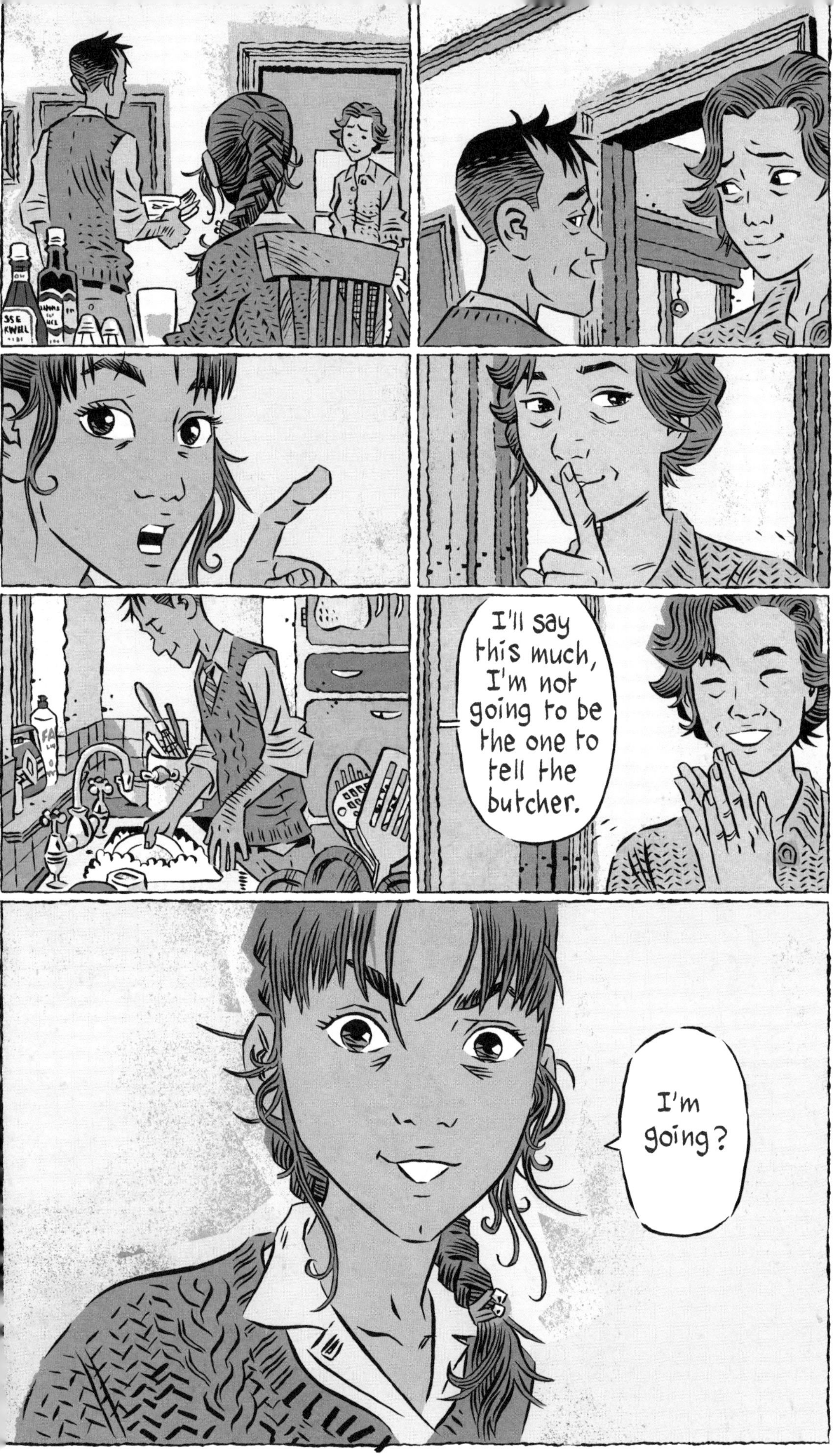
I'll say this much, I'm not going to be the one to tell the butcher.
I'm going?

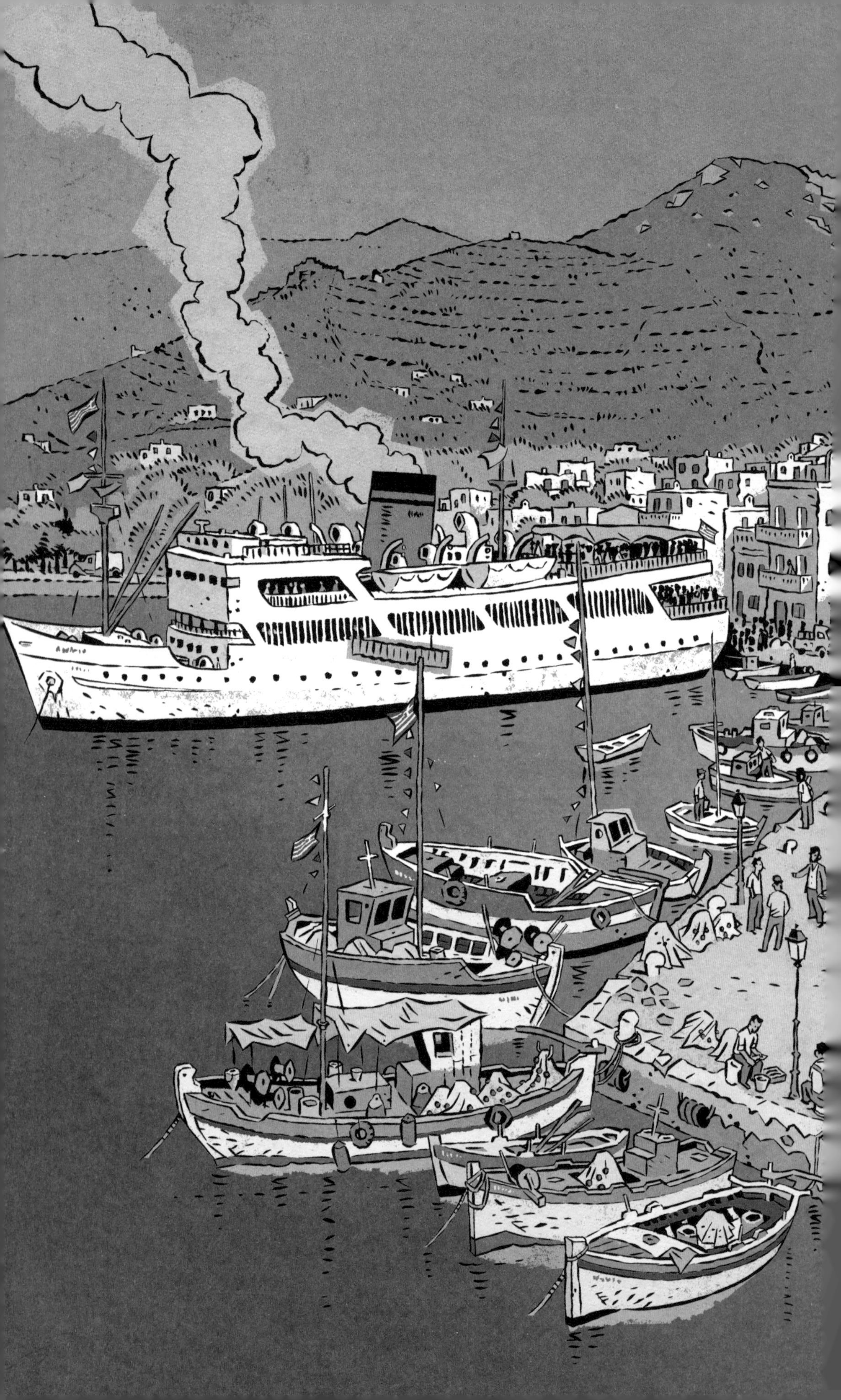

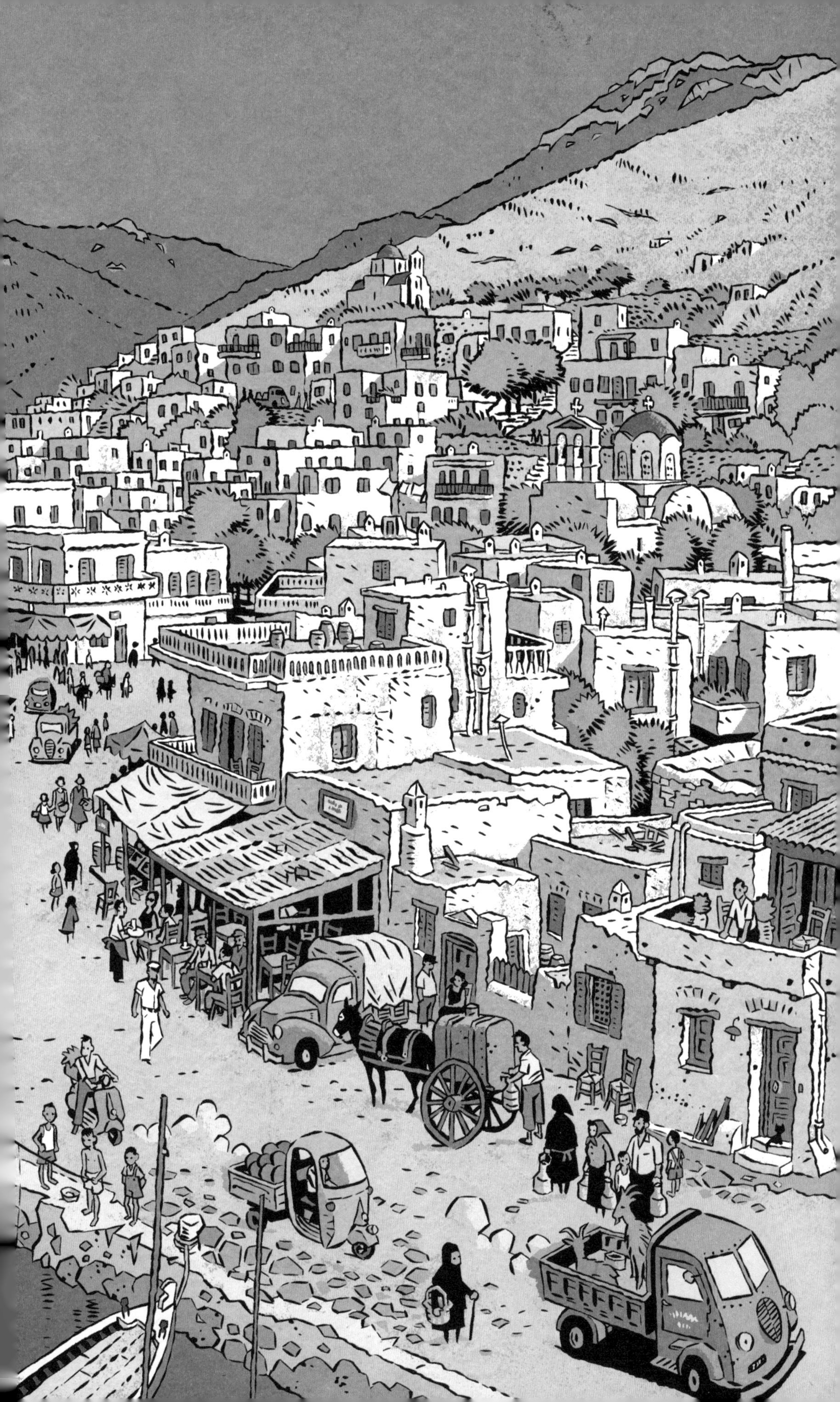

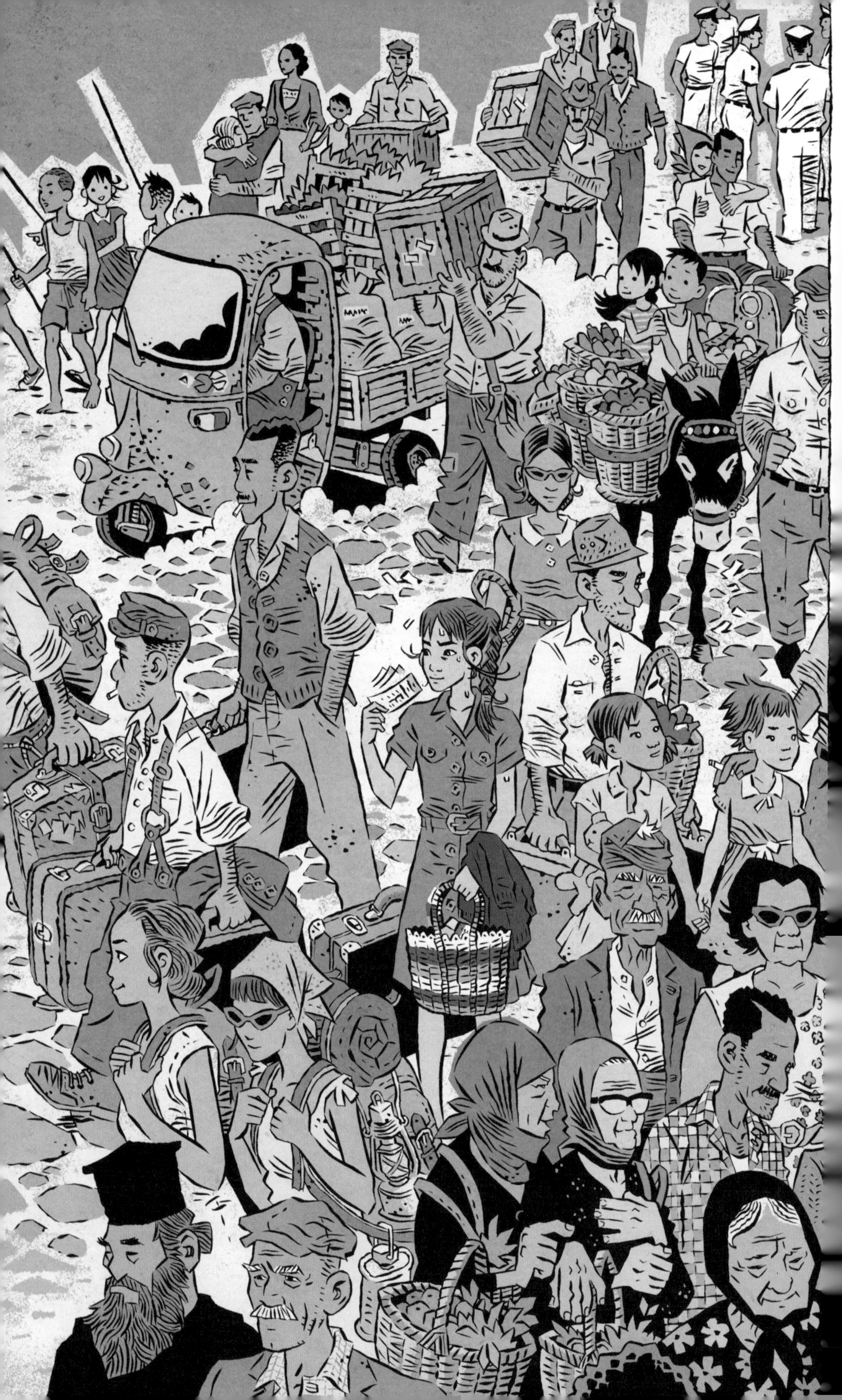

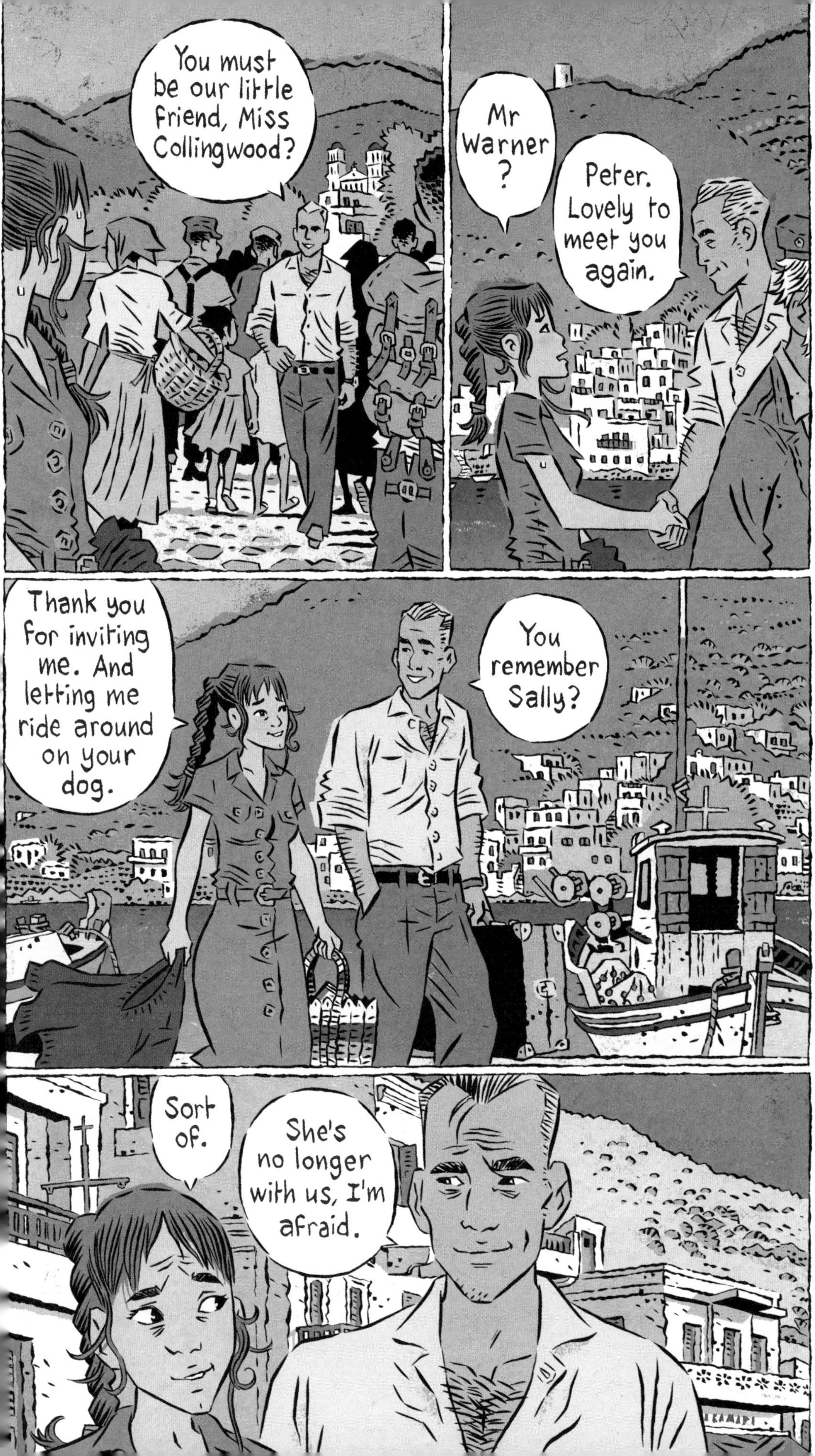
You must be our little friend, Miss Collingwood?
Mr Warner?
Peter. Lovely to meet you again.
Thank you for inviting me. And letting me ride around on your dog.
You remember Sally?
Sort of.
She's no longer with us, I'm afraid.

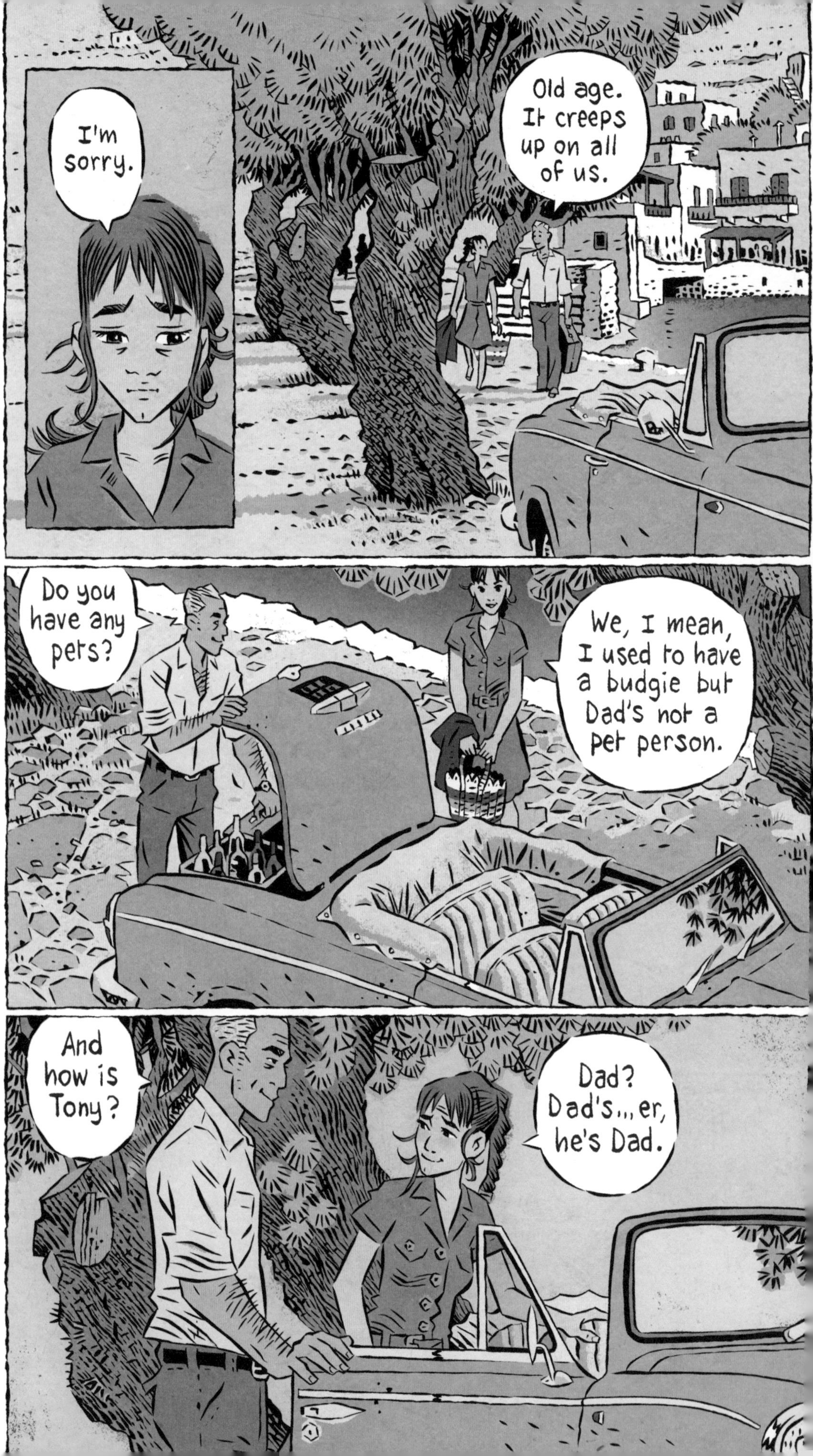
I'm sorry.
Old age. It creeps up on all of us.
Do you have any pets?
We, I mean, I used to have a budgie but Dad's not a pet person.
And how is Tony?
Dad? Dad's..., er, he's Dad.

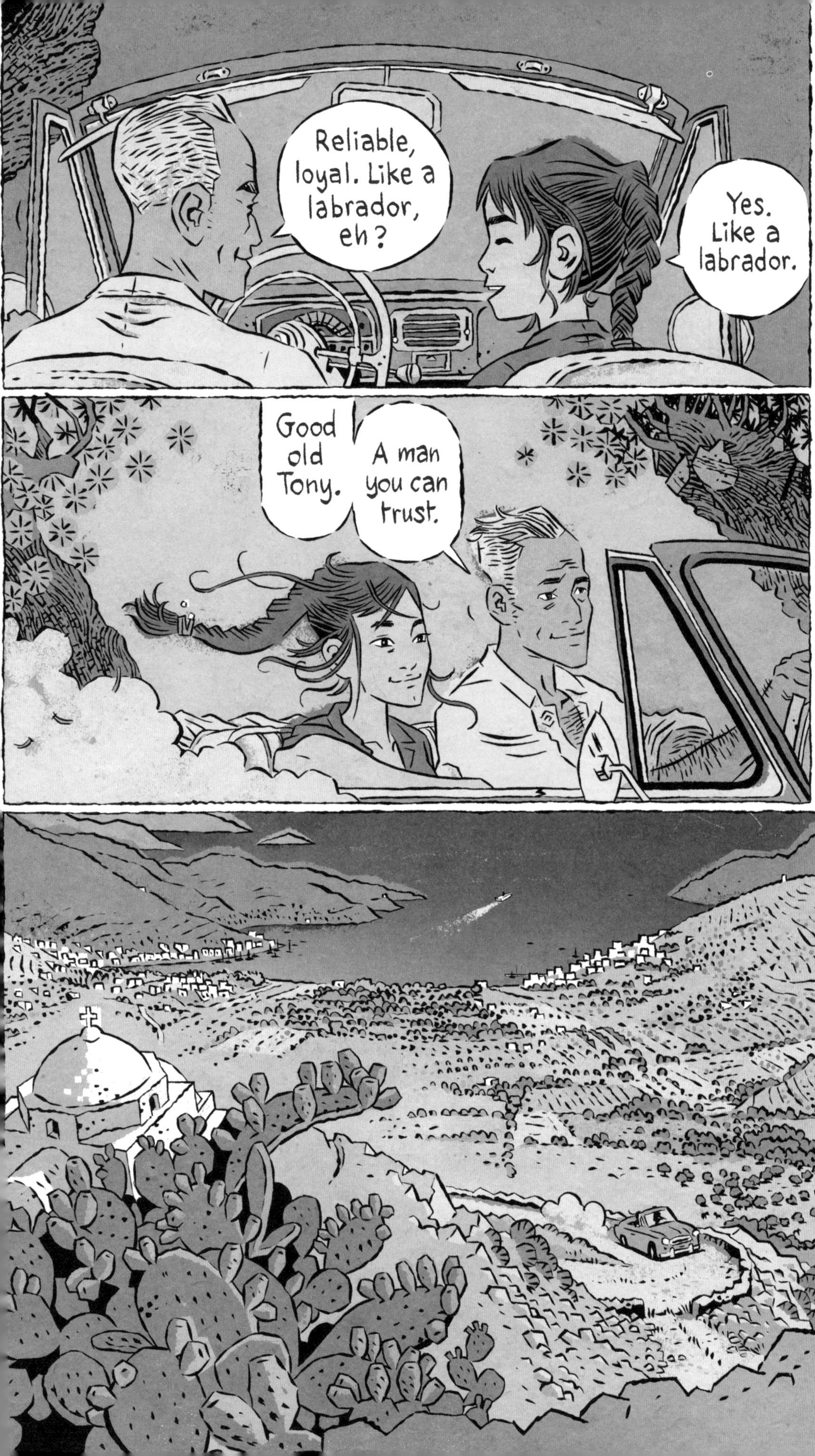
Reliable, loyal. Like a labrador, eh?
Yes. Like a labrador.
Good old Tony.
A man you can trust.

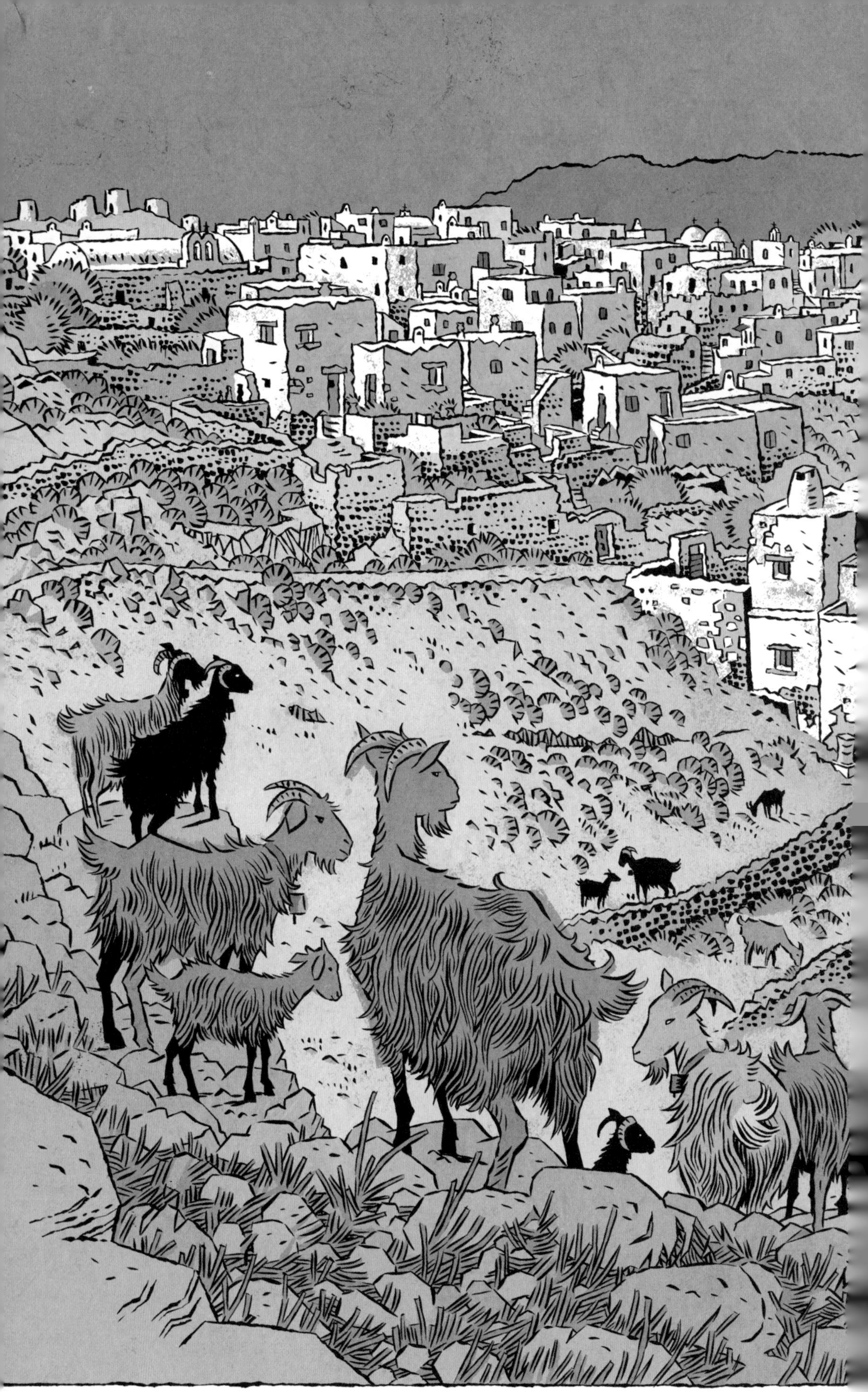

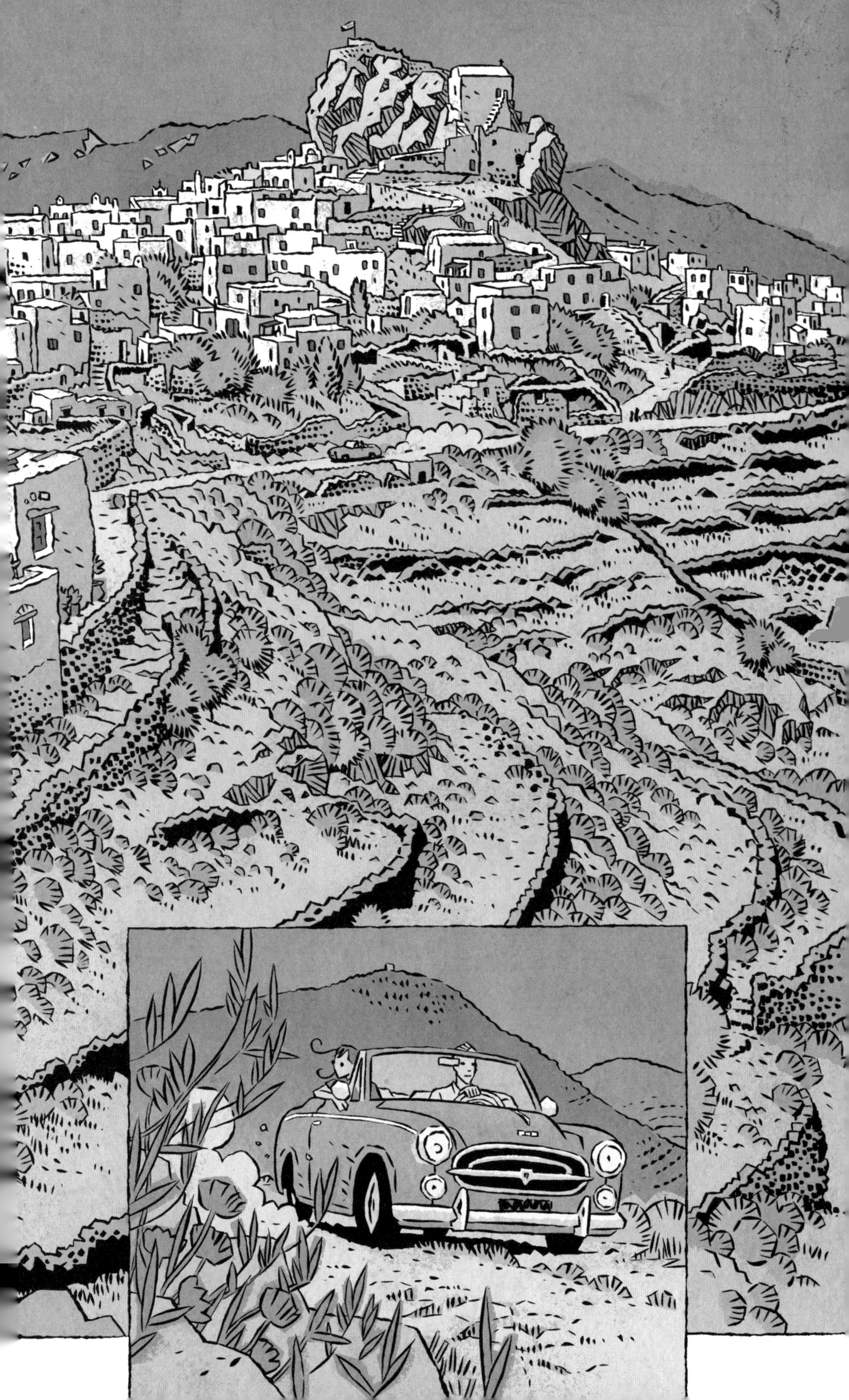

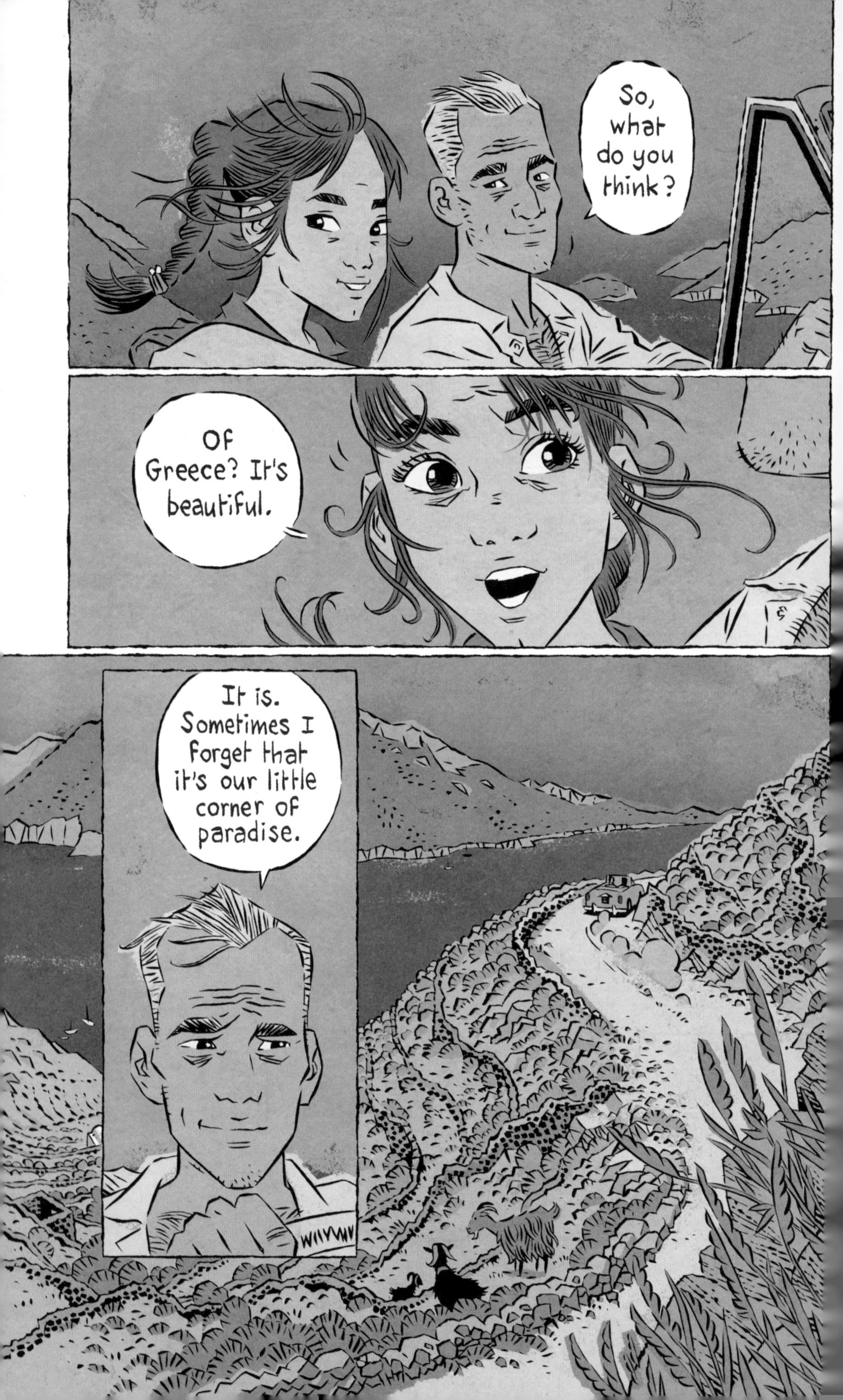
So, what do you think?
Of Greece? It's beautiful.
It is. Sometimes I forget that it's our little corner of paradise.

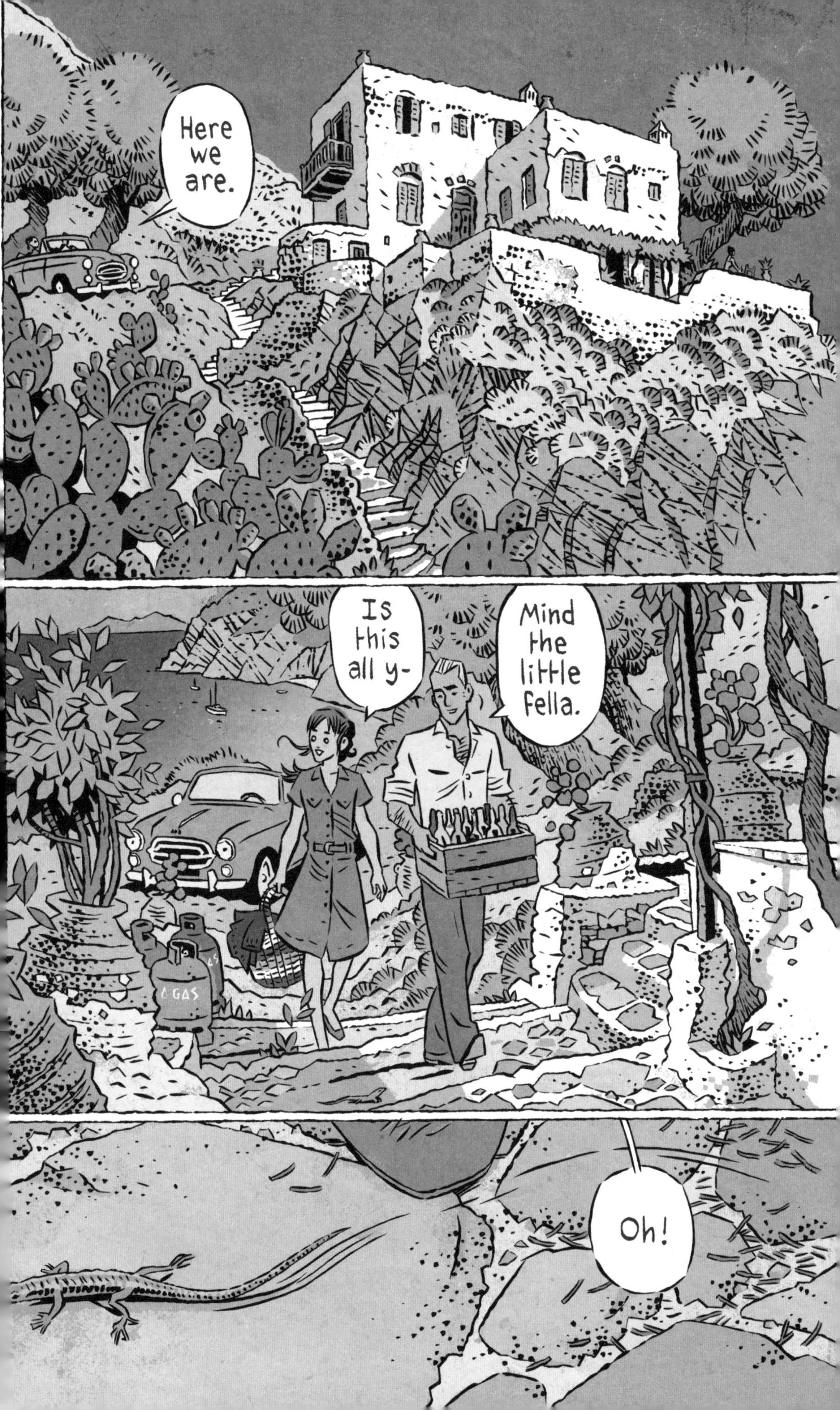
Here we are.
Is this all y-
Mind the little fella.
O GAS
Oh!

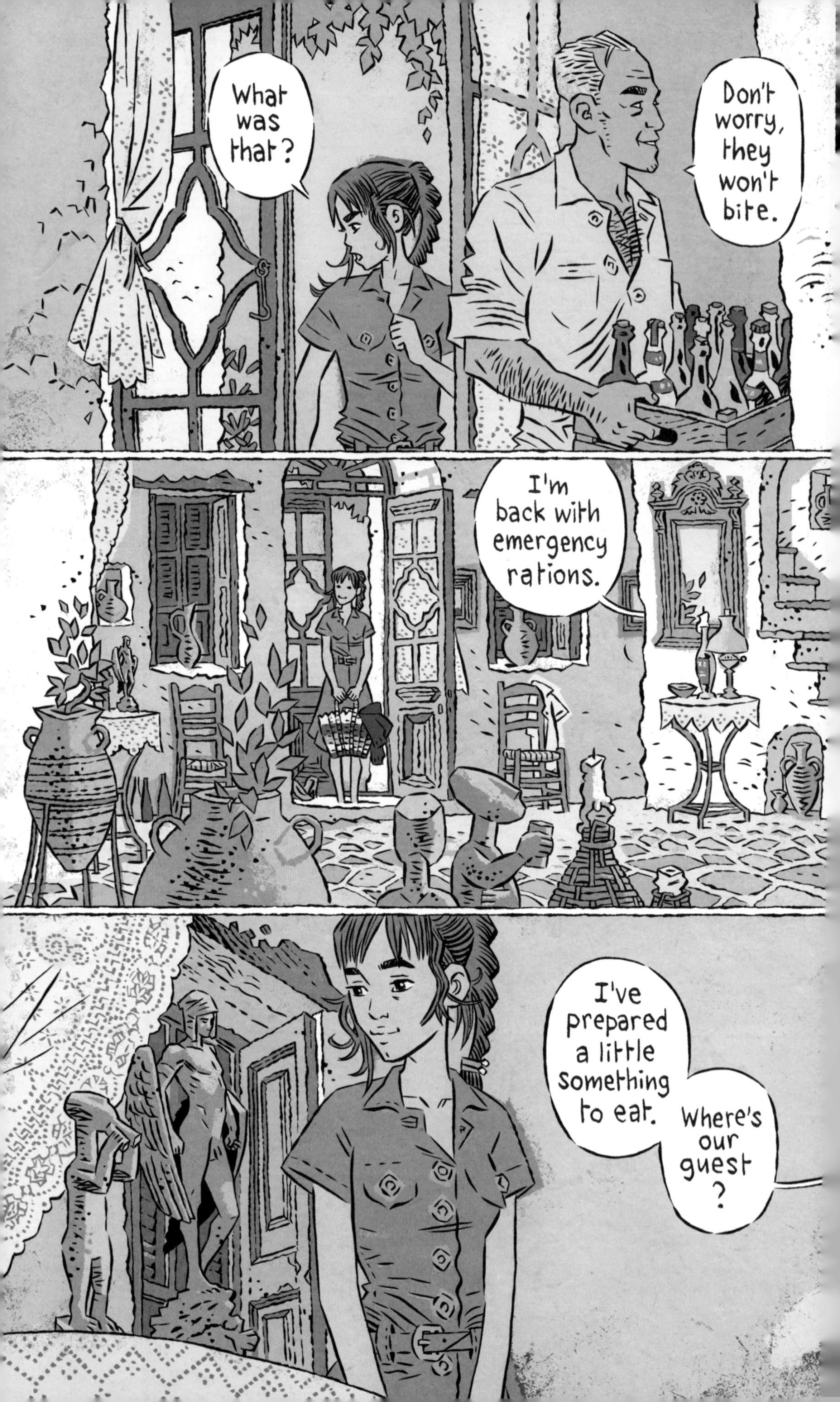
What was that?
Don't worry, they won't bite.
I'm back with emergency rations.
I've prepared a little something to eat.
Where's our guest?

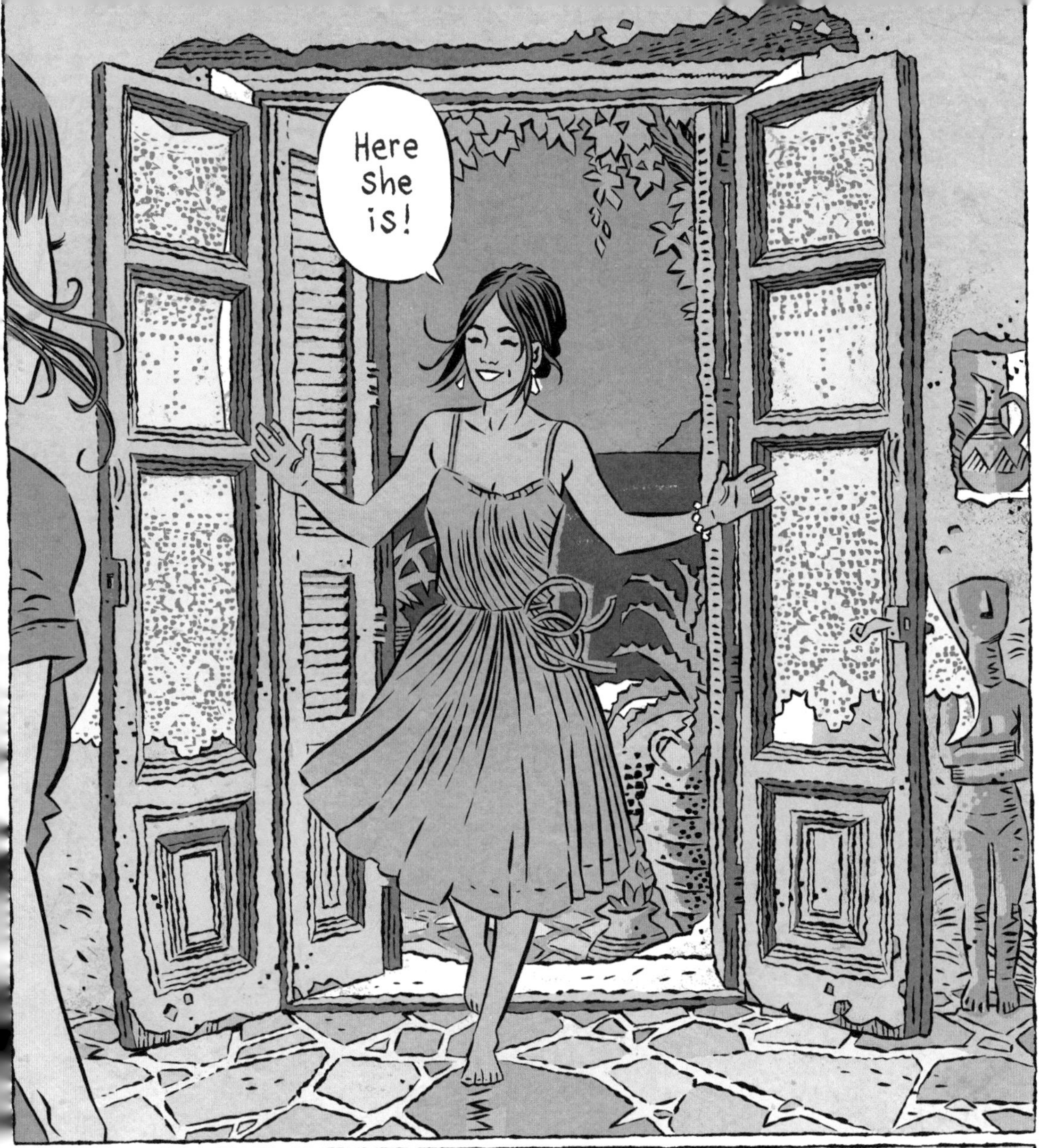
Here she is!
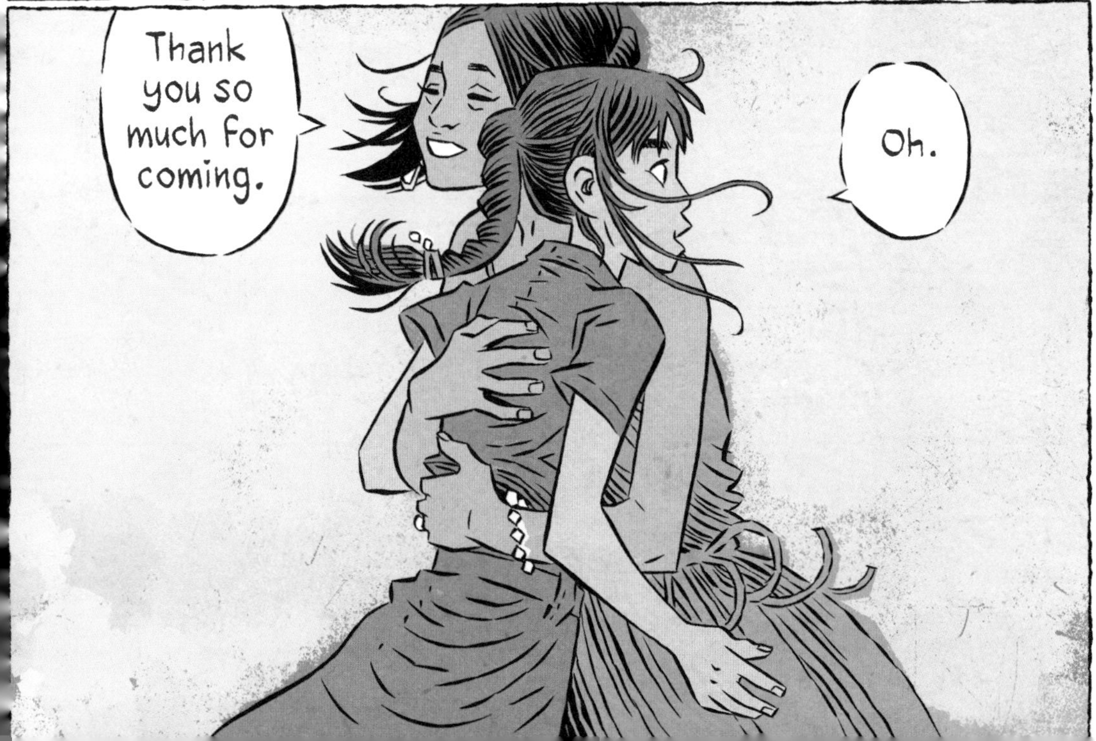
Thank you so much for coming.
Oh.

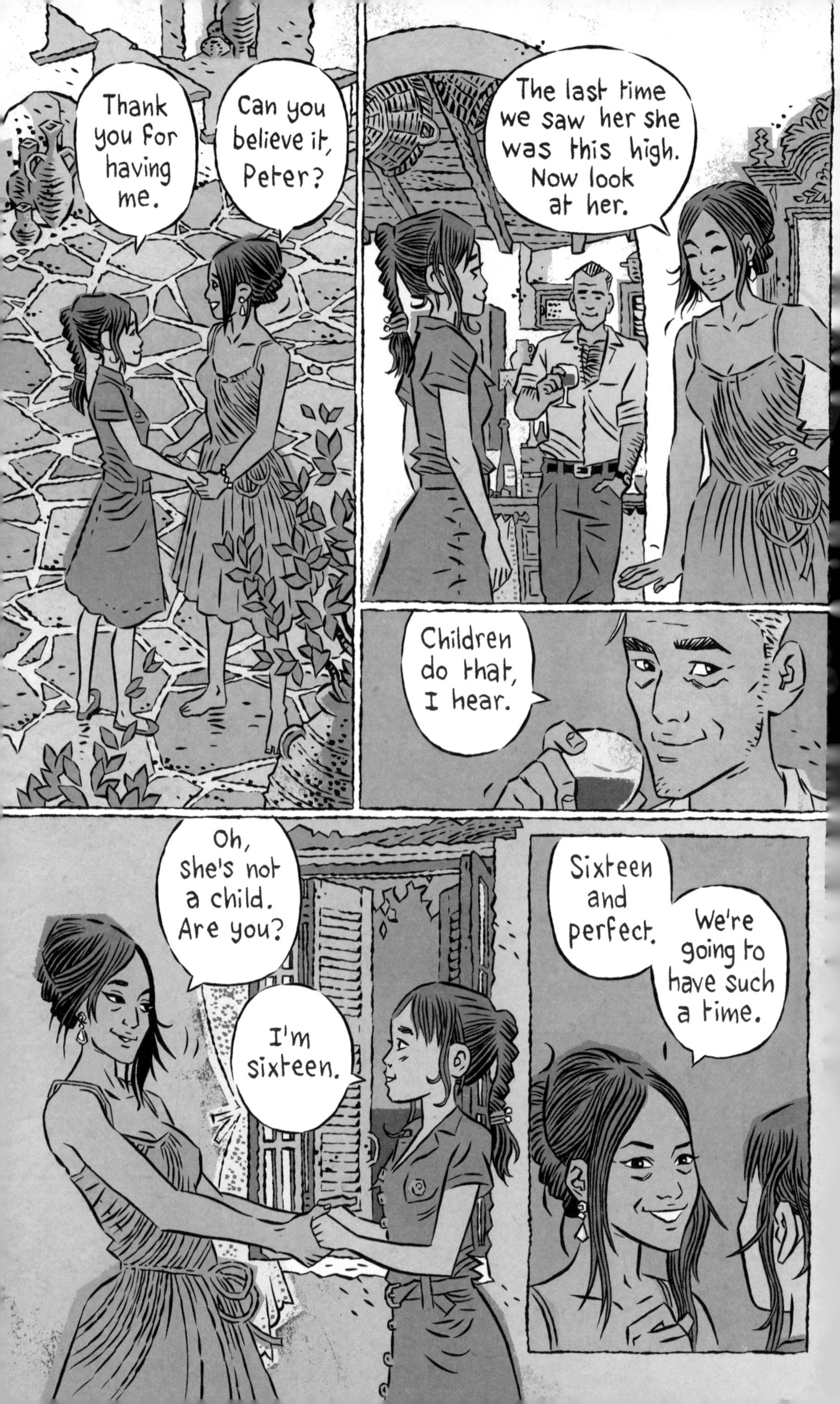
Thank you for having me.
Can you believe it, Peter?
The last time we saw her she was this high. Now look at her.
Children do that, I hear.
Oh, she's not a child. Are you?
I'm sixteen.
Sixteen and perfect.
We're going to have such a time.

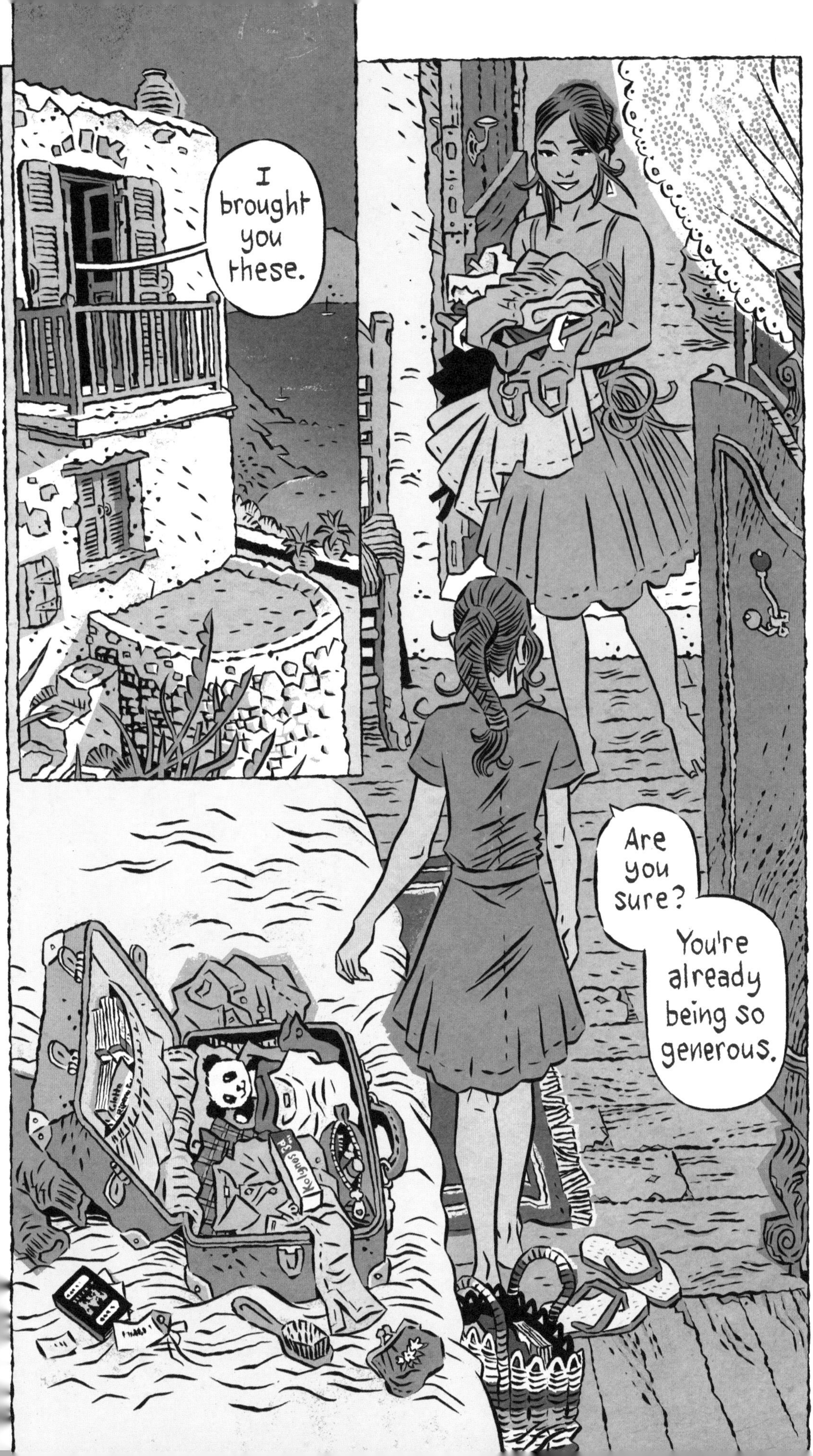
I brought you these.
Are you sure?
You're already being so generous.

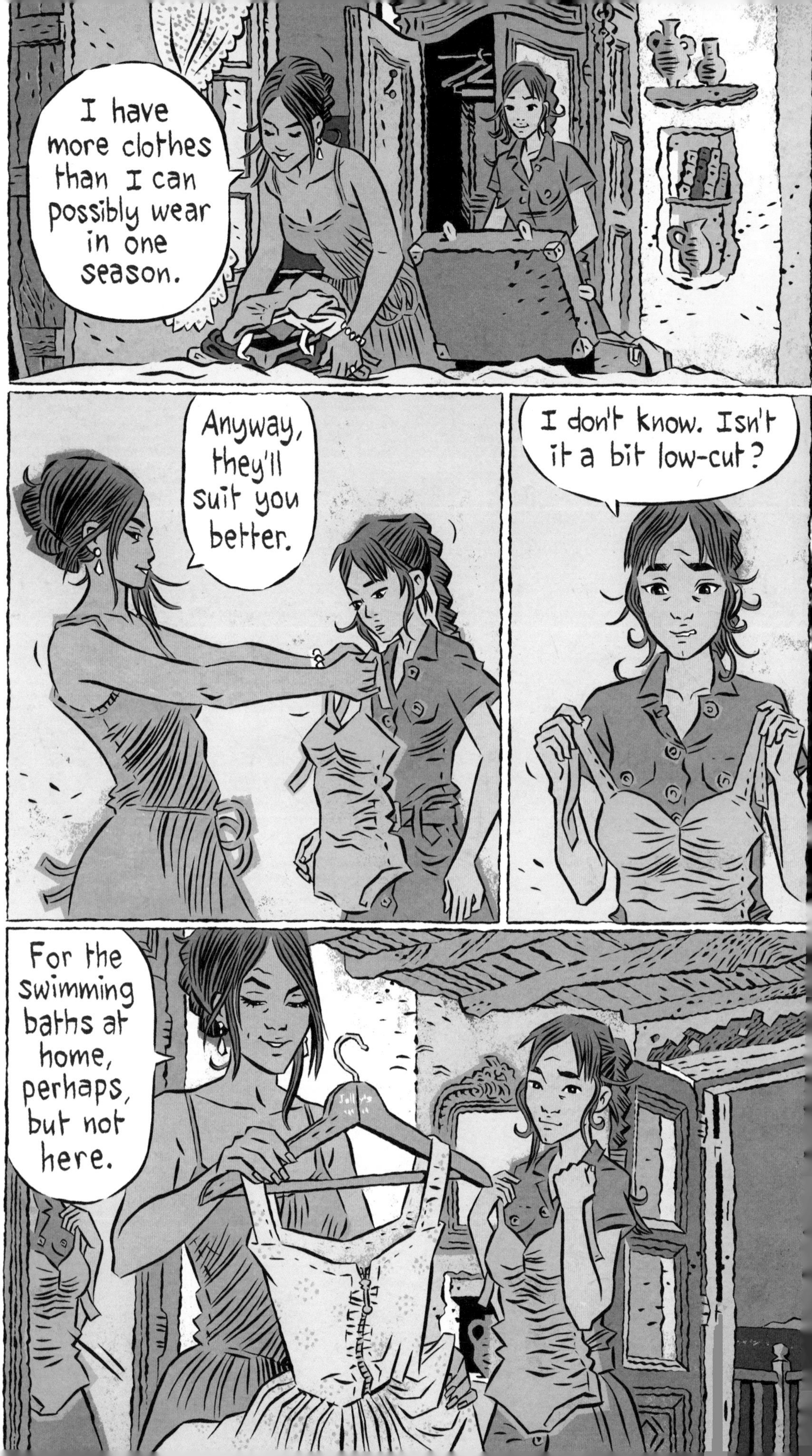
I have more clothes than I can possibly wear in one season.
Anyway, they'll suit you better.
I don't know. Isn't it a bit low-cut?
For the swimming baths at home, perhaps, but not here.

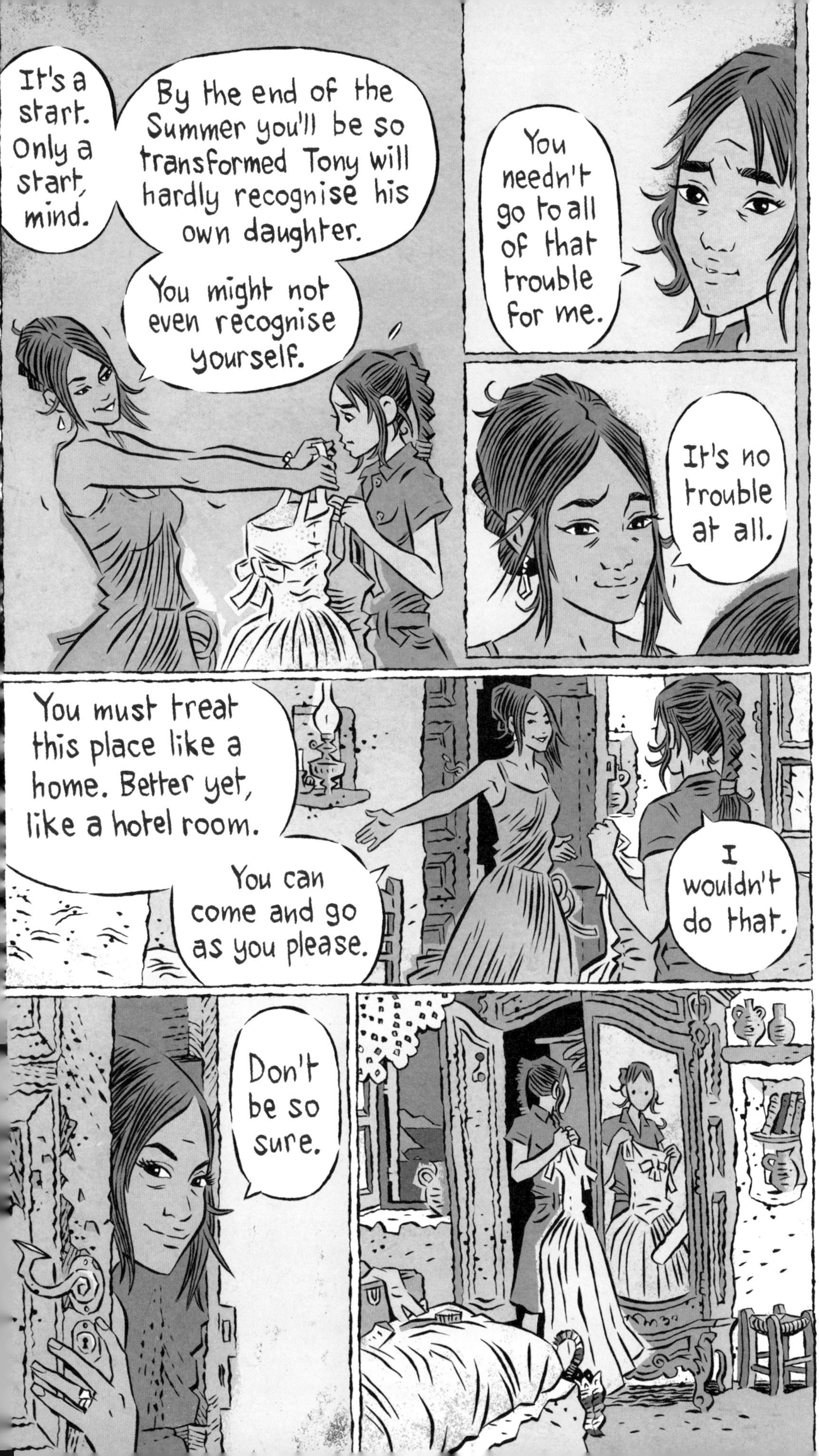
It's a start. Only a start, mind.
By the end of the Summer you'll be so transformed Tony will hardly recognise his own daughter.
You might not even recognise yourself.
You needn't go to all of that trouble for me.
It's no trouble at all.
You must treat this place like a home. Better yet, like a hotel room.
You can come and go as you please.
I wouldn't do that.
Don't be so sure.

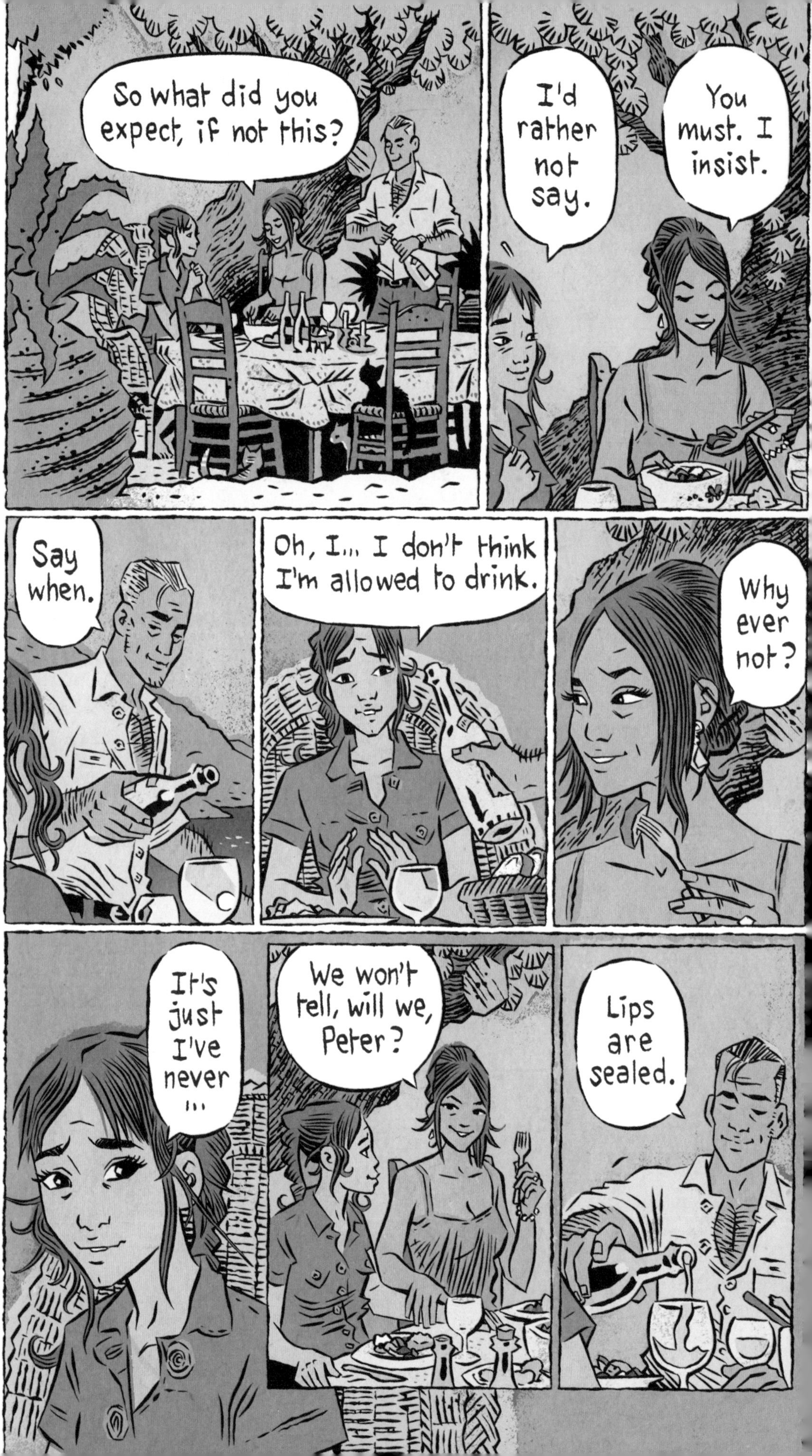
So what did you expect, if not this?
I'd rather not say.
You must. I insist.
Say when.
Oh, I... I don't think I'm allowed to drink.
Why ever not?
It's just I've never ...
We won't tell, will we, Peter?
Lips are sealed.

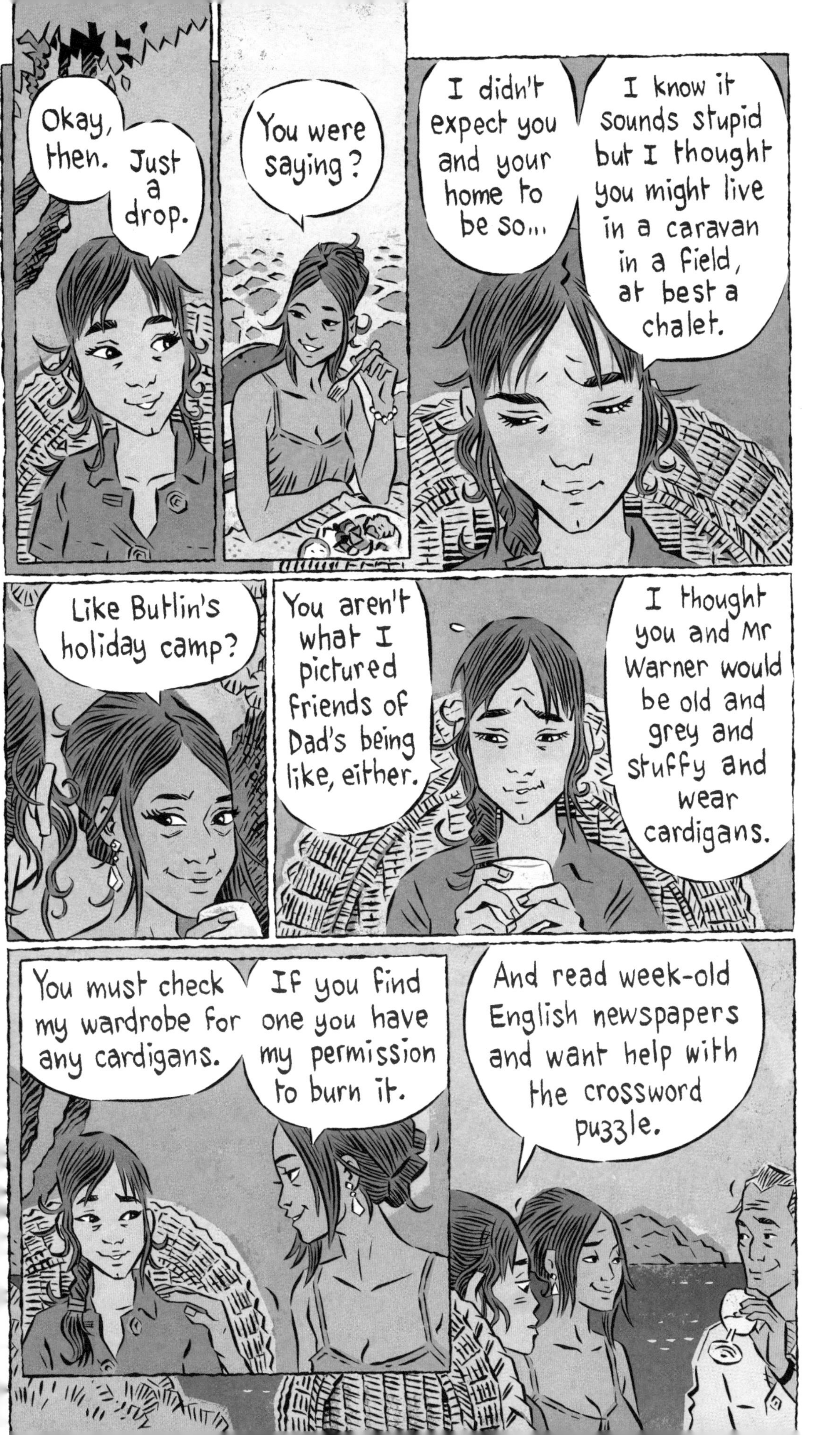

Okay, then.
Just a drop.
You were saying?
I didn't expect you and your home to be so...
I know it sounds stupid but I thought you might live in a caravan in a field, at best a chalet.
Like Butlin's holiday camp?
You aren't what I pictured friends of Dad's being like, either.
I thought you and Mr Warner would be old and grey and stuffy and wear cardigans.
You must check my wardrobe for any cardigans.
If you find one you have my permission to burn it.
And read week-old English newspapers and want help with the crossword puzzle.

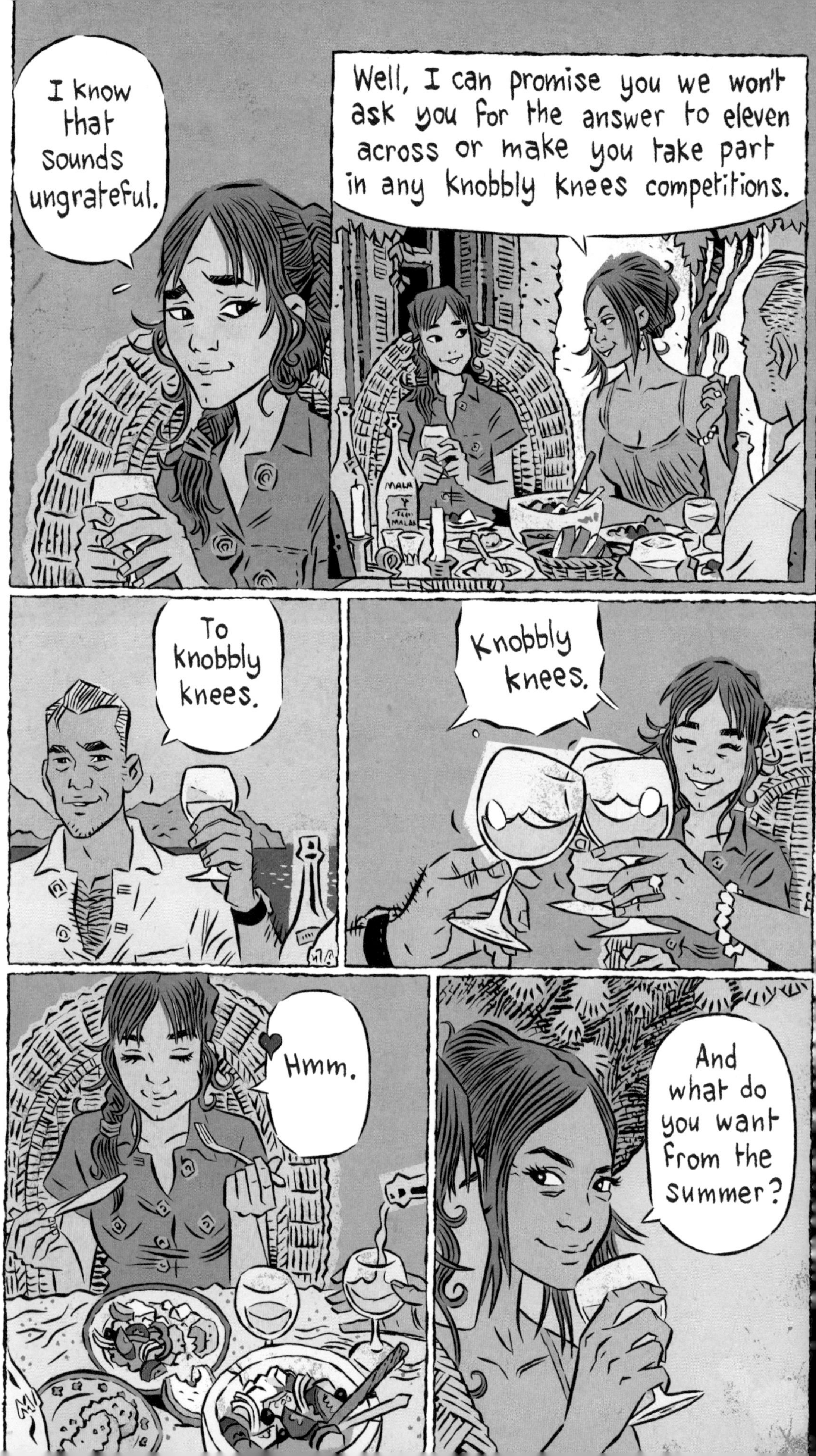
I know that sounds ungrateful.
Well, I can promise you we won't ask you for the answer to eleven across or make you take part in any knobbly knees competitions.
To knobbly knees.
Knobbly knees.
Hmm.
And what do you want from the summer?

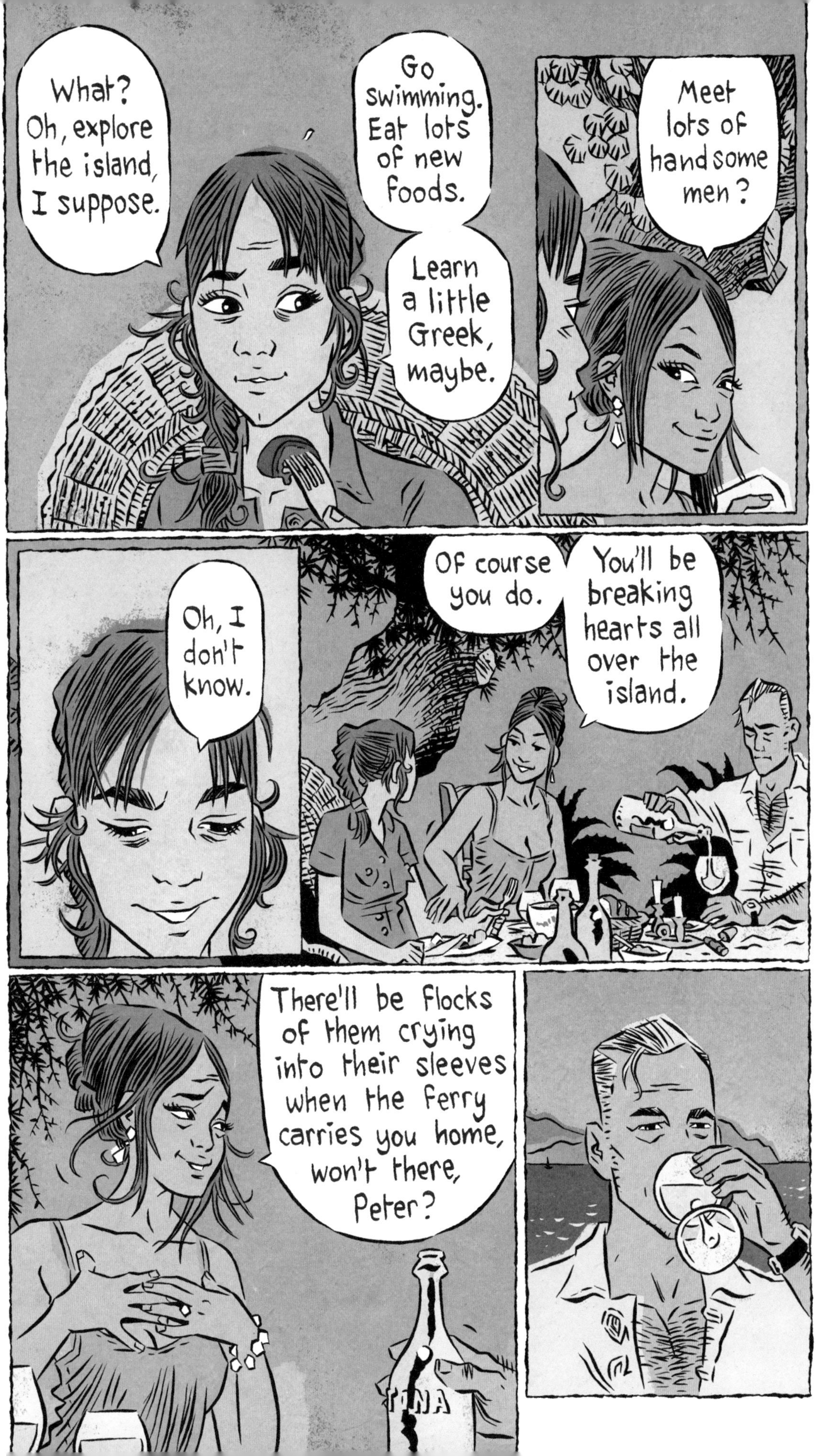
What? Oh, explore the island, I suppose.
Go swimming. Eat lots of new foods.
Learn a little Greek, maybe.
Meet lots of handsome men?
Oh, I don't know.
Of course you do.
You'll be breaking hearts all over the island.
There'll be flocks of them crying into their sleeves when the ferry carries you home, won't there, Peter?

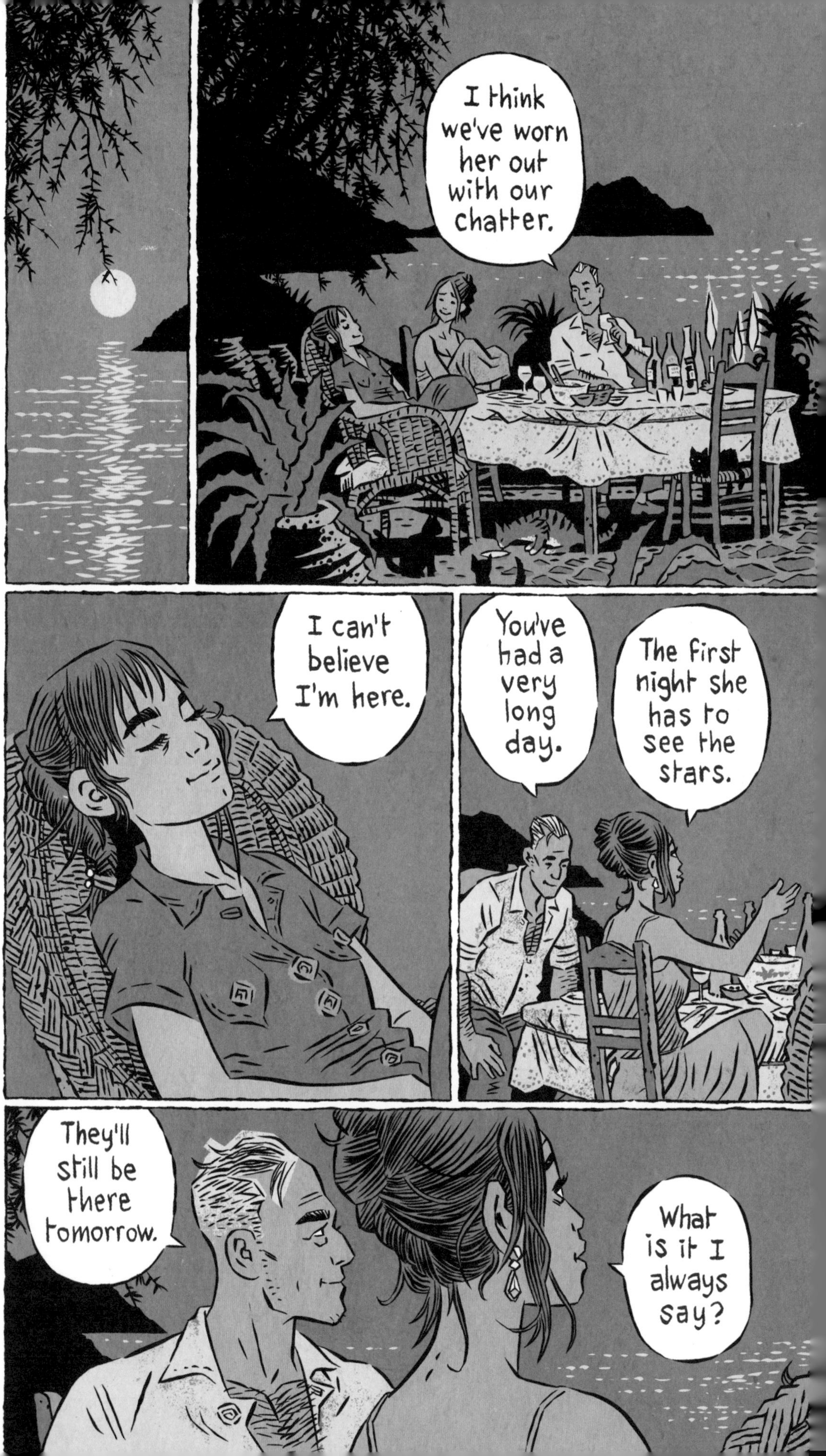
I think we've worn her out with our chatter.
I can't believe I'm here.
You've had a very long day.
The first night she has to see the stars.
They'll still be there tomorrow.
What is it I always say?

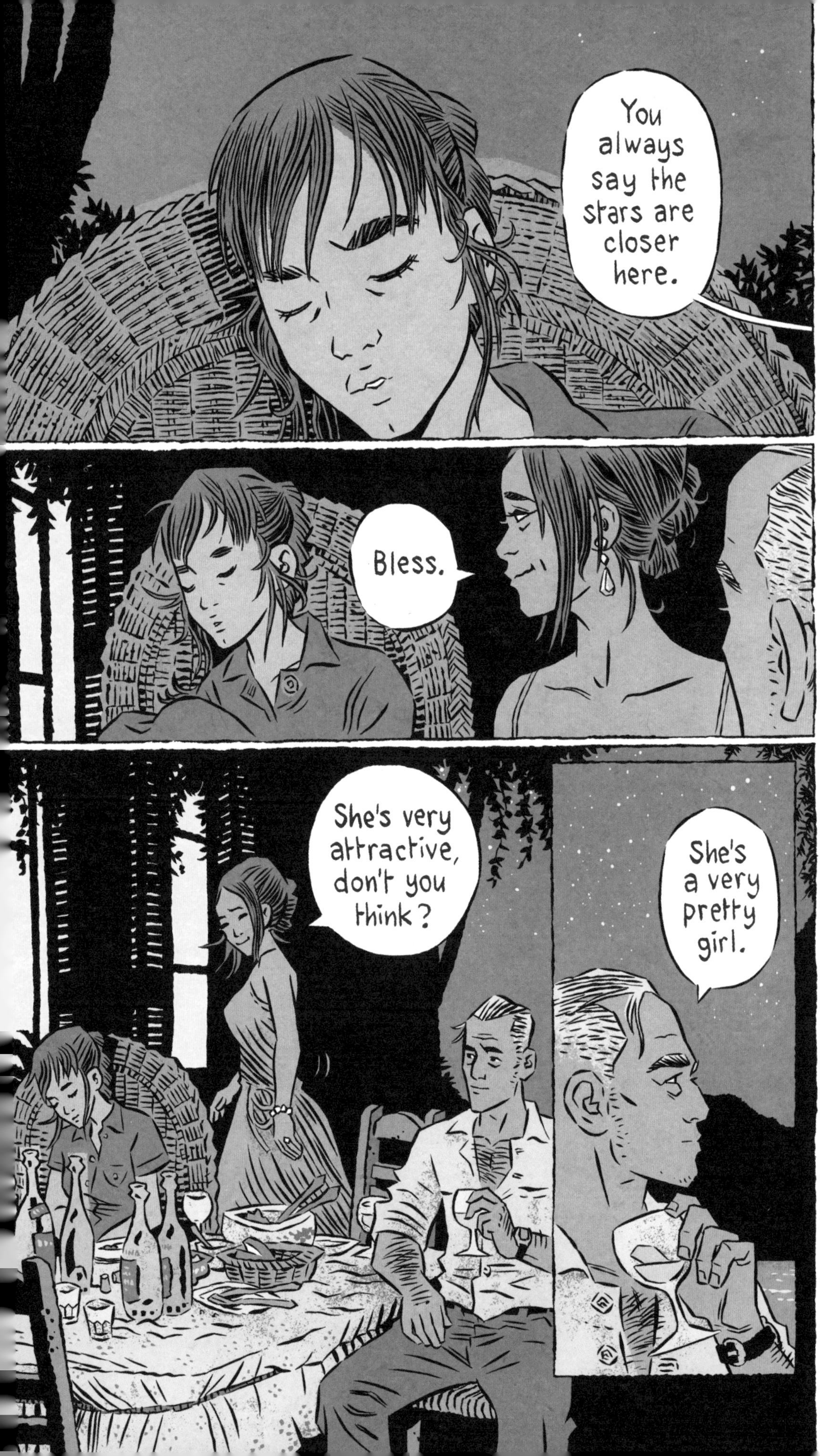
You always say the stars are closer here.
Bless.
She's very attractive, don't you think?
She's a very pretty girl.

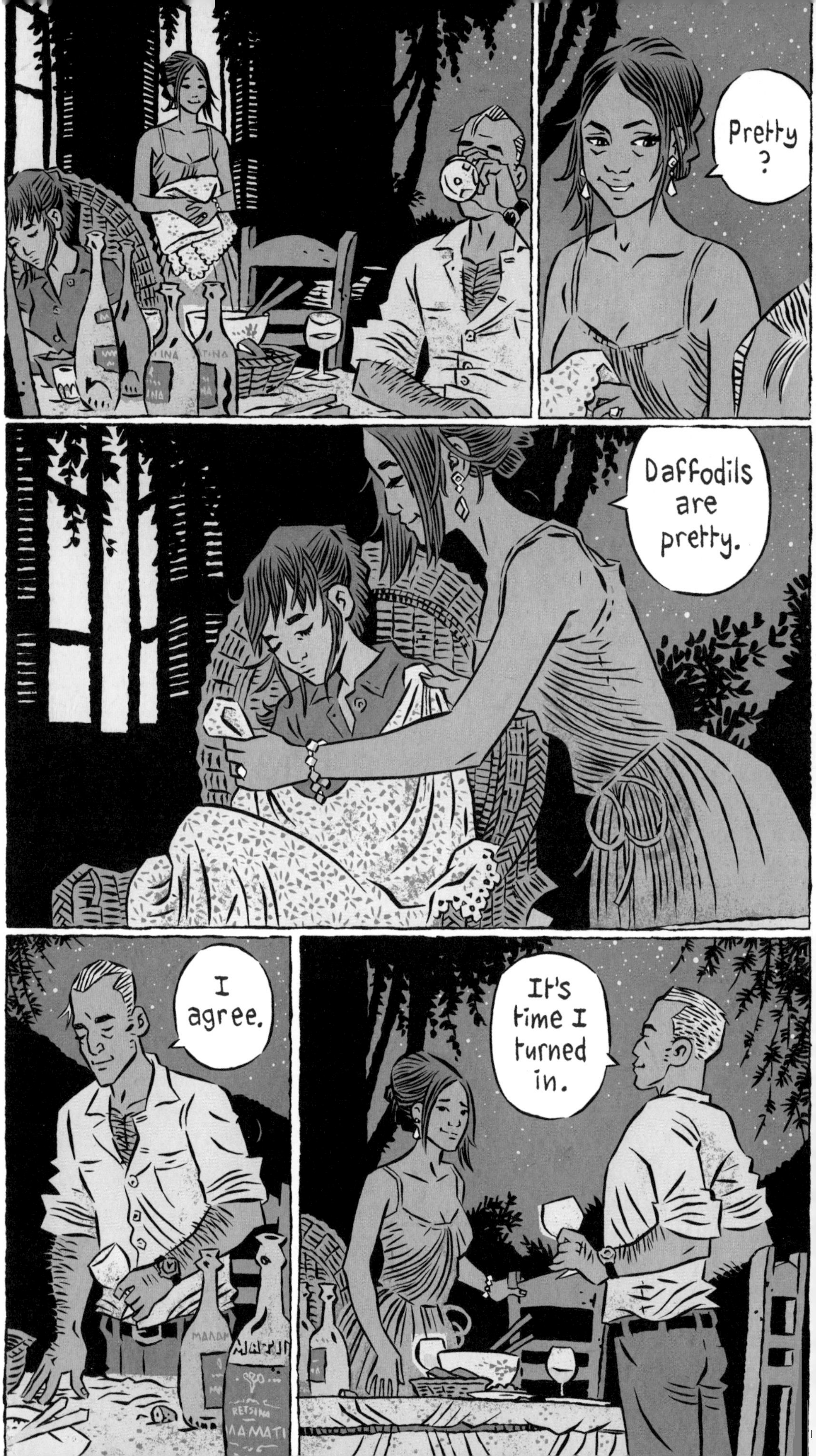
Pretty?
Daffodils are pretty.
I agree.
It's time I turned in.

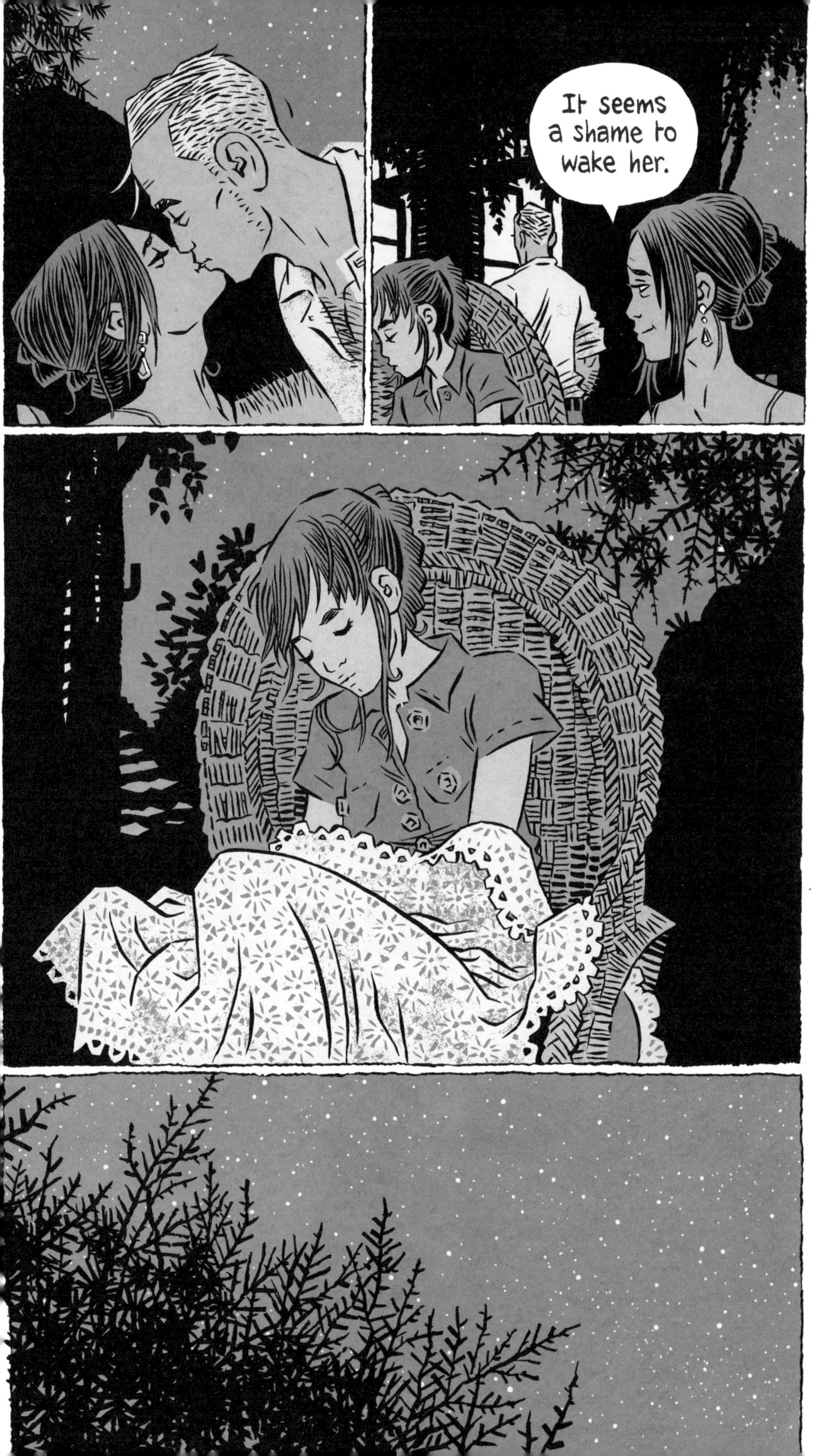
It seems a shame to wake her.

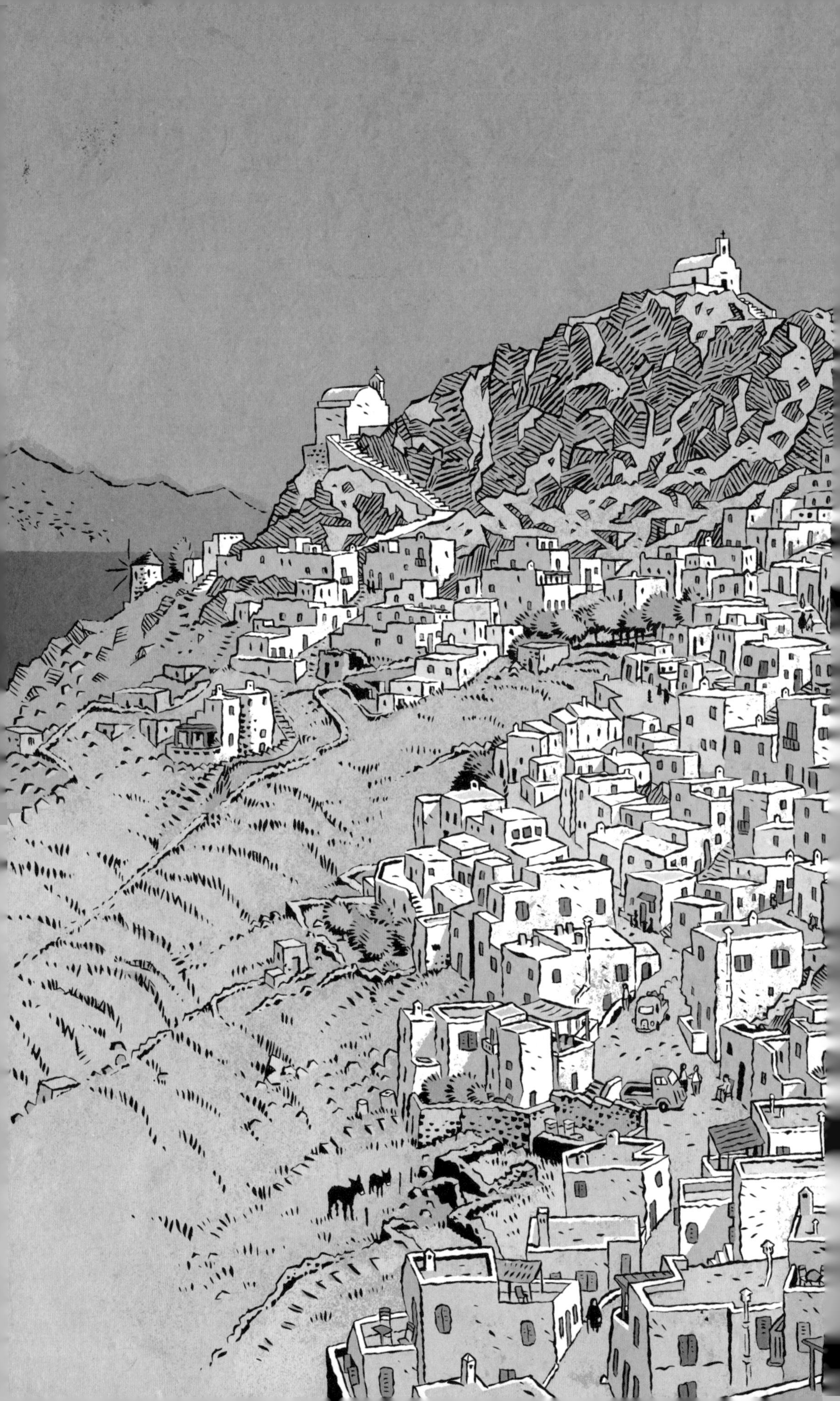

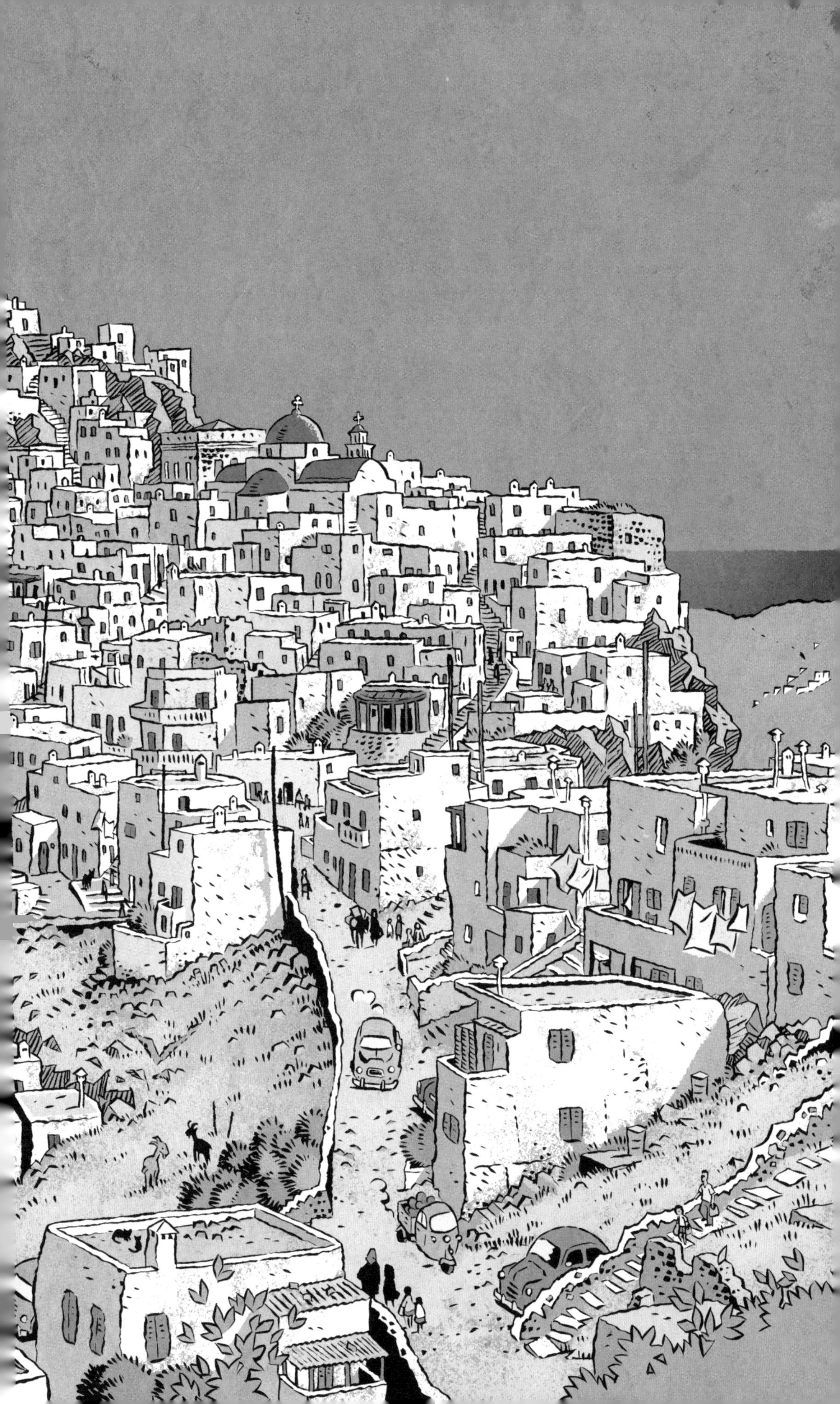

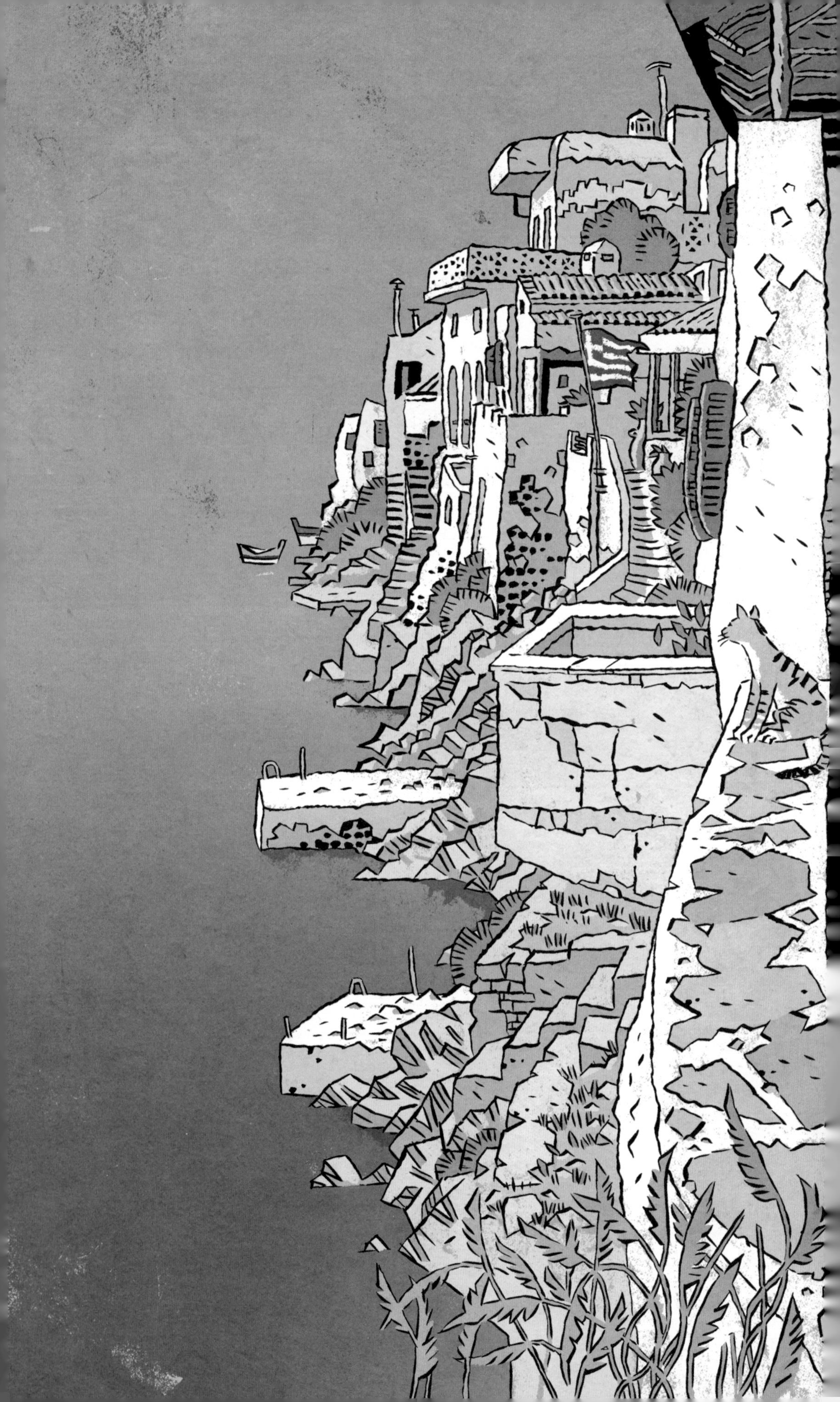

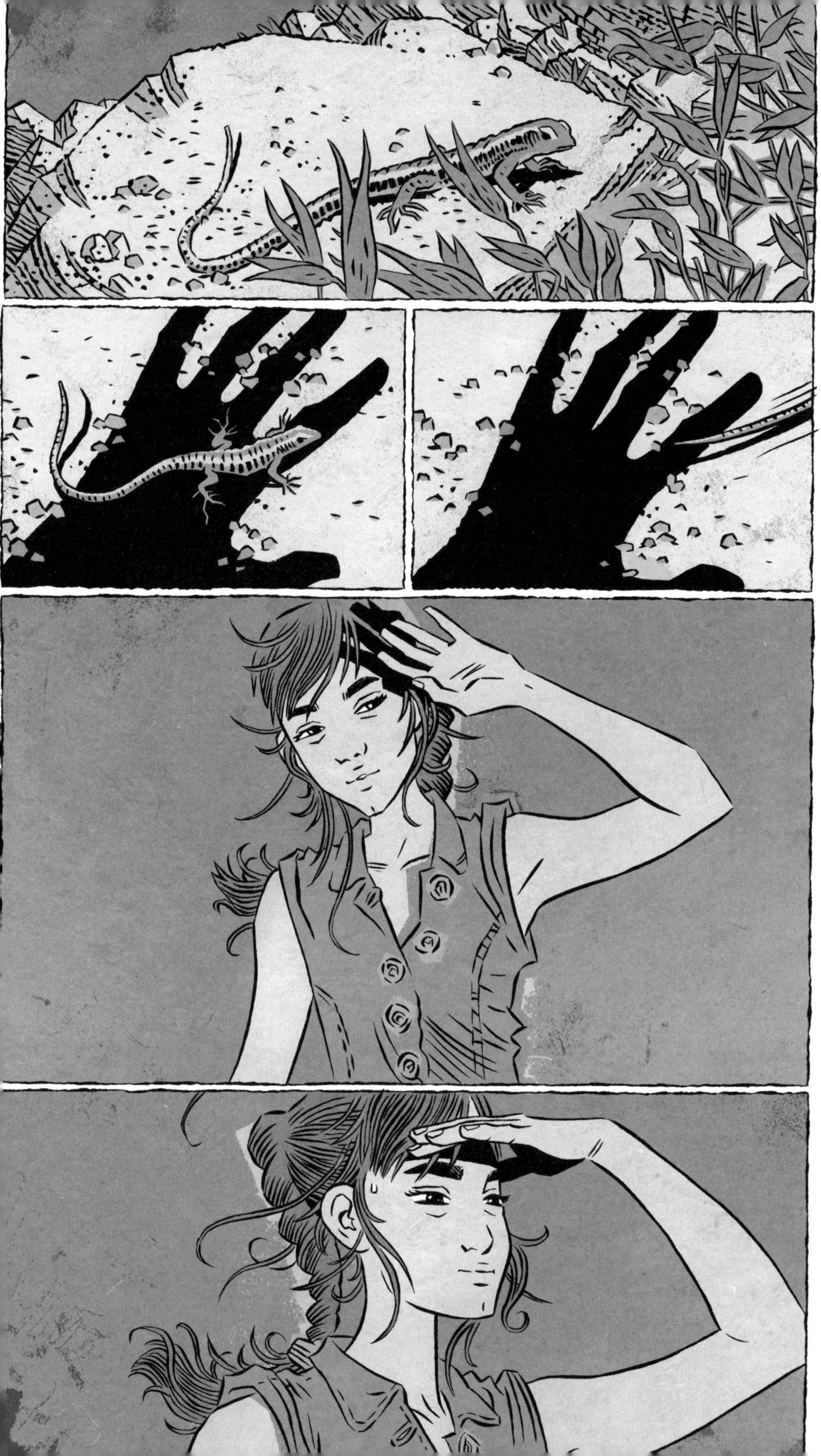

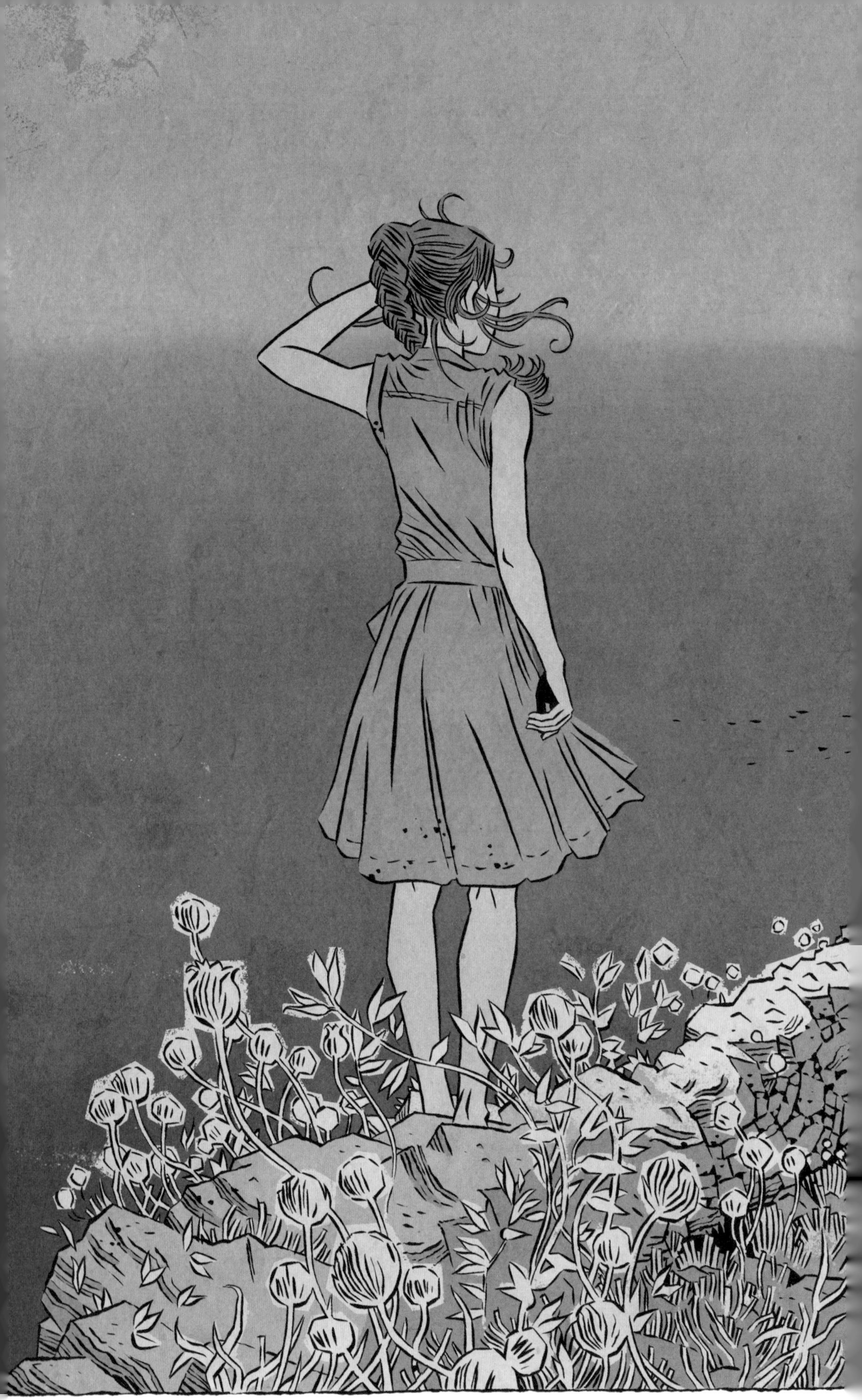

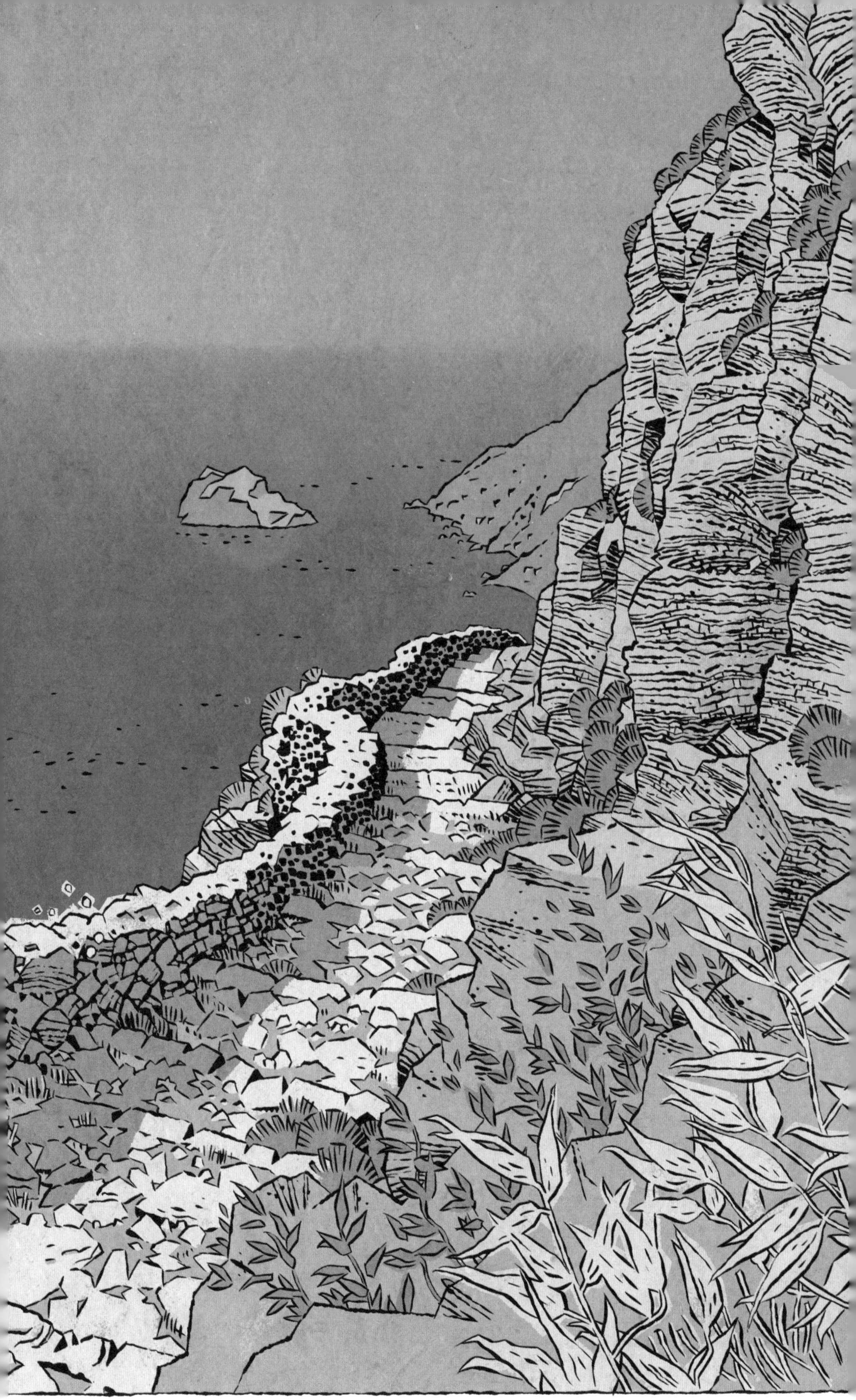

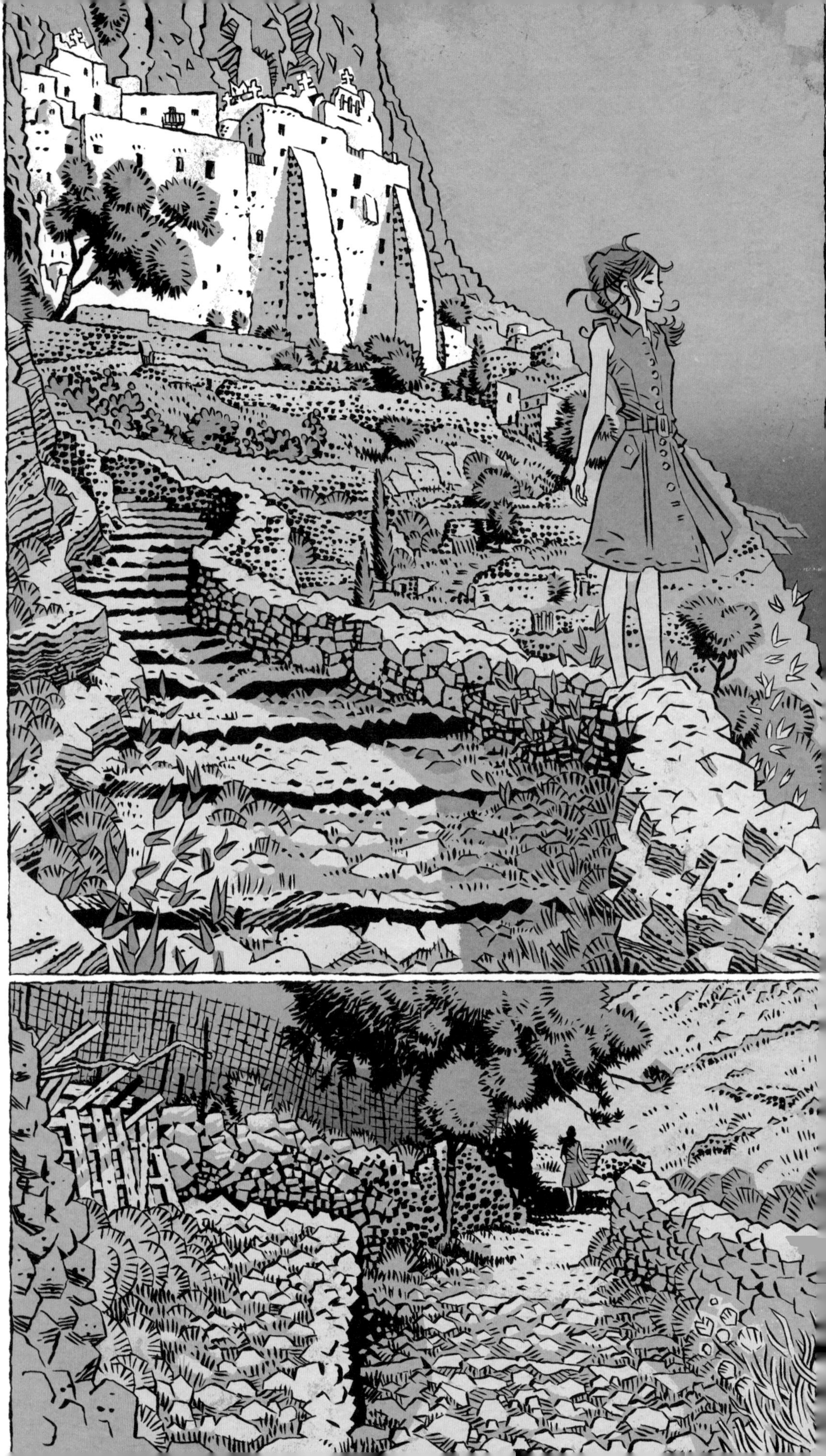

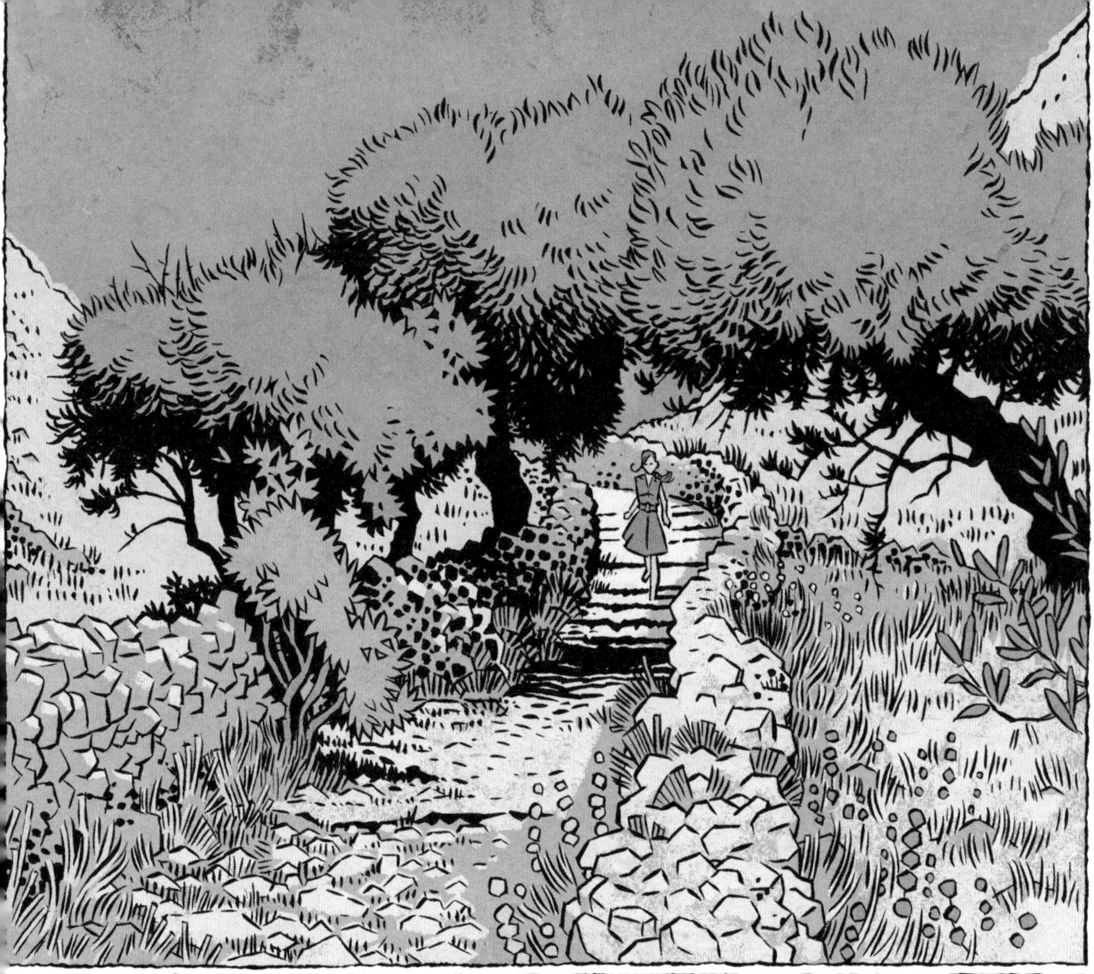

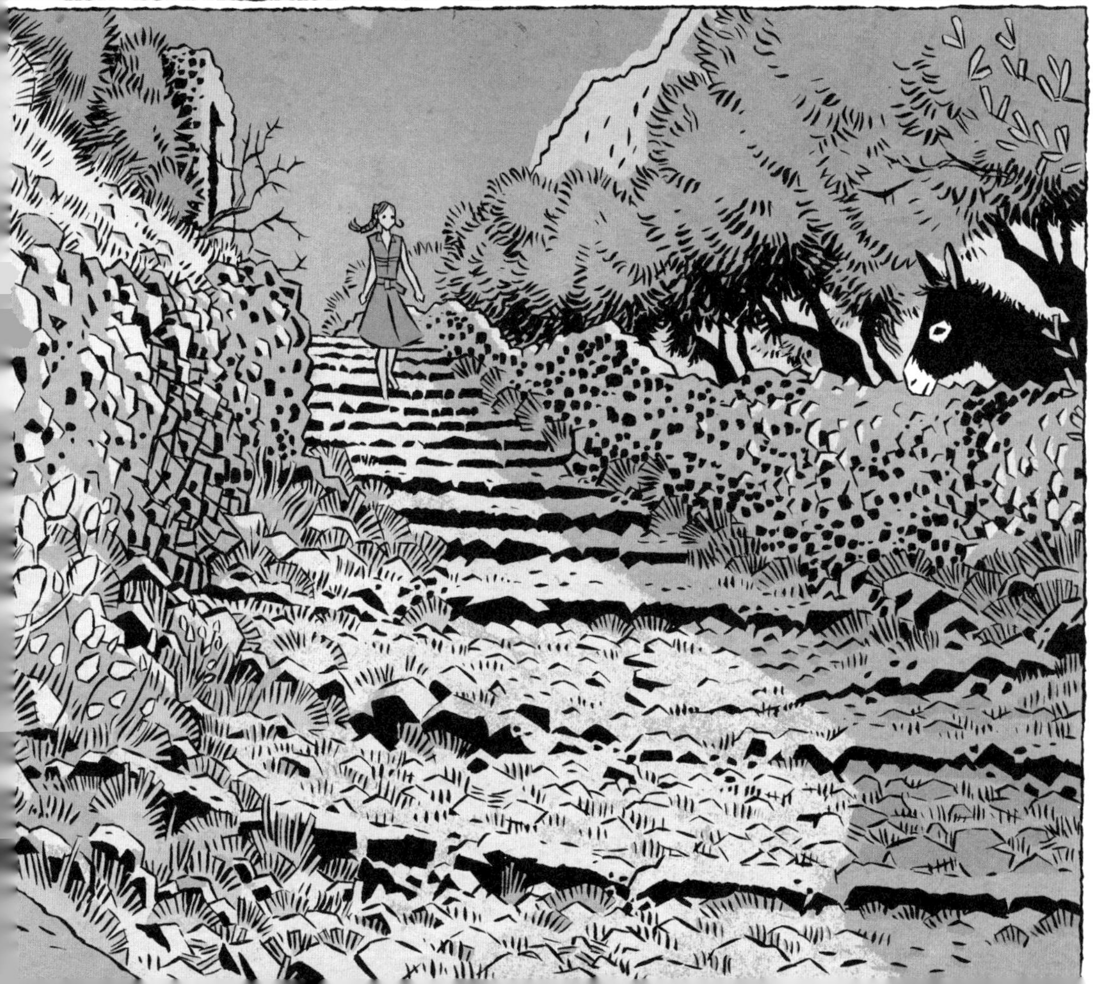

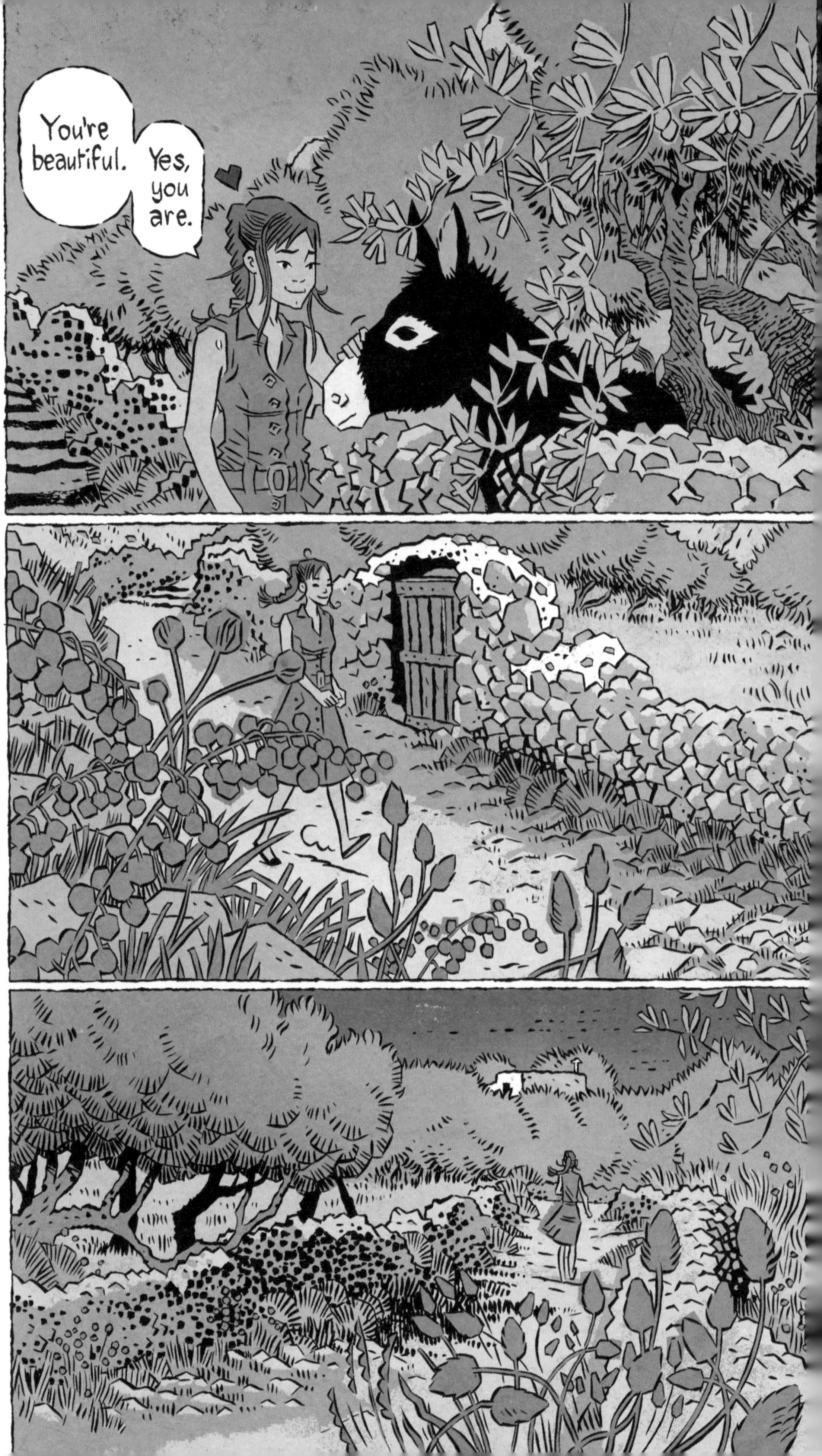
You're beautiful.
Yes, you are.

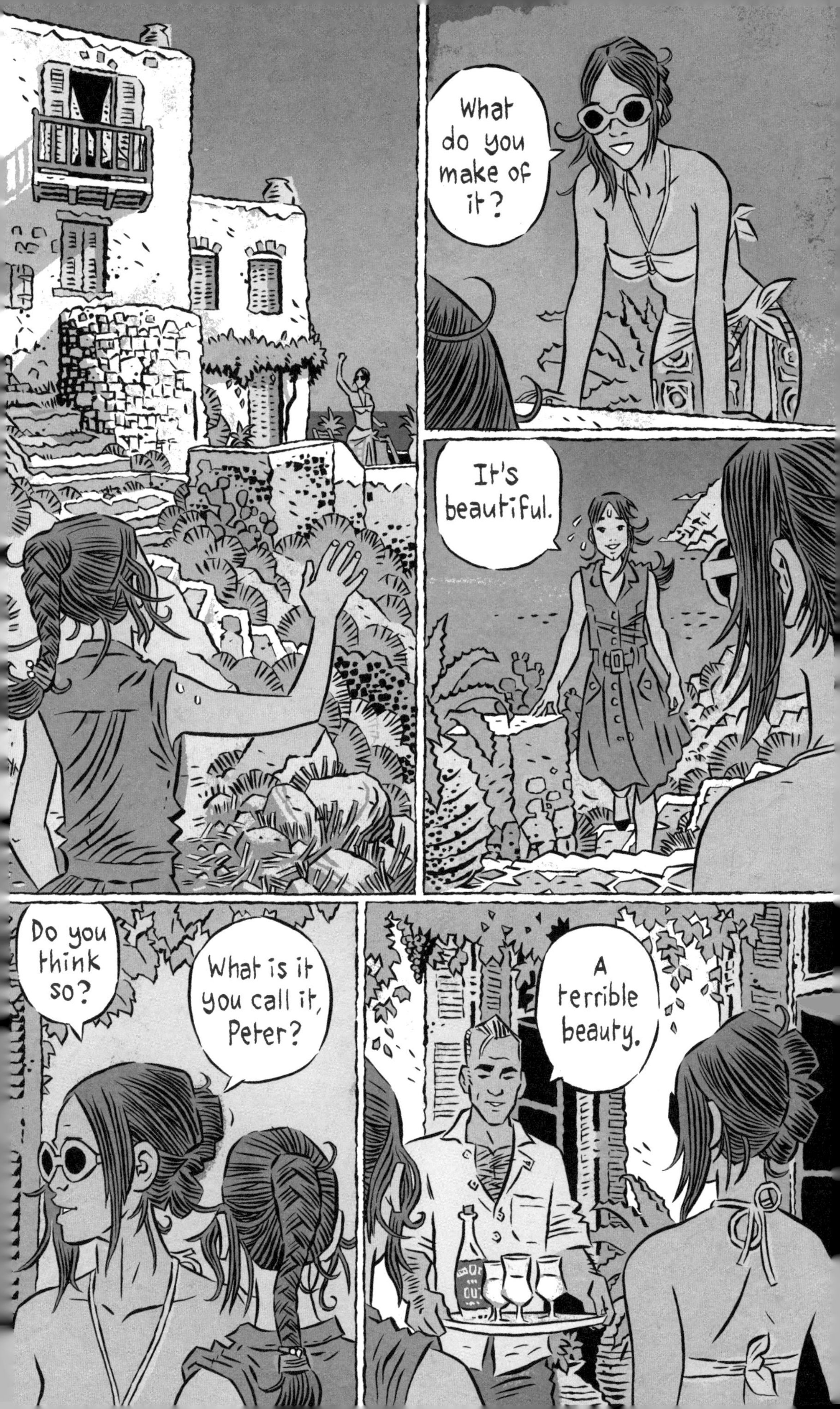
What do you make of it?
It's beautiful.
Do you think so?
What is it you call it, Peter?
A terrible beauty.

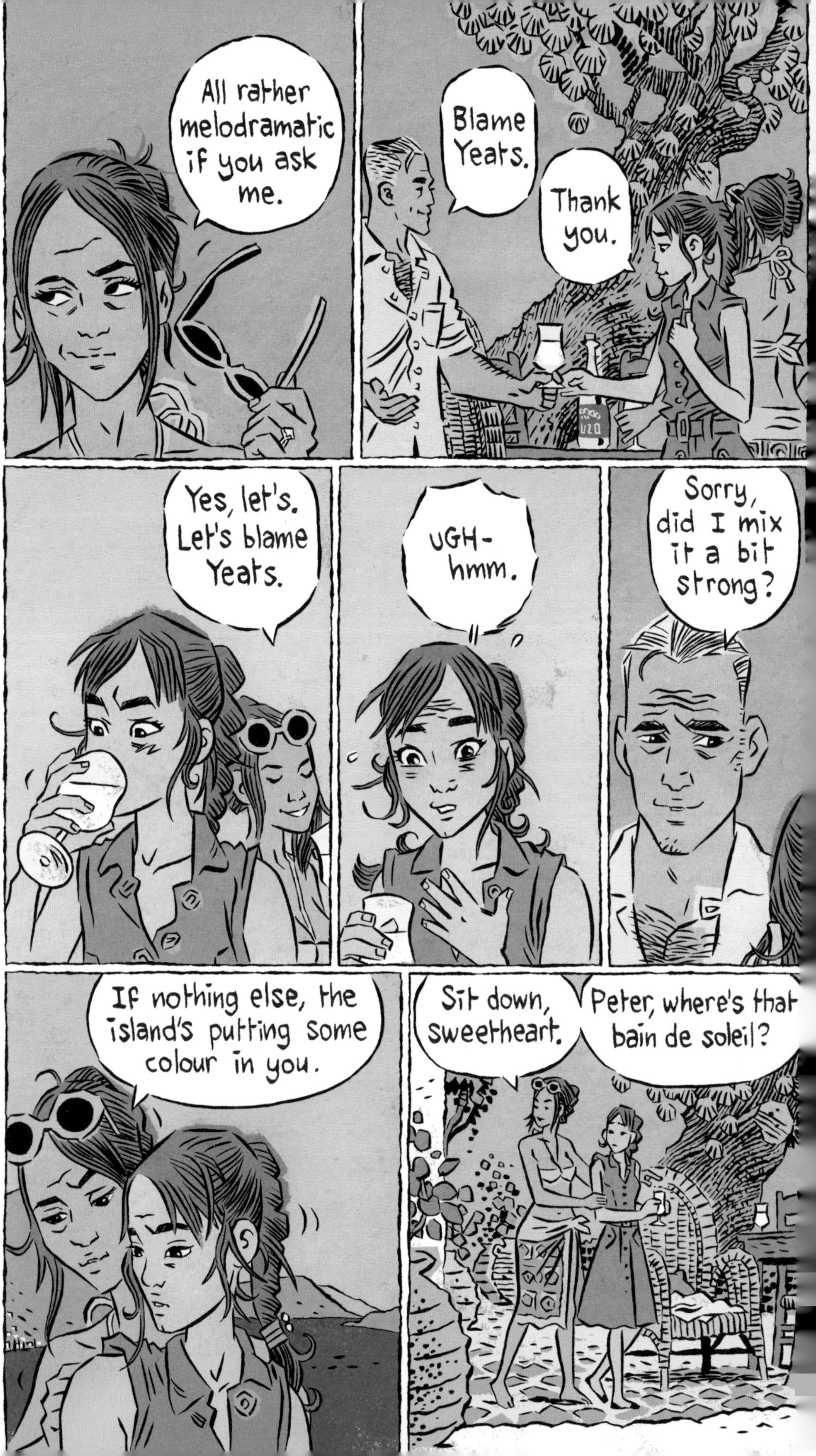
All rather melodramatic if you ask me.
Blame Yeats.
Thank you.
Yes, let's. Let's blame Yeats.
UGH-hmm.
Sorry, did I mix it a bit strong?
If nothing else, the island's putting some colour in you.
Sit down, sweetheart.
Peter, where's that bain de soleil?

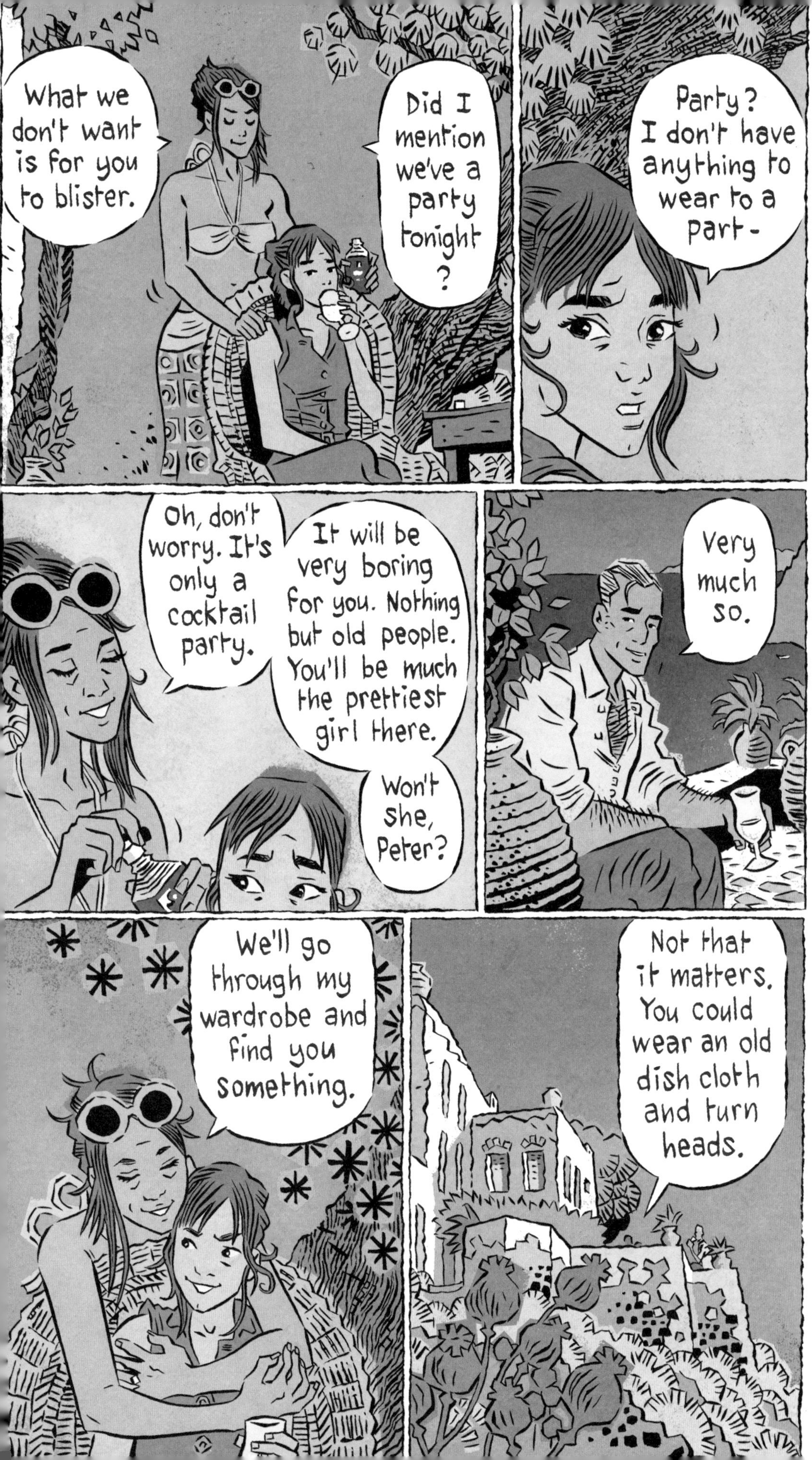
What we don't want is for you to blister.
Did I mention we've a party tonight?
Party? I don't have anything to wear to a part-
Oh, don't worry. It's only a cocktail party.
It will be very boring for you. Nothing but old people. You'll be much the prettiest girl there.
Won't she, Peter?
Very much so.
We'll go through my wardrobe and find you something.
Not that it matters. You could wear an old dish cloth and turn heads.

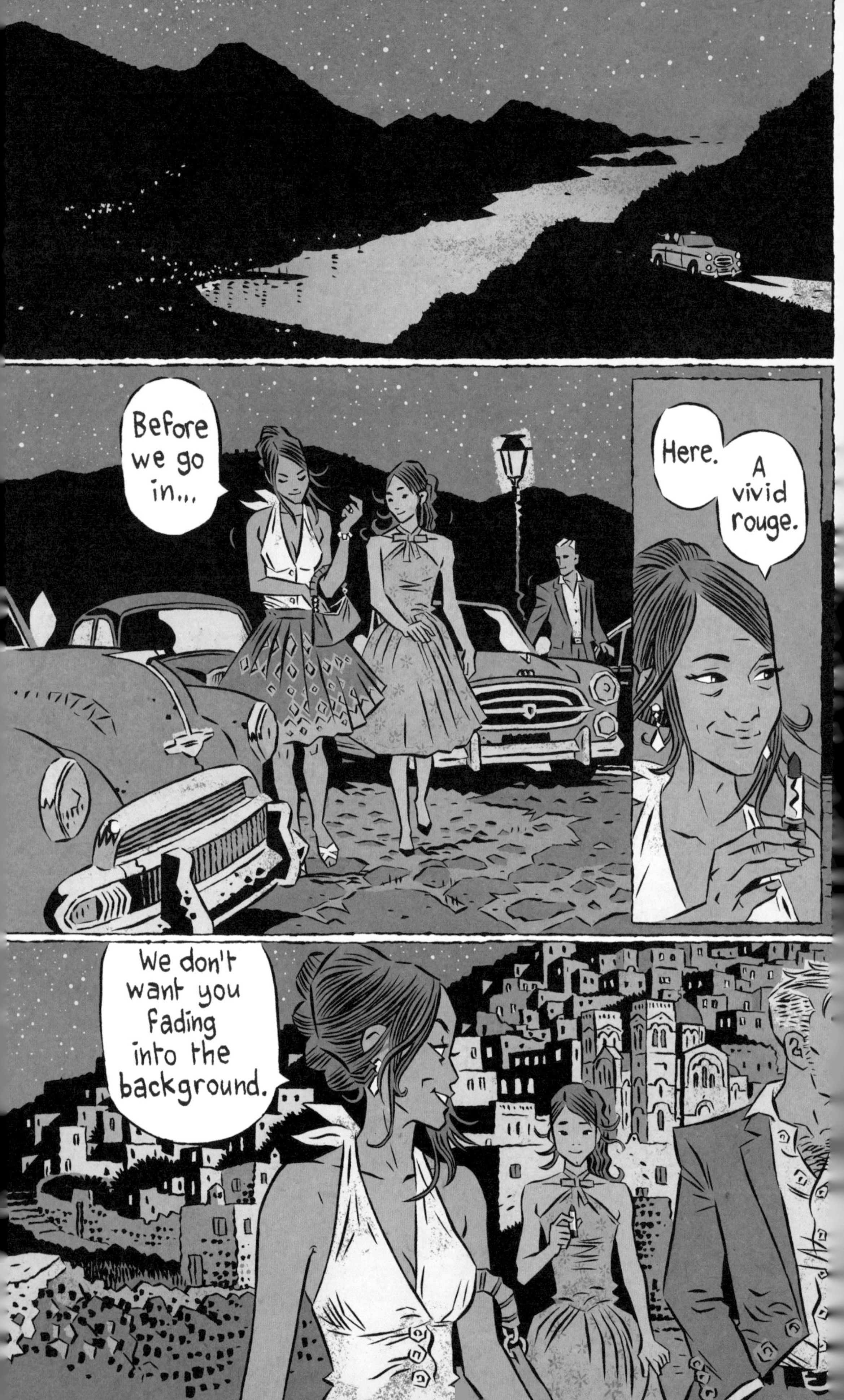
Before we go in...
Here.
A vivid rouge.
We don't want you fading into the background.

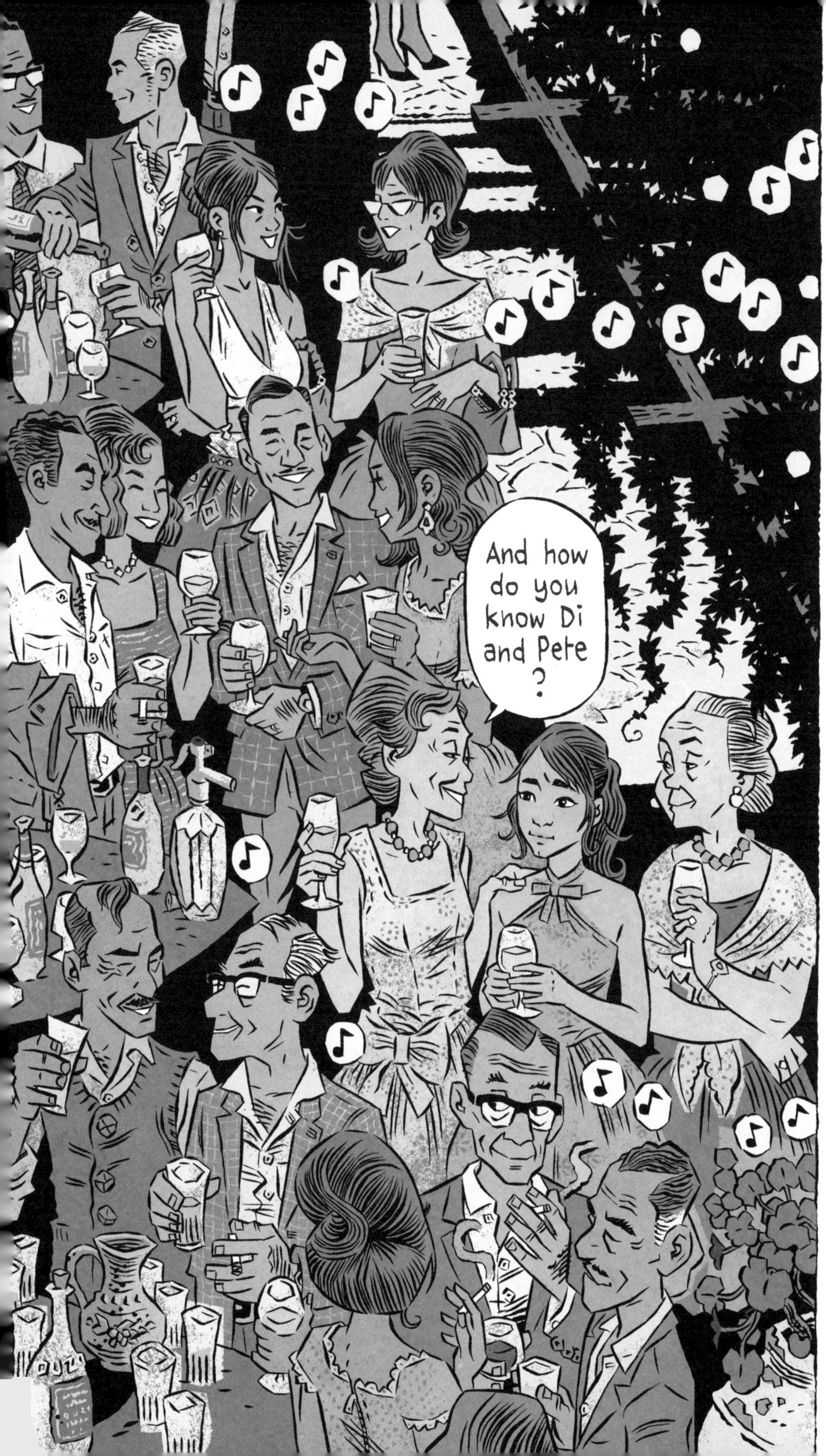
And how do you know Di and Pete ?

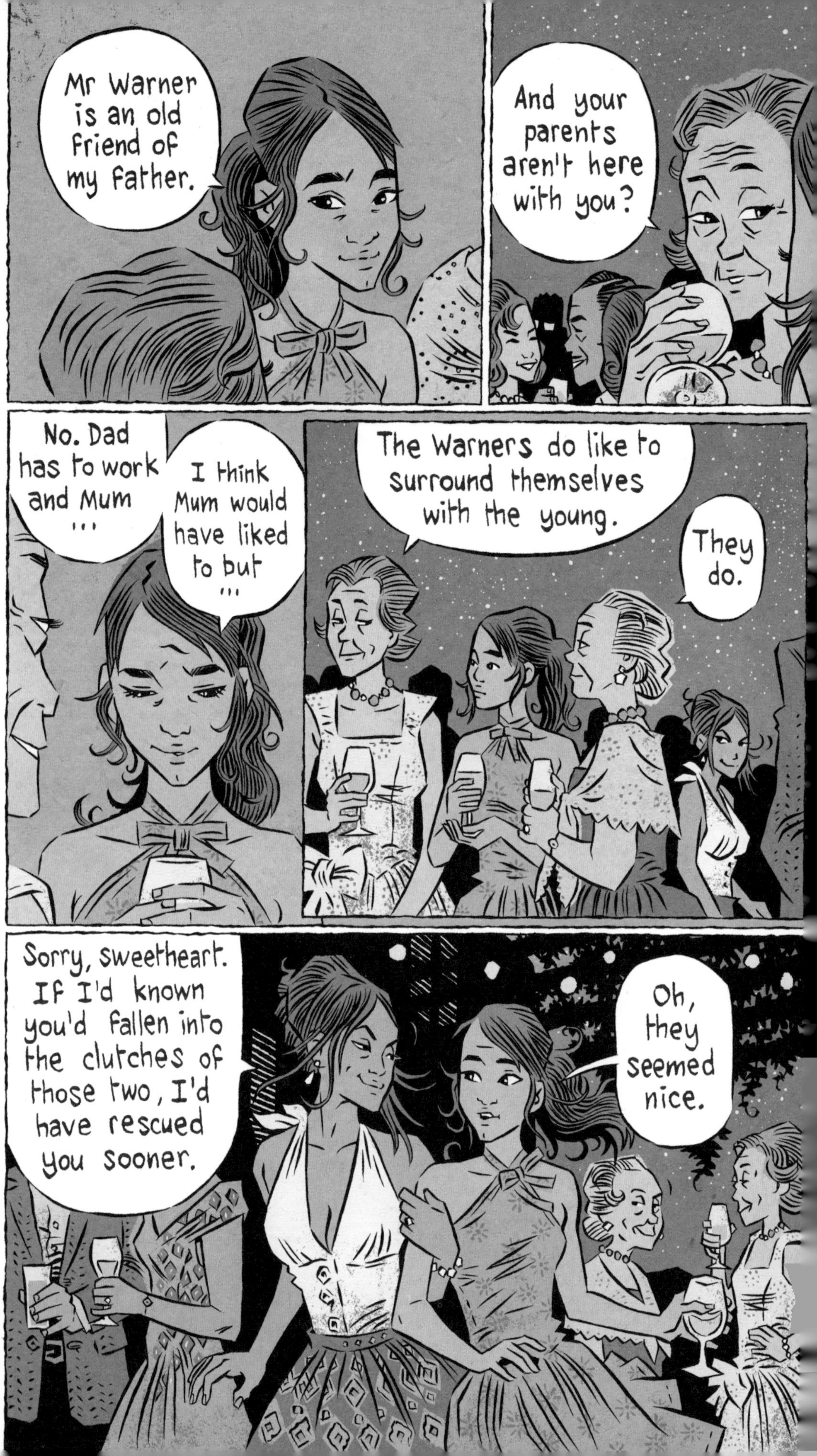
Mr Warner is an old friend of my father.
And your parents aren't here with you?
No. Dad has to work and Mum ...
I think Mum would have liked to but ...
The Warners do like to surround themselves with the young.
They do.
Sorry, sweetheart. If I'd known you'd fallen into the clutches of those two, I'd have rescued you sooner.
Oh, they seemed nice.

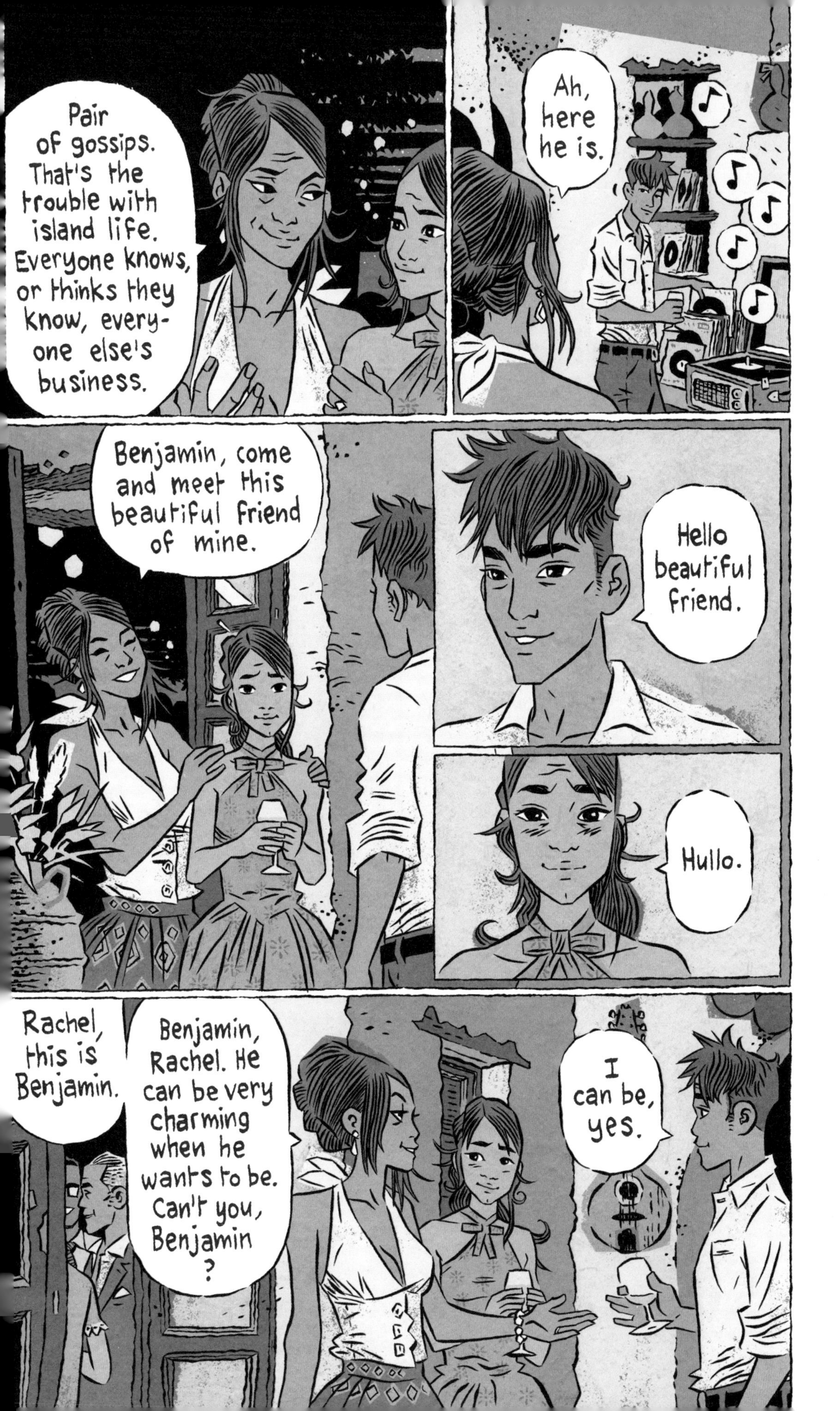
Pair of gossips. That's the trouble with island life. Everyone knows, or thinks they know, every-one else's business.
Ah, here he is.
Benjamin, come and meet this beautiful friend of mine.
Hello beautiful friend.
Hullo.
Rachel, this is Benjamin.
Benjamin, Rachel. He can be very charming when he wants to be. Can't you, Benjamin?
I can be, yes.

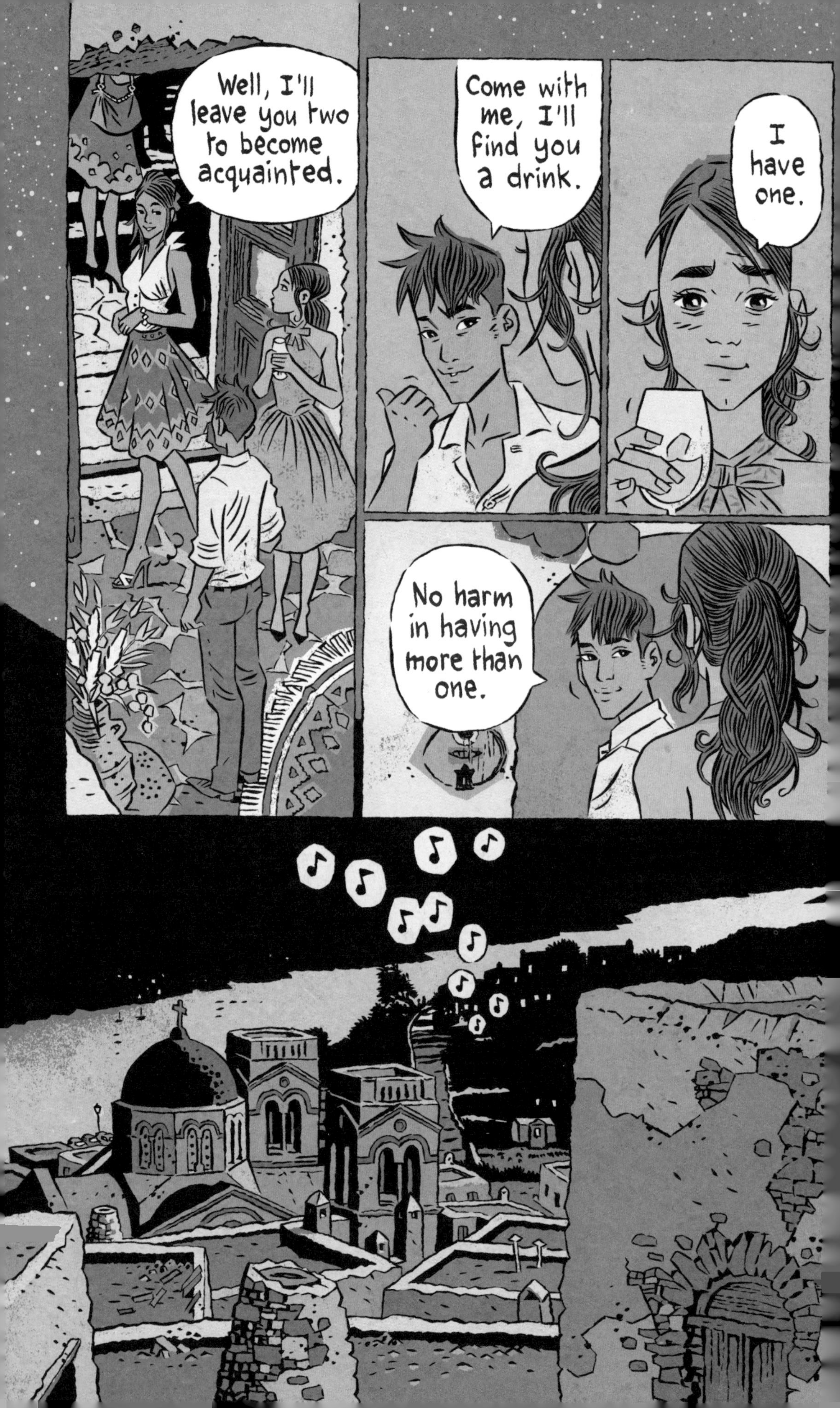
Well, I'll leave you two to become acquainted.
Come with me, I'll find you a drink.
I have one.
No harm in having more than one.

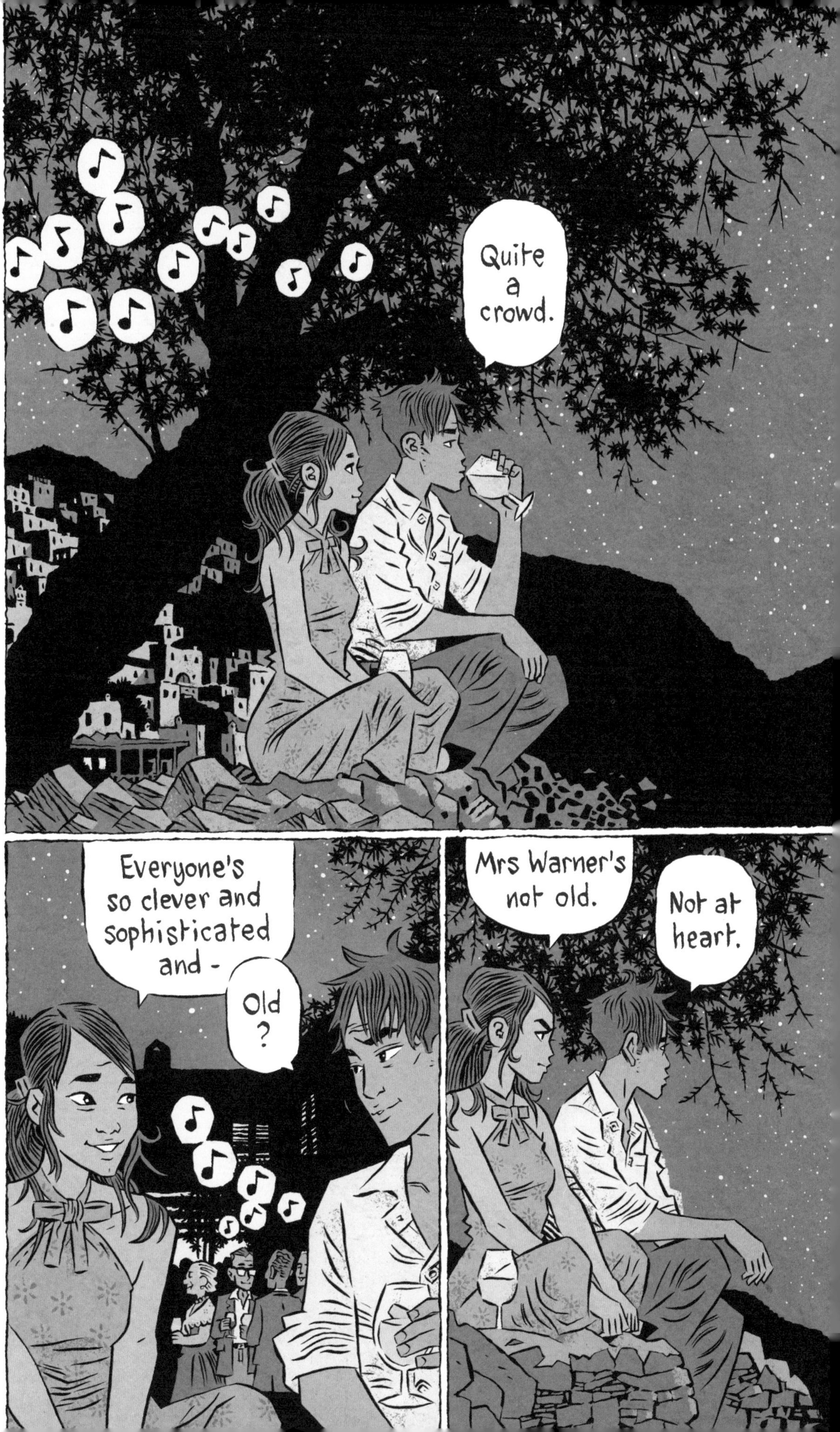
Quite a crowd.
Everyone's so clever and sophisticated and -
Old?
Mrs Warner's not old.
Not at heart.

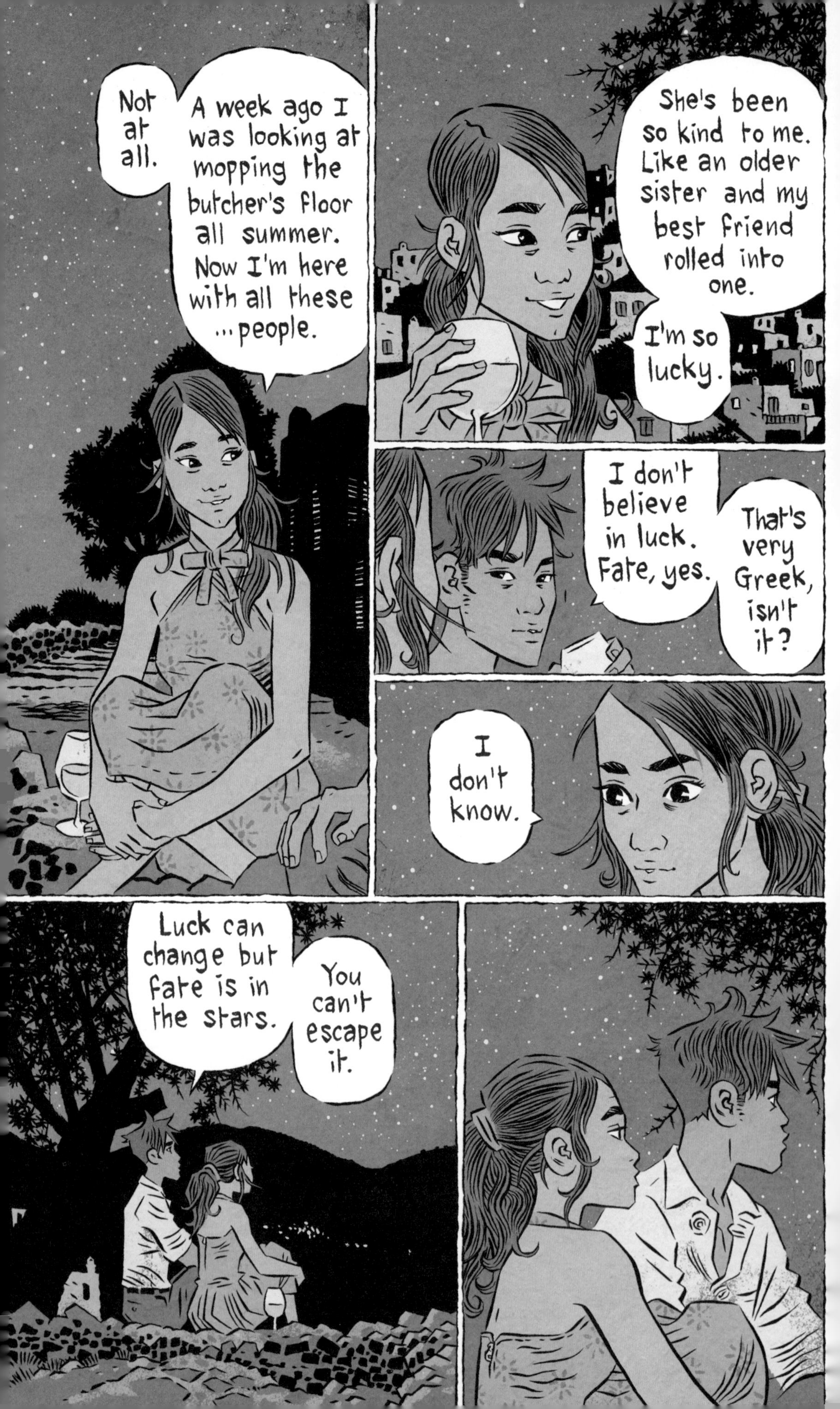
Not at all.
A week ago I was looking at mopping the butcher's floor all summer. Now I'm here with all these ...people.
She's been so kind to me. Like an older sister and my best friend rolled into one.
I'm so lucky.
I don't believe in luck. Fate, yes.
That's very Greek, isn't it?
I don't know.
Luck can change but fate is in the stars.
You can't escape it.

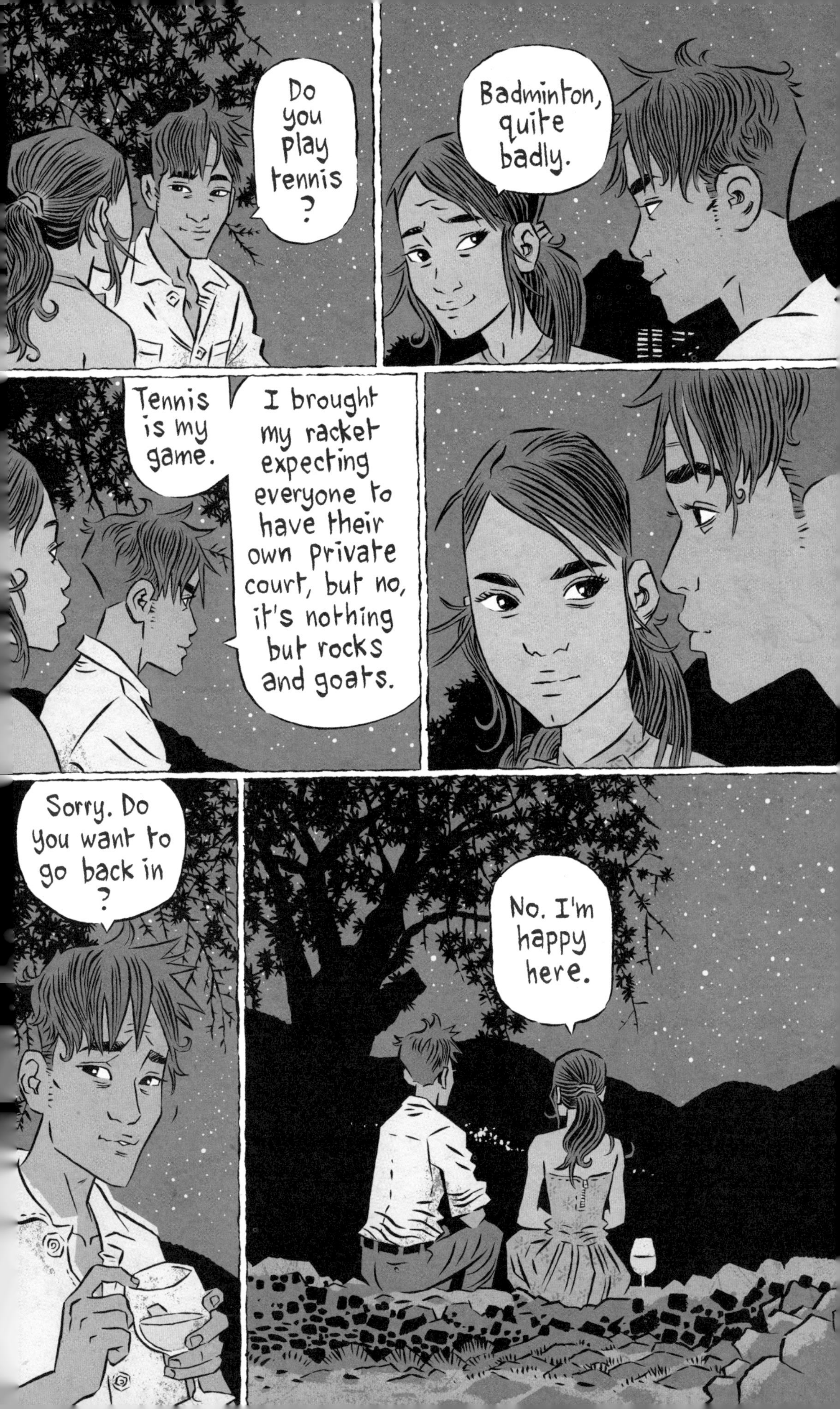
Do you play tennis?
Badminton, quite badly.
Tennis is my game.
I brought my racket expecting everyone to have their own private court, but no, it's nothing but rocks and goats.
Sorry. Do you want to go back in?
No. I'm happy here.

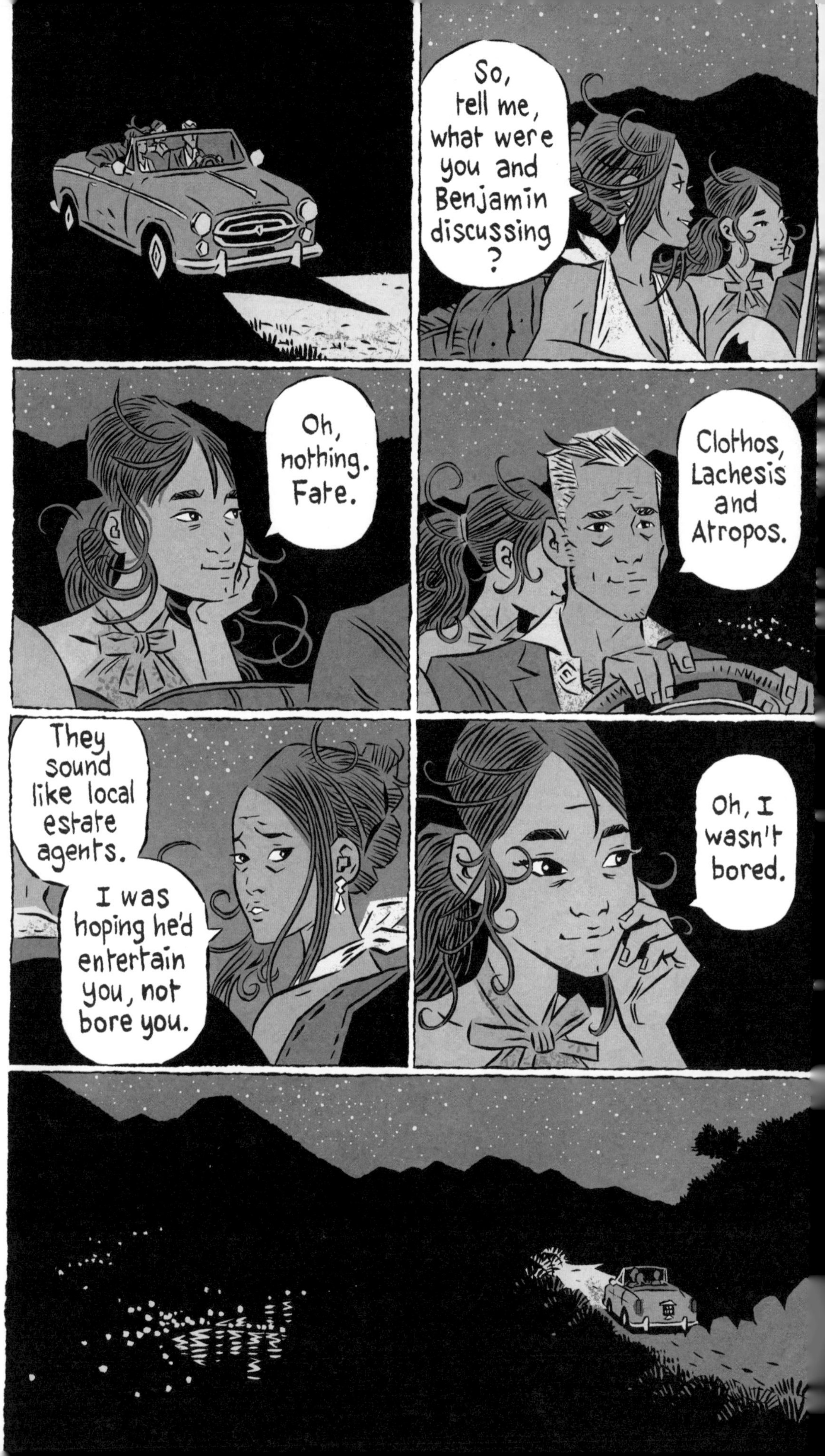

So, tell me, what were you and Benjamin discussing?
Oh, nothing. Fate.
Clothos, Lachesis and Atropos.
They sound like local estate agents.
I was hoping he'd entertain you, not bore you.
Oh, I wasn't bored.

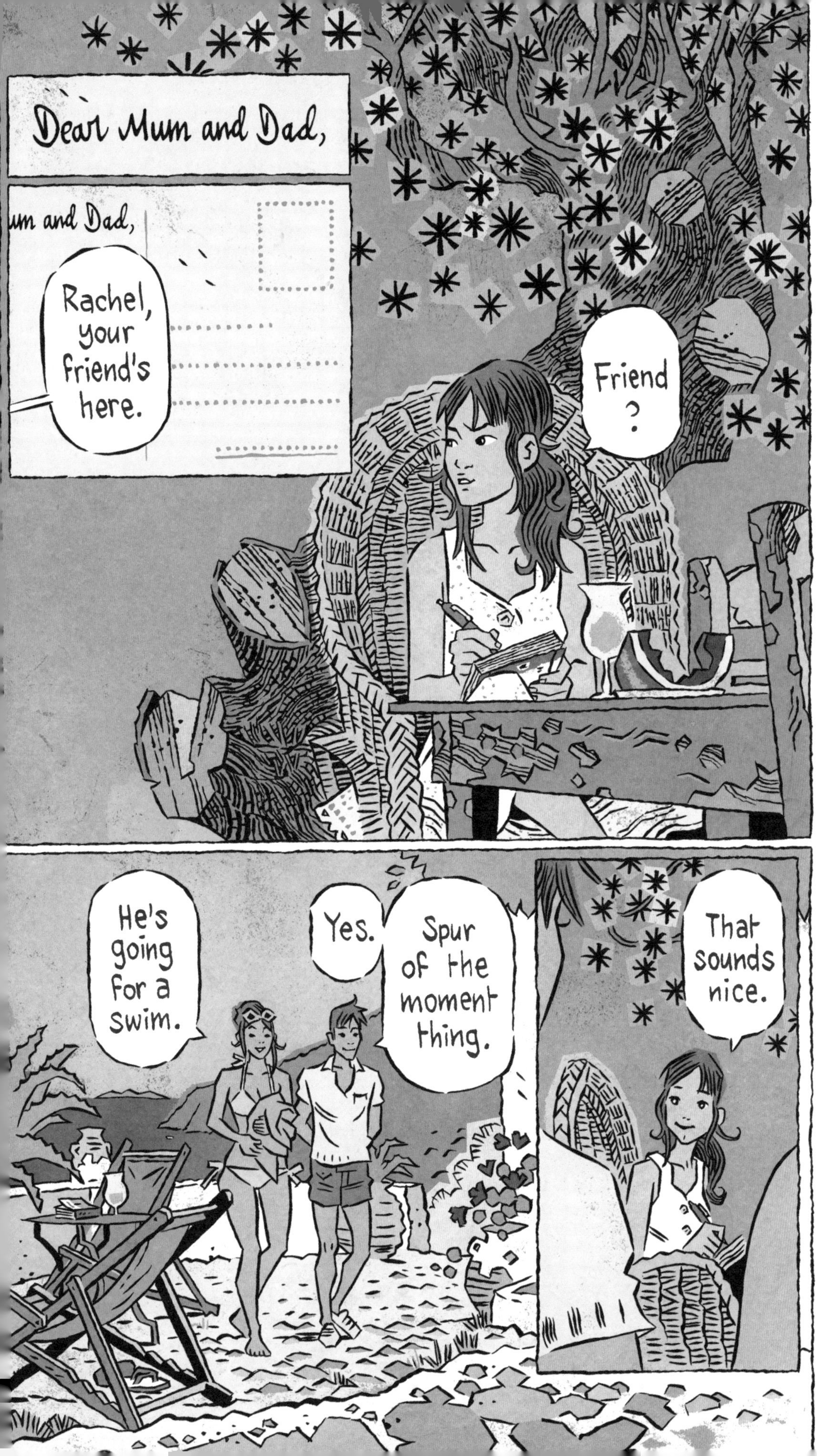
Dear Mum and Dad,
um and Dad,
Rachel, your friend's here.
Friend ?
He's going for a swim.
Yes.
Spur of the moment thing.
That sounds nice.

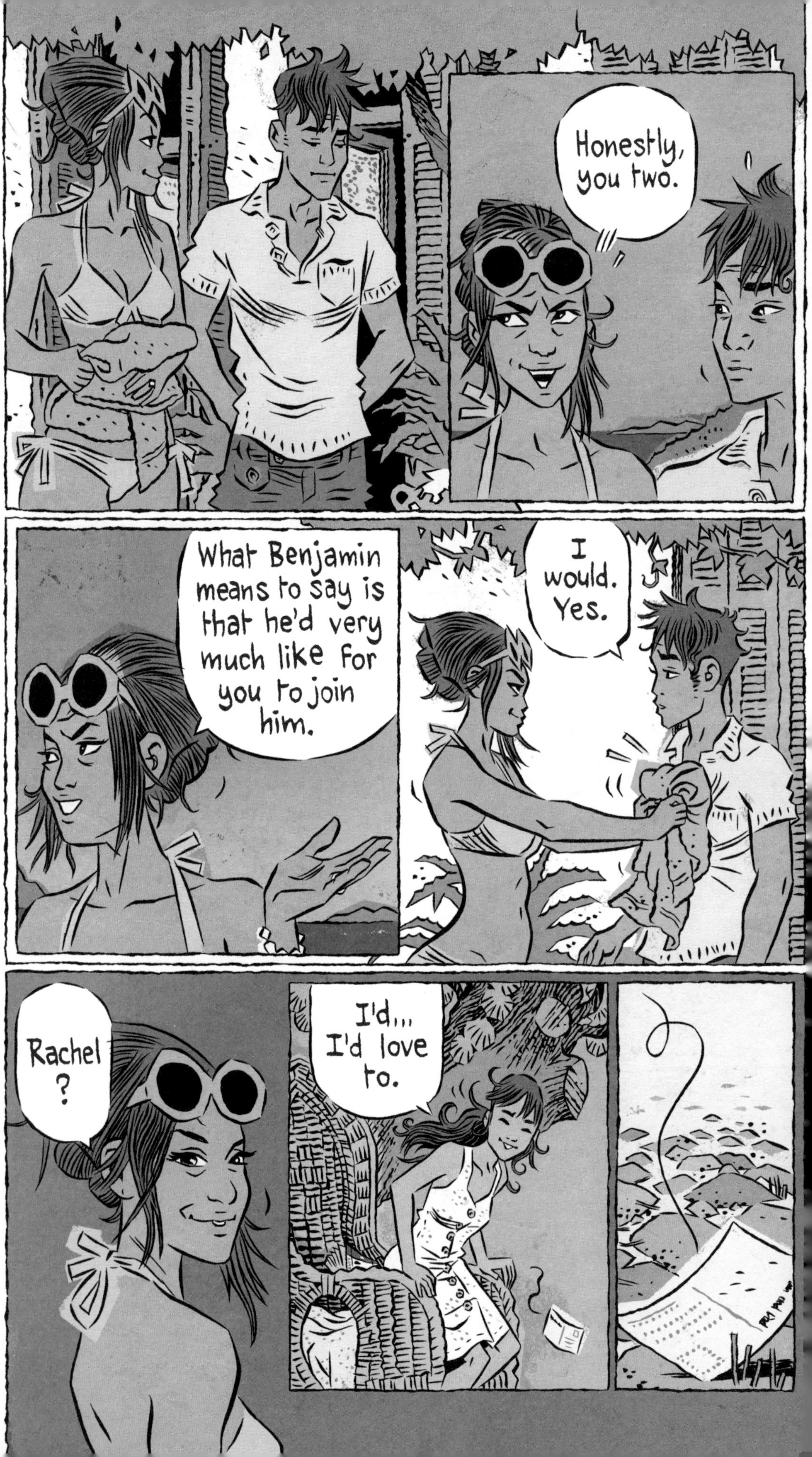
Honestly, you two.
What Benjamin means to say is that he'd very much like for you to join him.
I would. Yes.
Rachel?
I'd... I'd love to.

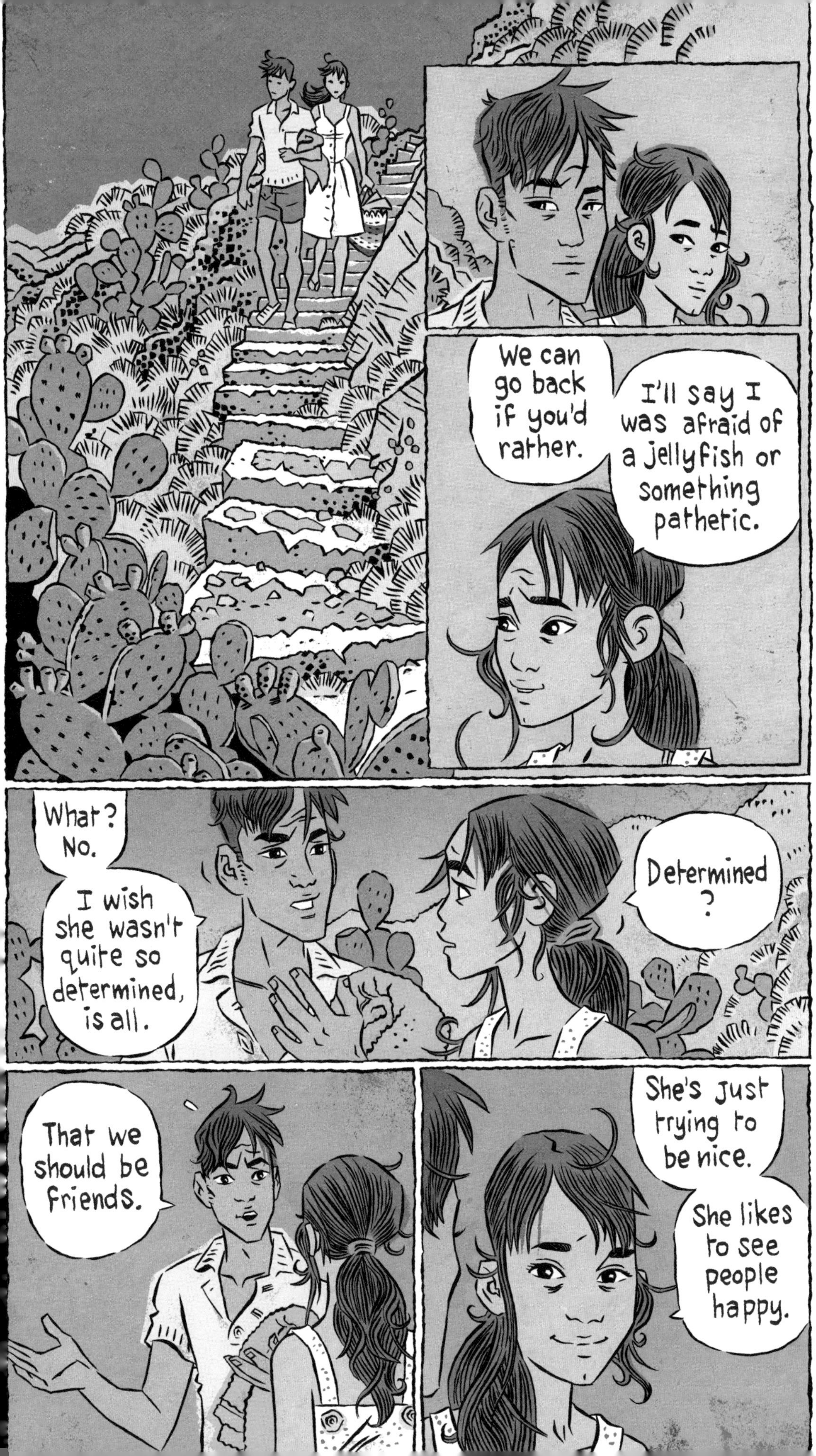
We can go back if you'd rather.
I'll say I was afraid of a jellyfish or something pathetic.
What? No.
I wish she wasn't quite so determined, is all.
Determined?
That we should be friends.
She's just trying to be nice.
She likes to see people happy.

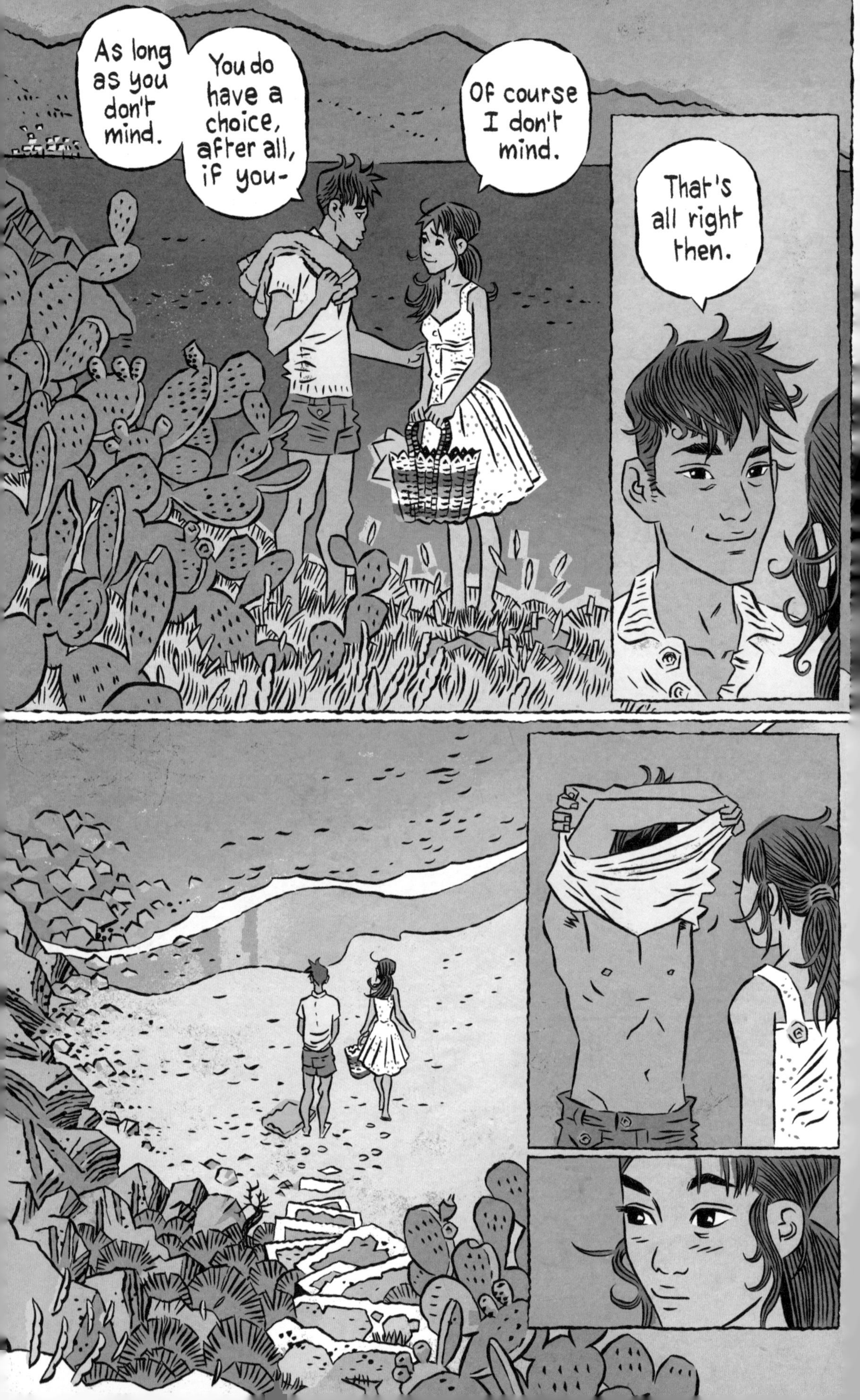
As long as you don't mind.
You do have a choice, after all, if you-
Of course I don't mind.
That's all right then.

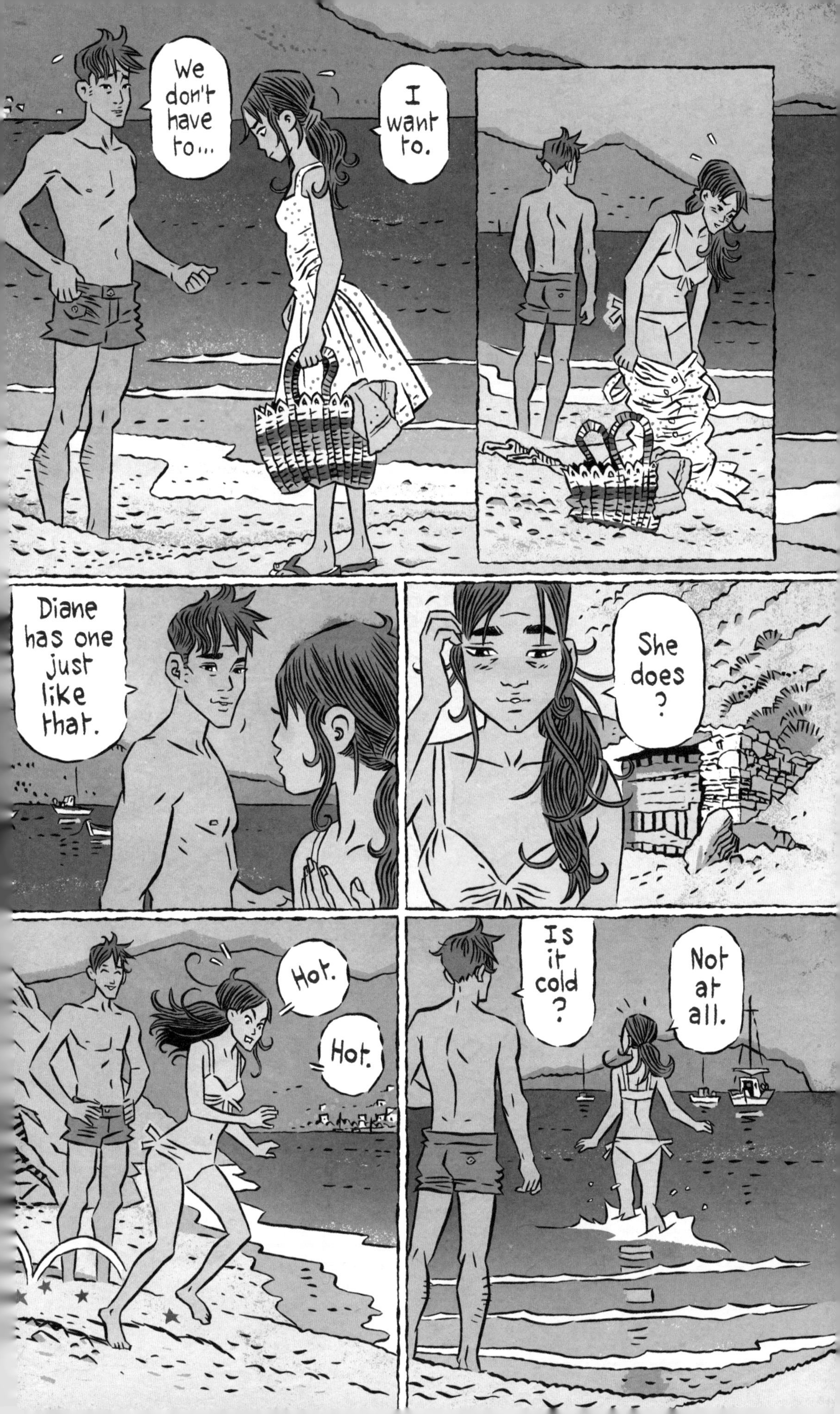
We don't have to...
I want to.
Diane has one just like that.
She does?
Hot.
Hot.
Is it cold?
Not at all.

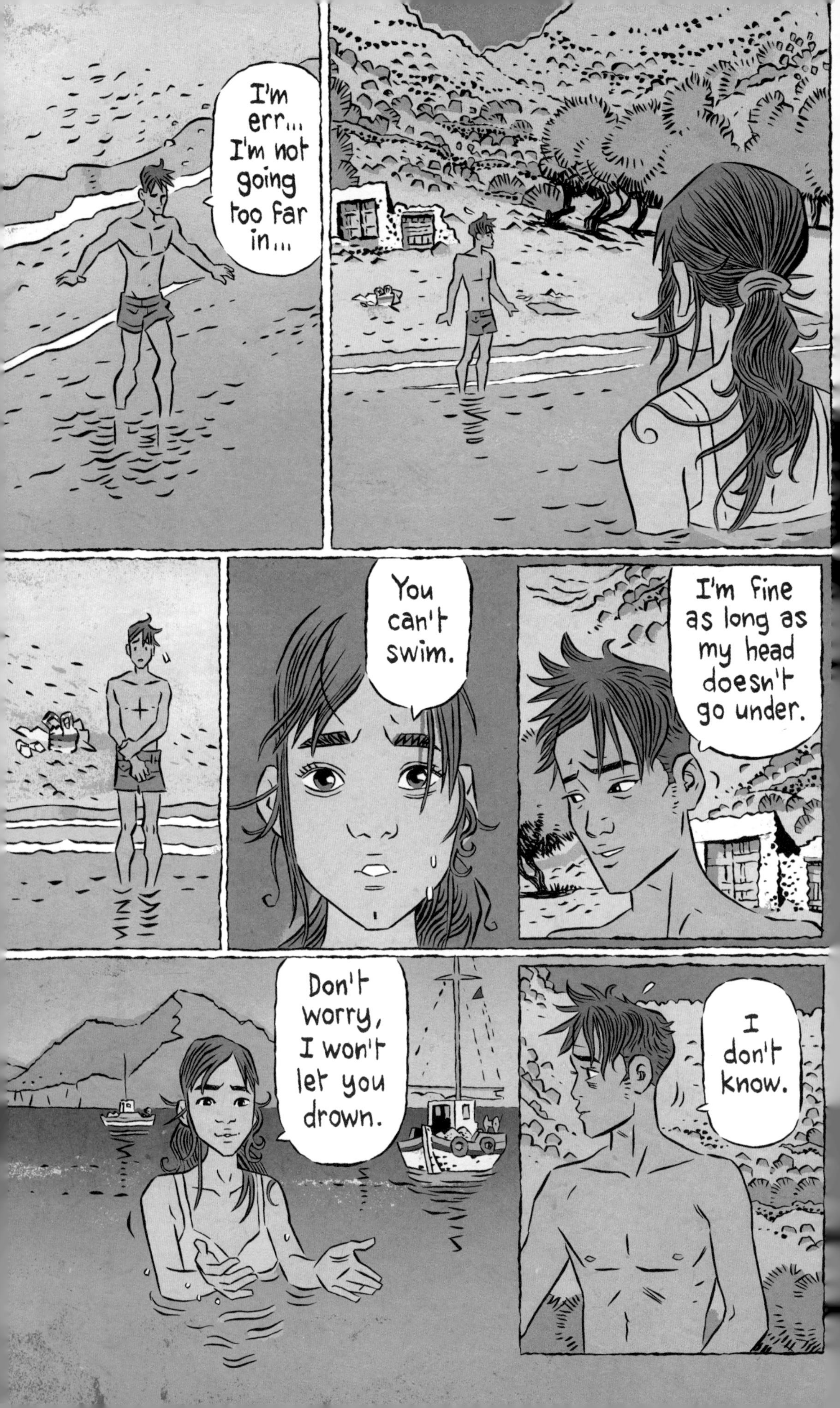
I'm err... I'm not going too far in...
You can't swim.
I'm fine as long as my head doesn't go under.
Don't worry, I won't let you drown.
I don't know.

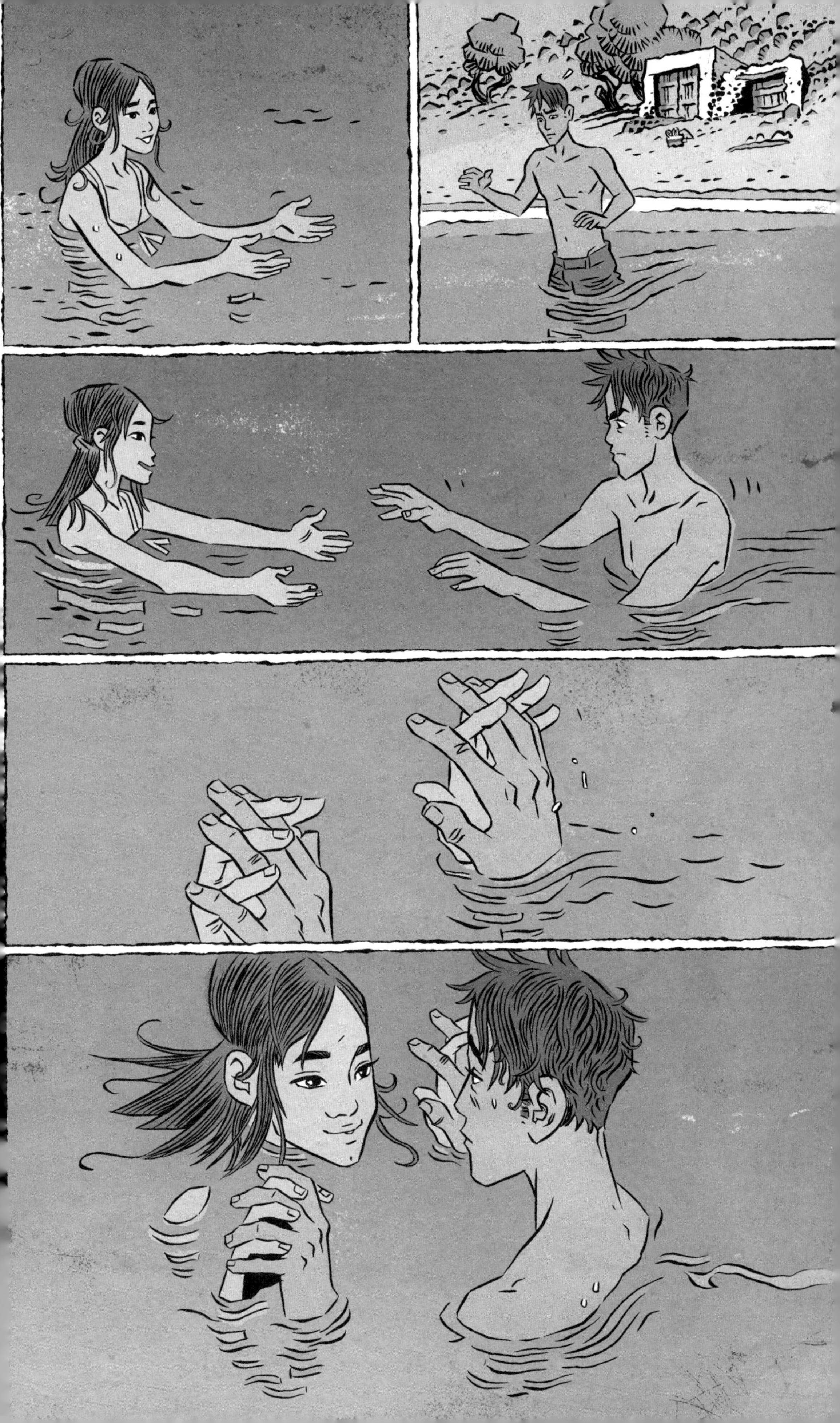

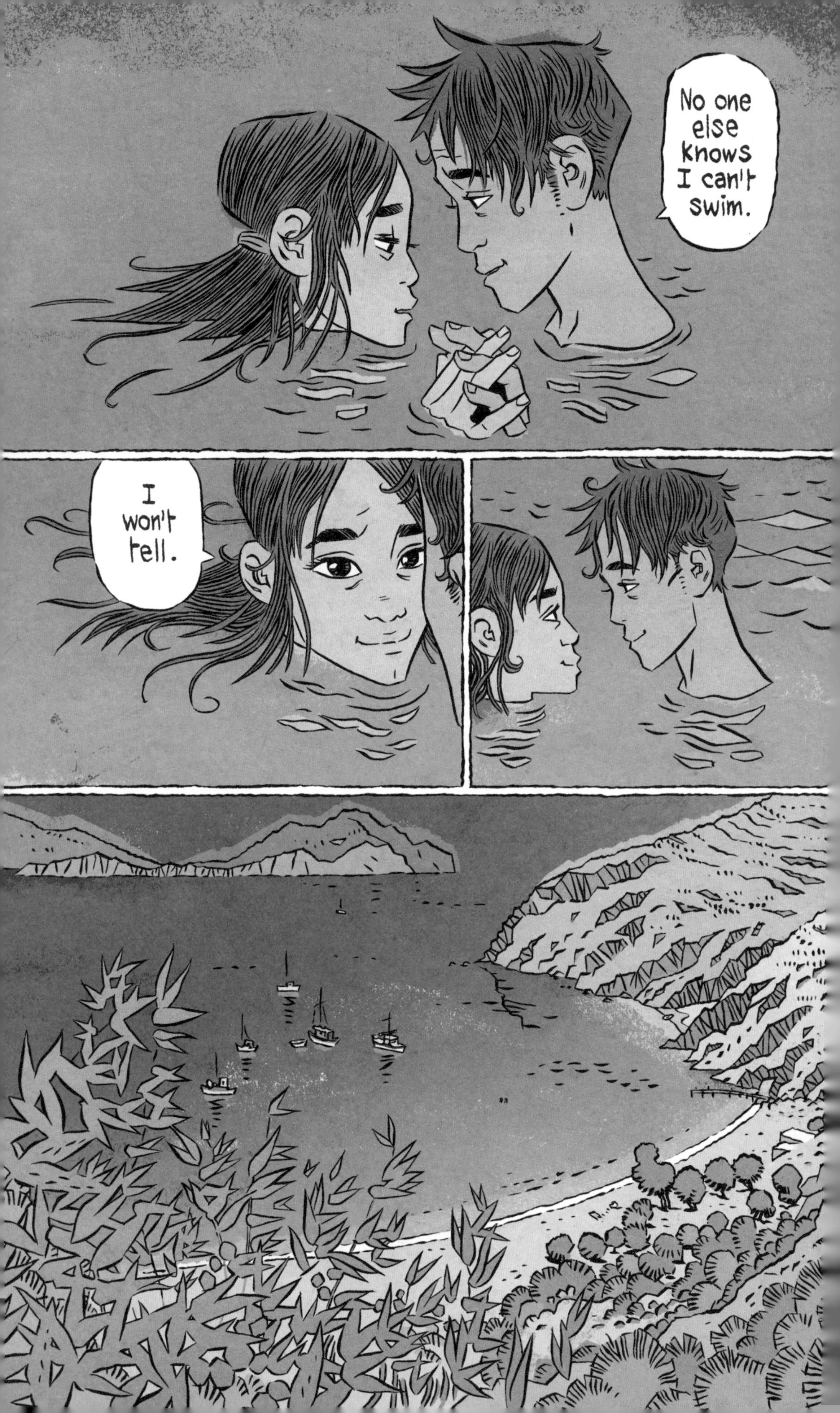
No one else knows I can't swim.
I won't tell.

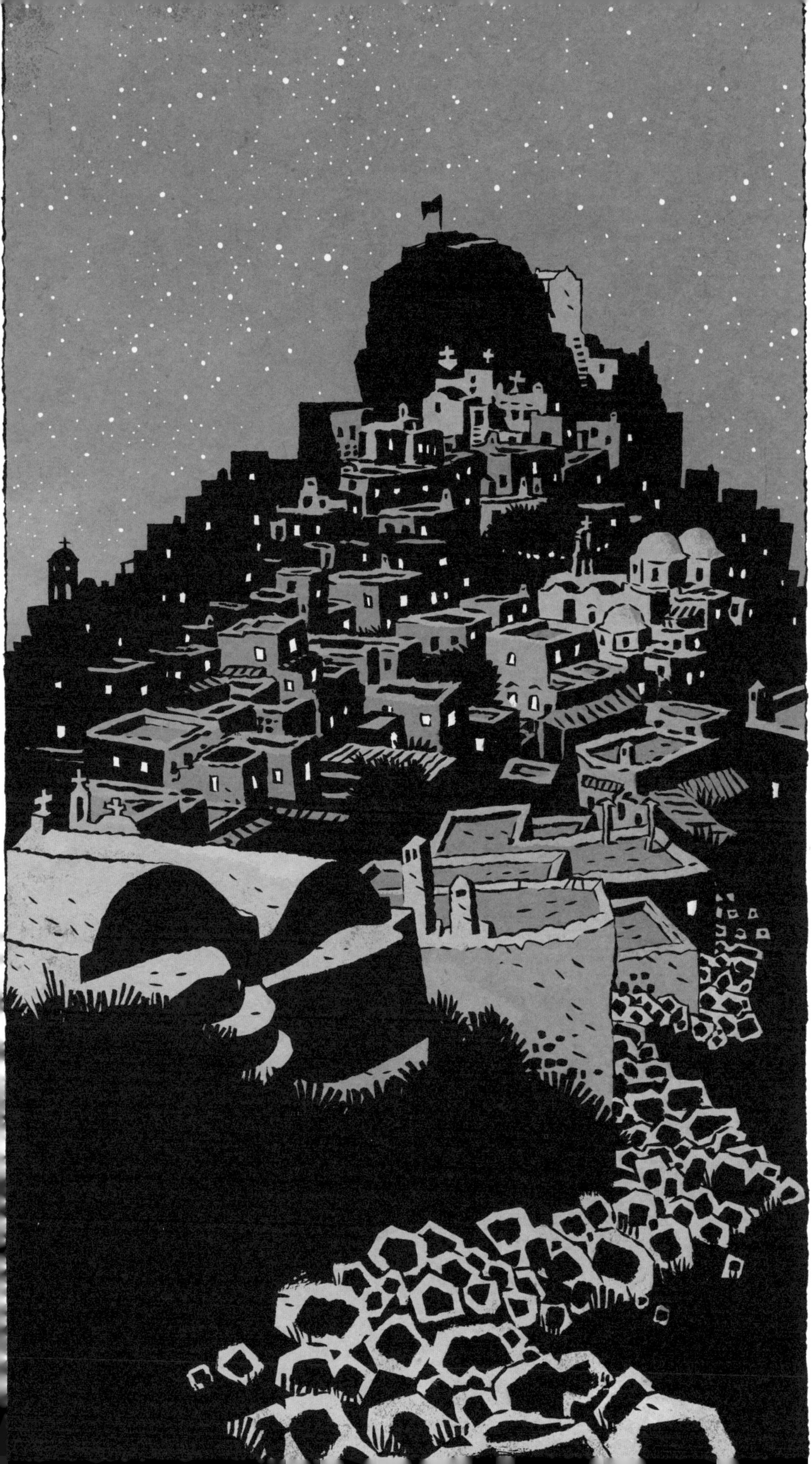

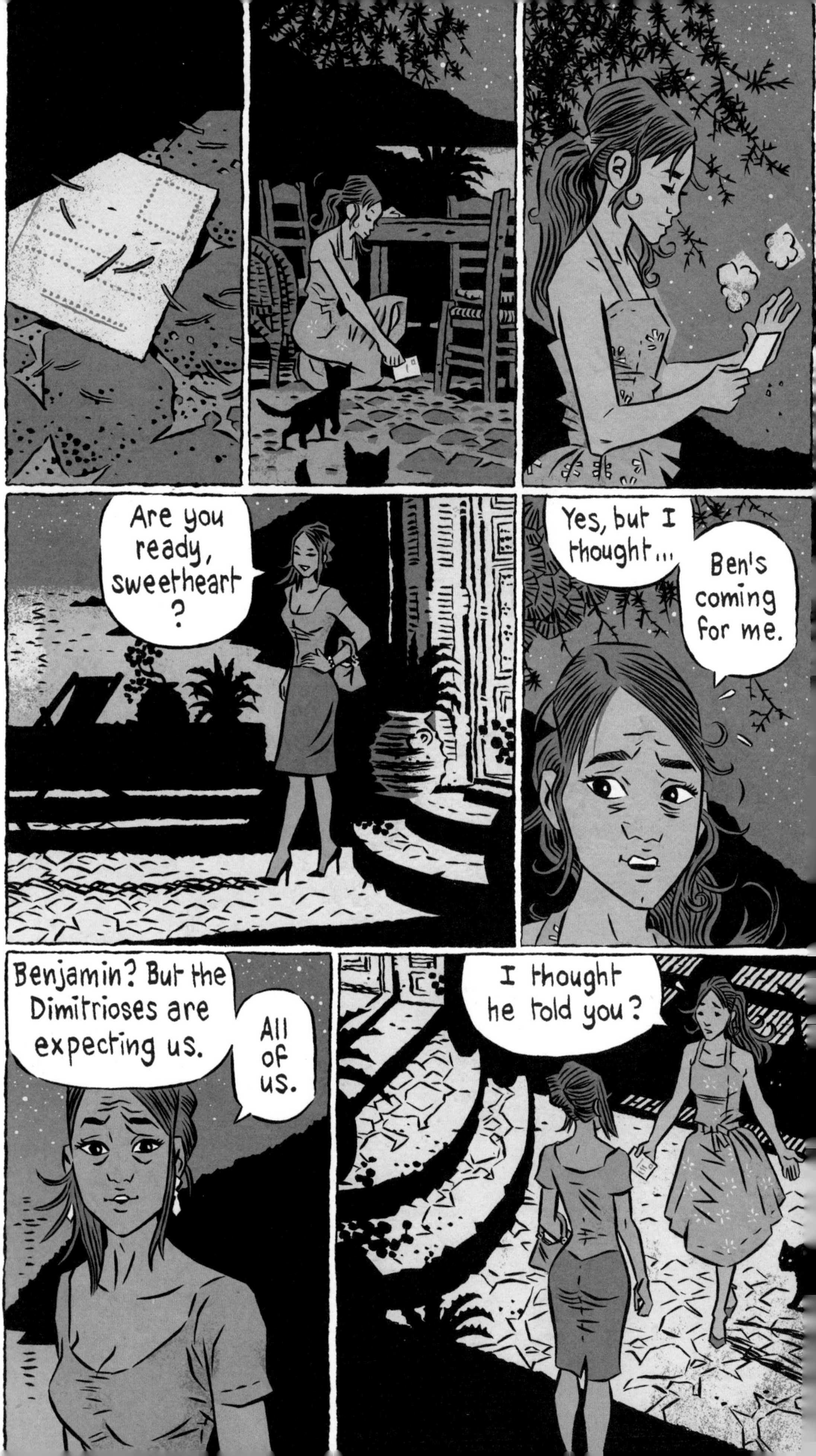
Are you ready, sweetheart?
Yes, but I thought...
Ben's coming for me.
Benjamin? But the Dimitrioses are expecting us.
All of us.
I thought he told you?

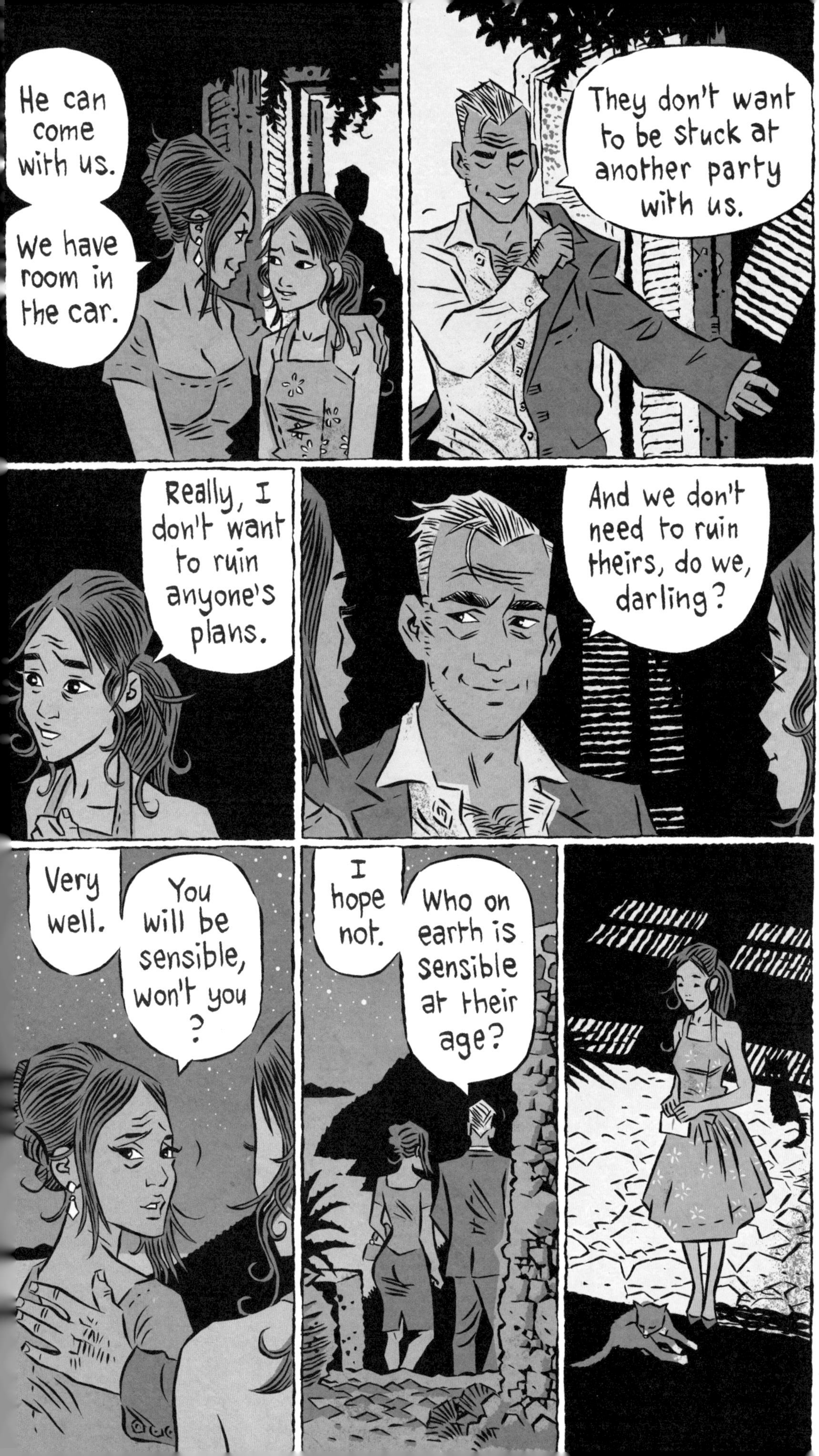
He can come with us.
We have room in the car.
They don't want to be stuck at another party with us.
Really, I don't want to ruin anyone's plans.
And we don't need to ruin theirs, do we, darling?
Very well.
You will be sensible, won't you?
I hope not.
Who on earth is sensible at their age?

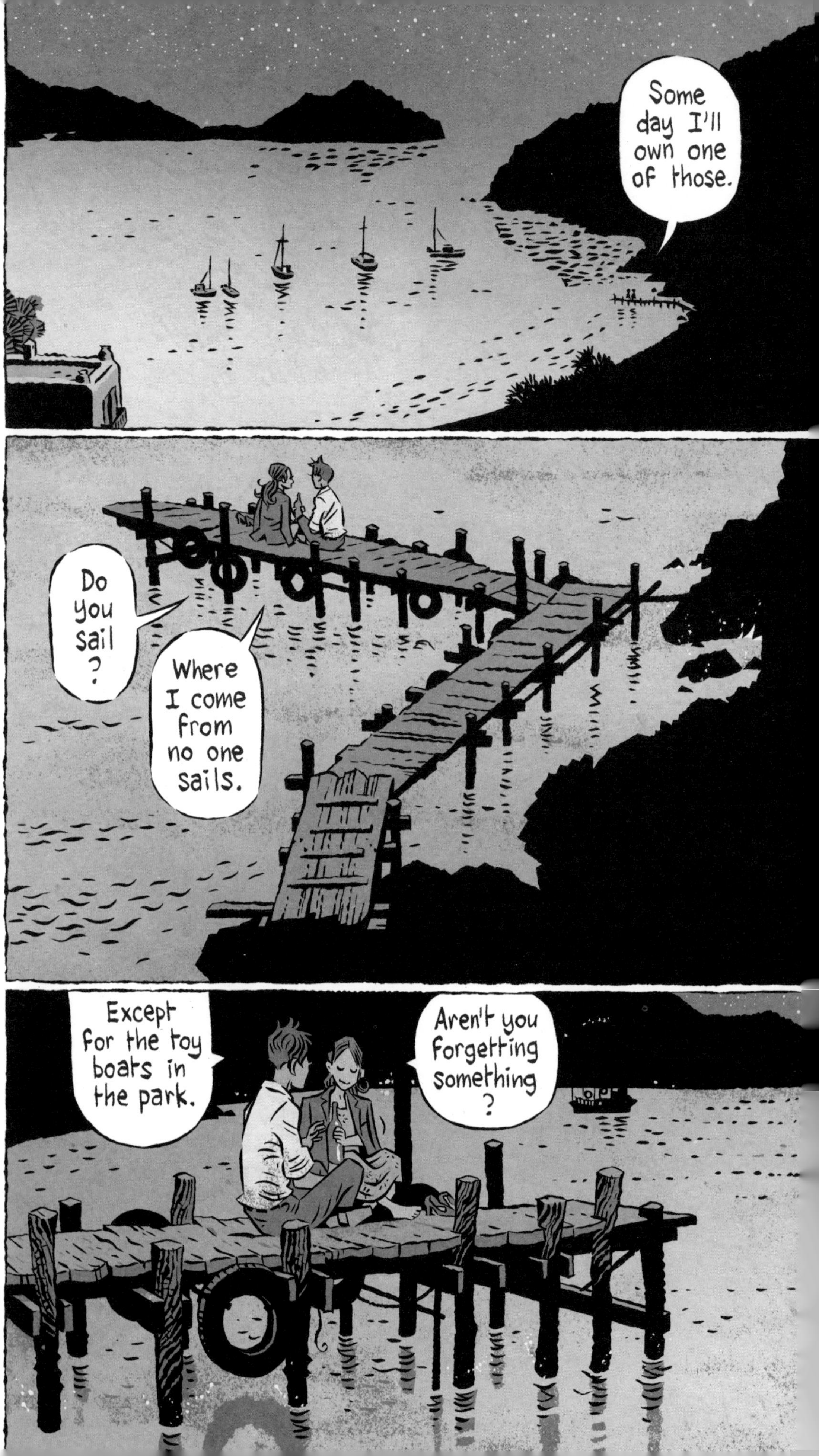
Some day I'll own one of those.
Do you sail?
Where I come from no one sails.
Except for the toy boats in the park.
Aren't you forgetting something?

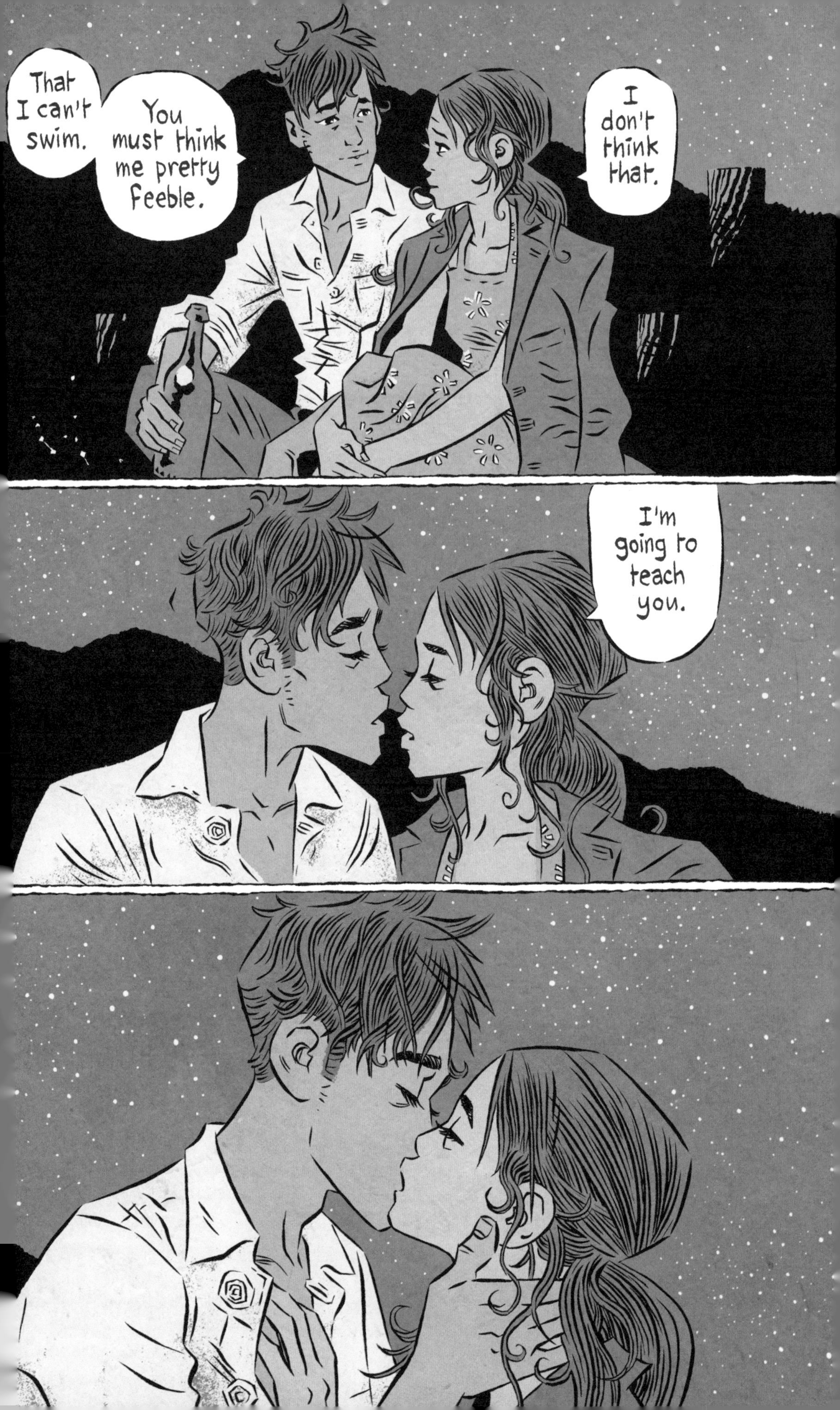
That I can't swim.
You must think me pretty feeble.
I don't think that.
I'm going to teach you.

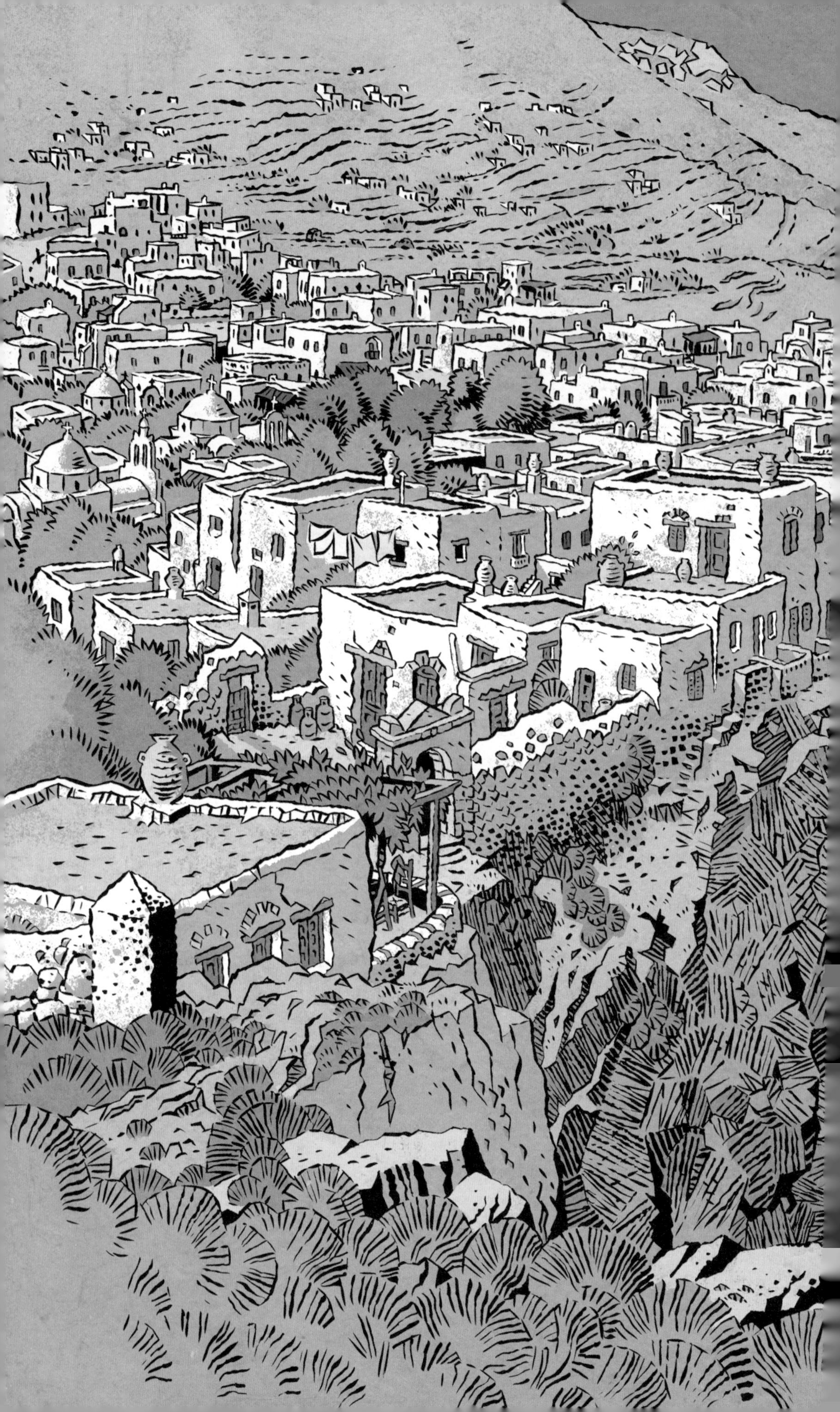

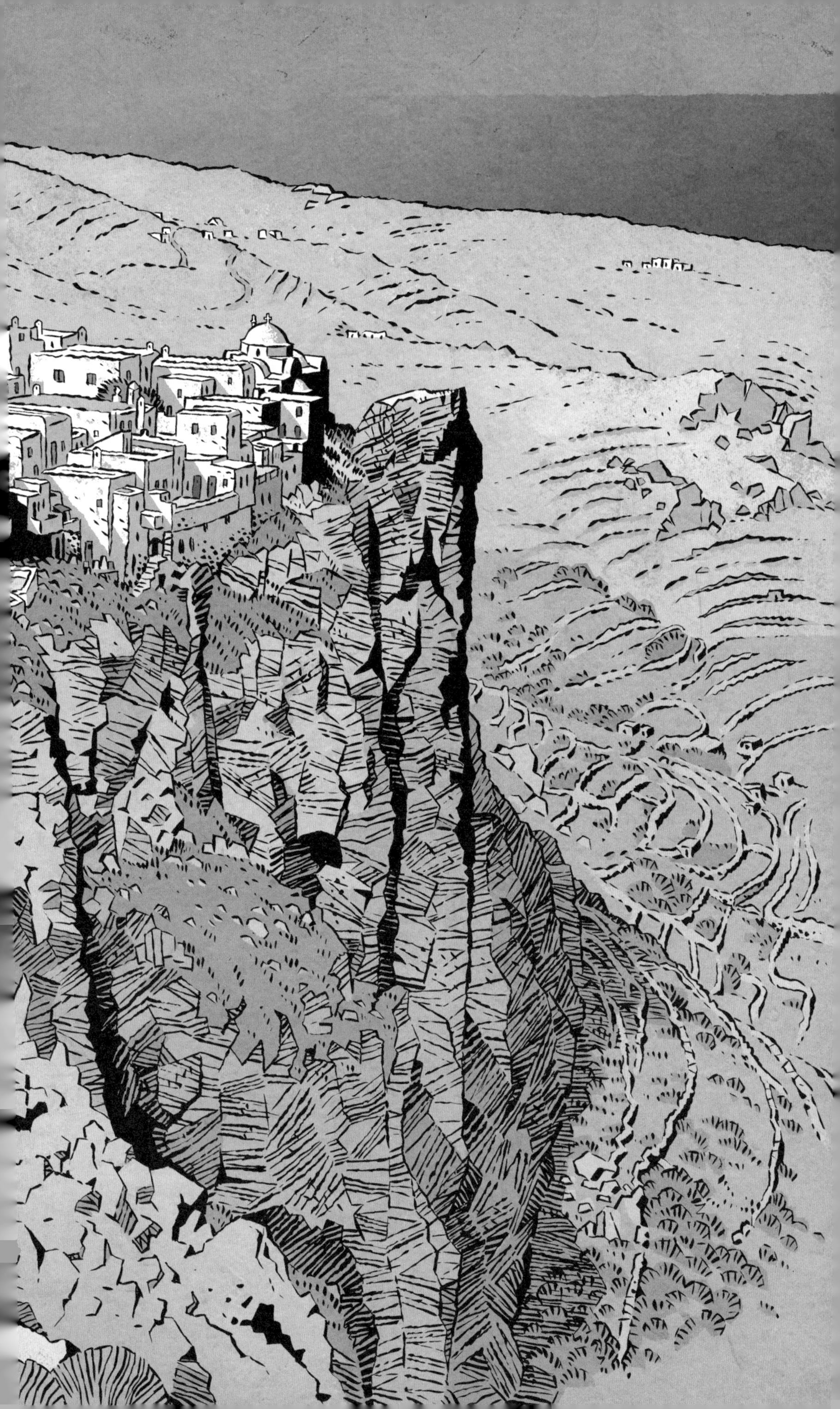

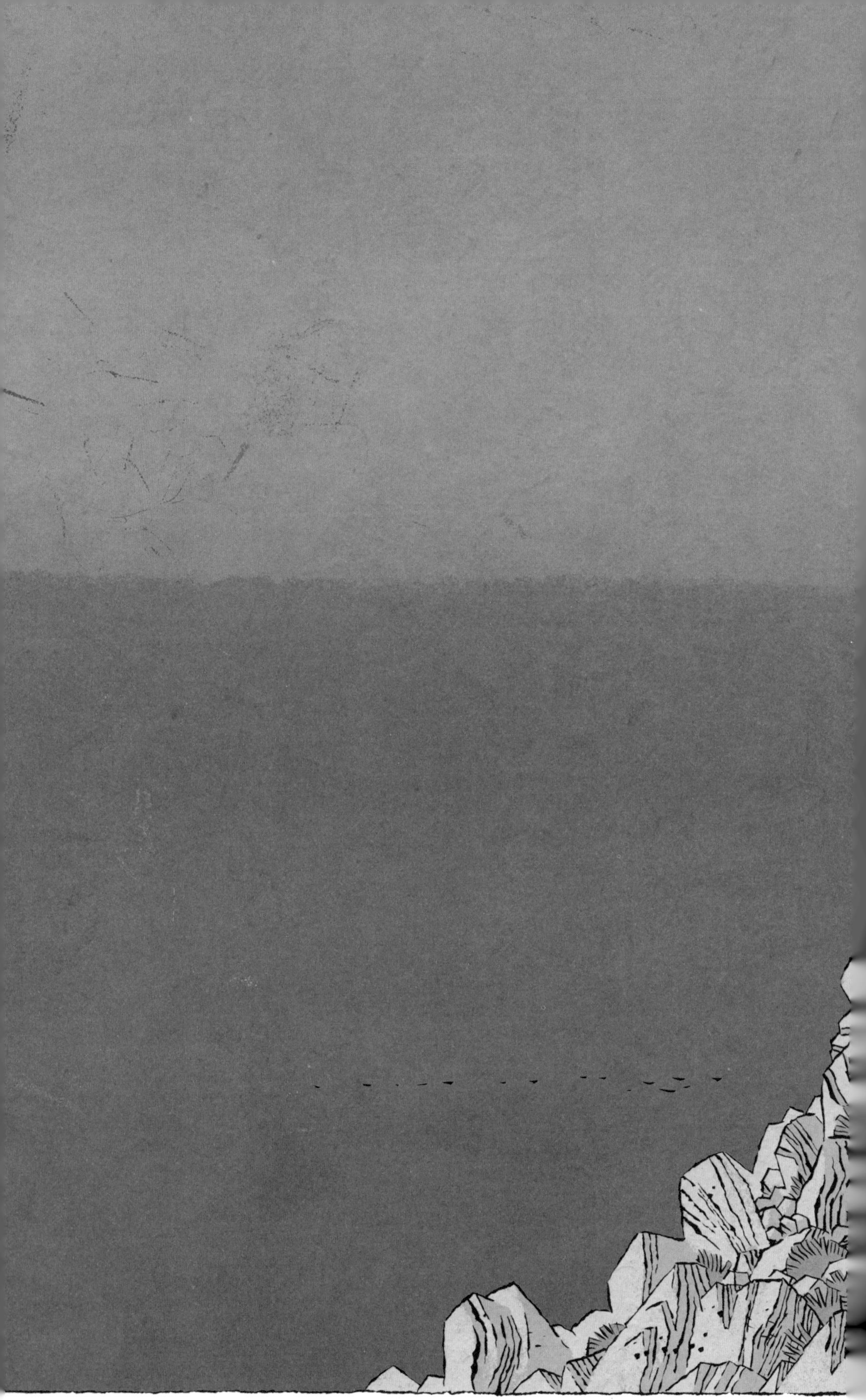

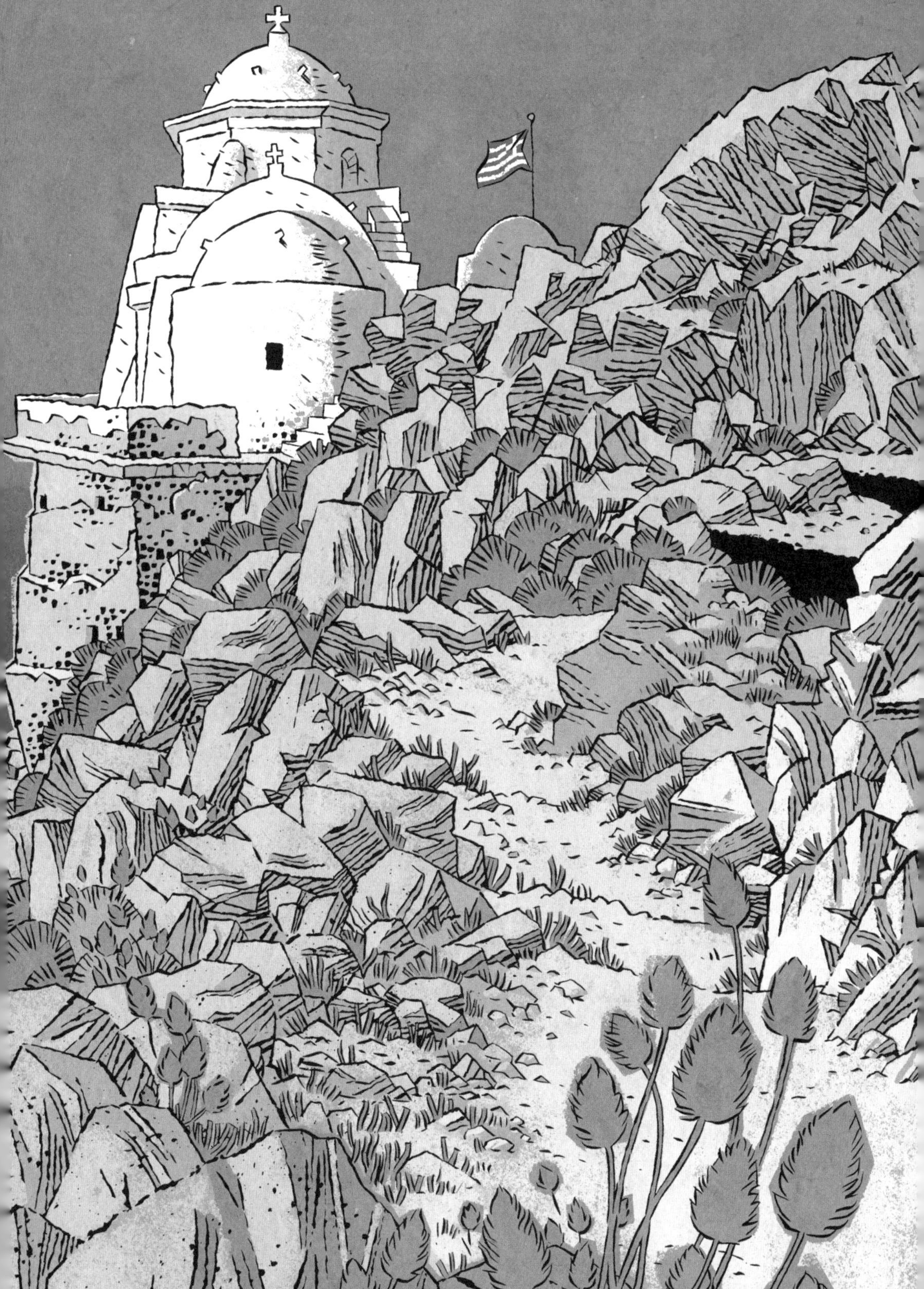

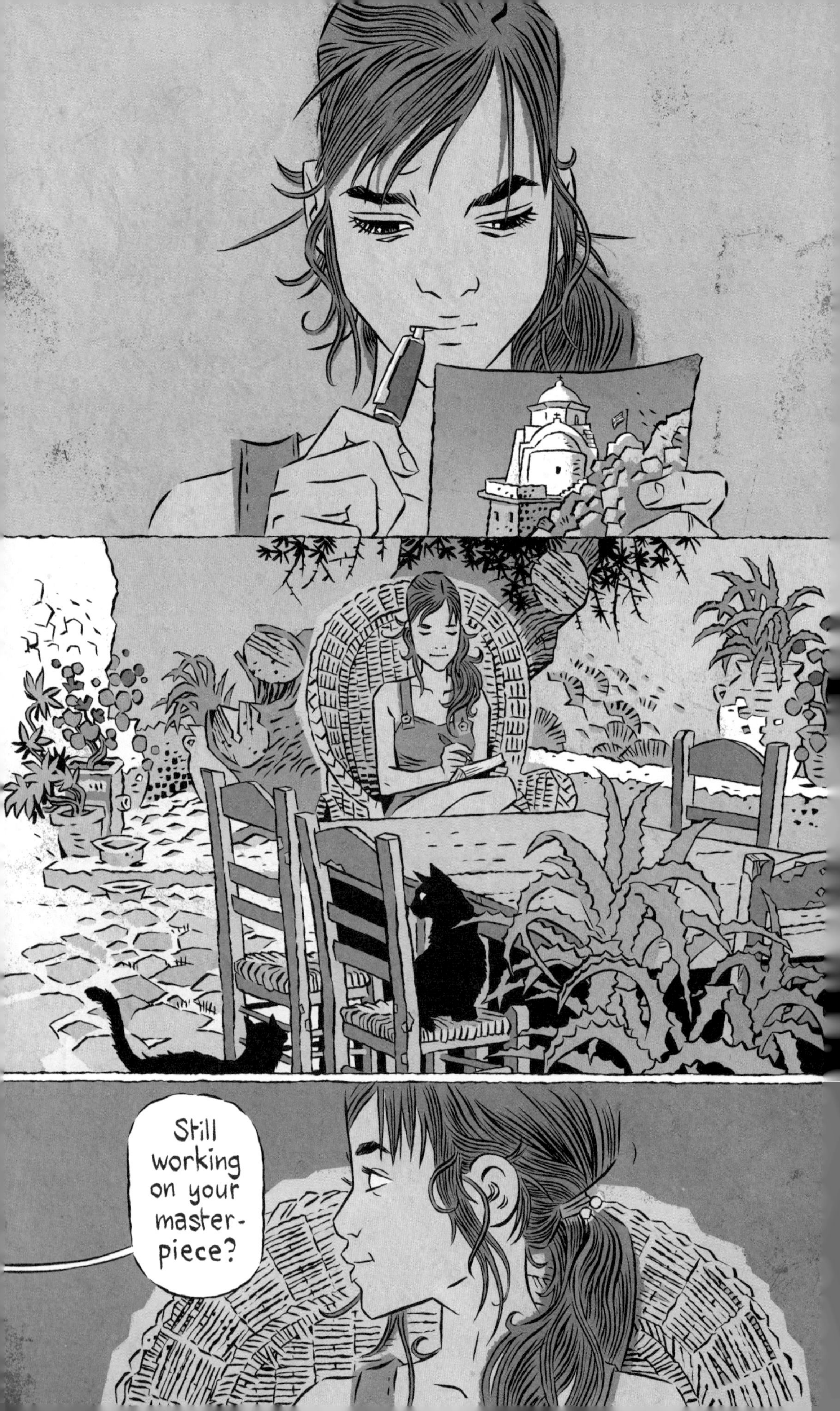
Still working on your masterpiece?

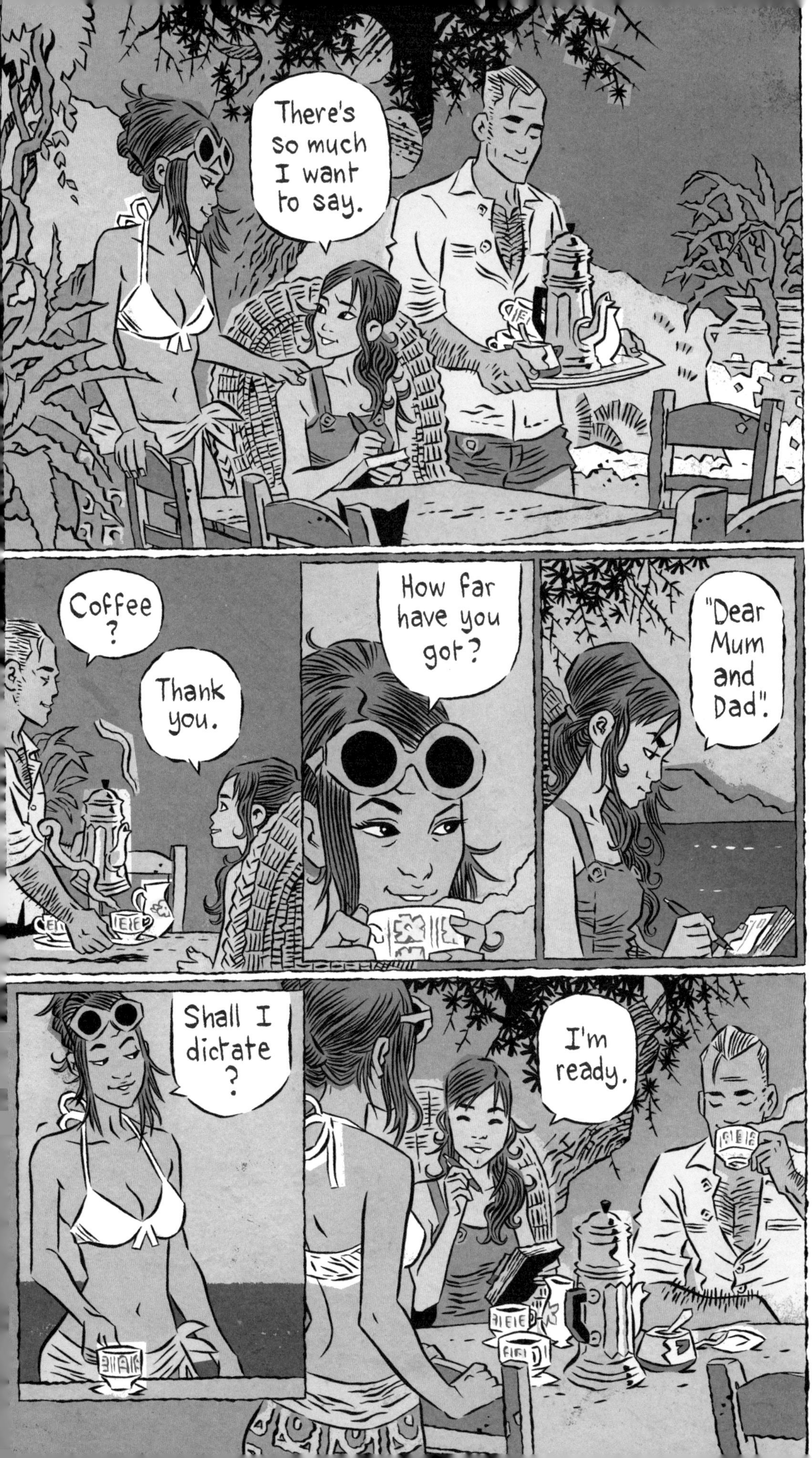
There's so much I want to say.
Coffee?
Thank you.
How far have you got?
"Dear Mum and Dad".
Shall I dictate?
I'm ready.

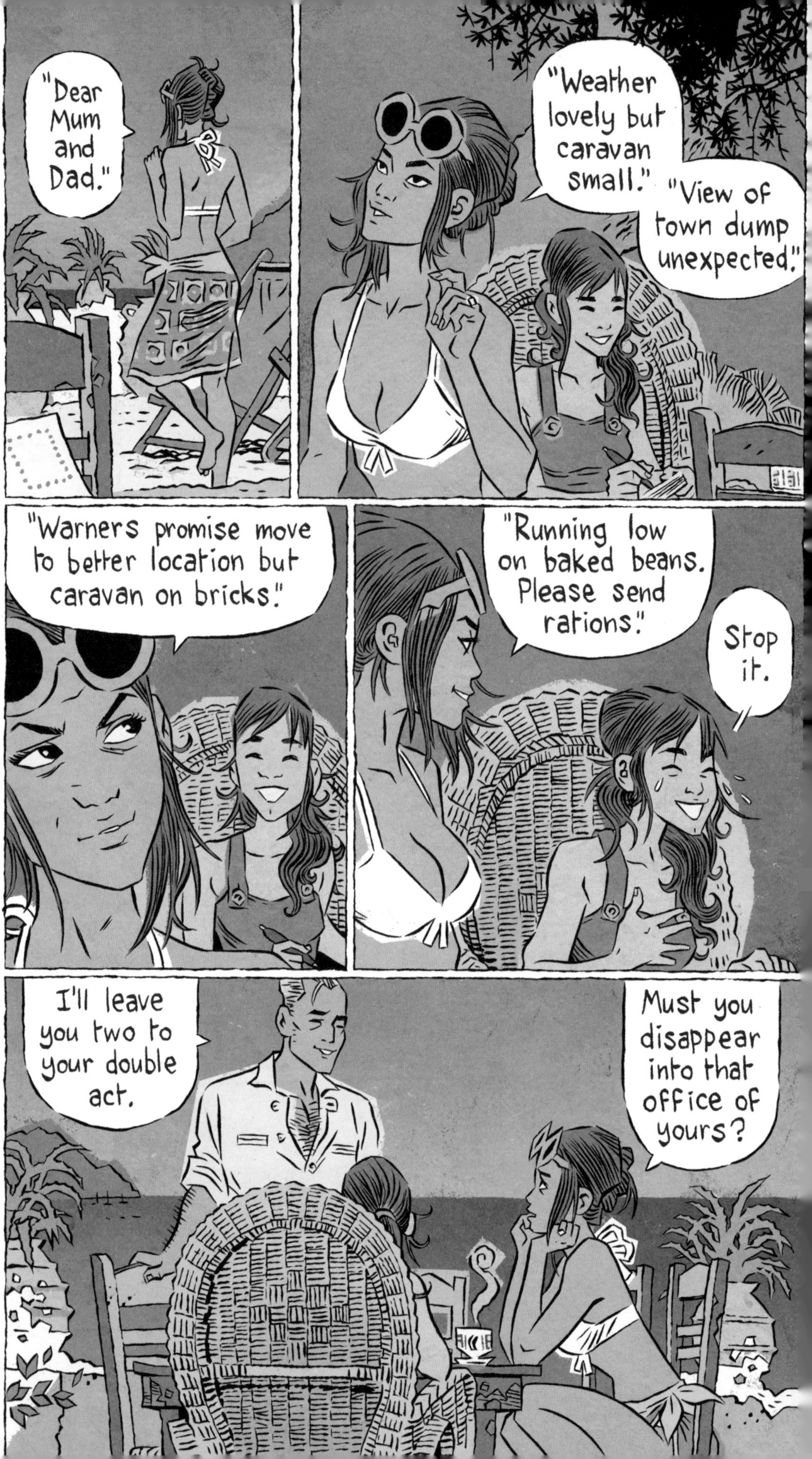
"Dear Mum and Dad."
"Weather lovely but caravan small."
"View of town dump unexpected."
"Warners promise move to better location but caravan on bricks."
"Running low on baked beans. Please send rations."
Stop it.
I'll leave you two to your double act.
Must you disappear into that office of yours?

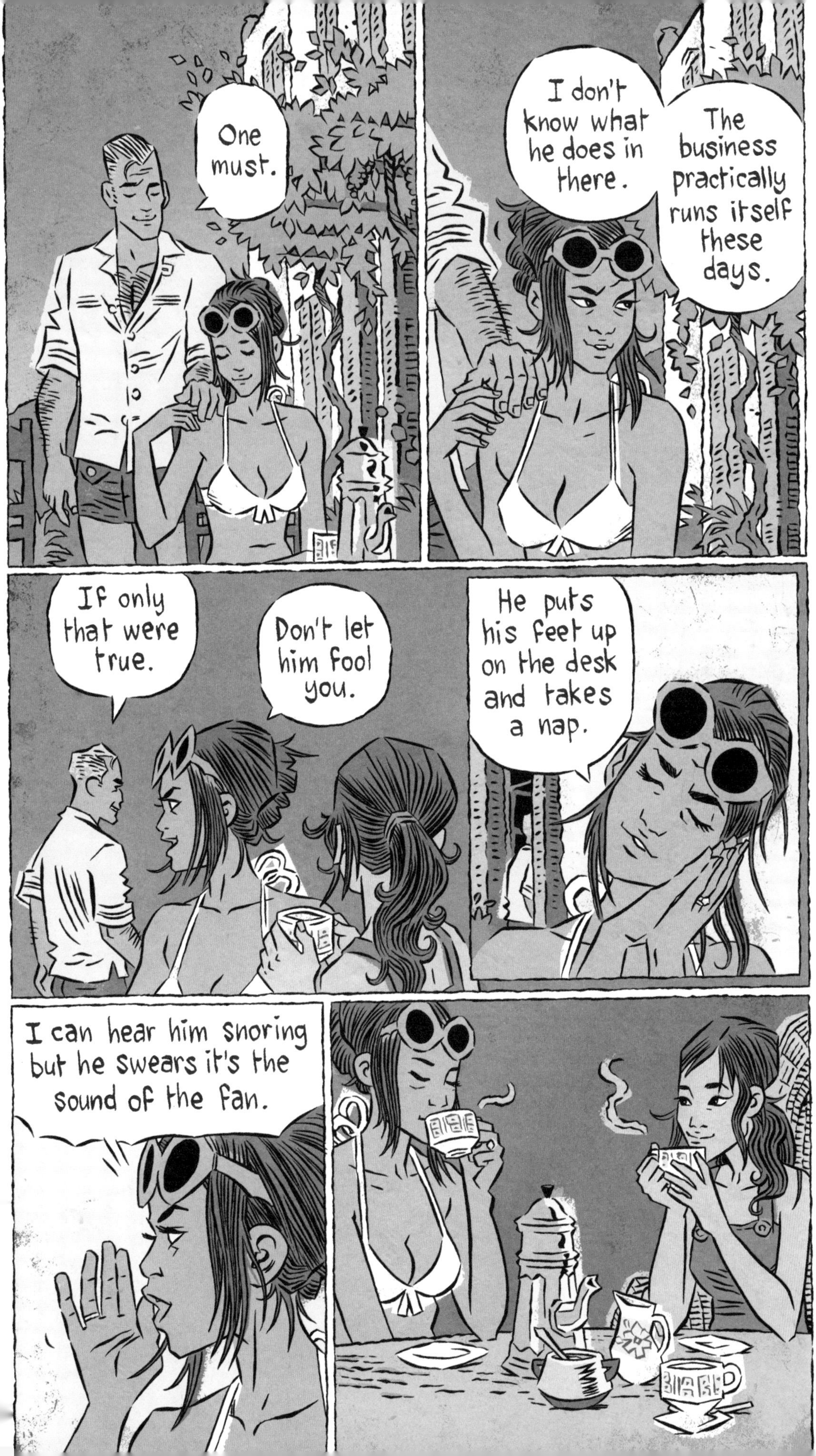
One must.
I don't know what he does in there.
The business practically runs itself these days.
If only that were true.
Don't let him fool you.
He puts his feet up on the desk and takes a nap.
I can hear him snoring but he swears it's the sound of the fan.

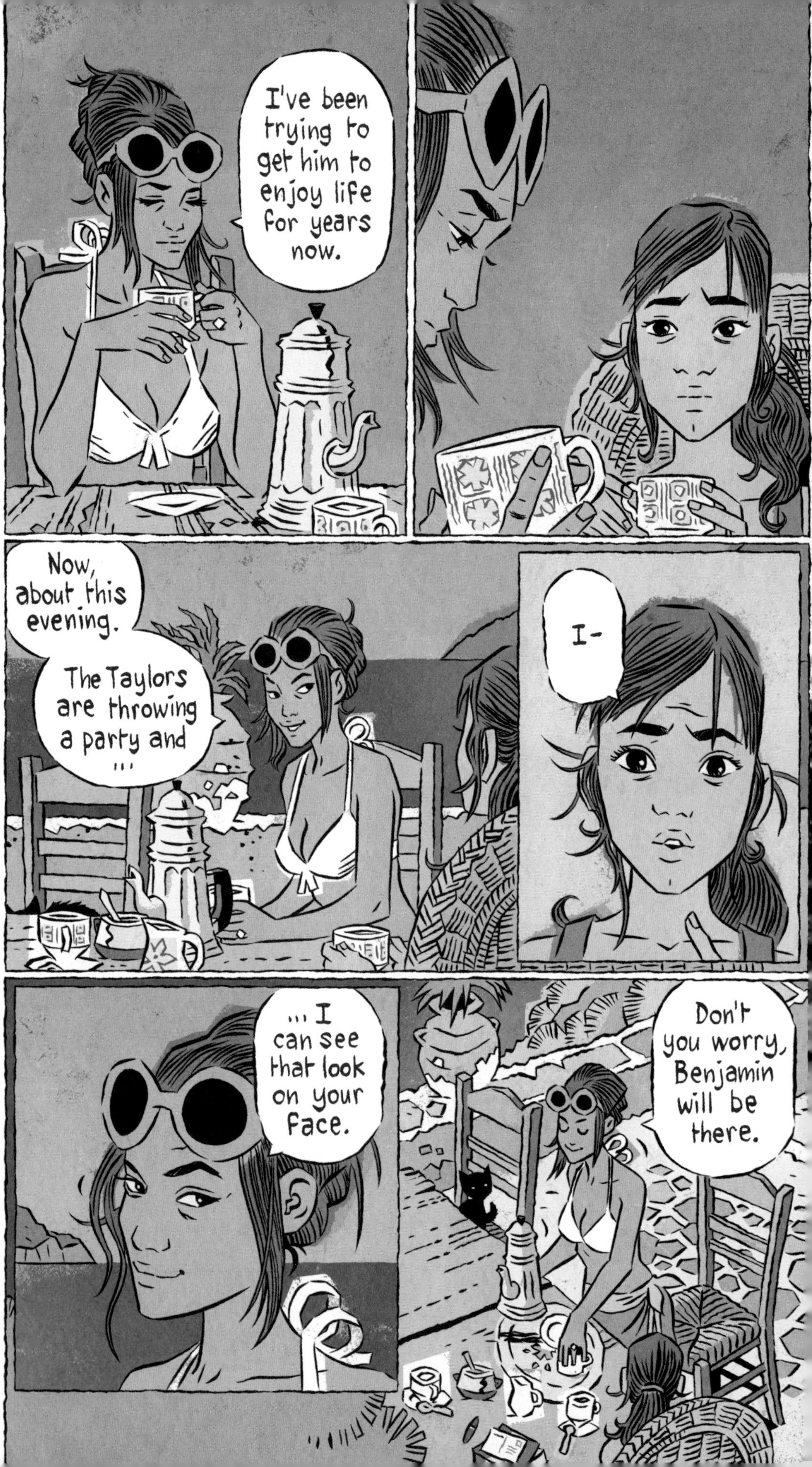
I've been trying to get him to enjoy life for years now.
Now, about this evening.
The Taylors are throwing a party and ...
I-
... I can see that look on your face.
Don't you worry, Benjamin will be there.

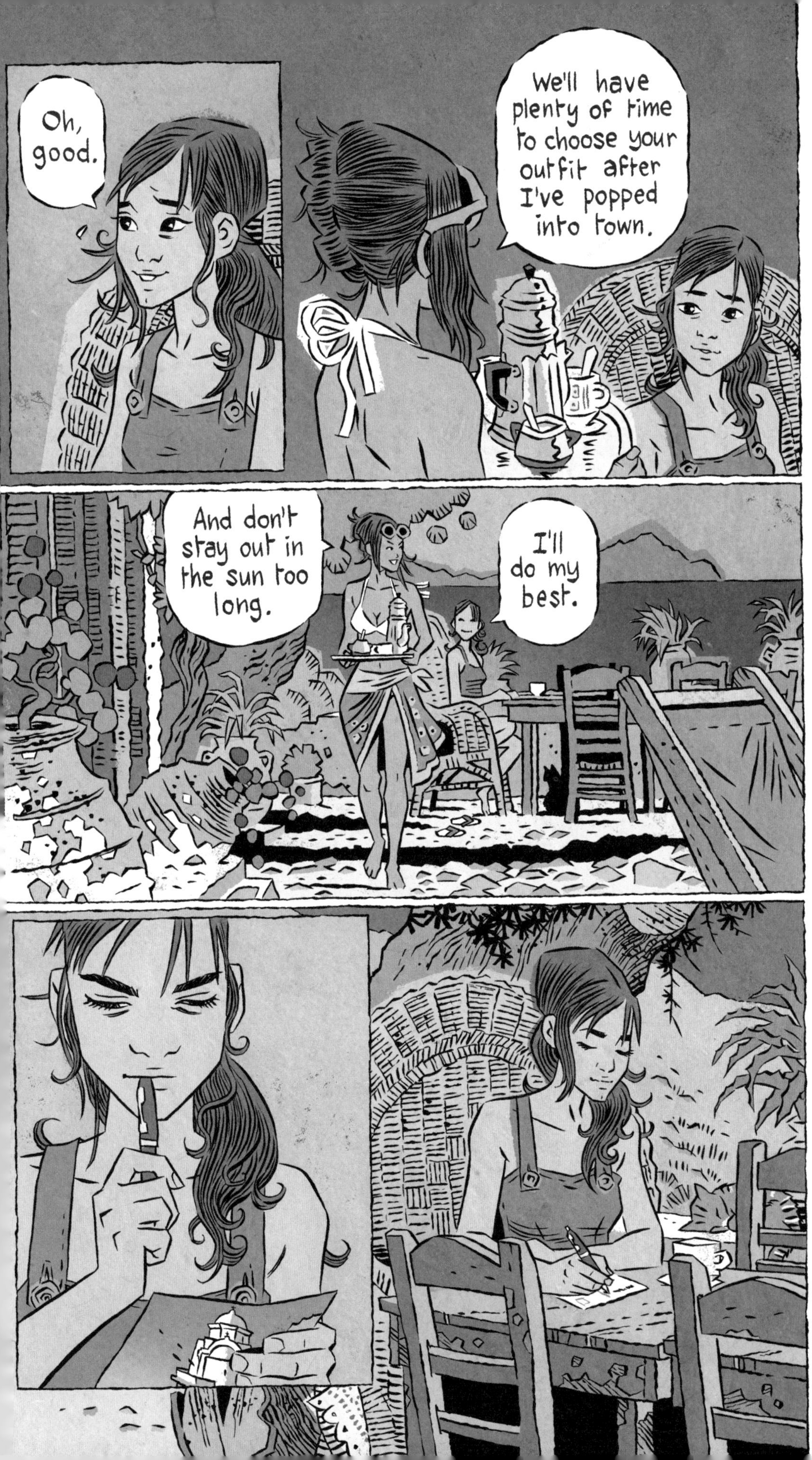
Oh, good.
We'll have plenty of time to choose your outfit after I've popped into town.
And don't stay out in the sun too long.
I'll do my best.

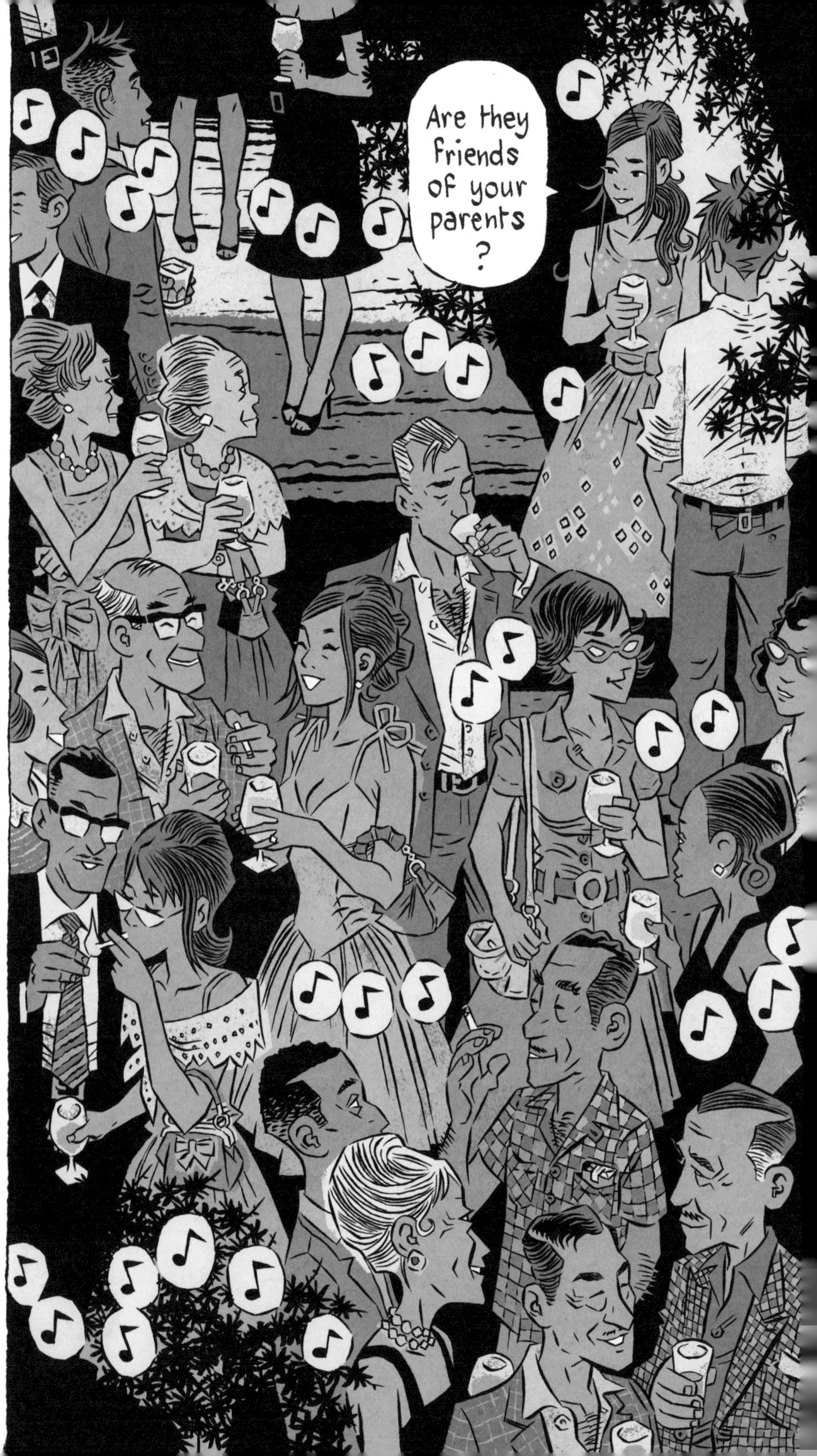
Are they friends of your parents ?

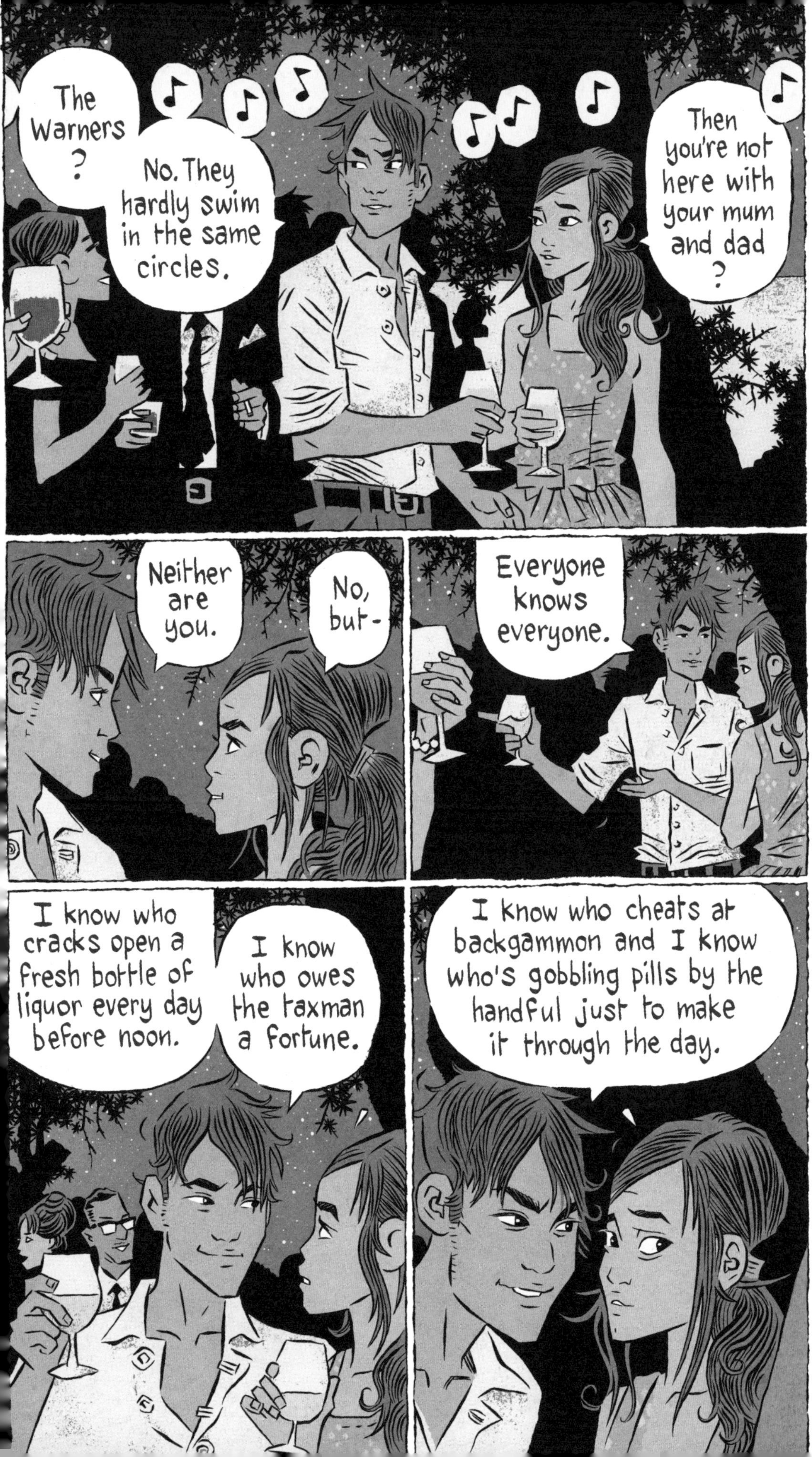
The Warners?
No. They hardly swim in the same circles.
Then you're not here with your mum and dad?
Neither are you.
No, but-
Everyone knows everyone.
I know who cracks open a fresh bottle of liquor every day before noon.
I know who owes the taxman a fortune.
I know who cheats at backgammon and I know who's gobbling pills by the handful just to make it through the day.

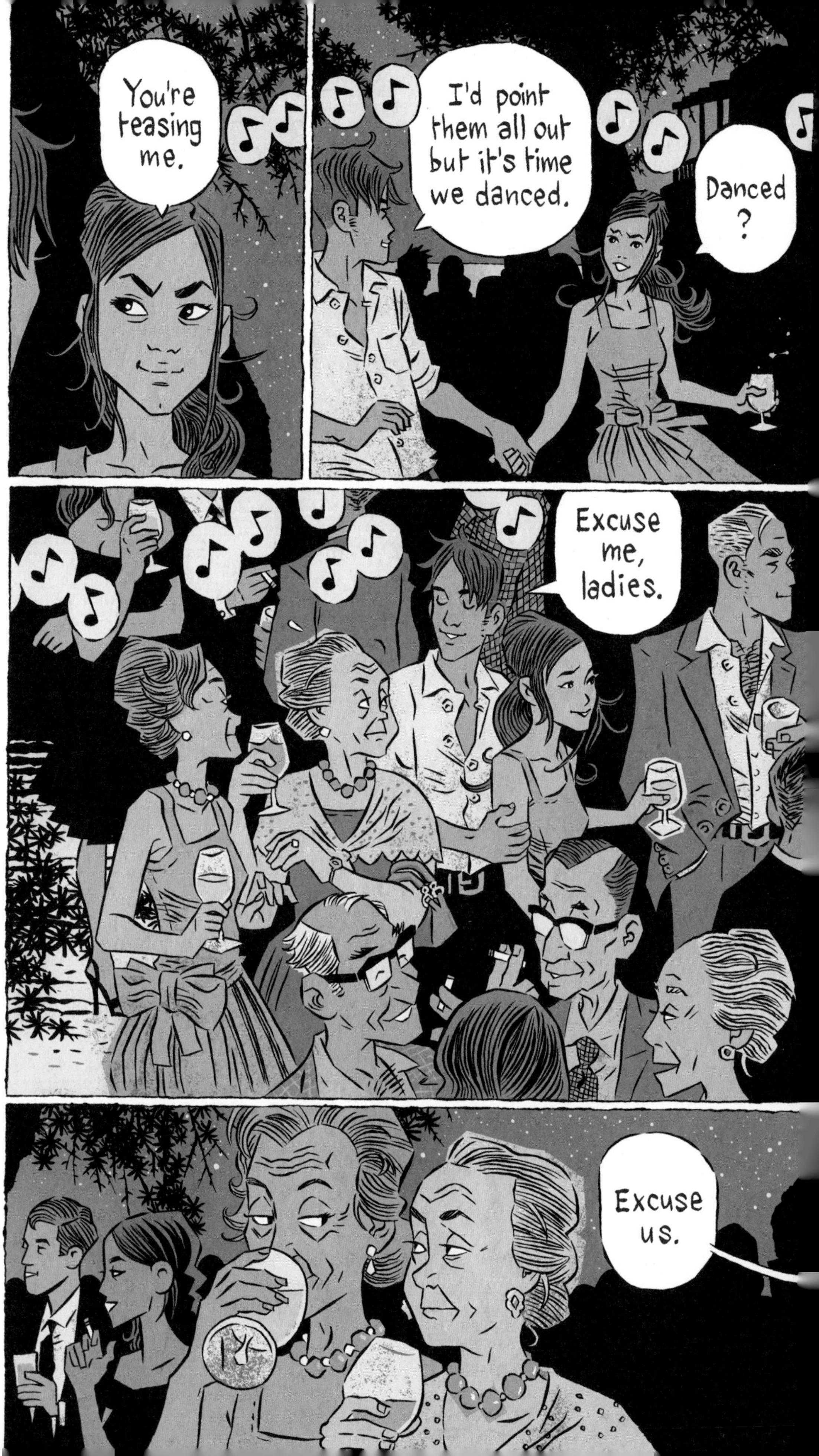
You're teasing me.
I'd point them all out but it's time we danced.
Danced?
Excuse me, ladies.
Excuse us.

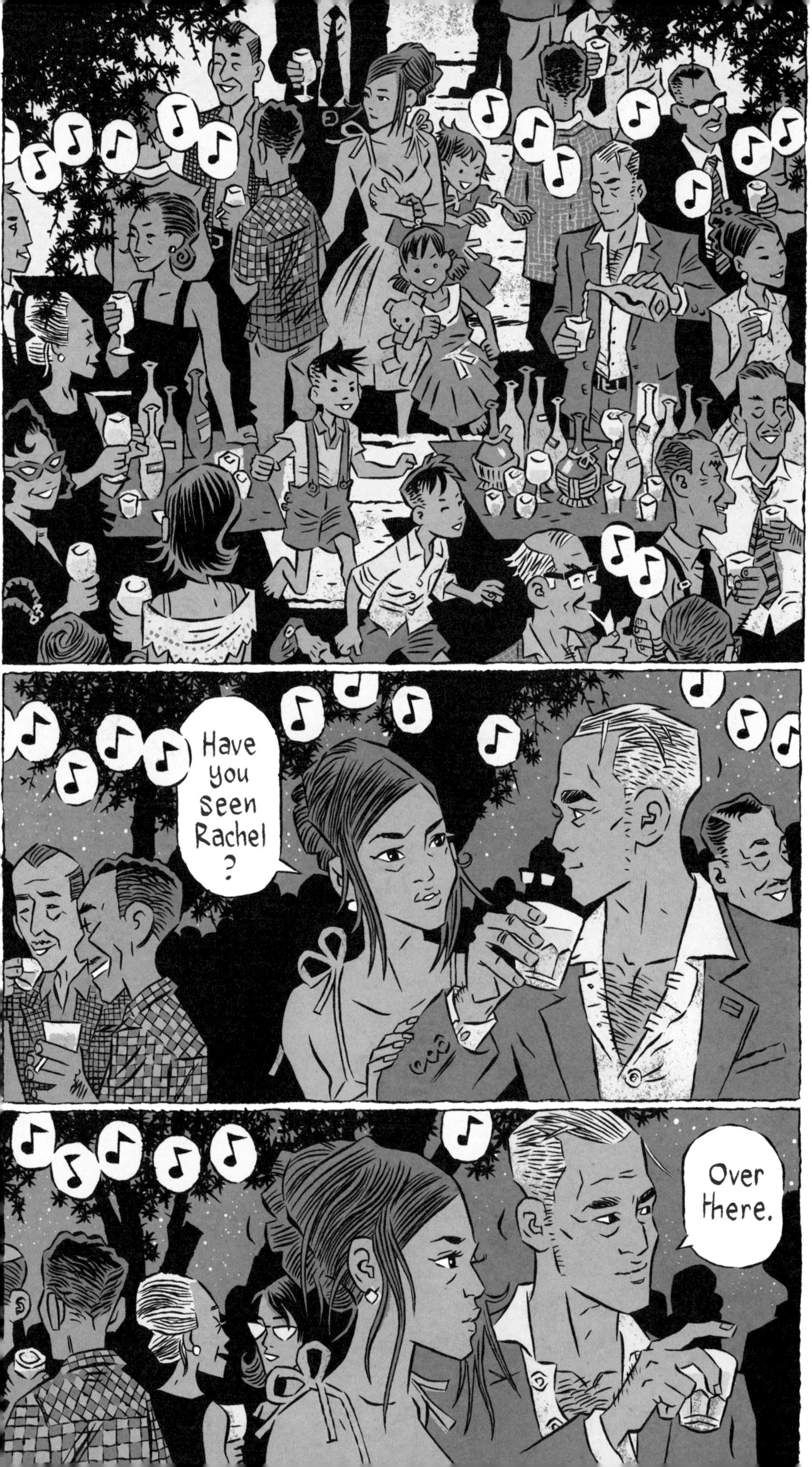
Have you seen Rachel?
Over there.

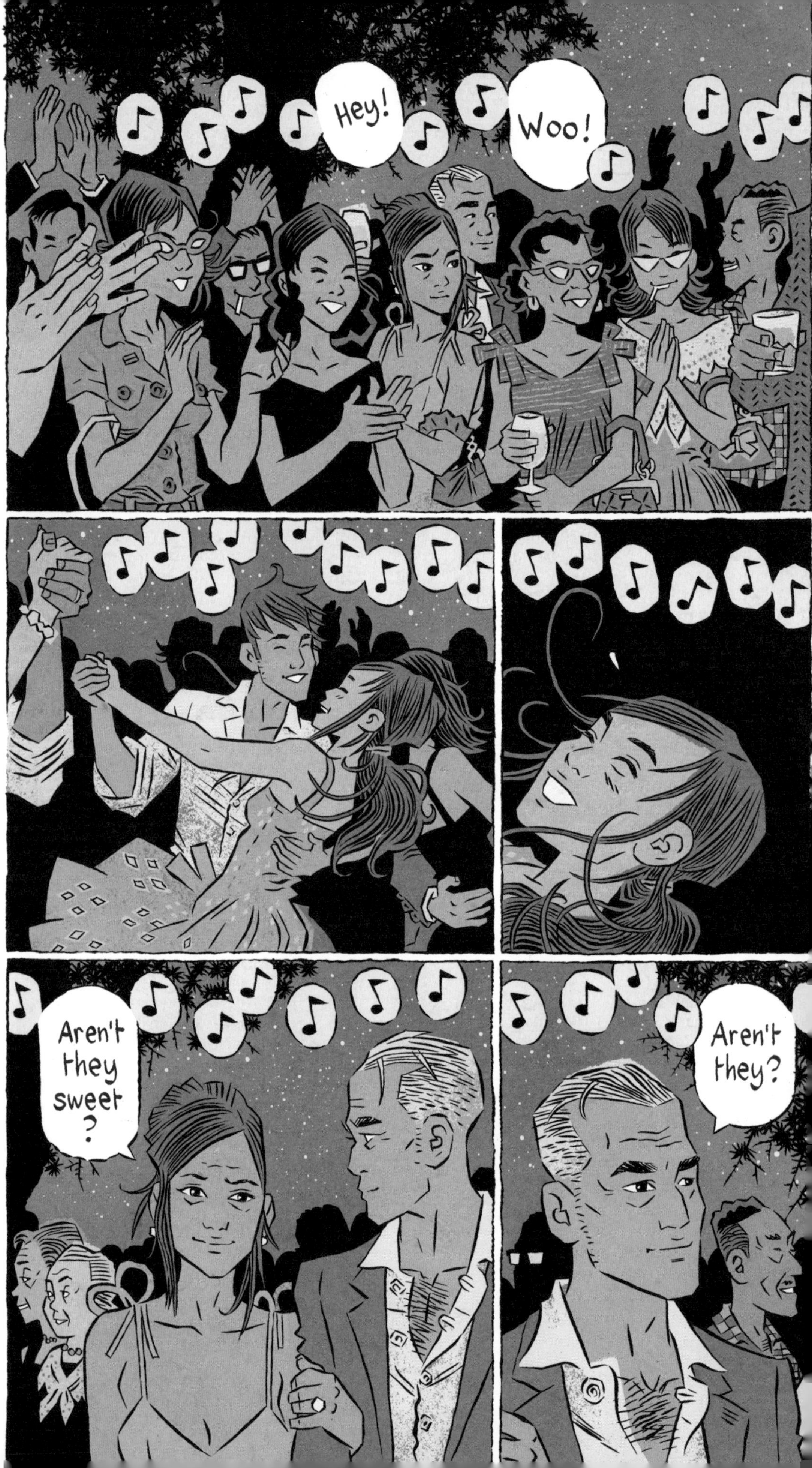
Hey!
Woo!
Aren't they sweet?
Aren't they?

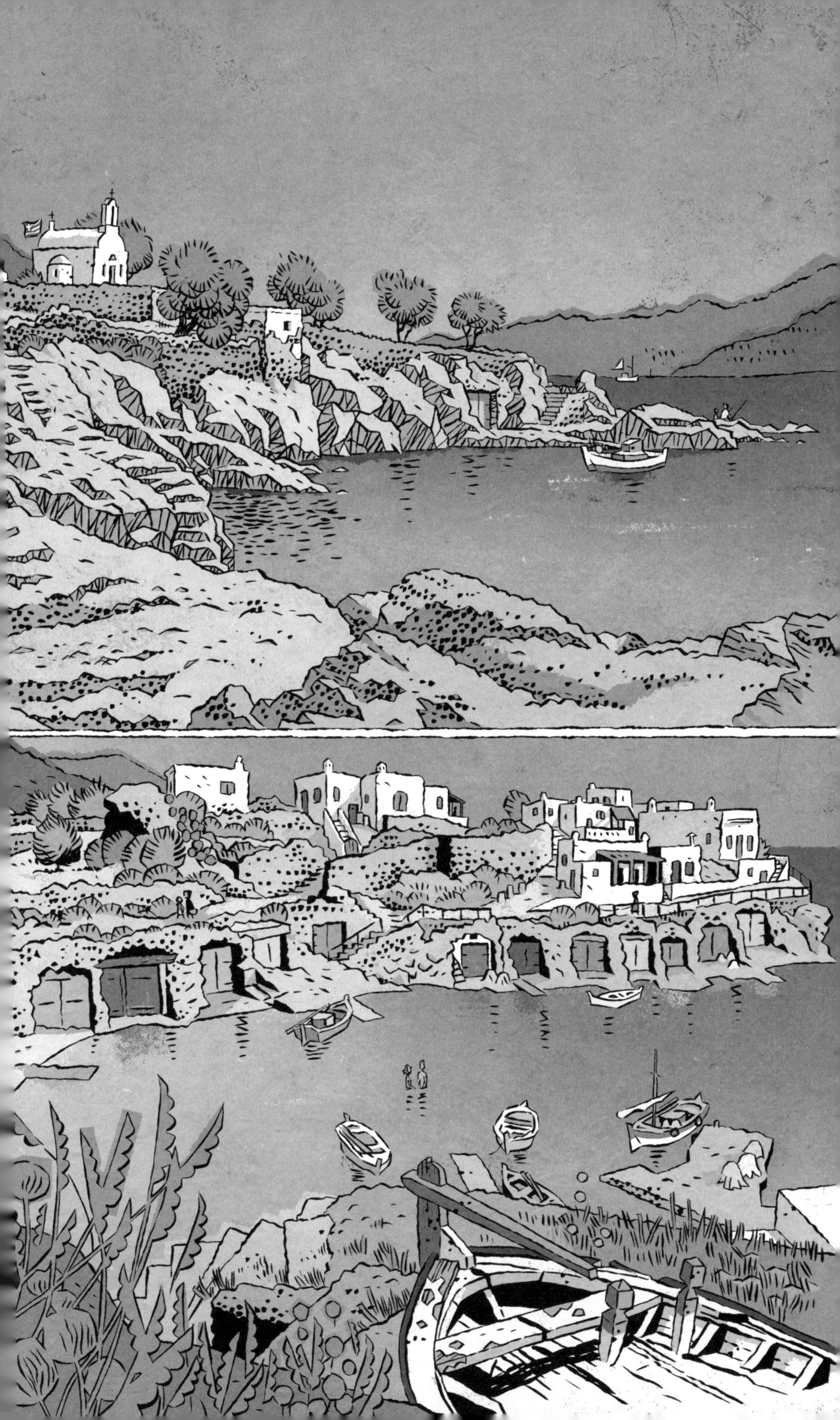

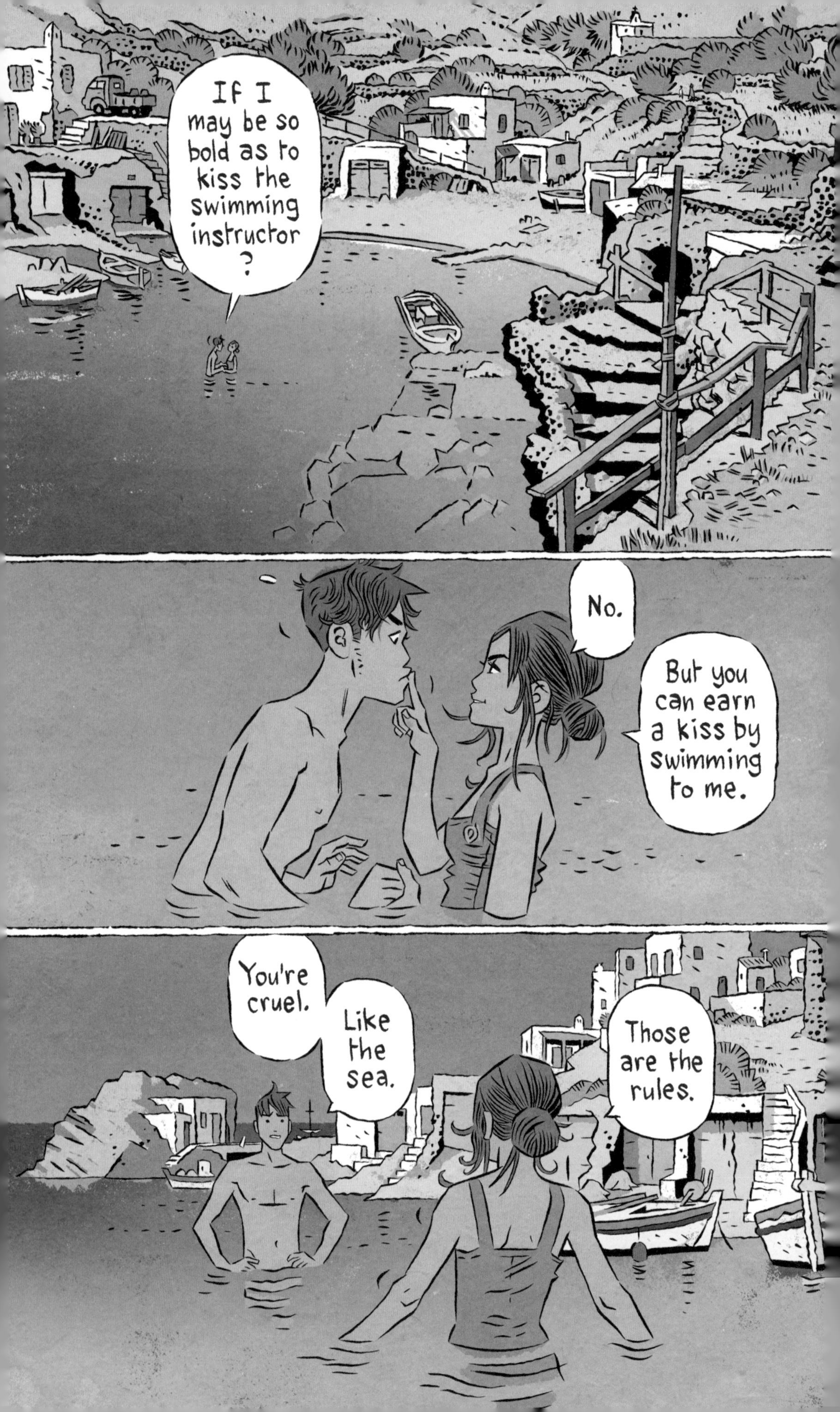
If I may be so bold as to kiss the swimming instructor?
No.
But you can earn a kiss by swimming to me.
You're cruel.
Like the sea.
Those are the rules.

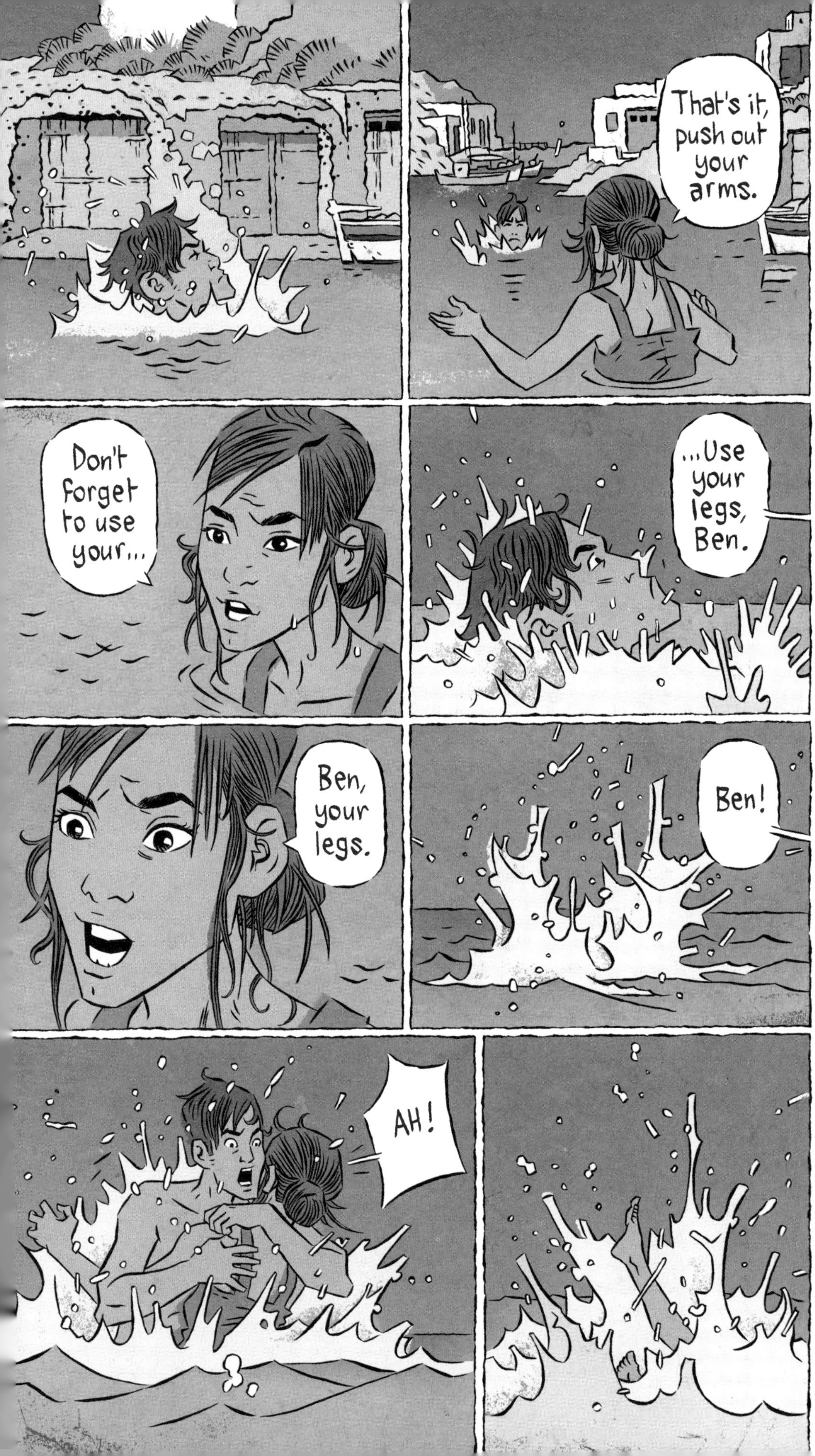
That's it, push out your arms.
Don't forget to use your...
...Use your legs, Ben.
Ben, your legs.
Ben!
AH!

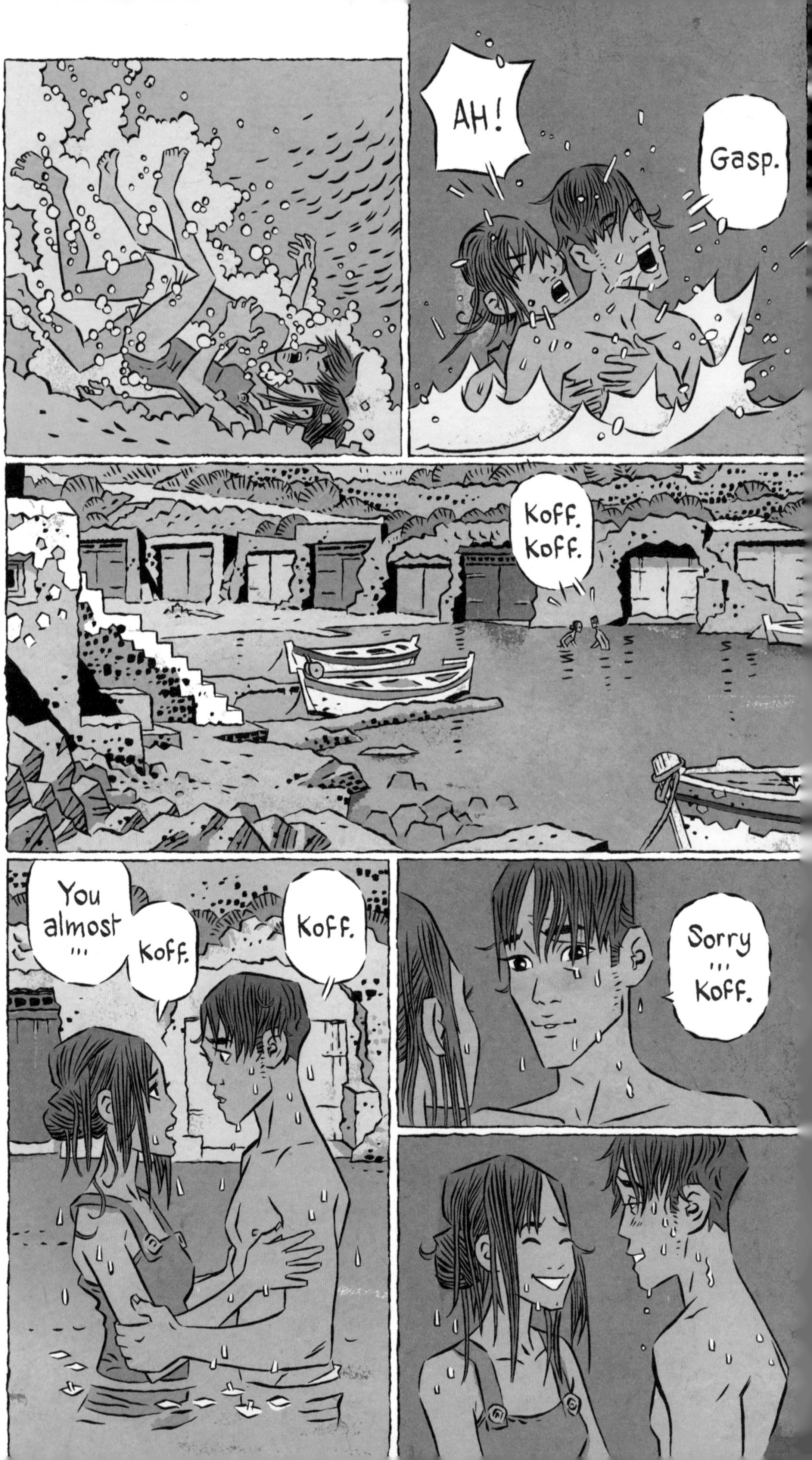
AH!
Gasp.
Koff. Koff.
You almost ...
Koff.
Koff.
Sorry ... Koff.

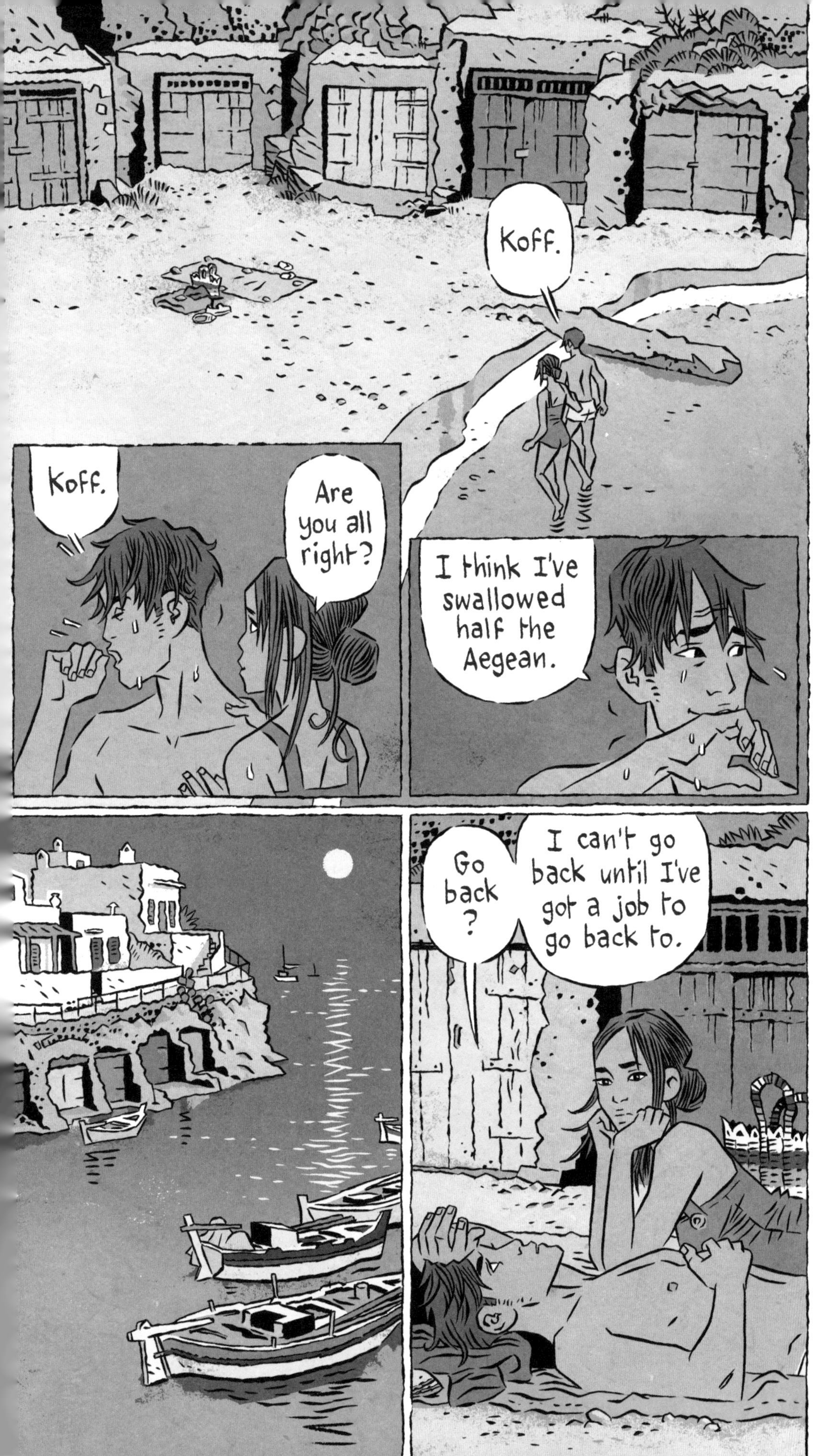
Koff.
Koff.
Are you all right?
I think I've swallowed half the Aegean.
Go back?
I can't go back until I've got a job to go back to.

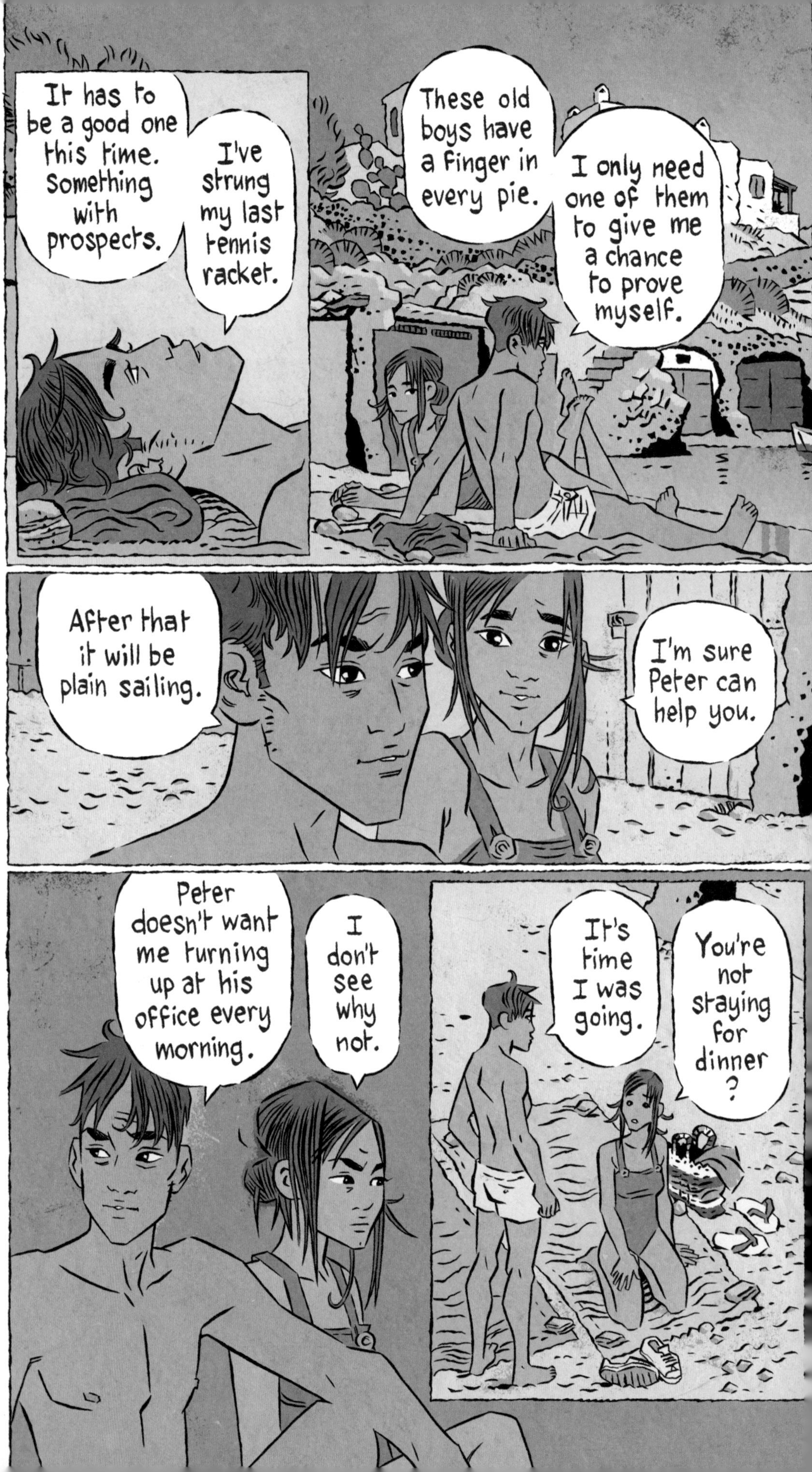
It has to be a good one this time. Something with prospects.
I've strung my last tennis racket.
These old boys have a finger in every pie.
I only need one of them to give me a chance to prove myself.
After that it will be plain sailing.
I'm sure Peter can help you.
Peter doesn't want me turning up at his office every morning.
I don't see why not.
It's time I was going.
You're not staying for dinner?

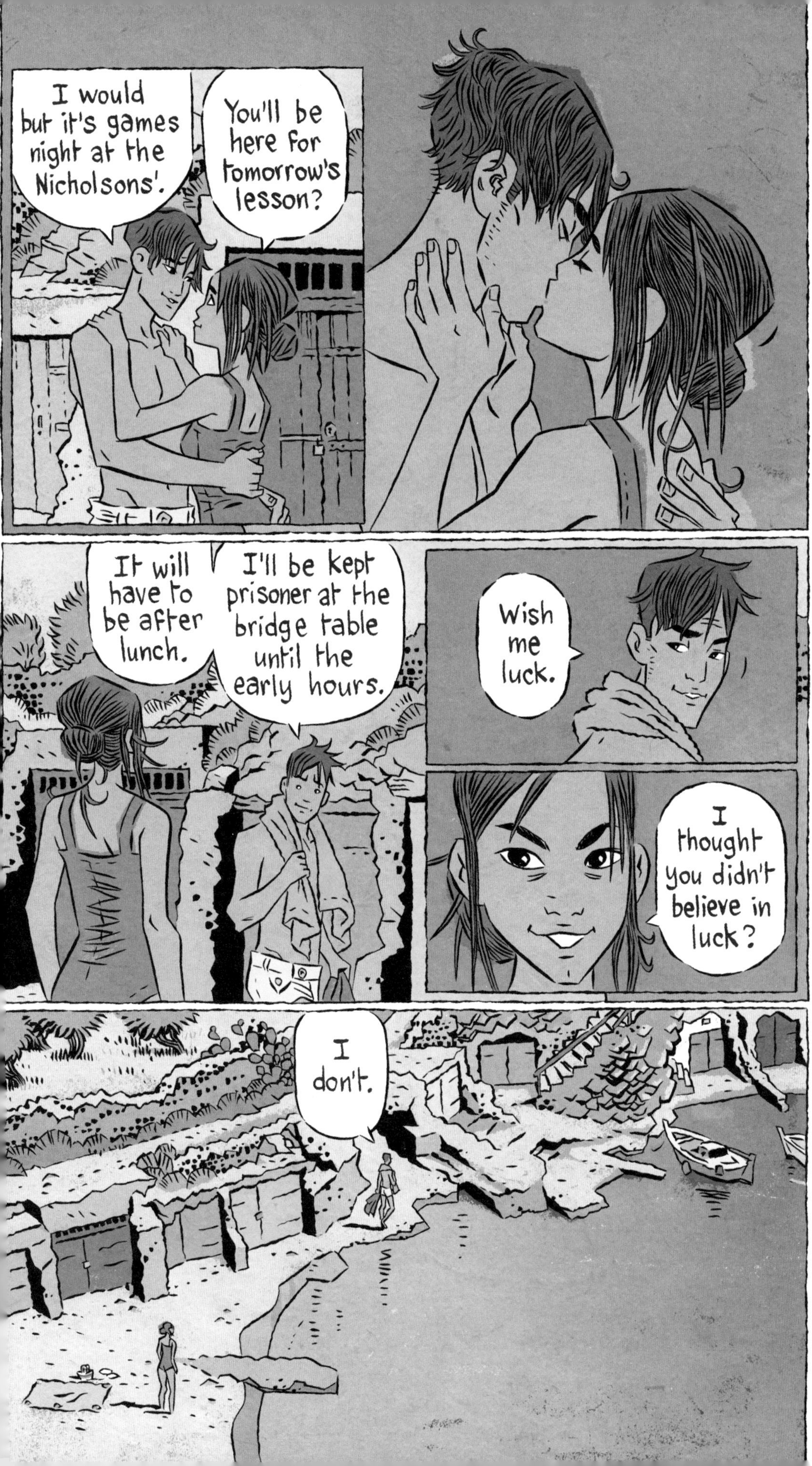
I would but it's games night at the Nicholsons'.
You'll be here for tomorrow's lesson?
It will have to be after lunch.
I'll be kept prisoner at the bridge table until the early hours.
Wish me luck.
I thought you didn't believe in luck?
I don't.

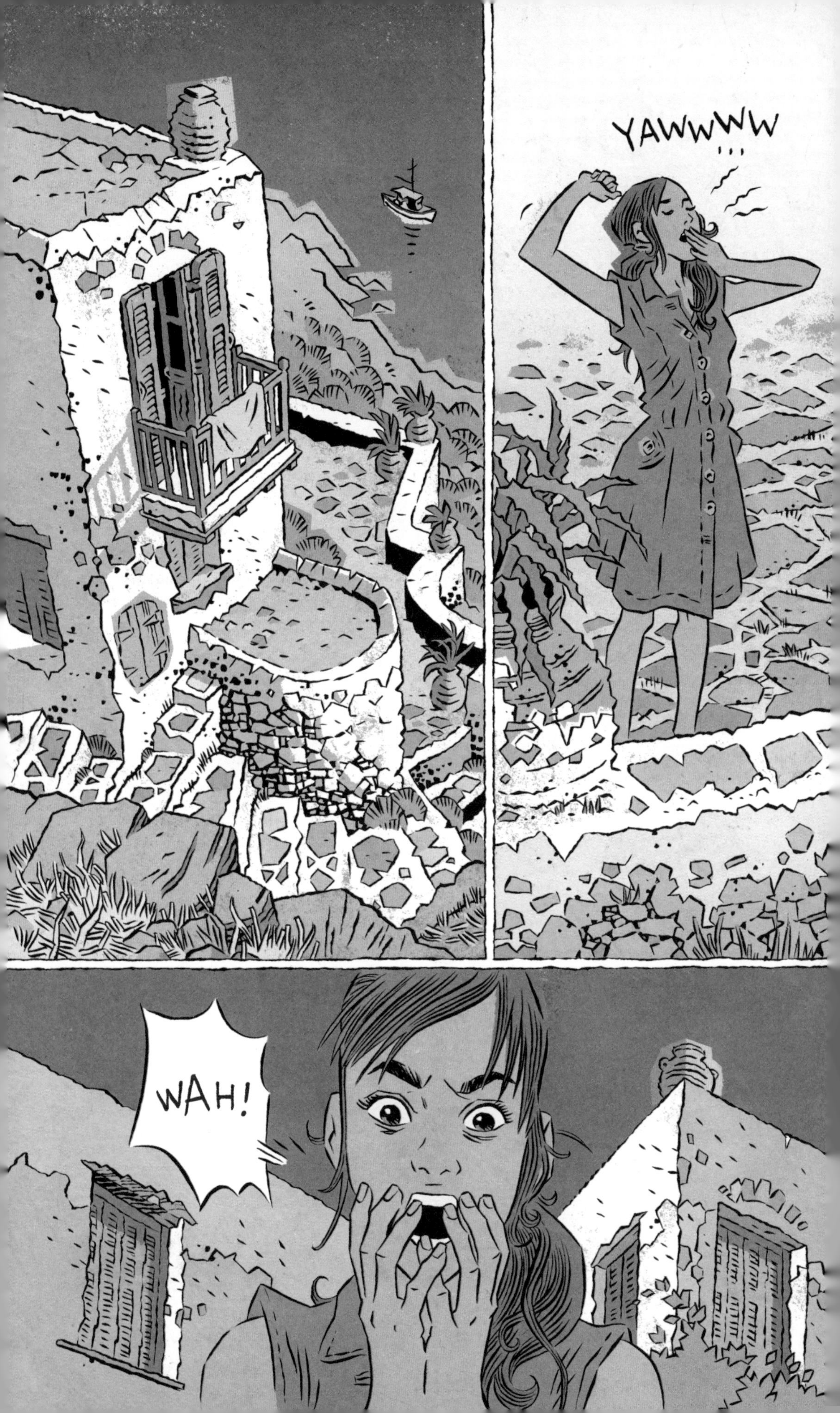
YAWWWW
WAH!

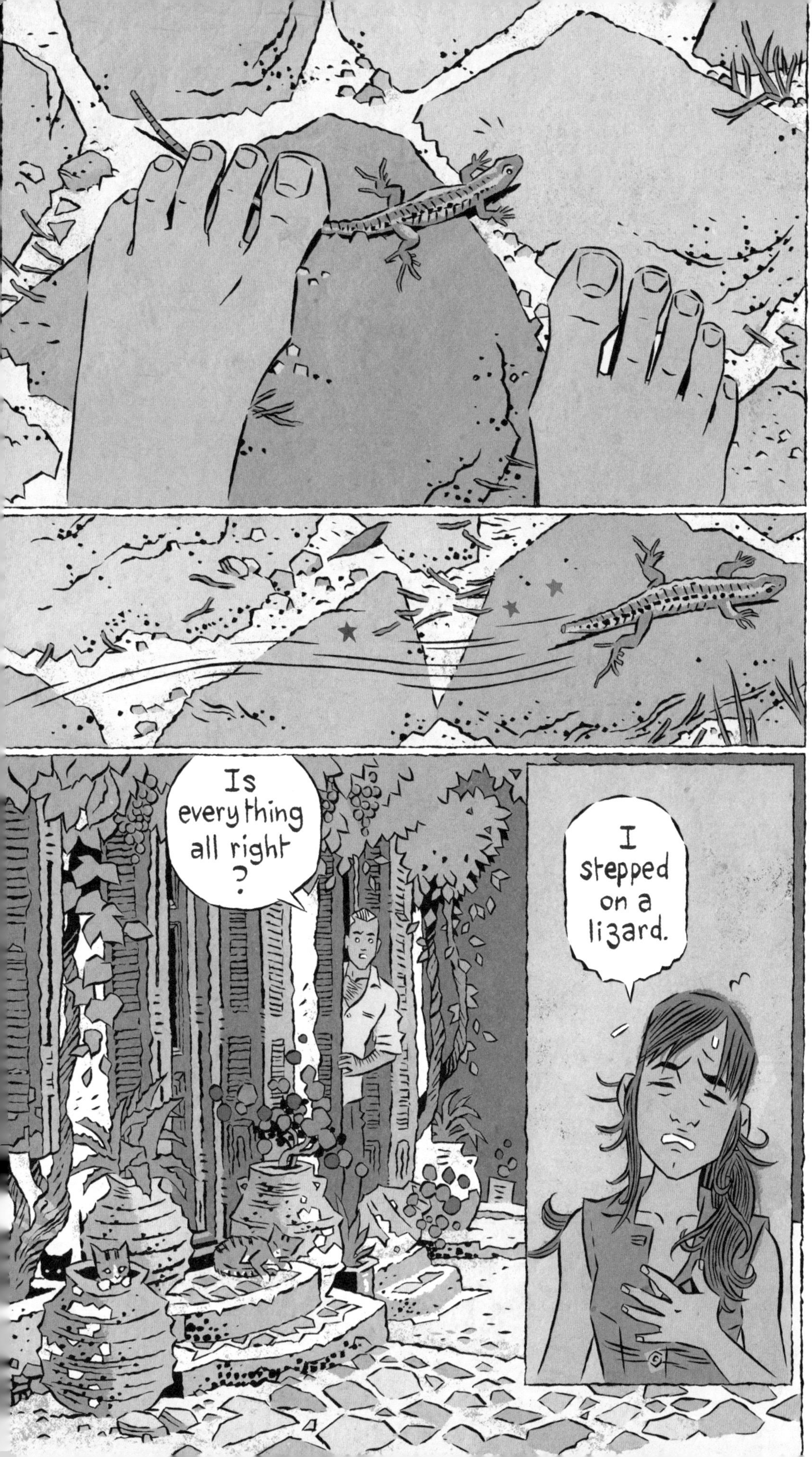
Is everything all right ?
I stepped on a lizard.

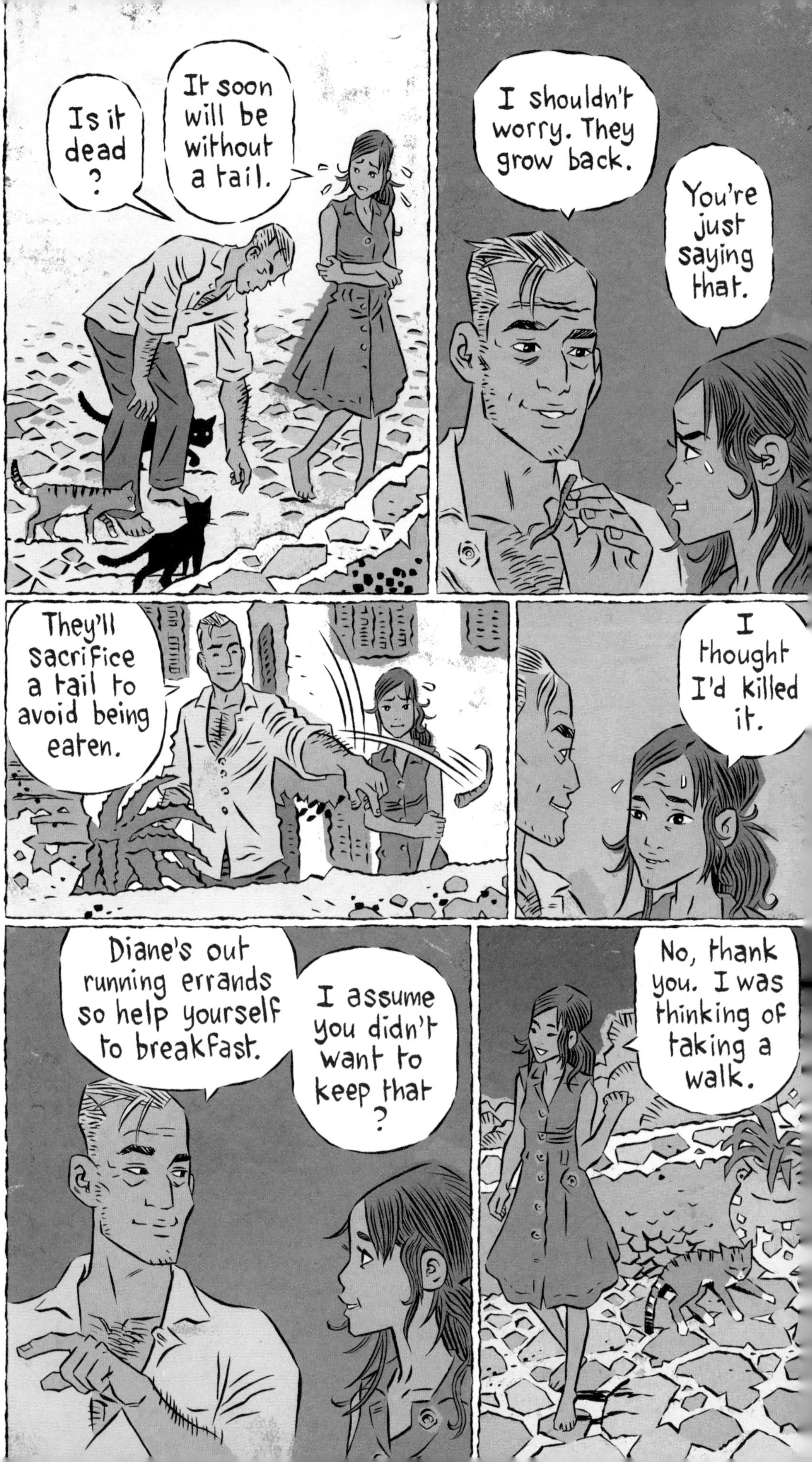

Is it dead?
It soon will be without a tail.
I shouldn't worry. They grow back.
You're just saying that.
They'll sacrifice a tail to avoid being eaten.
I thought I'd killed it.
Diane's out running errands so help yourself to breakfast.
I assume you didn't want to keep that?
No, thank you. I was thinking of taking a walk.

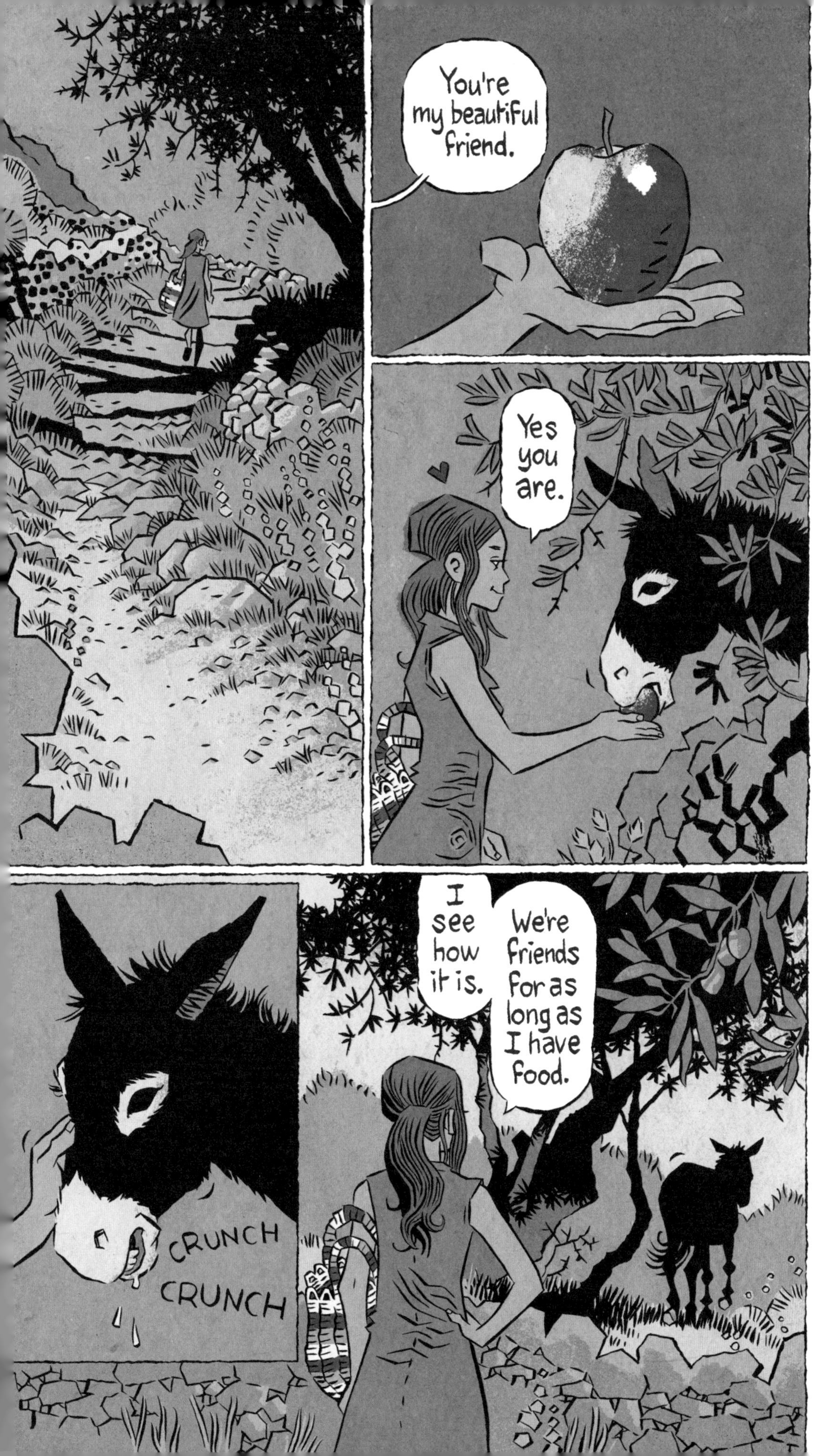
You're my beautiful friend.
Yes you are.
CRUNCH
CRUNCH
I see how it is.
We're friends for as long as I have food.

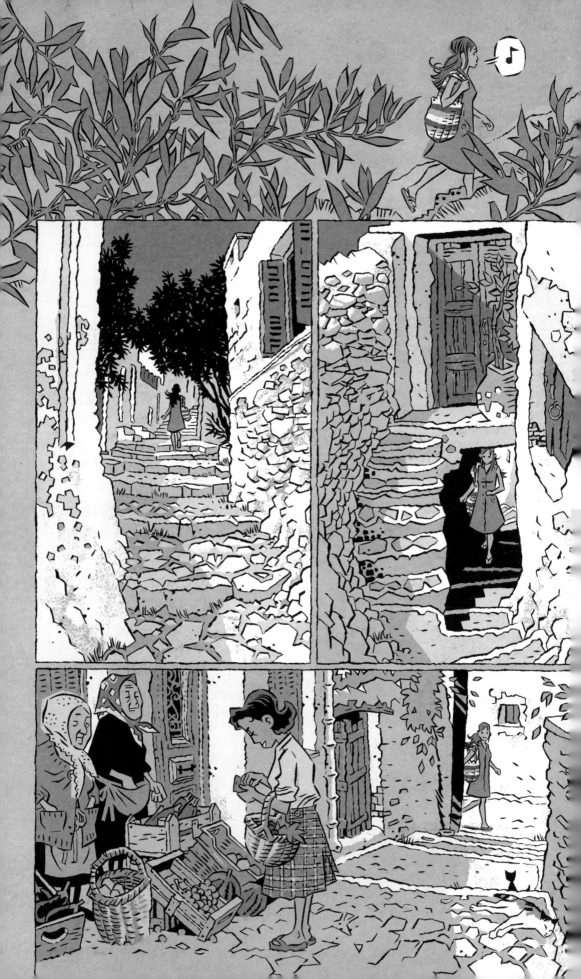

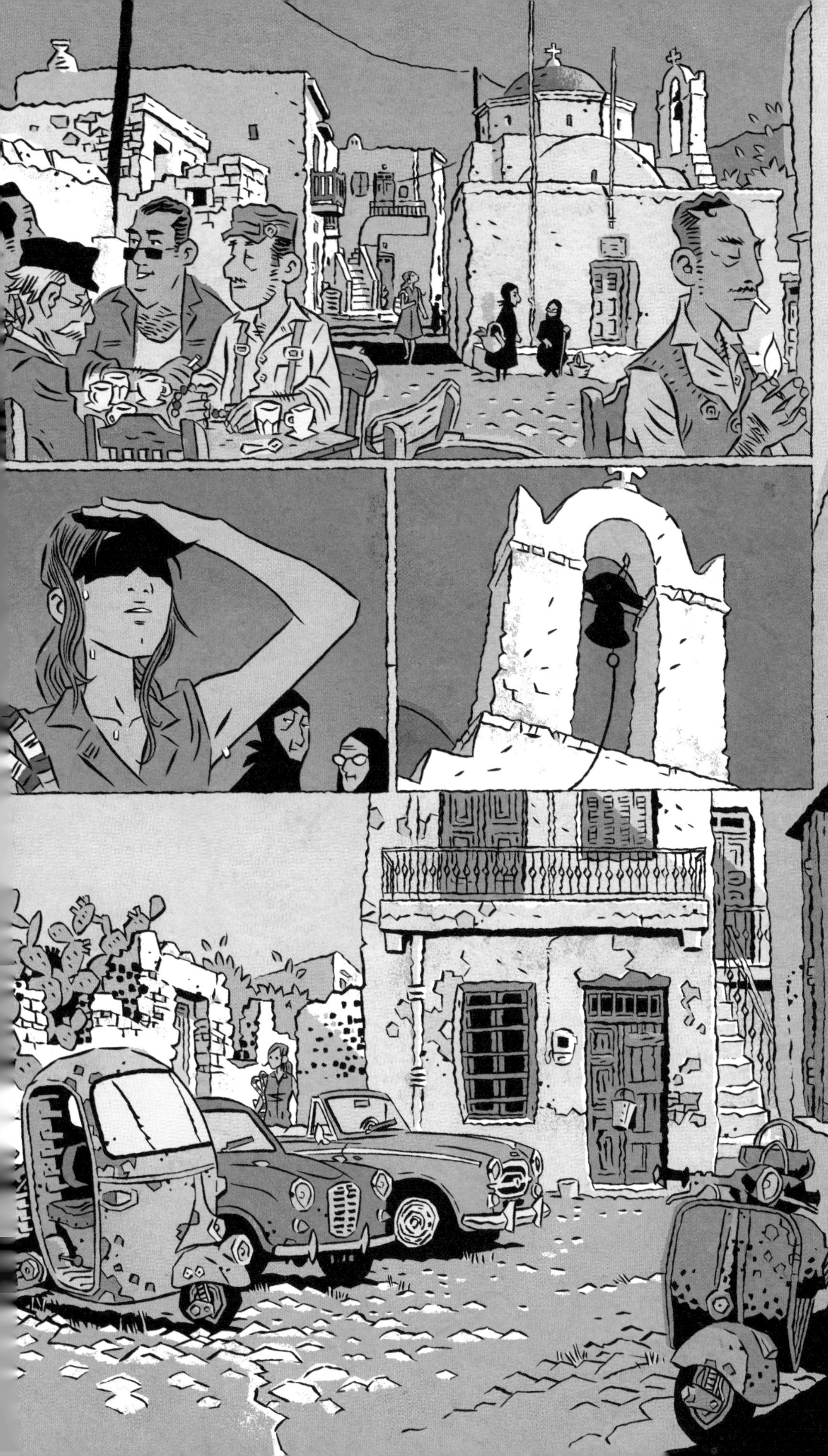

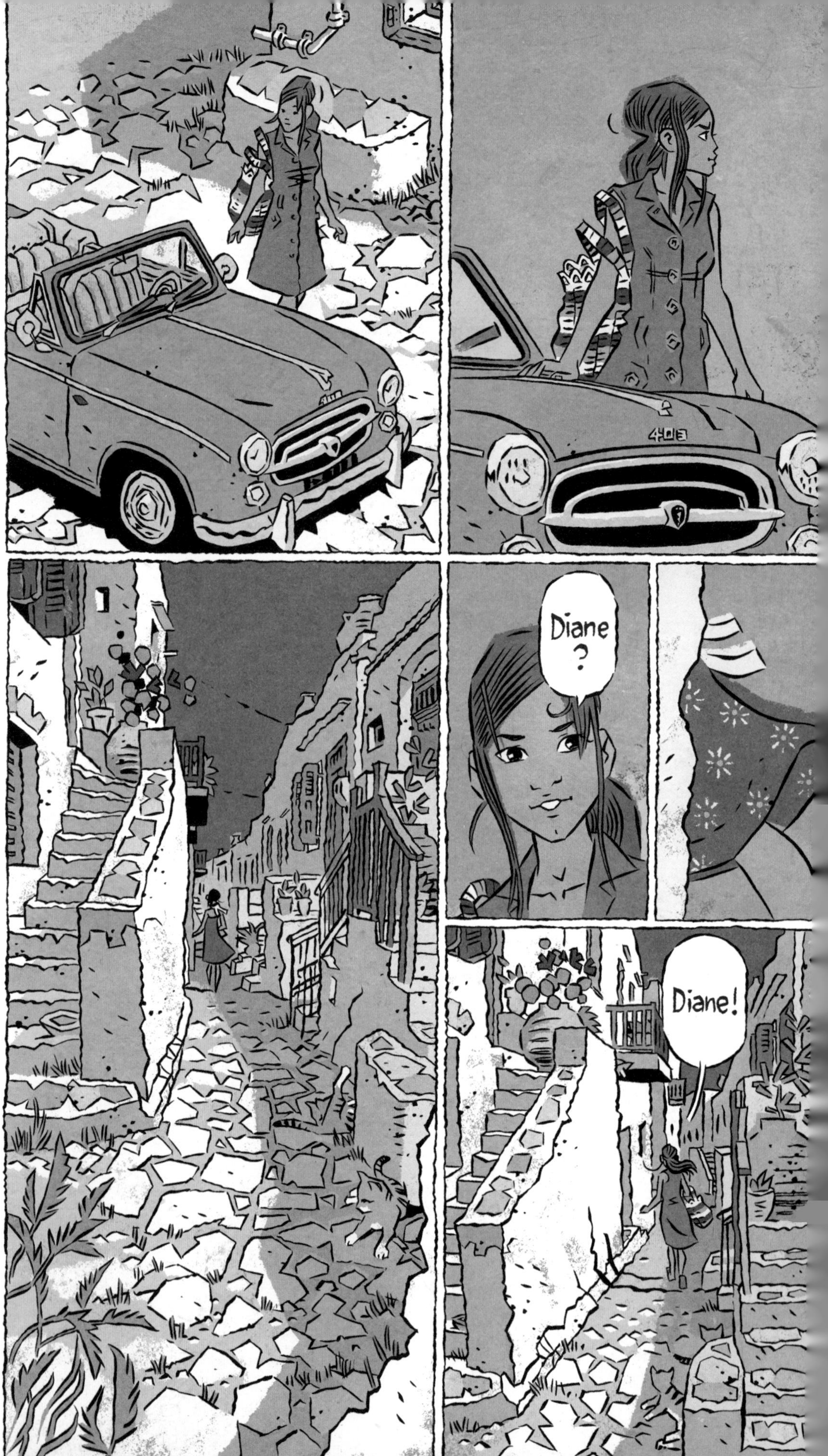
Diane ?
Diane!

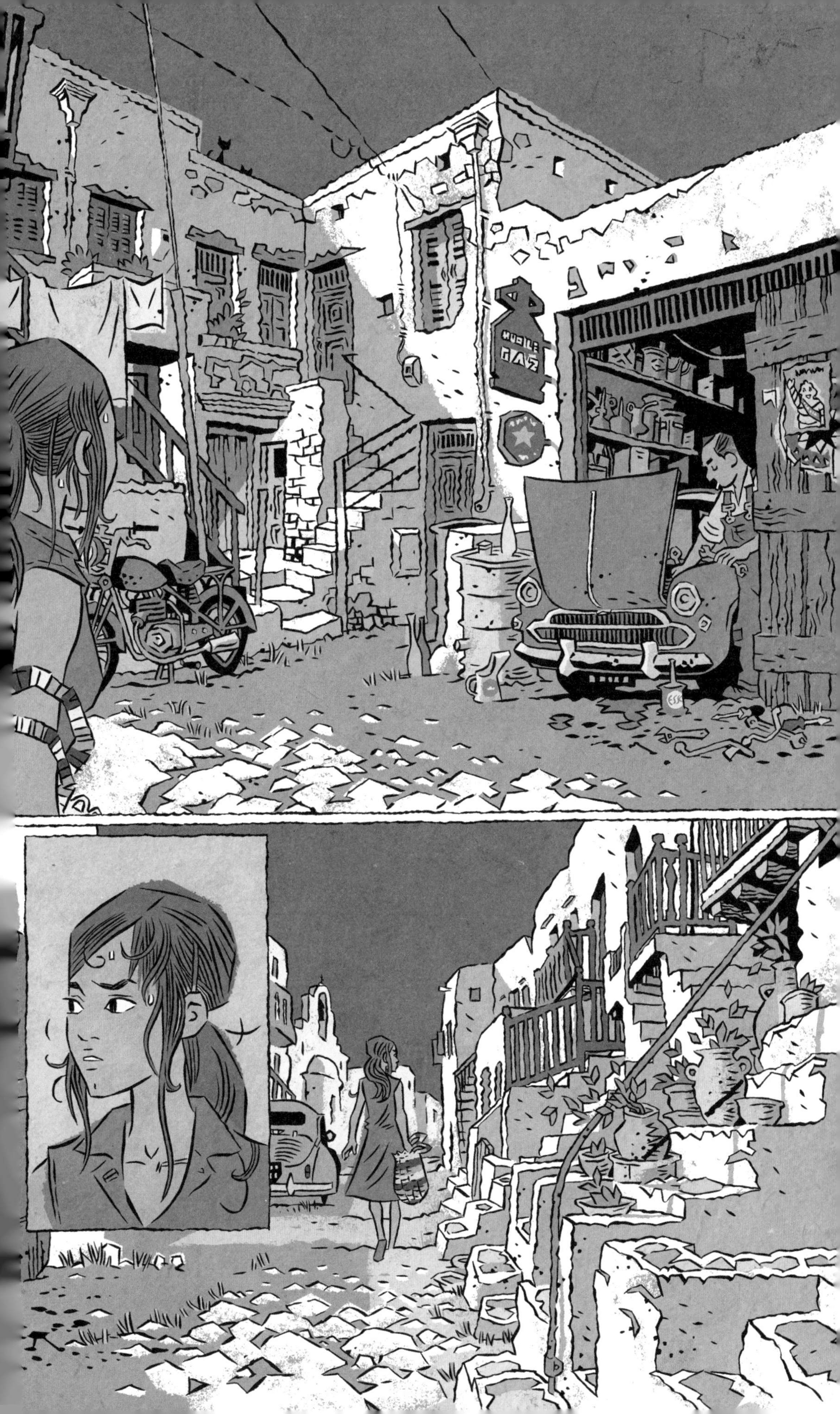
GAZ

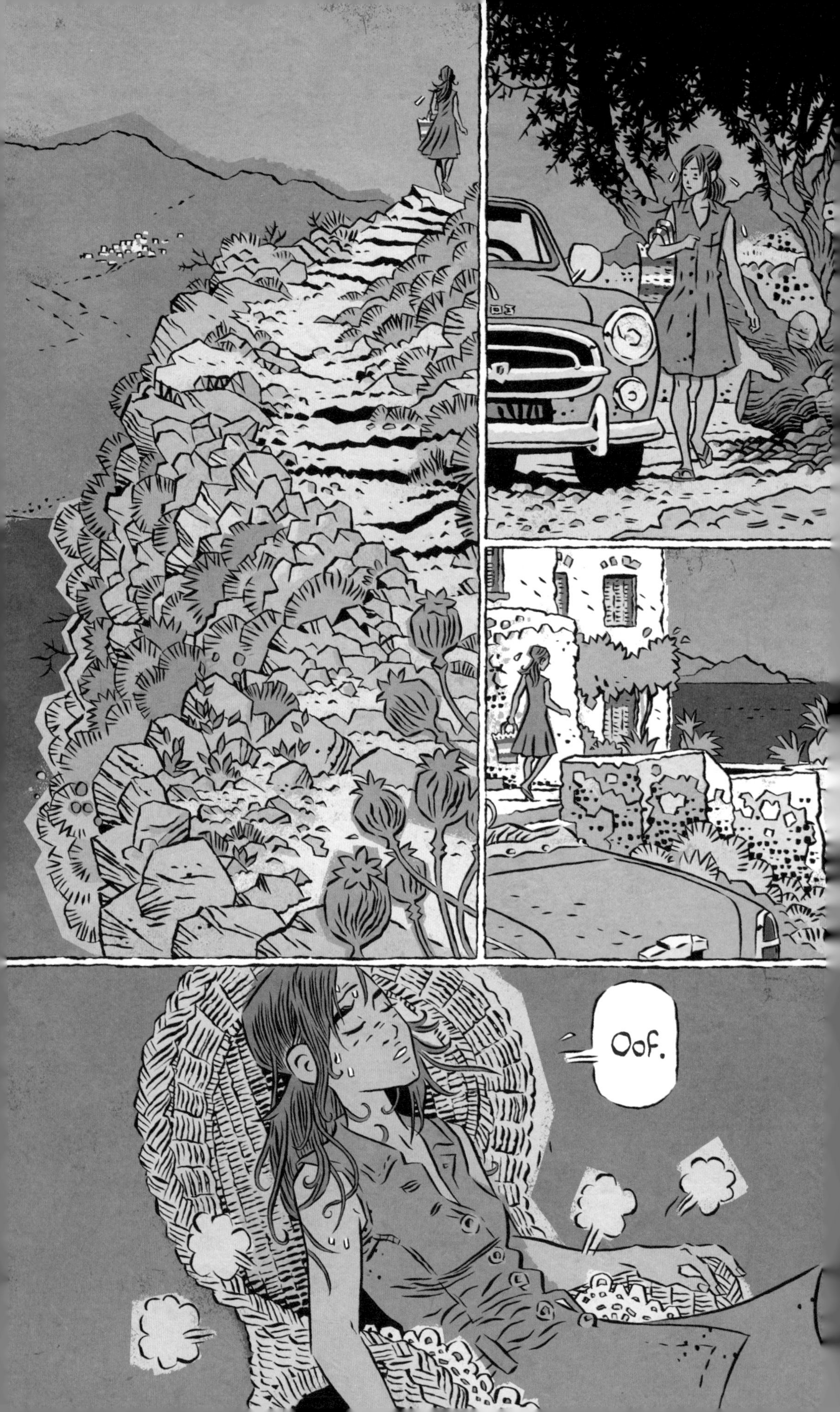
Oof.

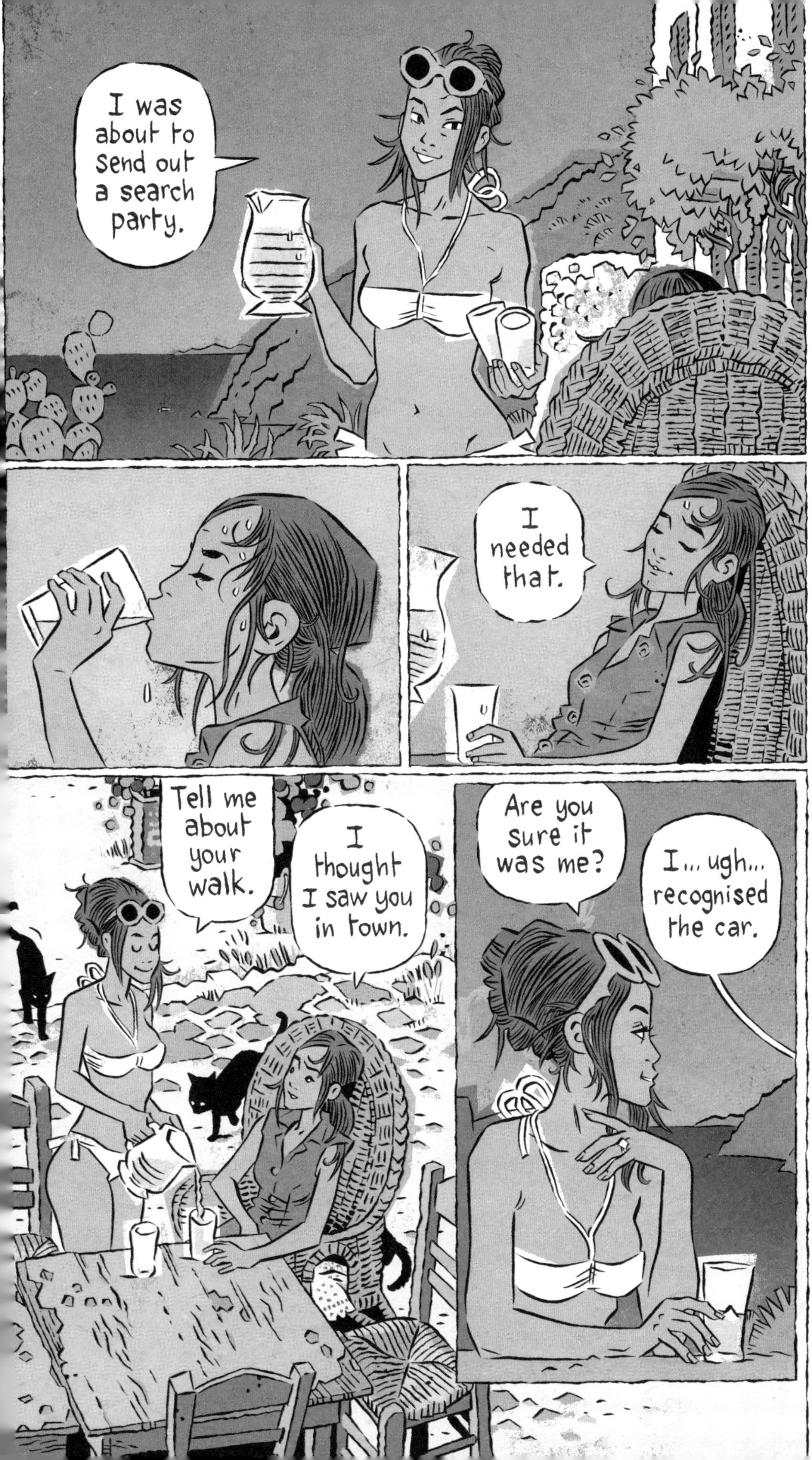
I was about to send out a search party.
I needed that.
Tell me about your walk.
I thought I saw you in town.
Are you sure it was me?
I... ugh... recognised the car.

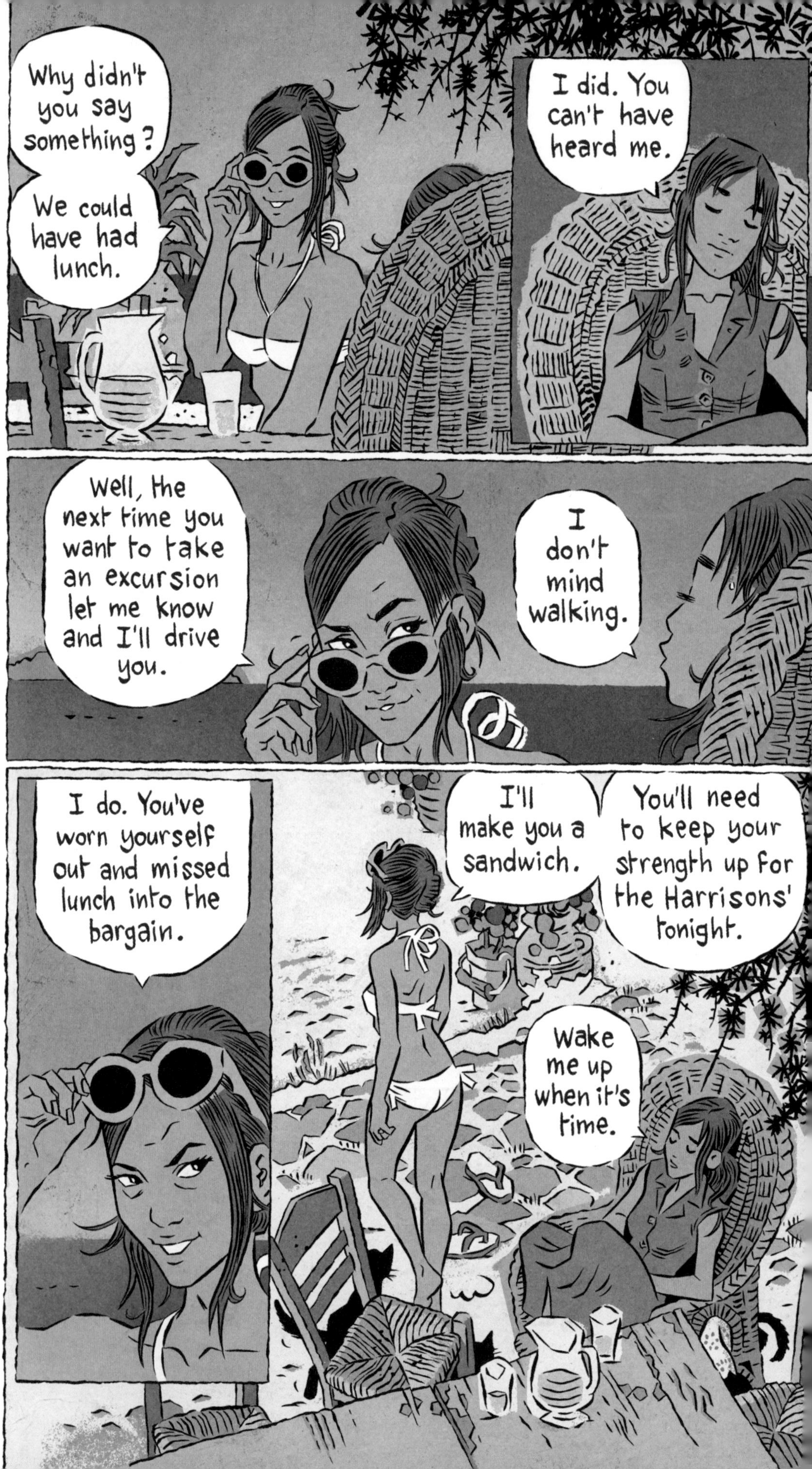
Why didn't you say something?
We could have had lunch.
I did. You can't have heard me.
Well, the next time you want to take an excursion let me know and I'll drive you.
I don't mind walking.
I do. You've worn yourself out and missed lunch into the bargain.
I'll make you a sandwich.
You'll need to keep your strength up for the Harrisons' tonight.
Wake me up when it's time.

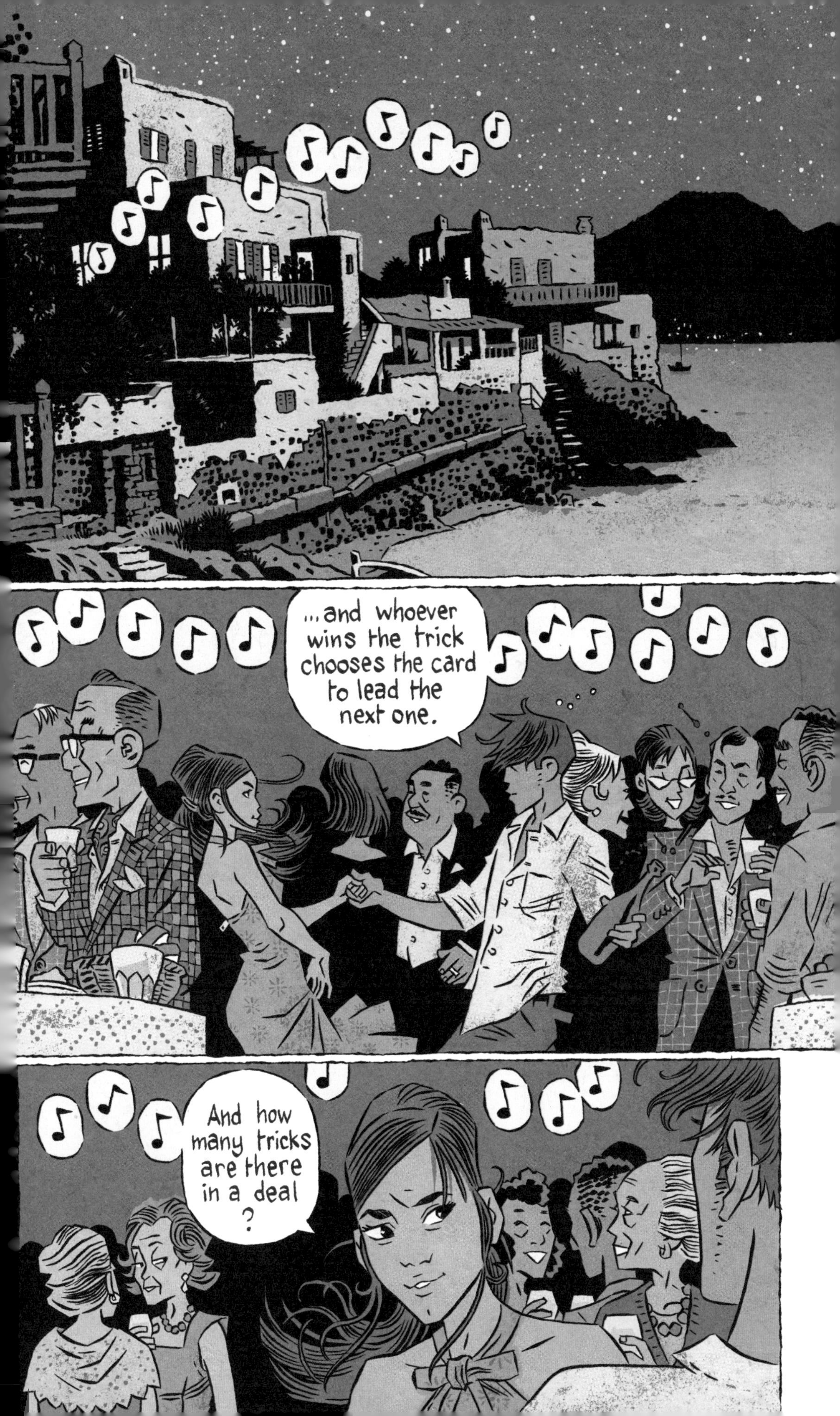
...and whoever wins the trick chooses the card to lead the next one.
And how many tricks are there in a deal ?

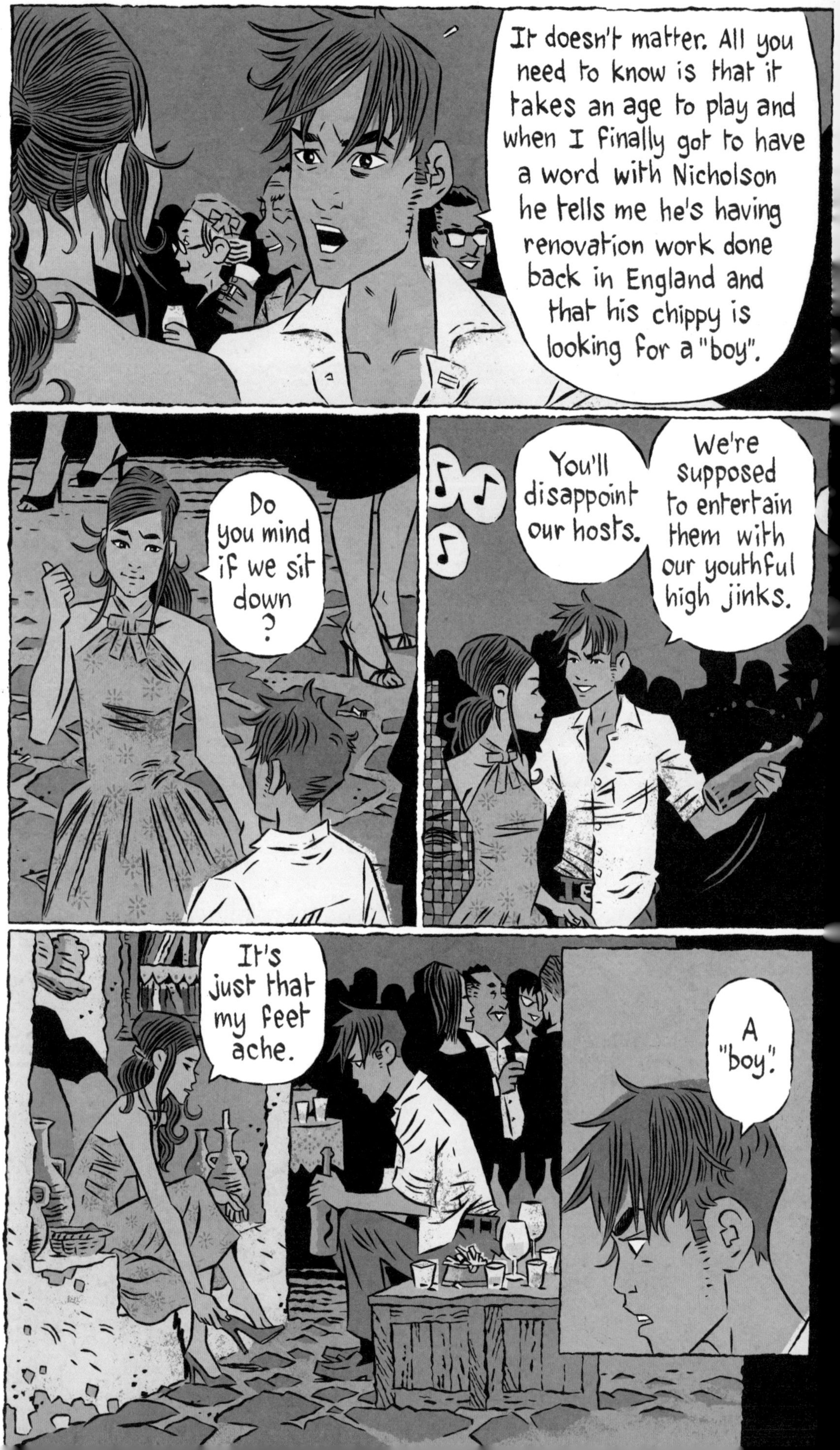
It doesn't matter. All you need to know is that it takes an age to play and when I finally got to have a word with Nicholson he tells me he's having renovation work done back in England and that his chippy is looking for a "boy".
Do you mind if we sit down?
You'll disappoint our hosts.
We're supposed to entertain them with our youthful high jinks.
It's just that my feet ache.
A "boy".

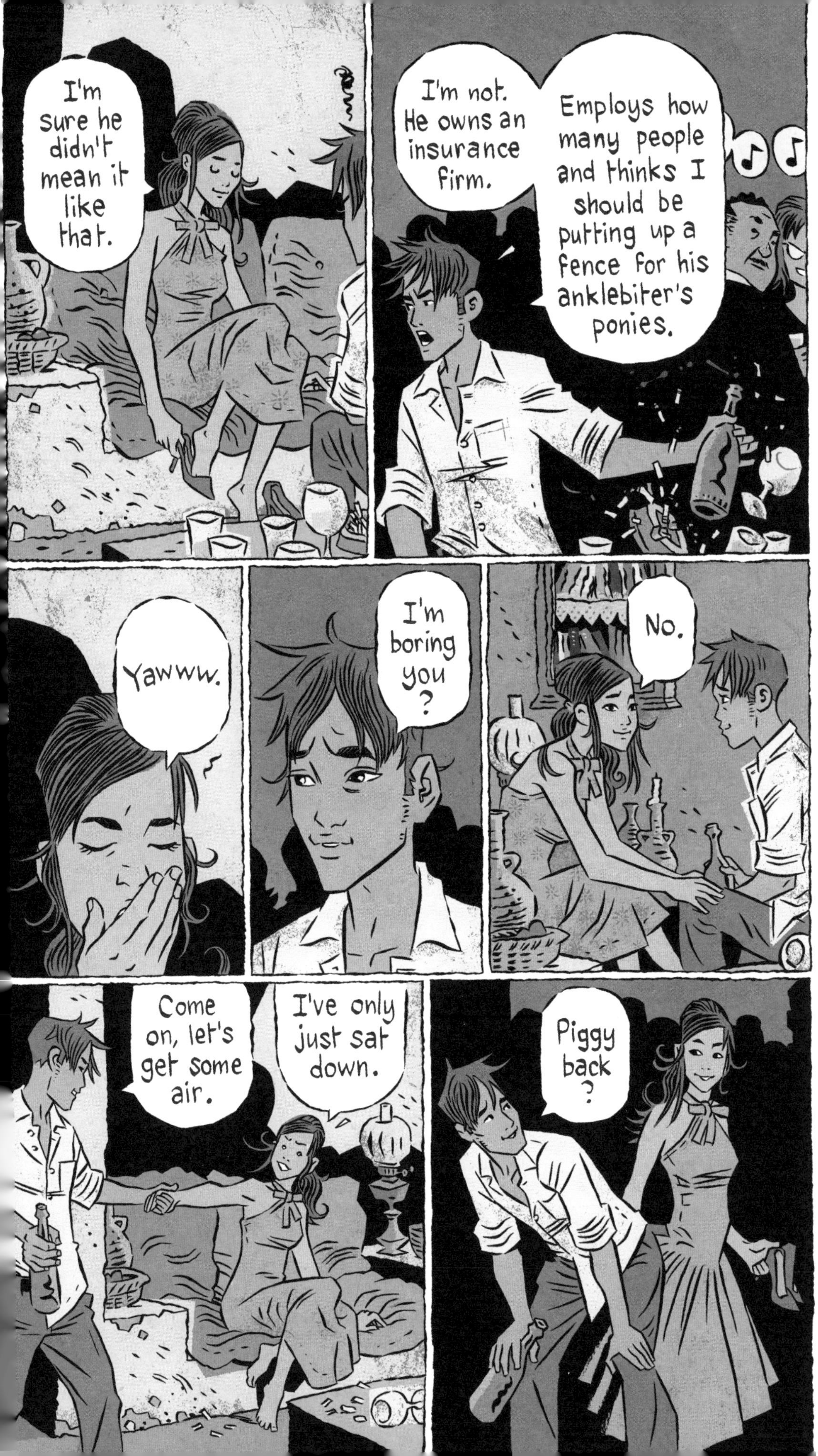
I'm sure he didn't mean it like that.
I'm not. He owns an insurance firm.
Employs how many people and thinks I should be putting up a fence for his anklebiter's ponies.
Yawww.
I'm boring you?
No.
Come on, let's get some air.
I've only just sat down.
Piggy back?

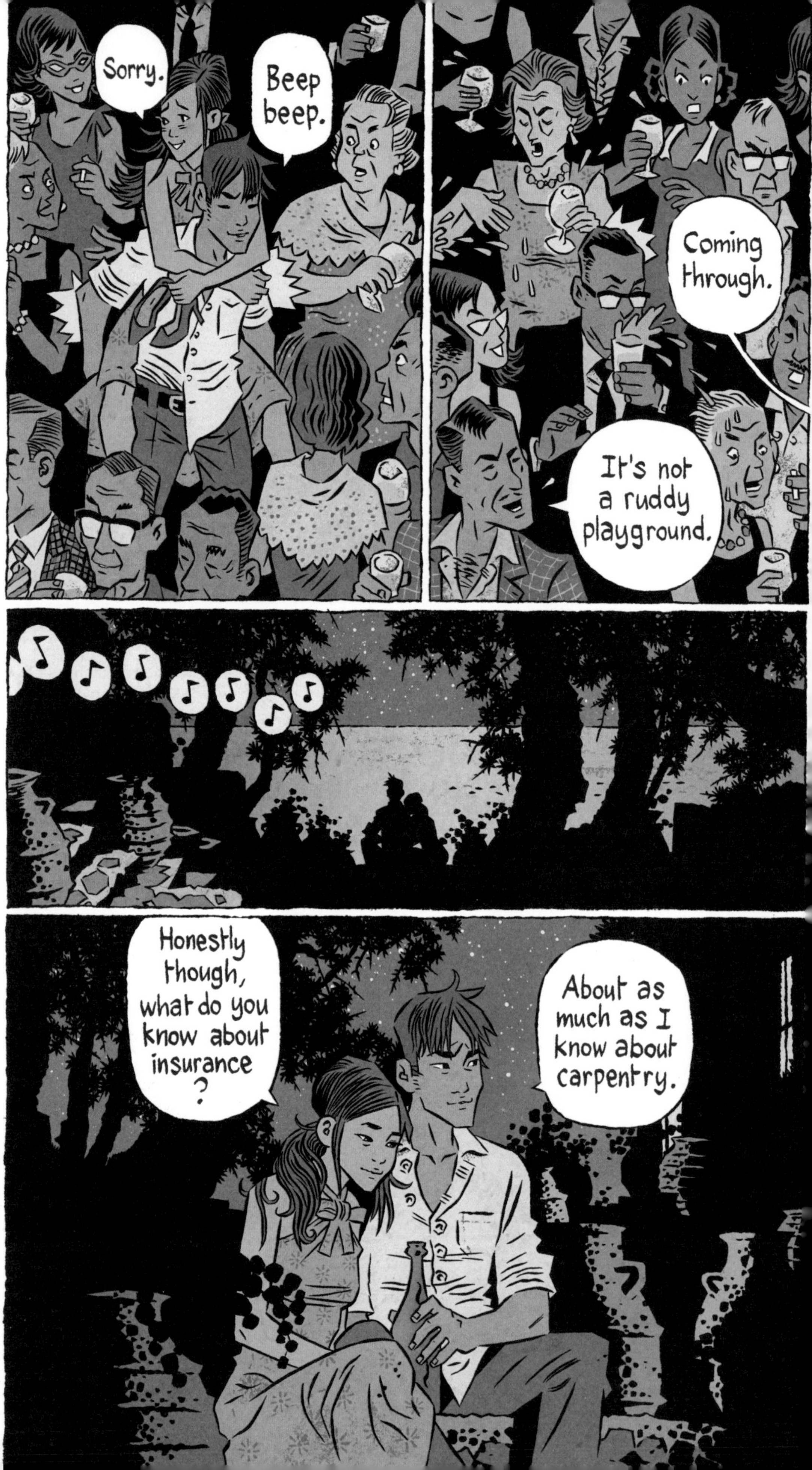
Sorry.
Beep beep.
Coming through.
It's not a ruddy playground.
Honestly though, what do you know about insurance ?
About as much as I know about carpentry.

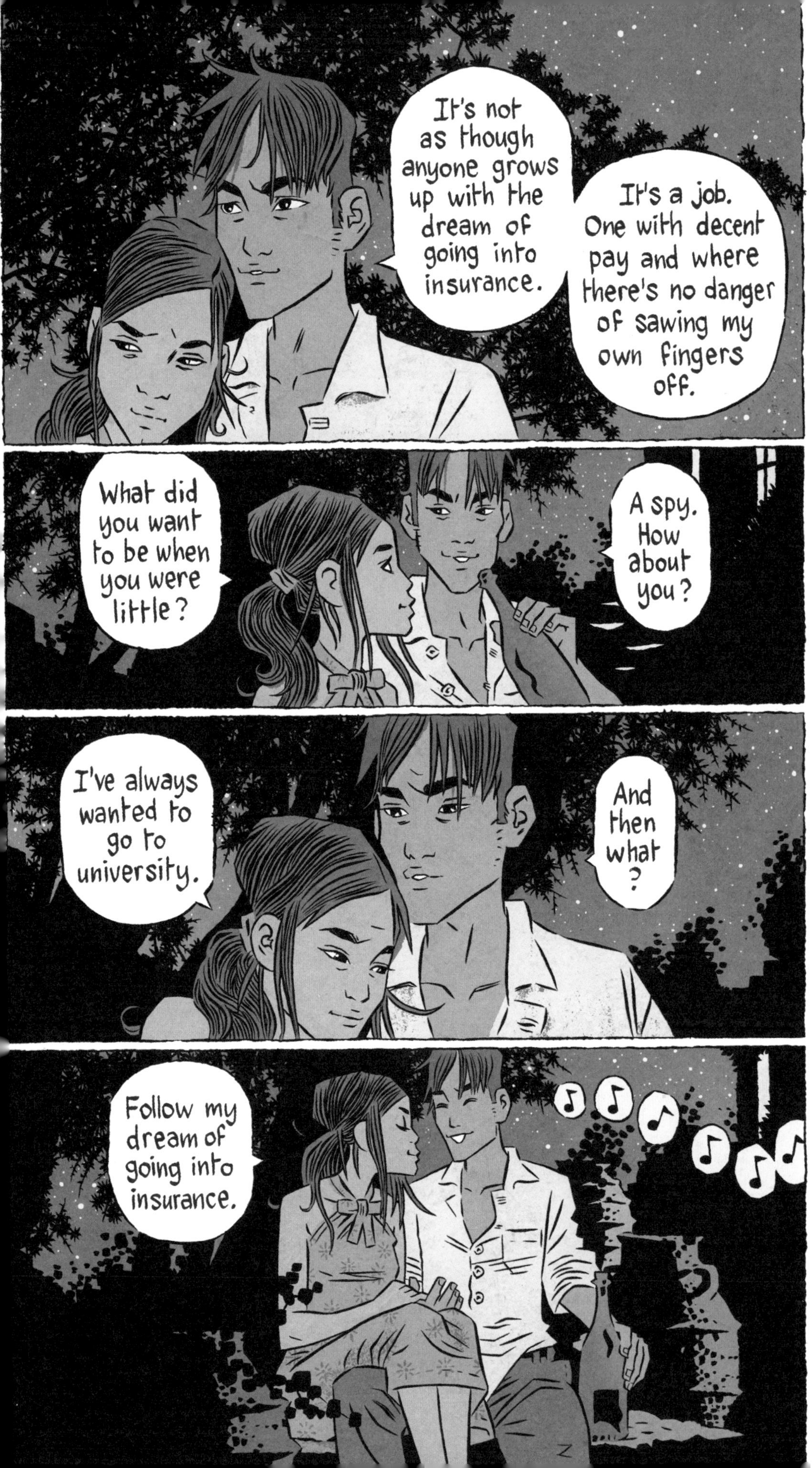
It's not as though anyone grows up with the dream of going into insurance.
It's a job. One with decent pay and where there's no danger of sawing my own fingers off.
What did you want to be when you were little?
A spy. How about you?
I've always wanted to go to university.
And then what?
Follow my dream of going into insurance.

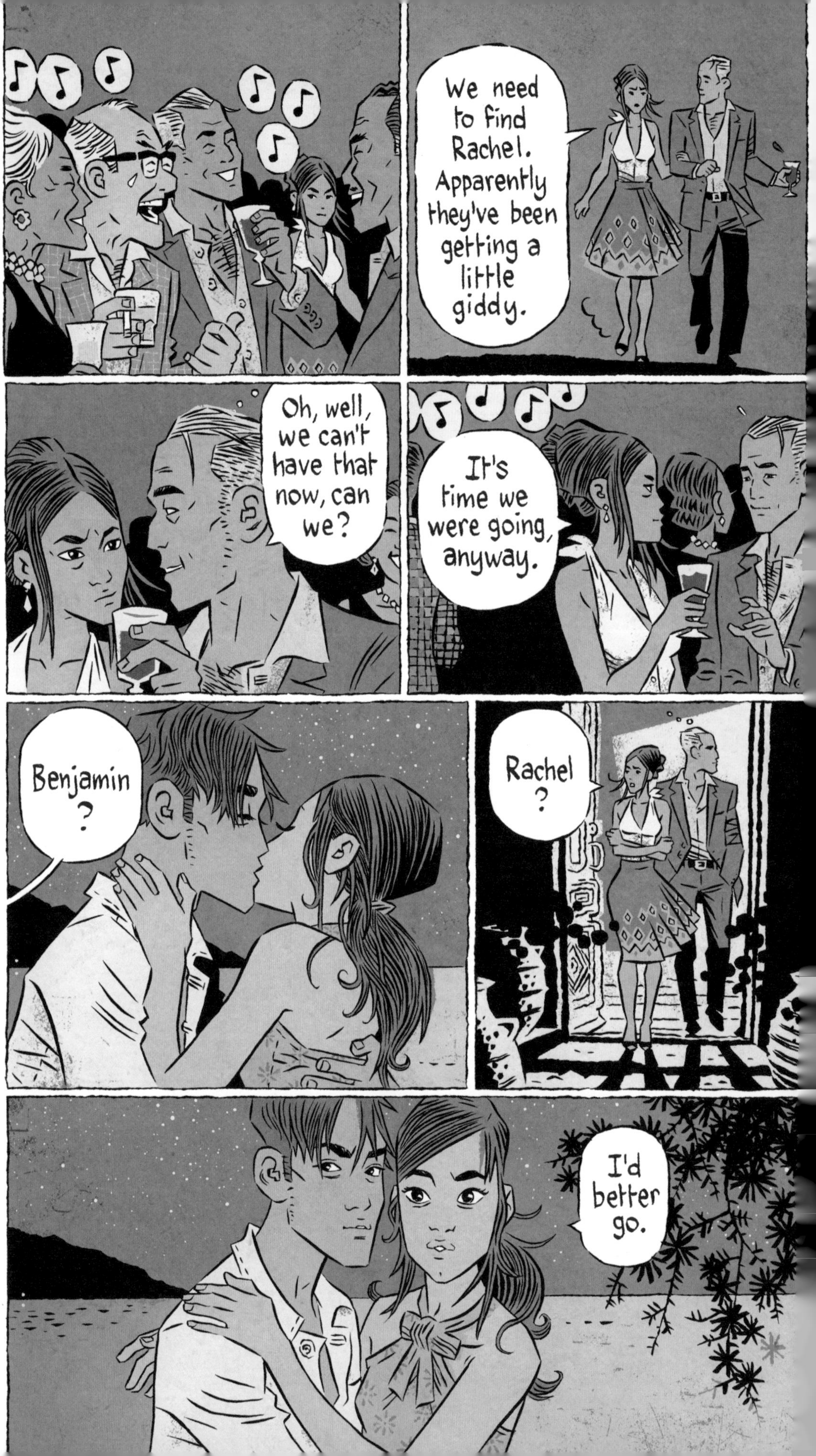
We need to find Rachel. Apparently they've been getting a little giddy.
Oh, well, we can't have that now, can we?
It's time we were going, anyway.
Benjamin?
Rachel?
I'd better go.

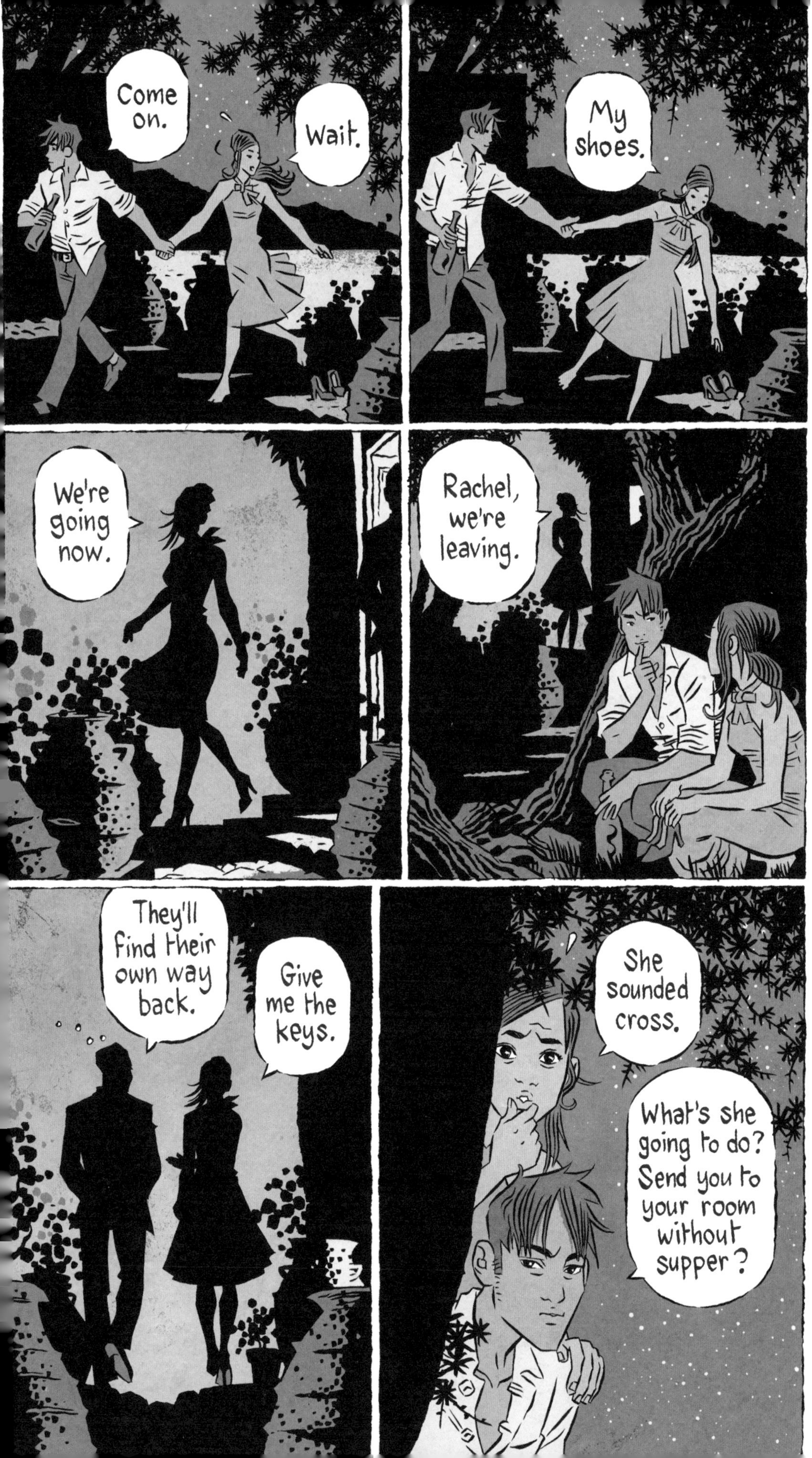
Come on.
Wait.
My shoes.
We're going now.
Rachel, we're leaving.
They'll find their own way back.
Give me the keys.
She sounded cross.
What's she going to do? Send you to your room without supper?

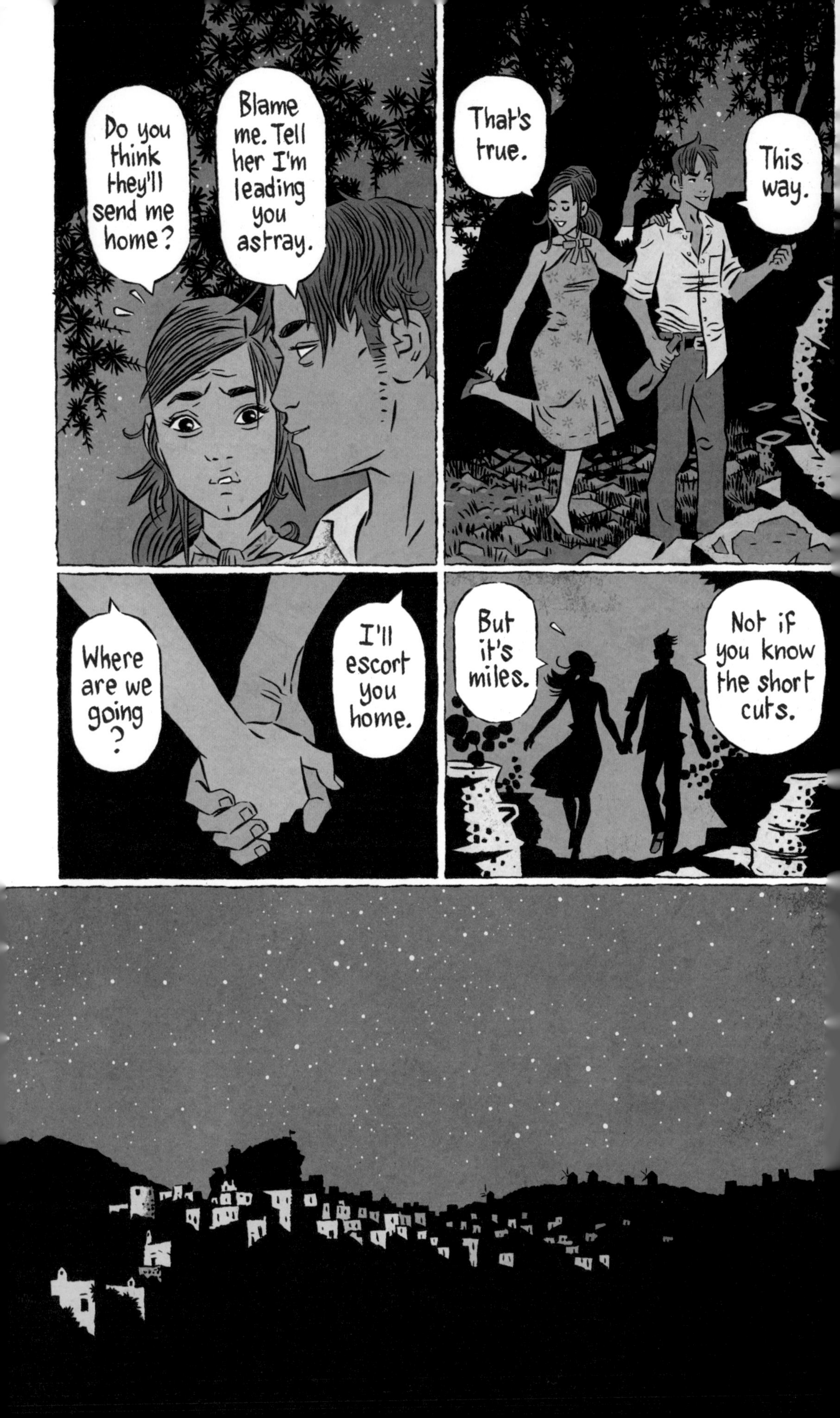
Do you think they'll send me home?
Blame me. Tell her I'm leading you astray.
That's true.
This way.
Where are we going?
I'll escort you home.
But it's miles.
Not if you know the short cuts.

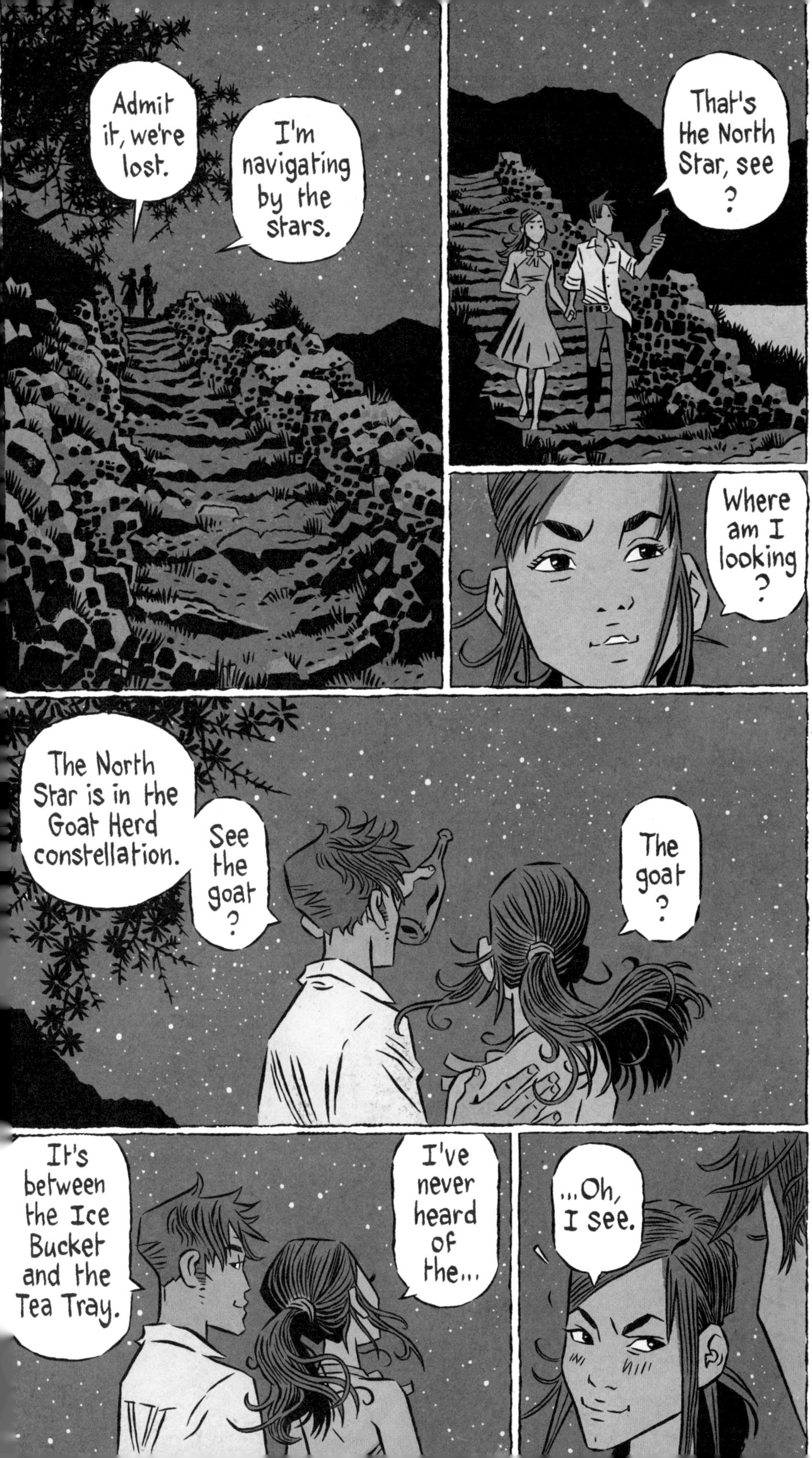
Admit it, we're lost.
I'm navigating by the stars.
That's the North Star, see?
Where am I looking?
The North Star is in the Goat Herd constellation.
See the goat?
The goat?
It's between the Ice Bucket and the Tea Tray.
I've never heard of the...
...Oh, I see.

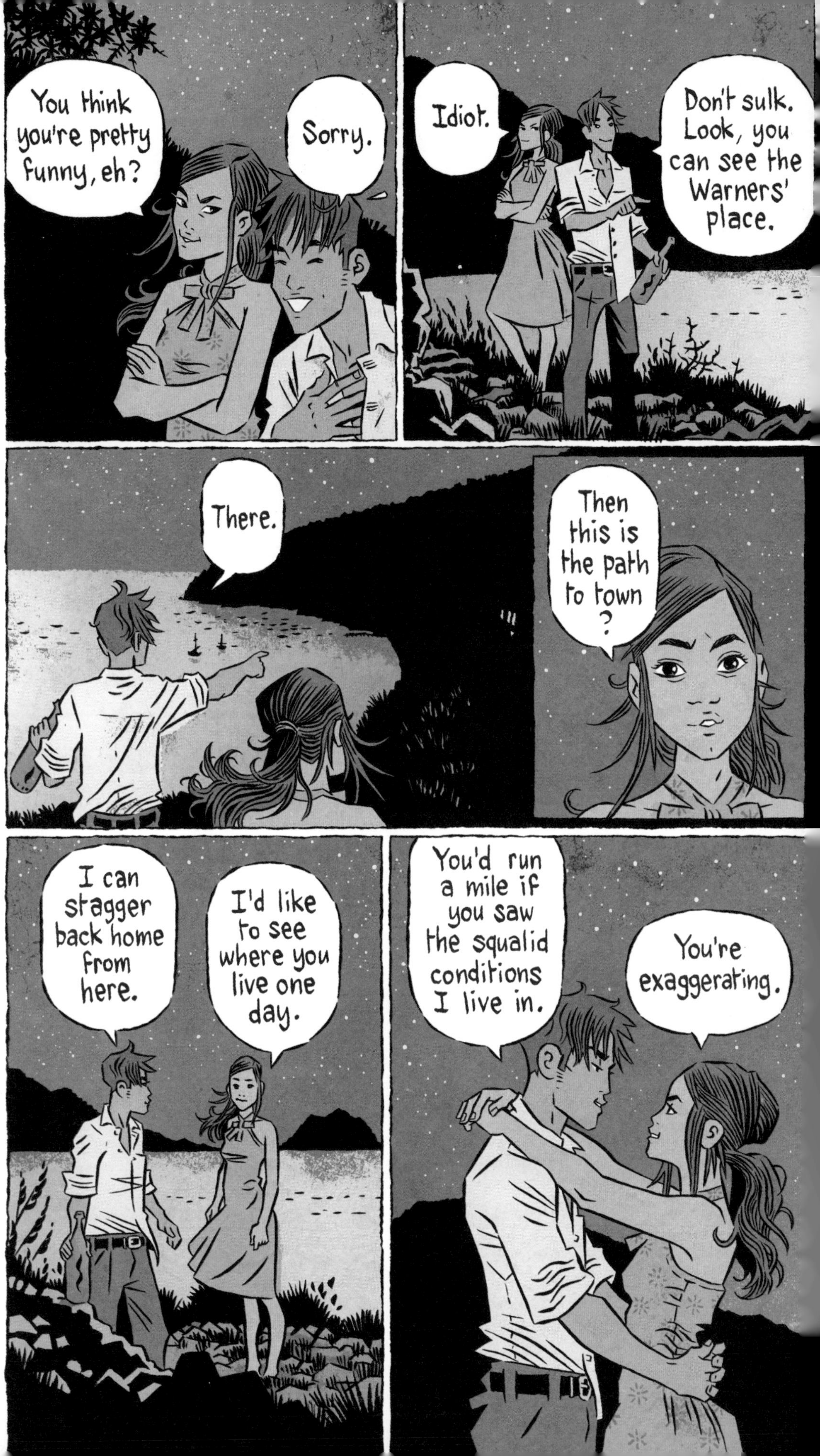
You think you're pretty funny, eh?
Sorry.
Idiot.
Don't sulk. Look, you can see the Warners' place.
There.
Then this is the path to town ?
I can stagger back home from here.
I'd like to see where you live one day.
You'd run a mile if you saw the squalid conditions I live in.
You're exaggerating.

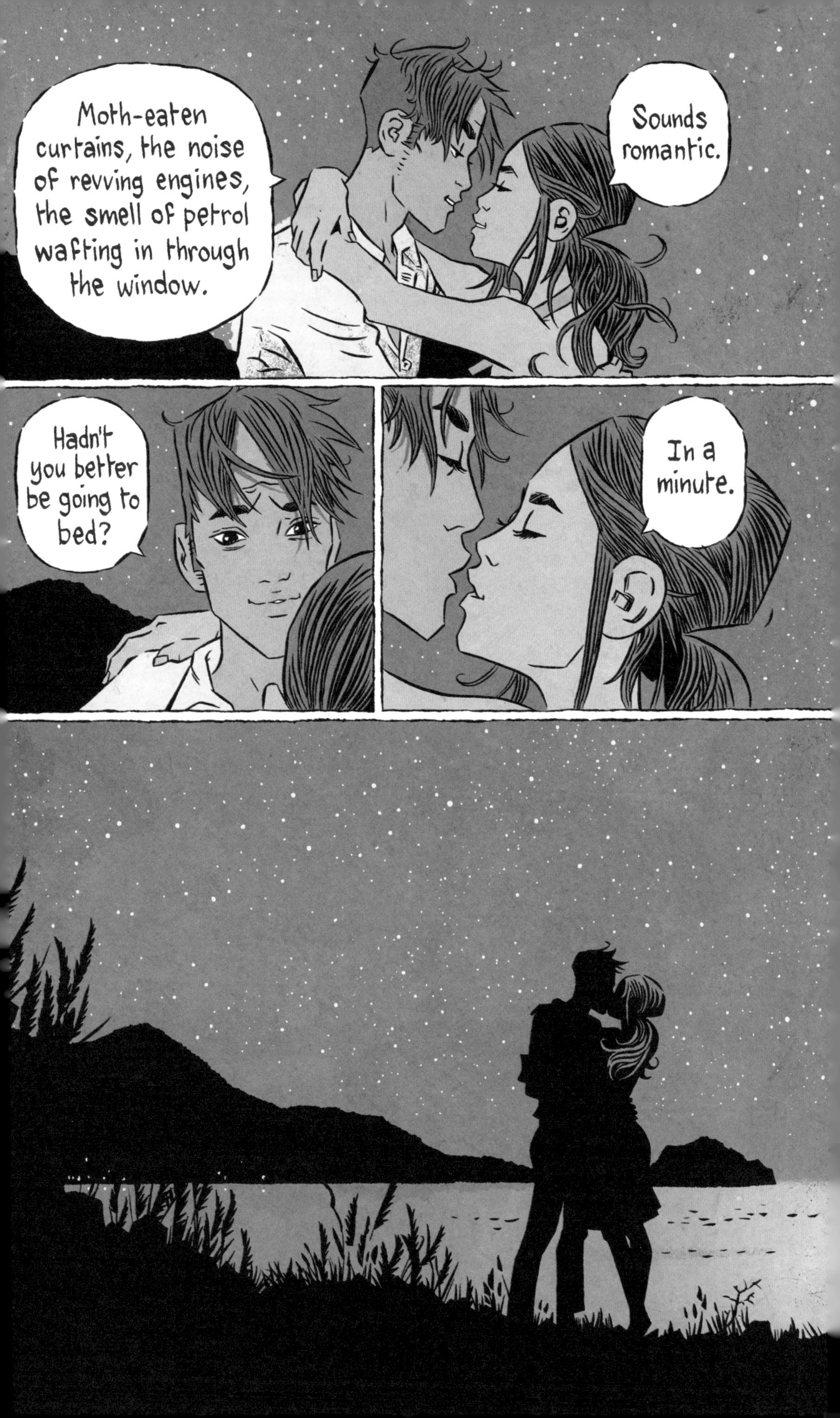
Moth-eaten curtains, the noise of revving engines, the smell of petrol wafting in through the window.
Sounds romantic.
Hadn't you better be going to bed?
In a minute.

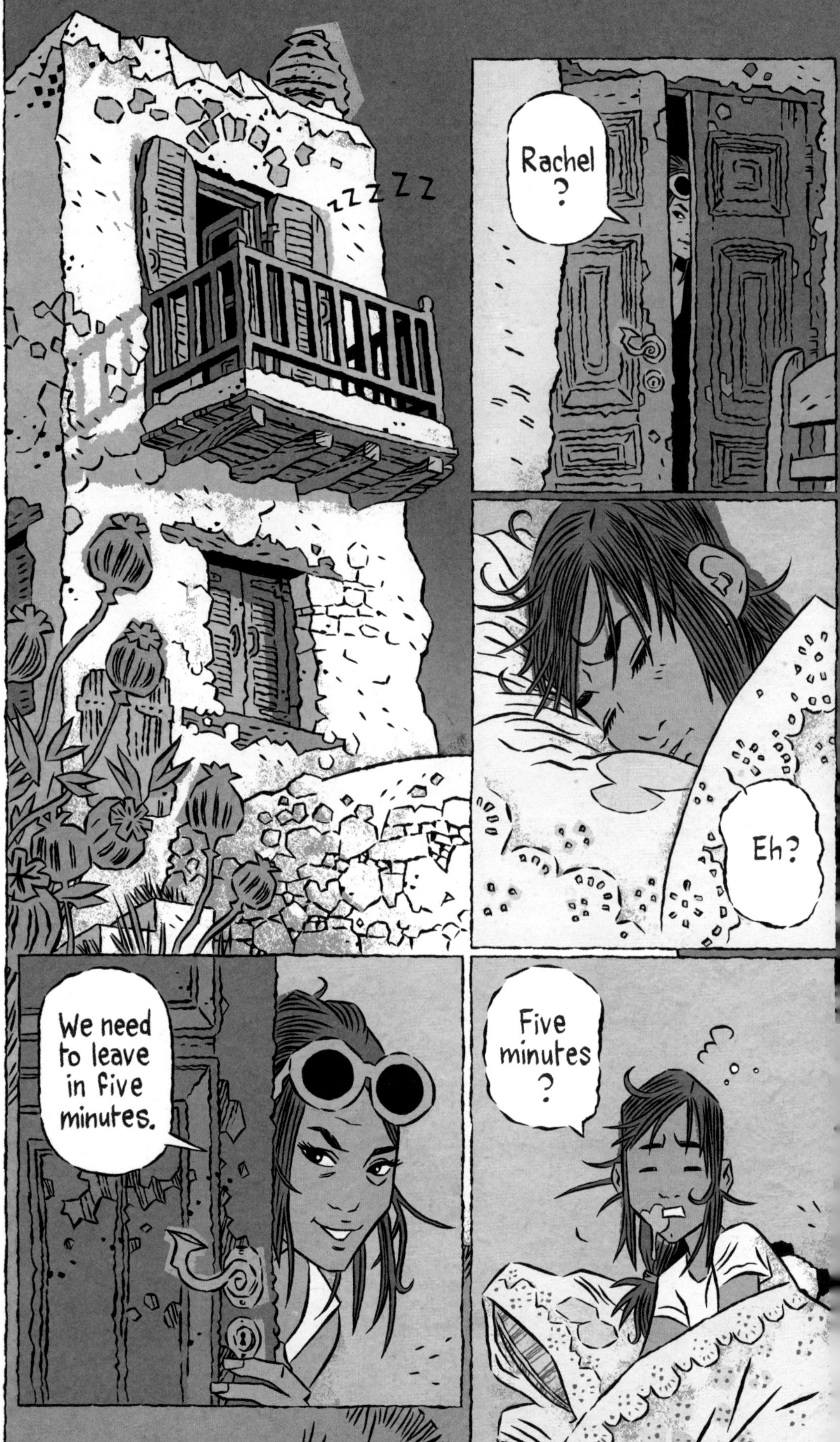
zzzzzz
Rachel?
Eh?
We need to leave in five minutes.
Five minutes?

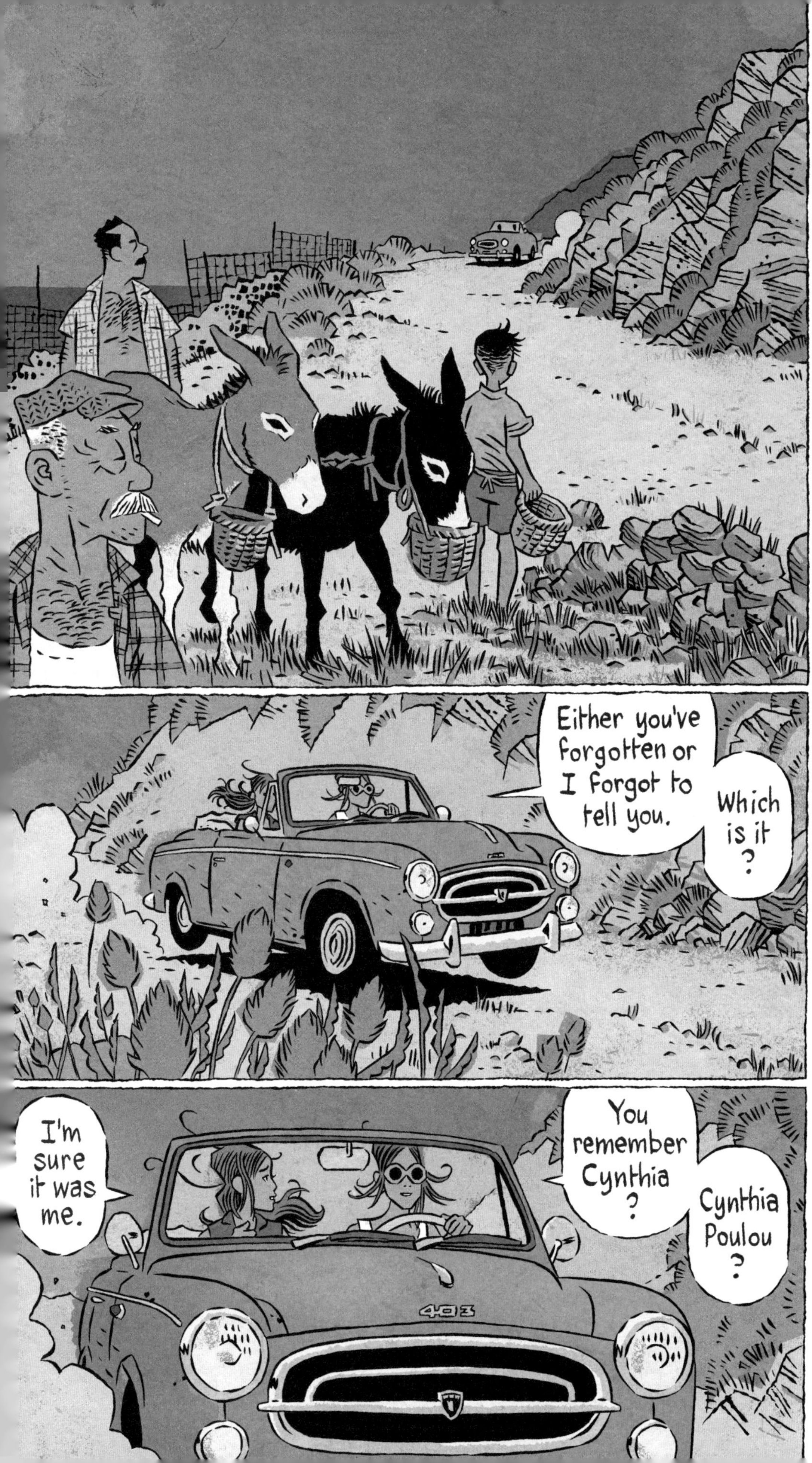
Either you've forgotten or I forgot to tell you.
Which is it ?
I'm sure it was me.
You remember Cynthia ?
Cynthia Poulou ?
403

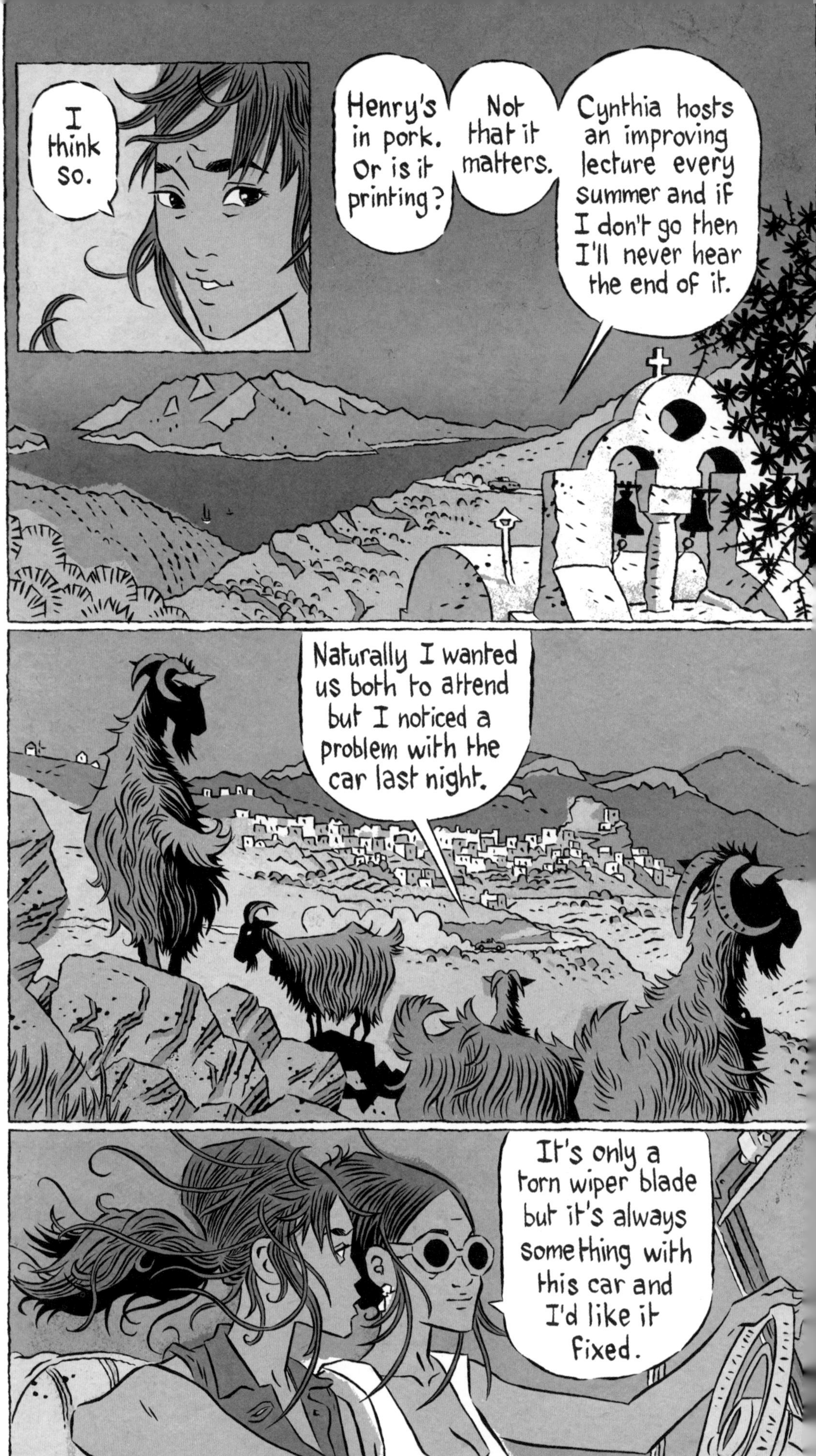
I think so.
Henry's in pork. Or is it printing?
Not that it matters.
Cynthia hosts an improving lecture every summer and if I don't go then I'll never hear the end of it.
Naturally I wanted us both to attend but I noticed a problem with the car last night.
It's only a torn wiper blade but it's always something with this car and I'd like it fixed.

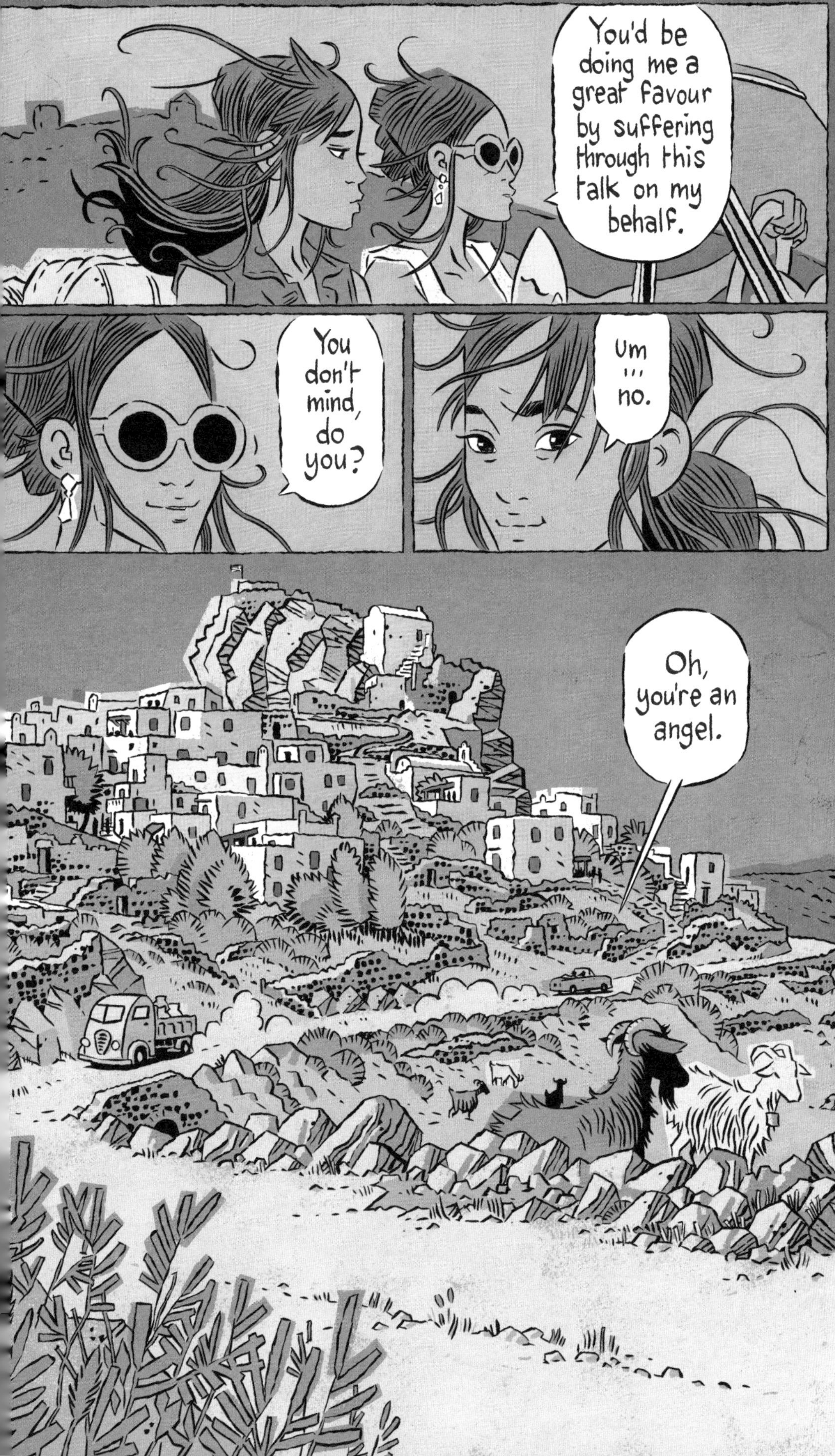
You'd be doing me a great favour by suffering through this talk on my behalf.
You don't mind, do you?
Um ... no.
Oh, you're an angel.

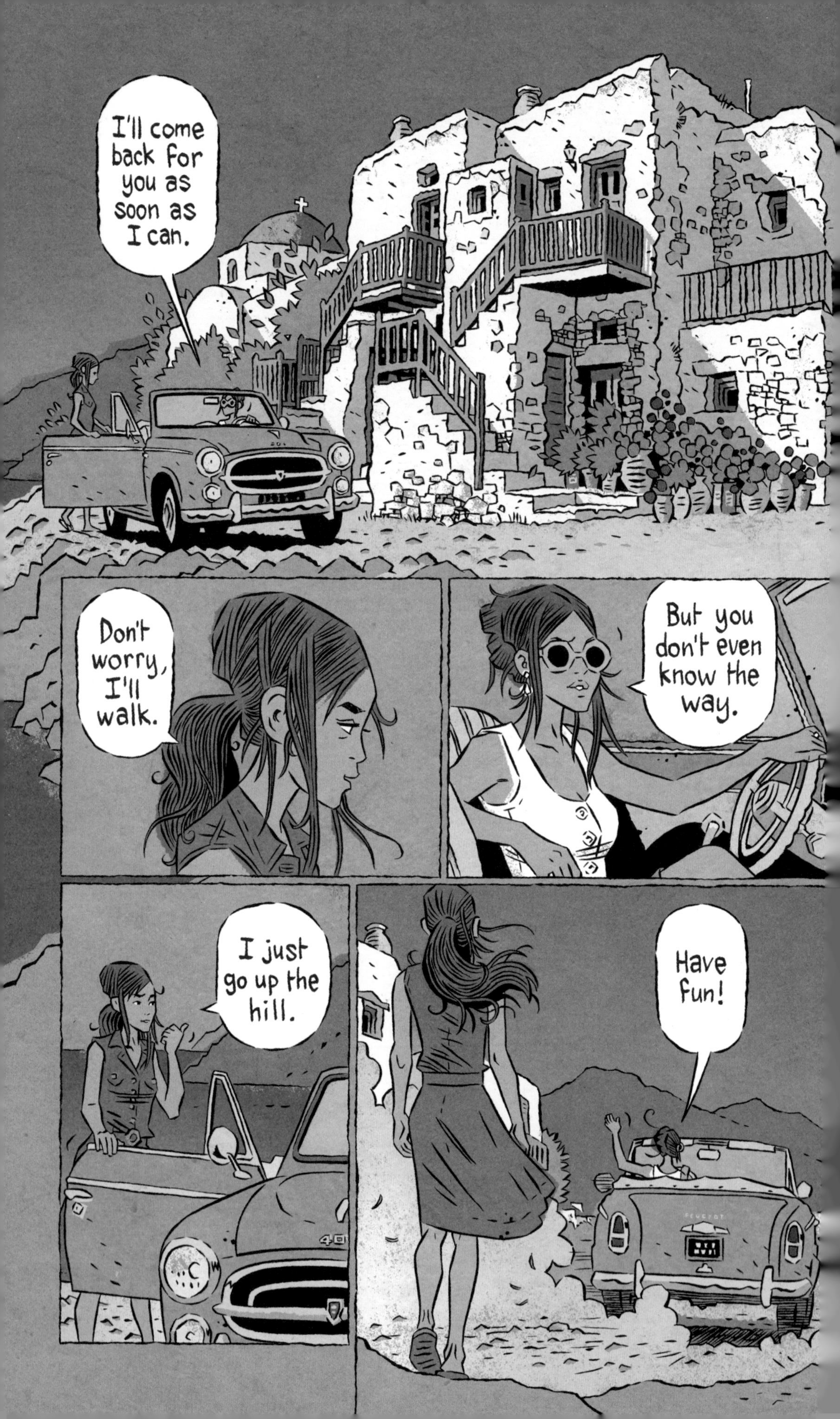
I'll come back for you as soon as I can.
Don't worry, I'll walk.
But you don't even know the way.
I just go up the hill.
Have fun!

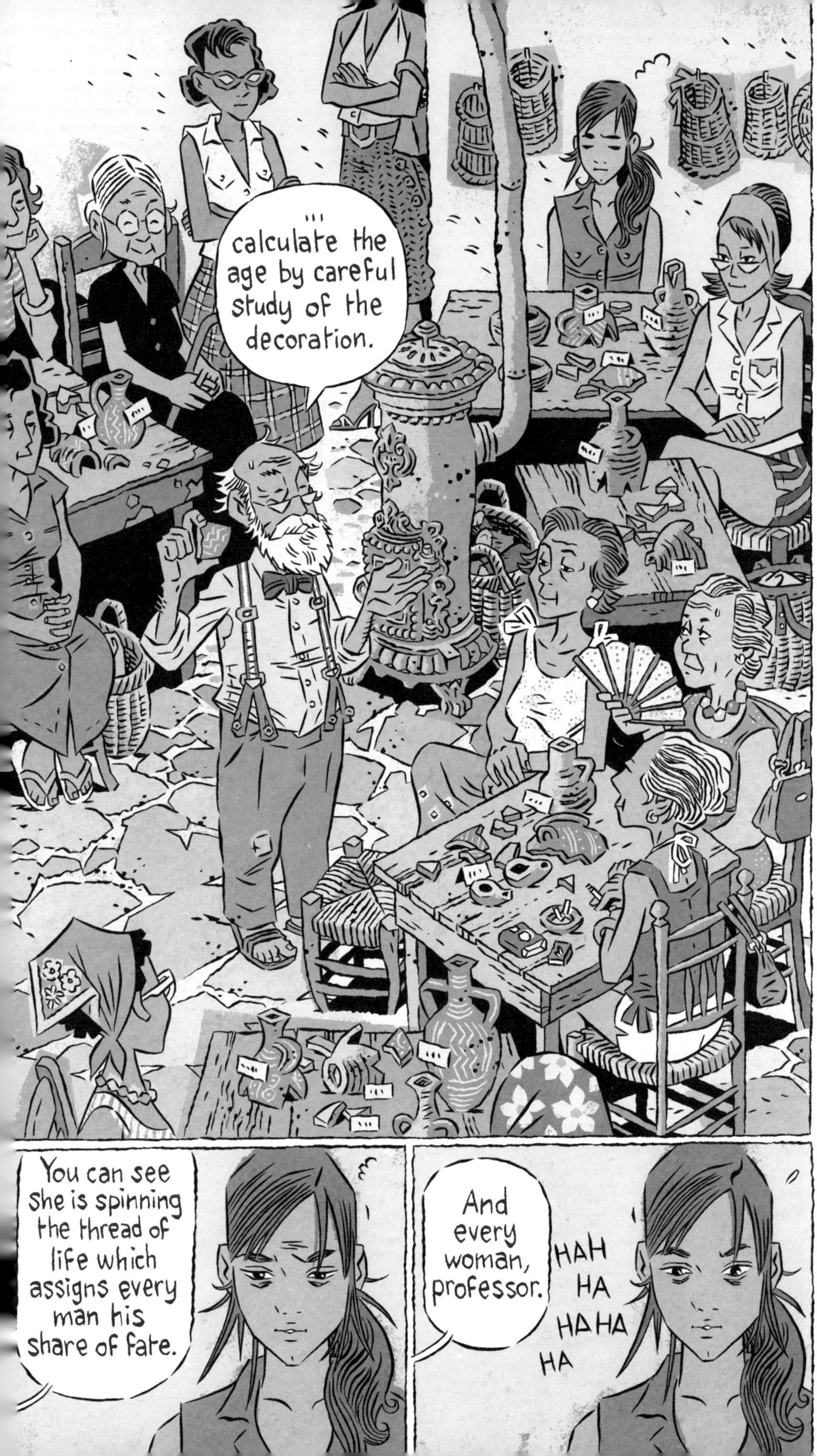
... calculate the age by careful study of the decoration.
You can see she is spinning the thread of life which assigns every man his share of fate.
And every woman, professor.
HAH HA HAHA HA

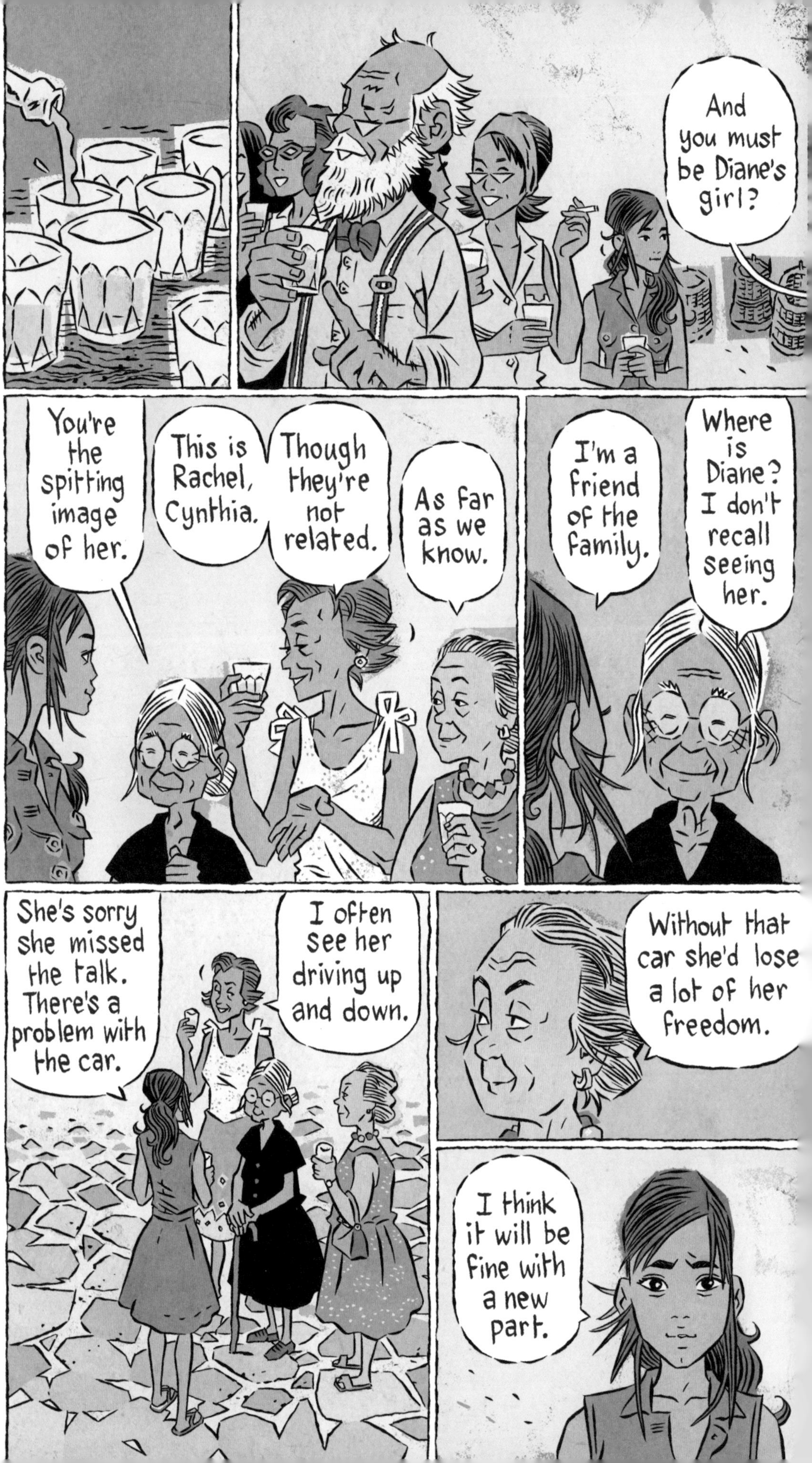
And you must be Diane's girl?
You're the spitting image of her.
This is Rachel, Cynthia.
Though they're not related.
As far as we know.
I'm a friend of the family.
Where is Diane? I don't recall seeing her.
She's sorry she missed the talk. There's a problem with the car.
I often see her driving up and down.
Without that car she'd lose a lot of her freedom.
I think it will be fine with a new part.

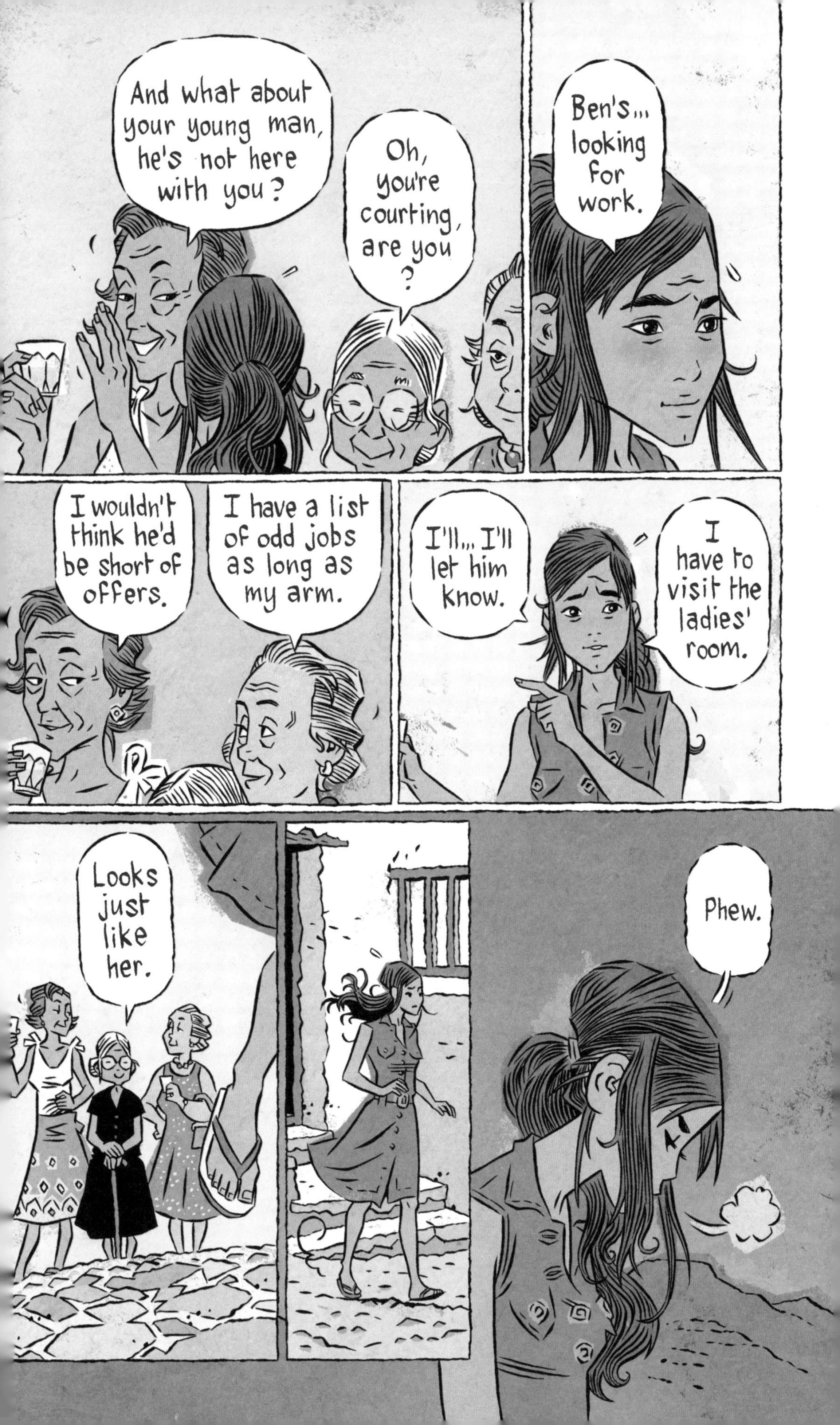
And what about your young man, he's not here with you?
Oh, you're courting, are you?
Ben's... looking for work.
I wouldn't think he'd be short of offers.
I have a list of odd jobs as long as my arm.
I'll... I'll let him know.
I have to visit the ladies' room.
Looks just like her.
Phew.

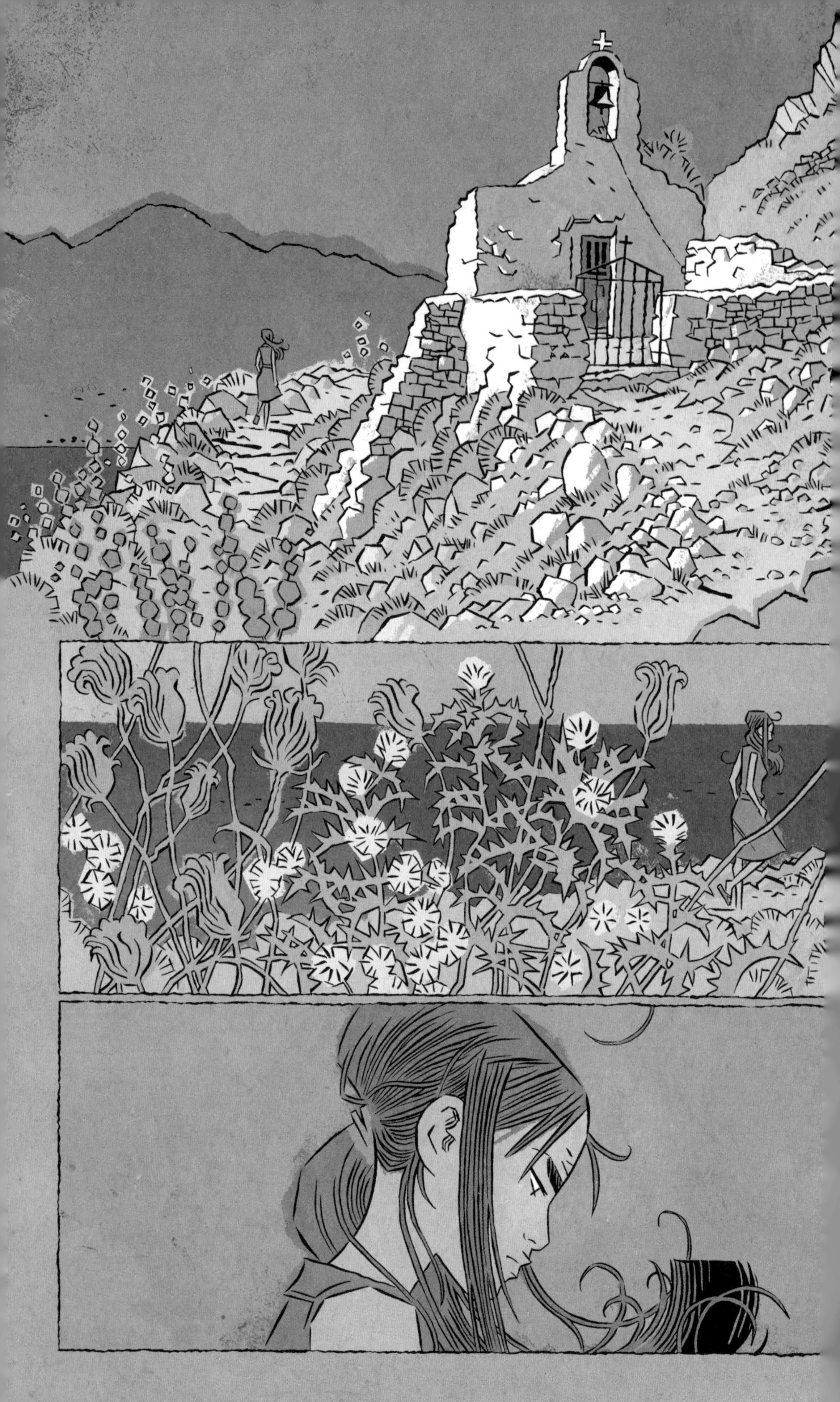

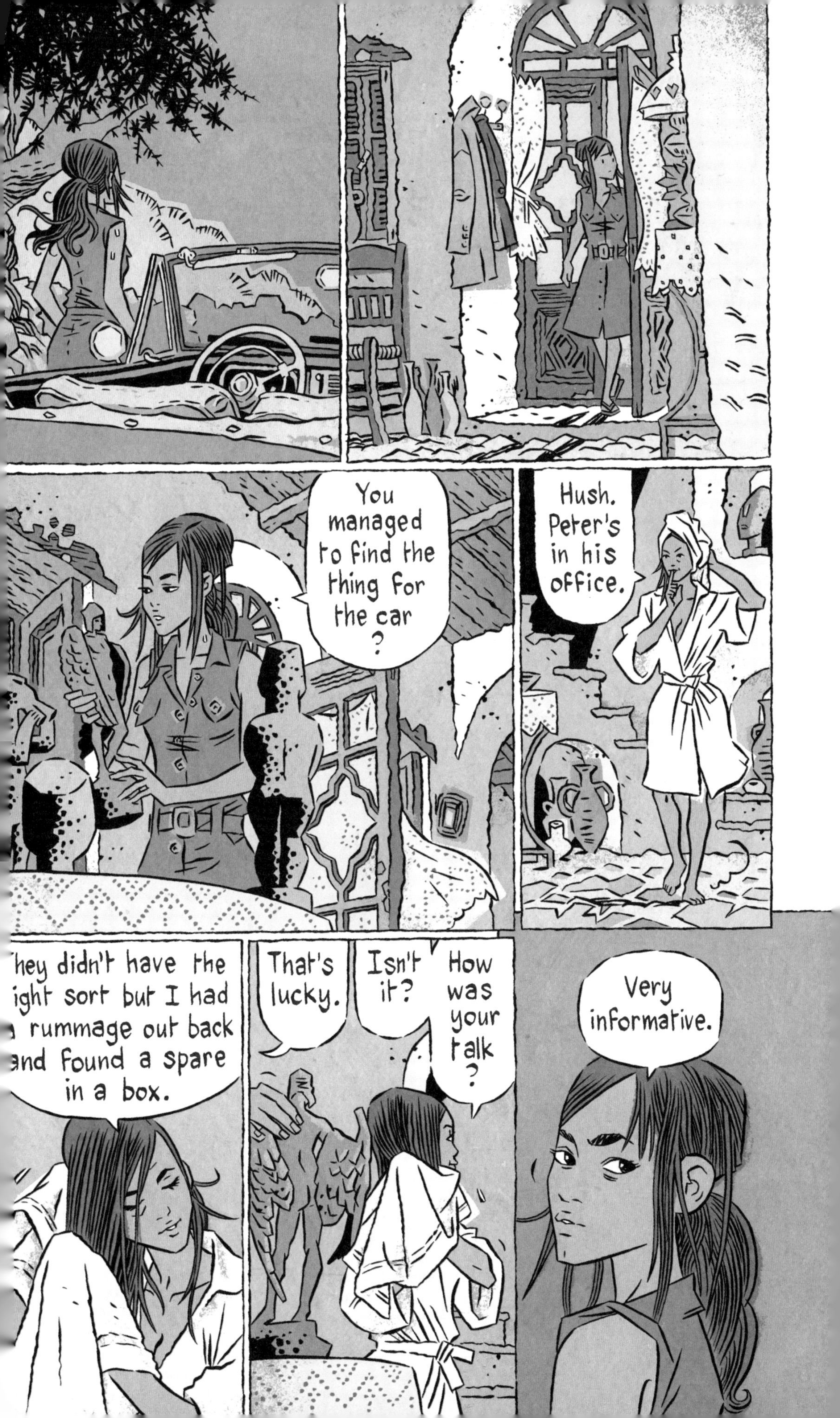
You managed to find the thing for the car ?
Hush. Peter's in his office.
hey didn't have the ight sort but I had rummage out back and found a spare in a box.
That's lucky.
Isn't it?
How was your talk ?
Very informative.

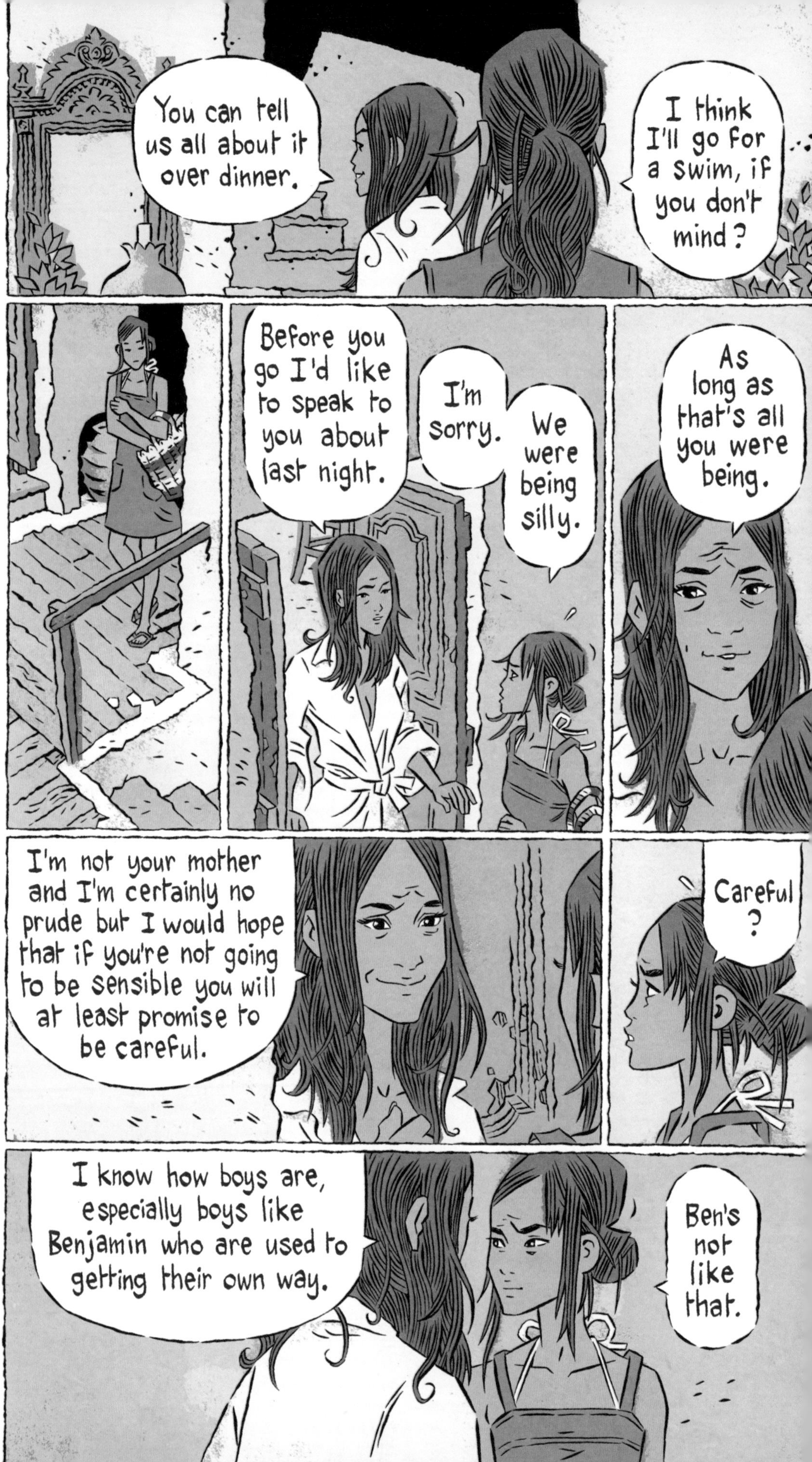
You can tell us all about it over dinner.
I think I'll go for a swim, if you don't mind?
Before you go I'd like to speak to you about last night.
I'm sorry.
We were being silly.
As long as that's all you were being.
I'm not your mother and I'm certainly no prude but I would hope that if you're not going to be sensible you will at least promise to be careful.
Careful?
I know how boys are, especially boys like Benjamin who are used to getting their own way.
Ben's not like that.

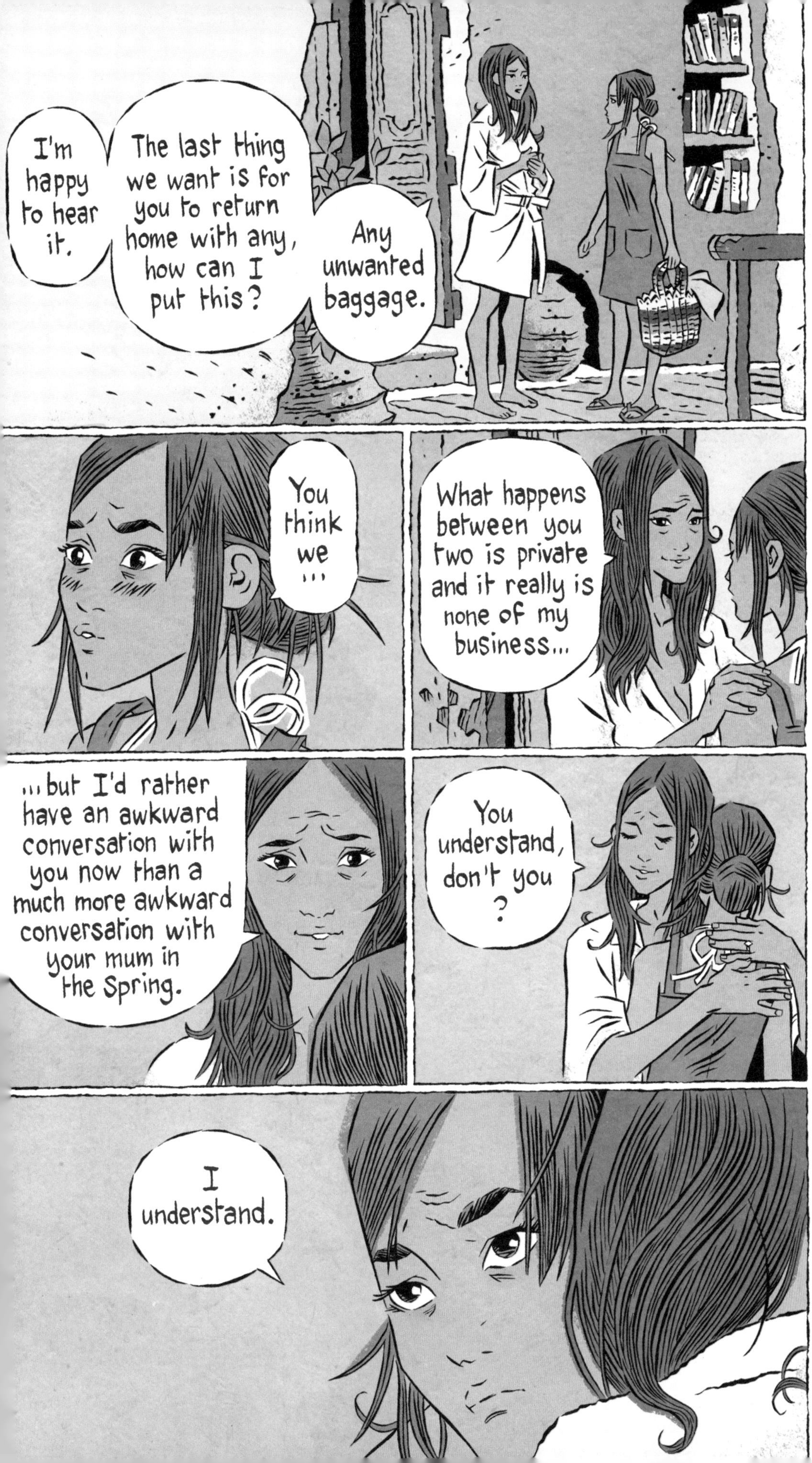
I'm happy to hear it.
The last thing we want is for you to return home with any, how can I put this?
Any unwanted baggage.
You think we ...
What happens between you two is private and it really is none of my business...
...but I'd rather have an awkward conversation with you now than a much more awkward conversation with your mum in the Spring.
You understand, don't you?
I understand.

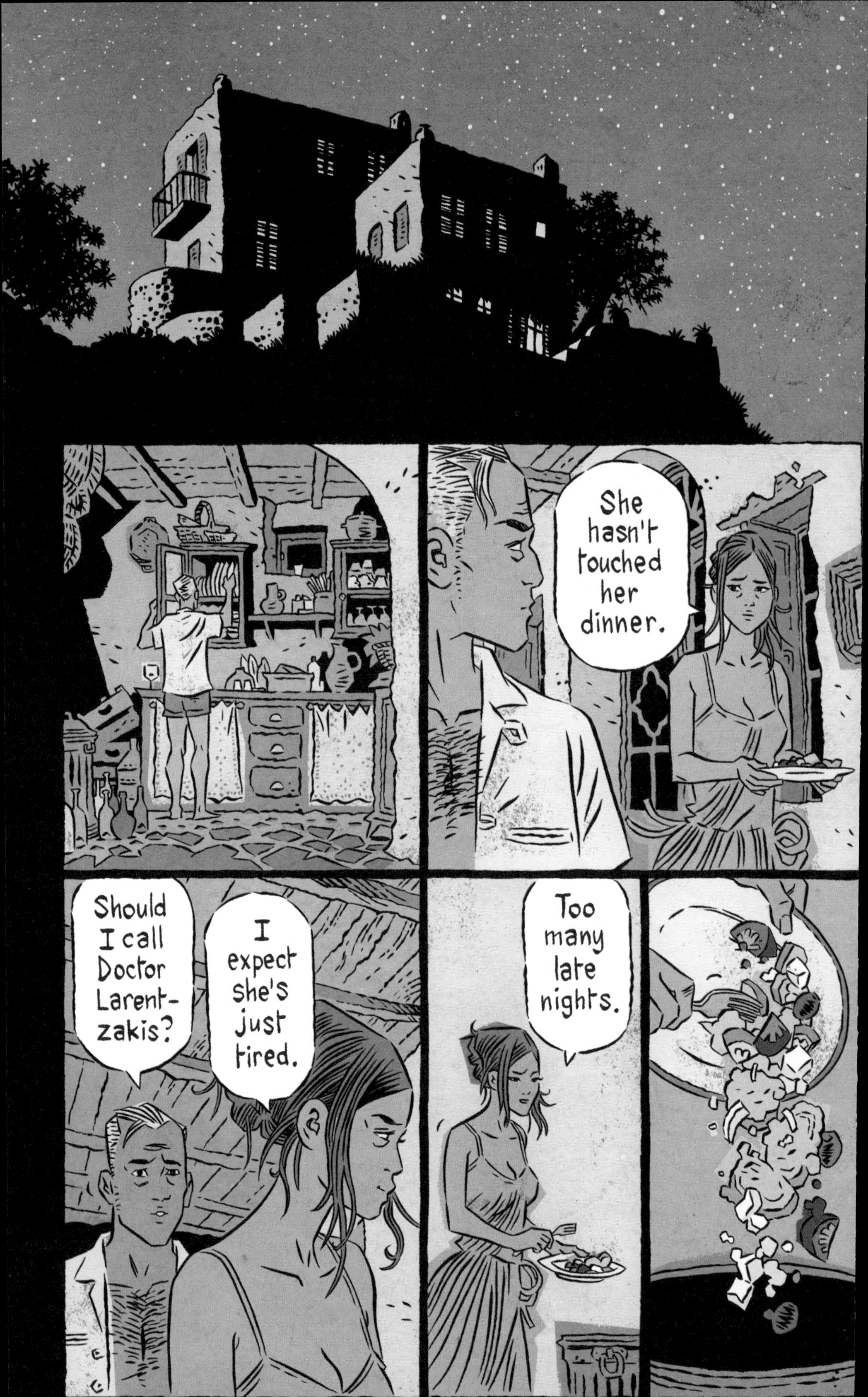
She hasn't touched her dinner.
Should I call Doctor Larent-zakis?
I expect she's just tired.
Too many late nights.

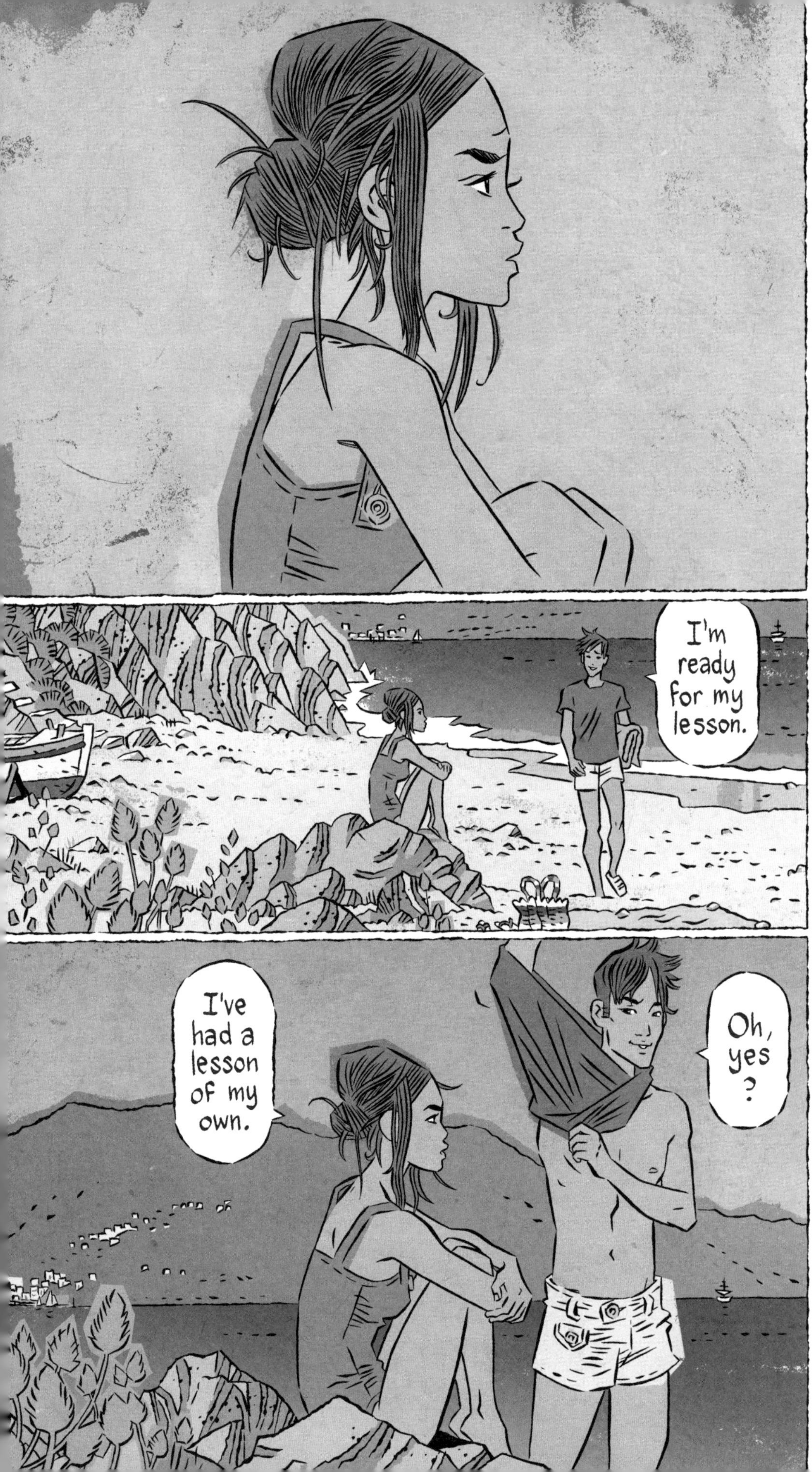
I'm ready for my lesson.
I've had a lesson of my own.
Oh, yes?

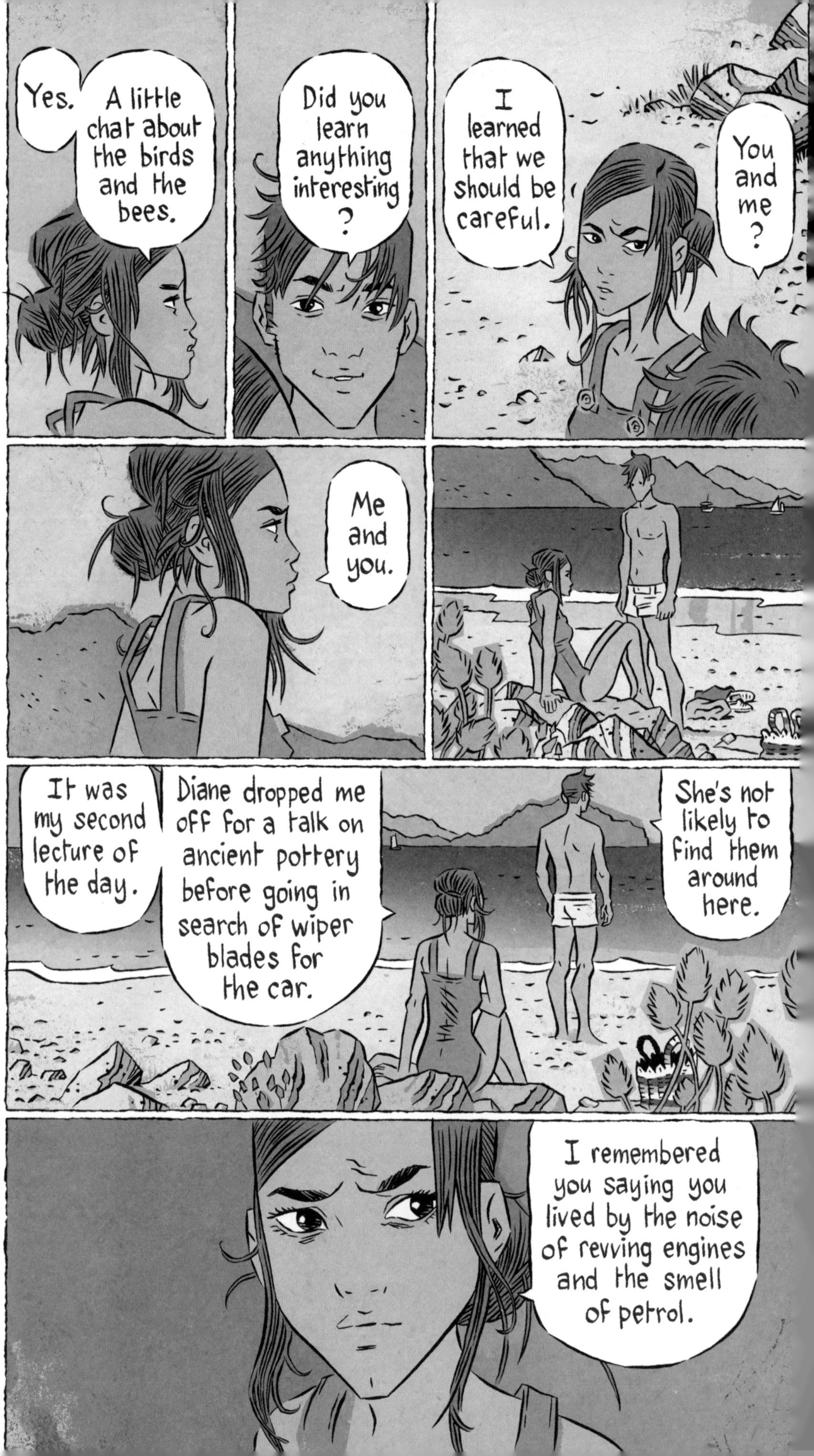
Yes.
A little chat about the birds and the bees.
Did you learn anything interesting ?
I learned that we should be careful.
You and me ?
Me and you.
It was my second lecture of the day.
Diane dropped me off for a talk on ancient pottery before going in search of wiper blades for the car.
She's not likely to find them around here.
I remembered you saying you lived by the noise of revving engines and the smell of petrol.

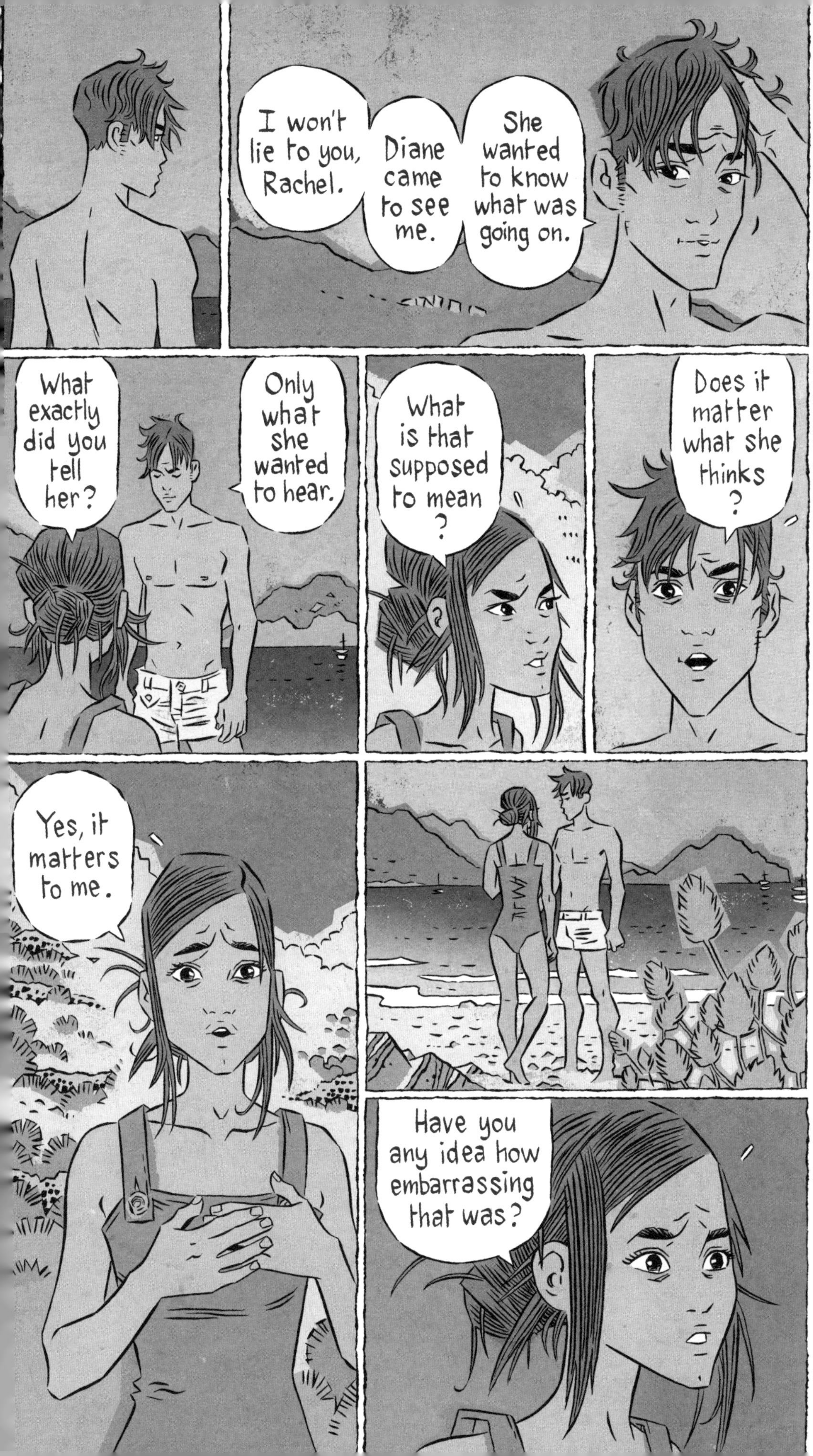
I won't lie to you, Rachel.
Diane came to see me.
She wanted to know what was going on.
What exactly did you tell her?
Only what she wanted to hear.
What is that supposed to mean?
Does it matter what she thinks?
Yes, it matters to me.
Have you any idea how embarrassing that was?

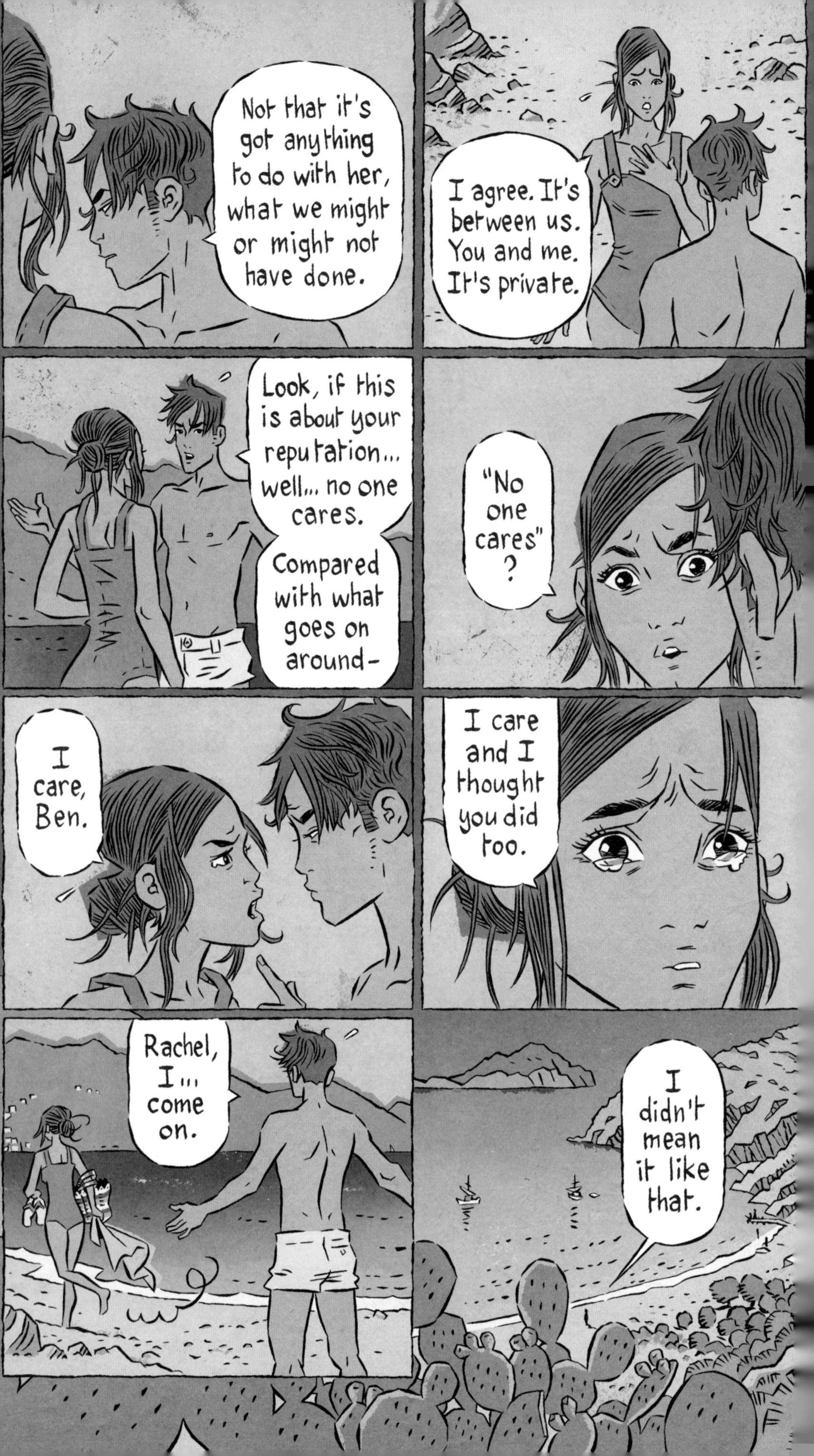
Not that it's got anything to do with her, what we might or might not have done.
I agree. It's between us. You and me. It's private.
Look, if this is about your reputation... well... no one cares.
Compared with what goes on around-
"No one cares"?
I care, Ben.
I care and I thought you did too.
Rachel, I... come on.
I didn't mean it like that.

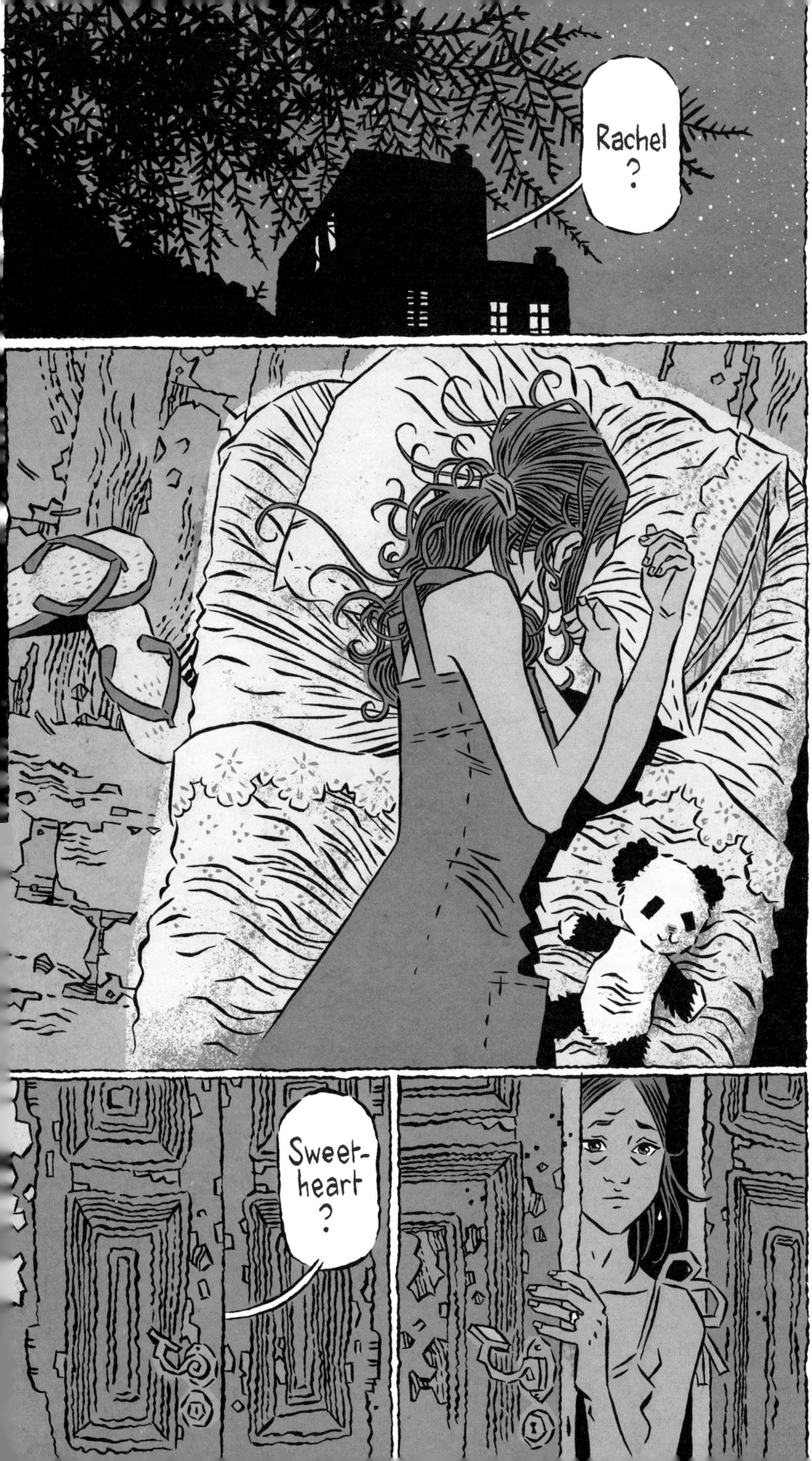
Rachel ?
Sweet-heart ?

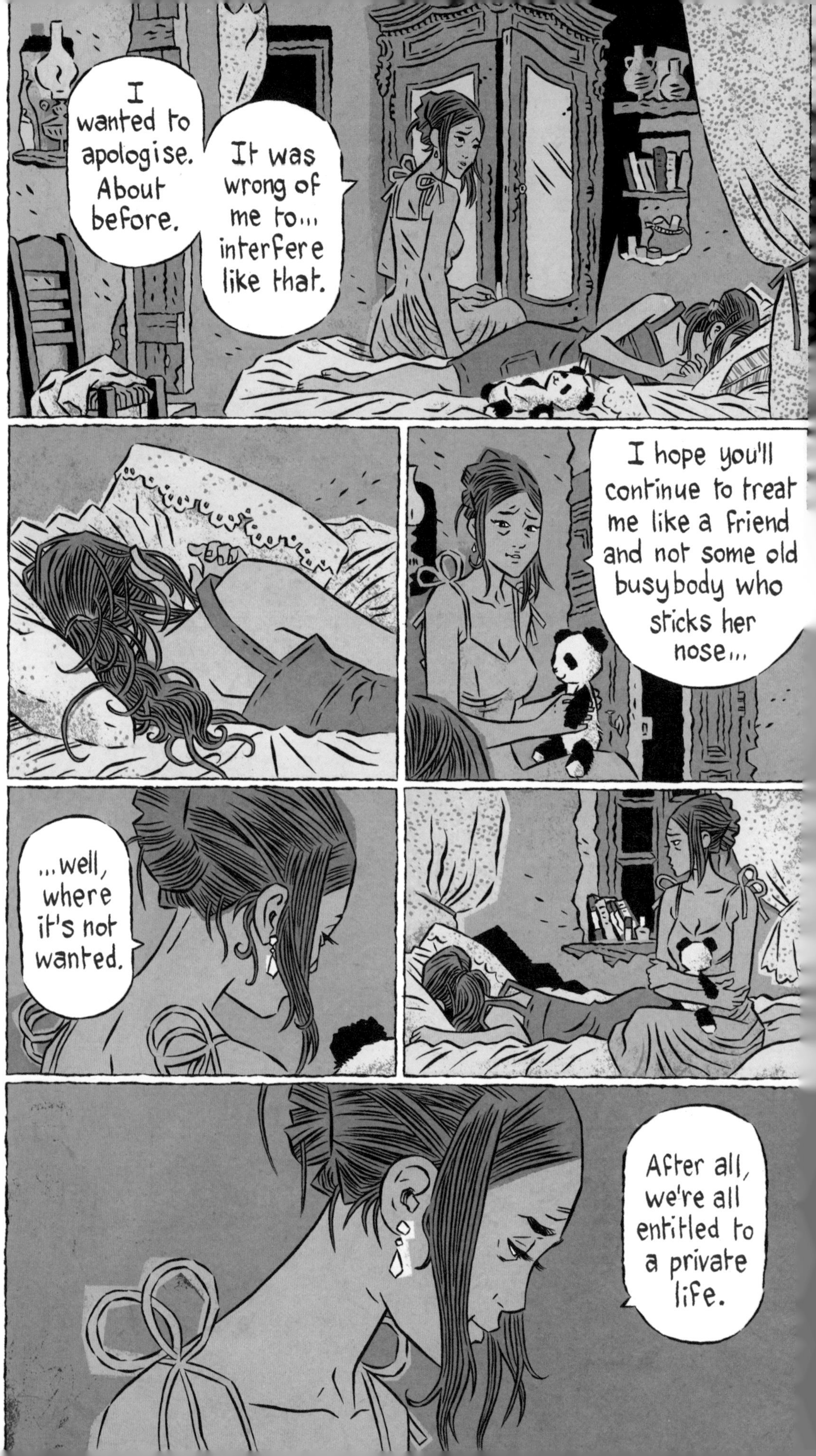
I wanted to apologise. About before.
It was wrong of me to... interfere like that.
I hope you'll continue to treat me like a friend and not some old busybody who sticks her nose...
...well, where it's not wanted.
After all, we're all entitled to a private life.

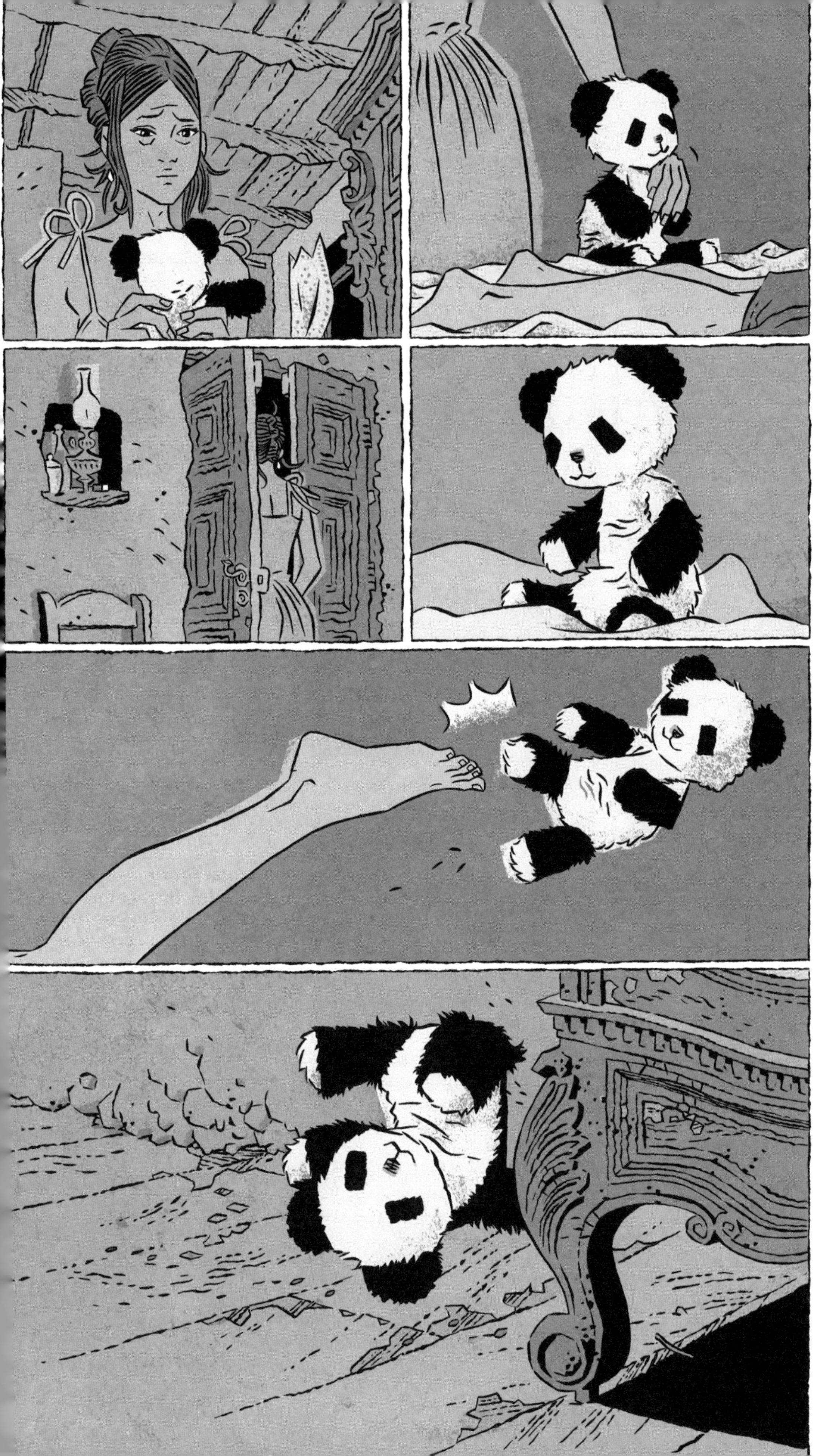

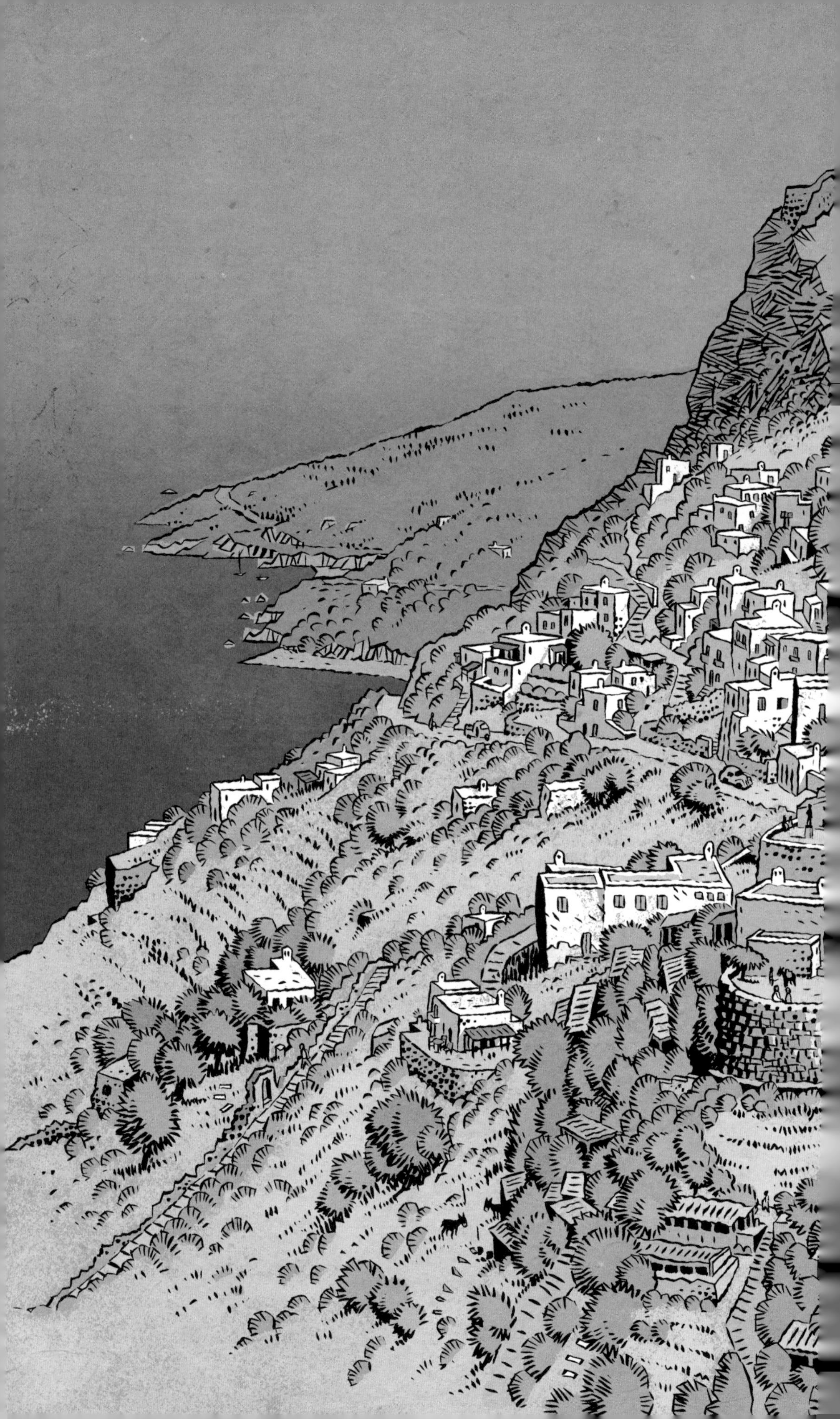

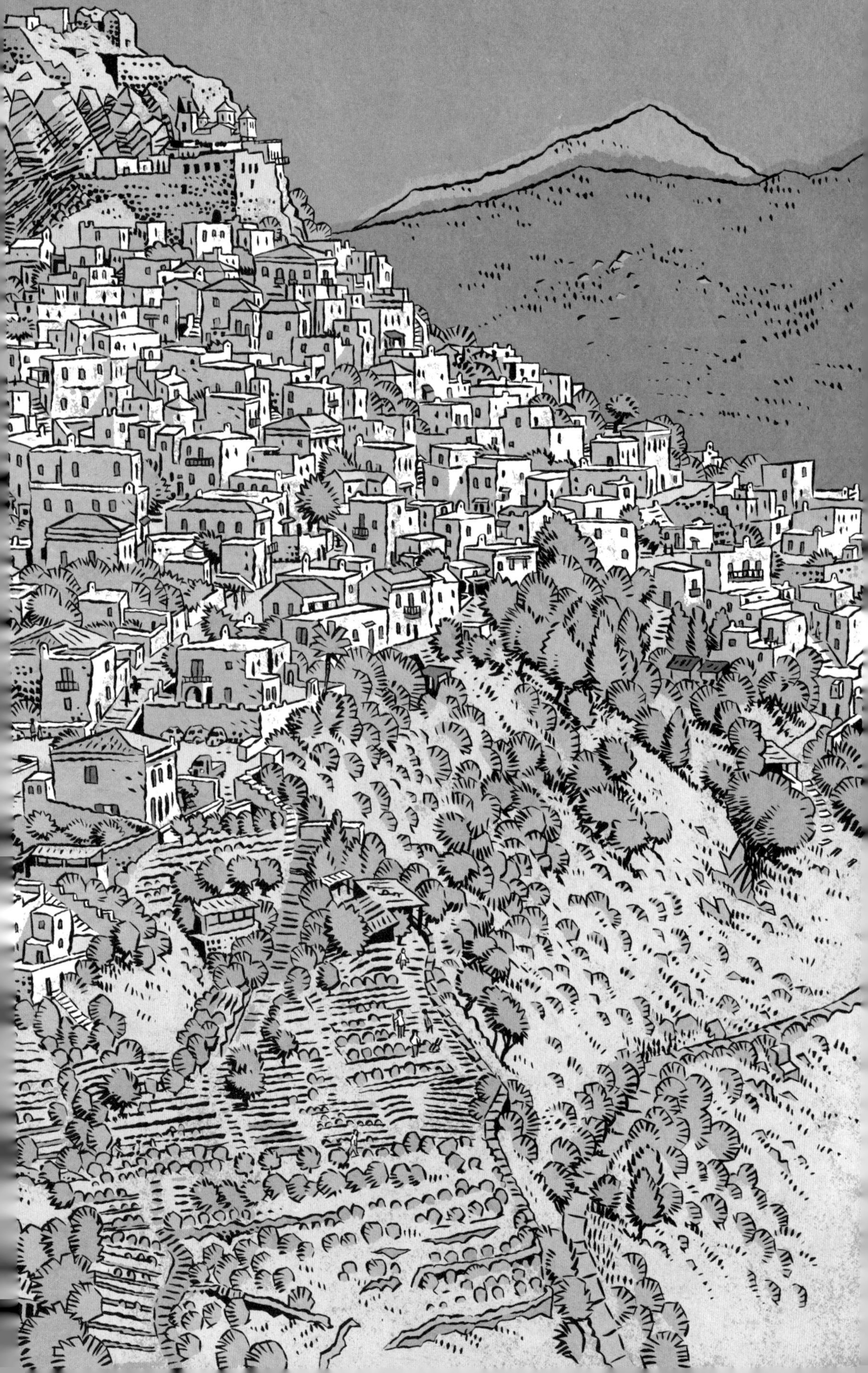

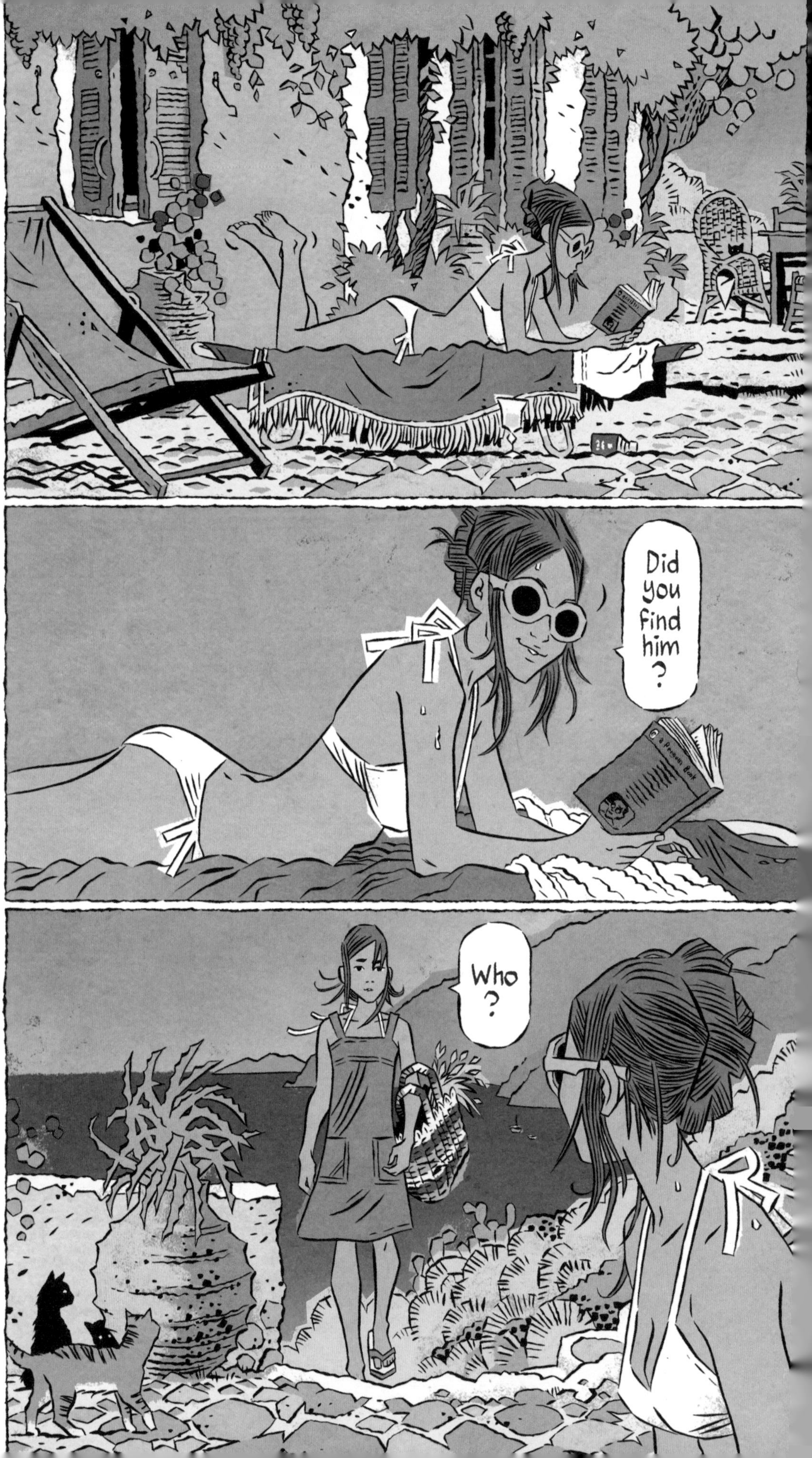
Did you find him?
Who?

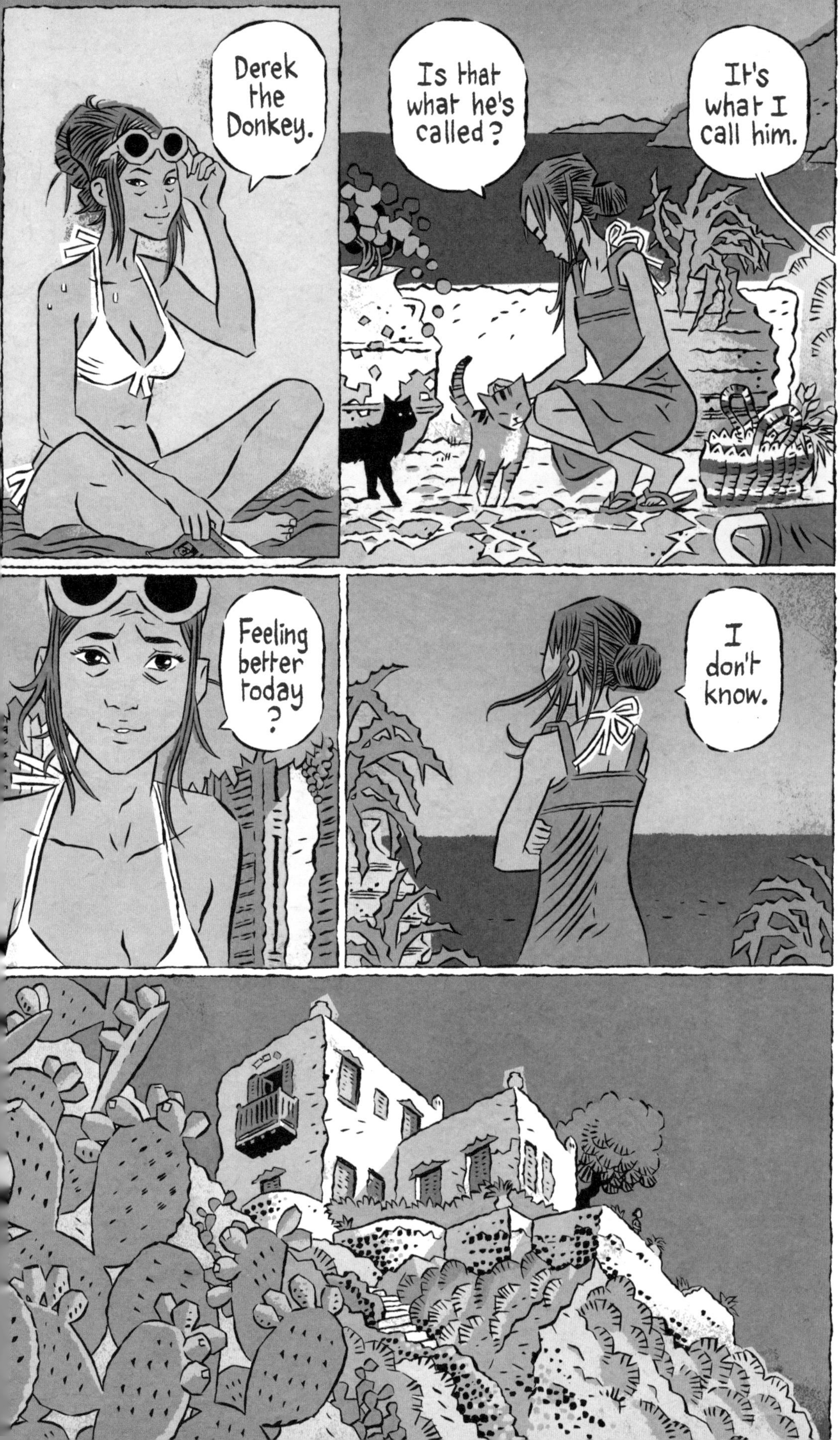
Derek the Donkey.
Is that what he's called?
It's what I call him.
Feeling better today?
I don't know.

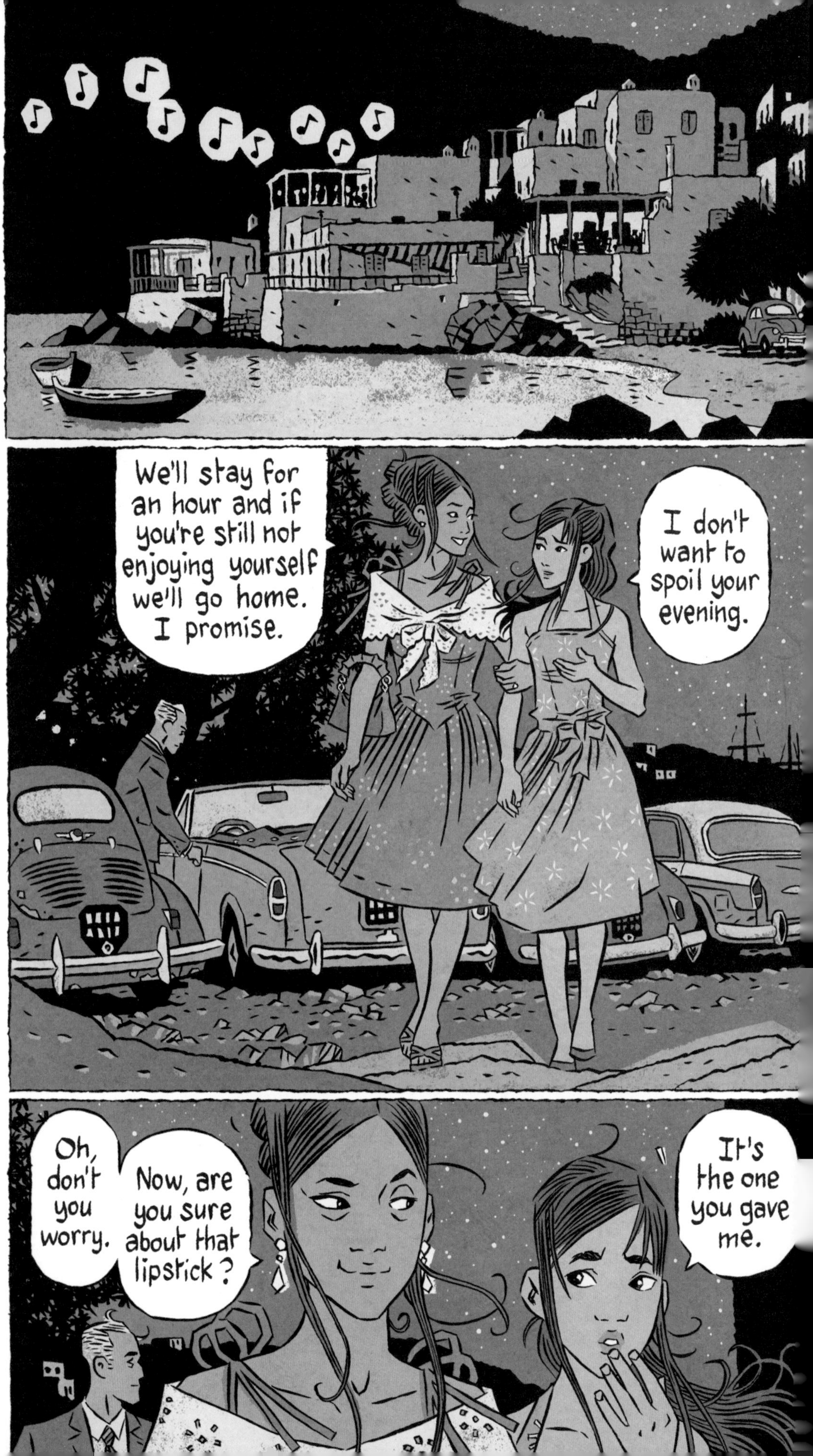
We'll stay for an hour and if you're still not enjoying yourself we'll go home. I promise.
I don't want to spoil your evening.
Oh, don't you worry.
Now, are you sure about that lipstick?
It's the one you gave me.

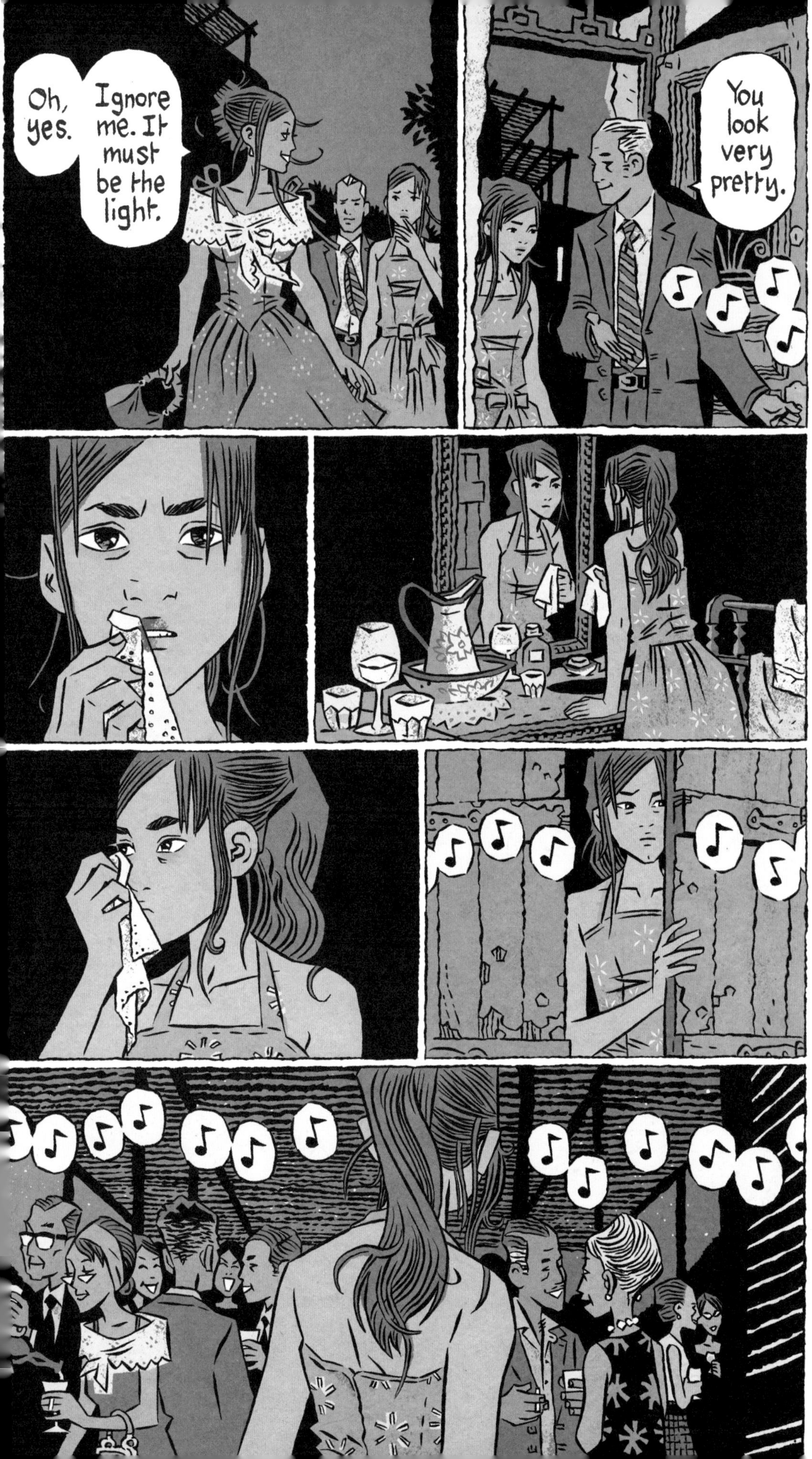
Oh, yes.
Ignore me. It must be the light.
You look very pretty.

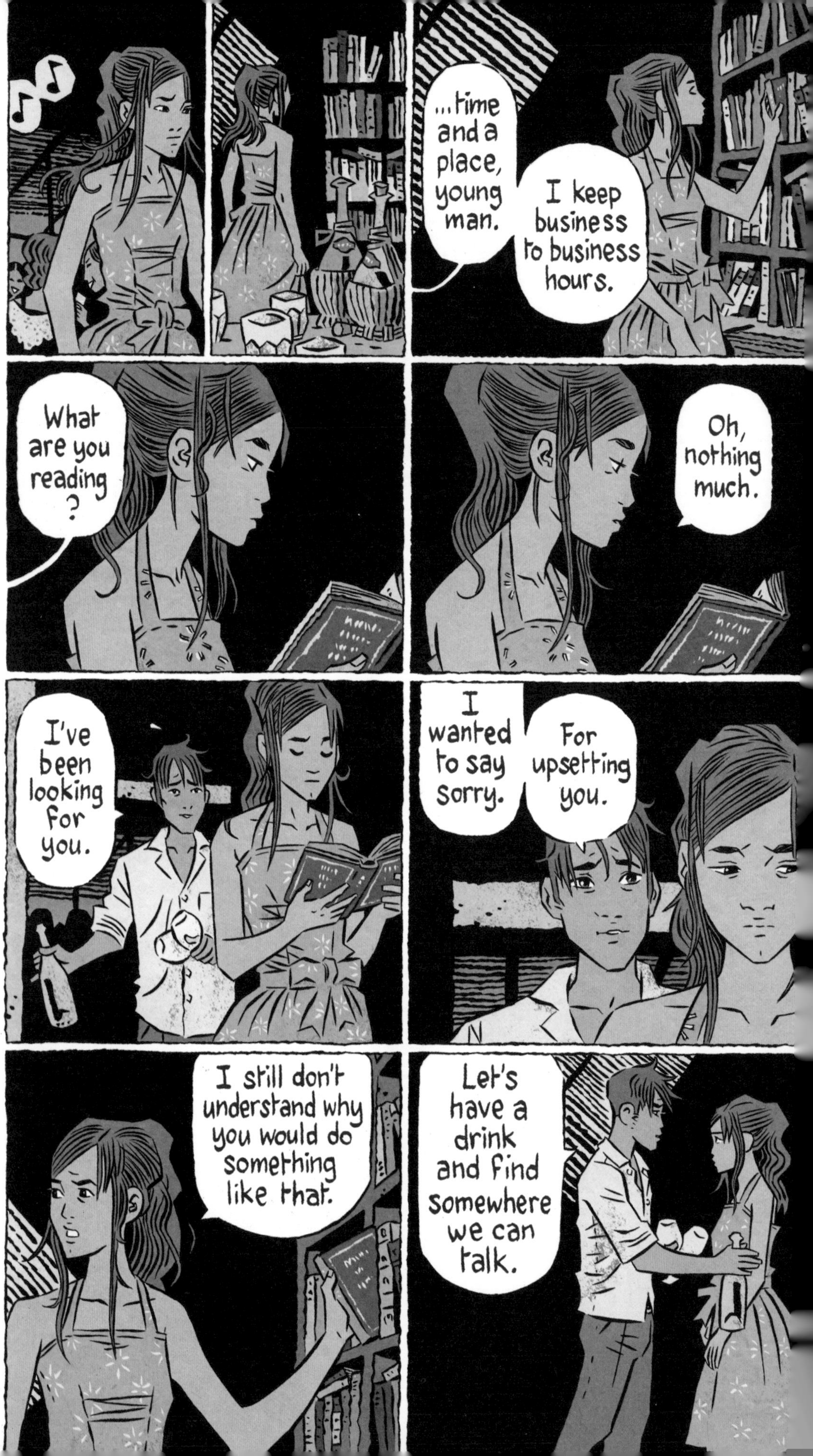
...time and a place, young man.
I keep business to business hours.
What are you reading?
Oh, nothing much.
I've been looking for you.
I wanted to say sorry.
For upsetting you.
I still don't understand why you would do something like that.
Let's have a drink and find somewhere we can talk.

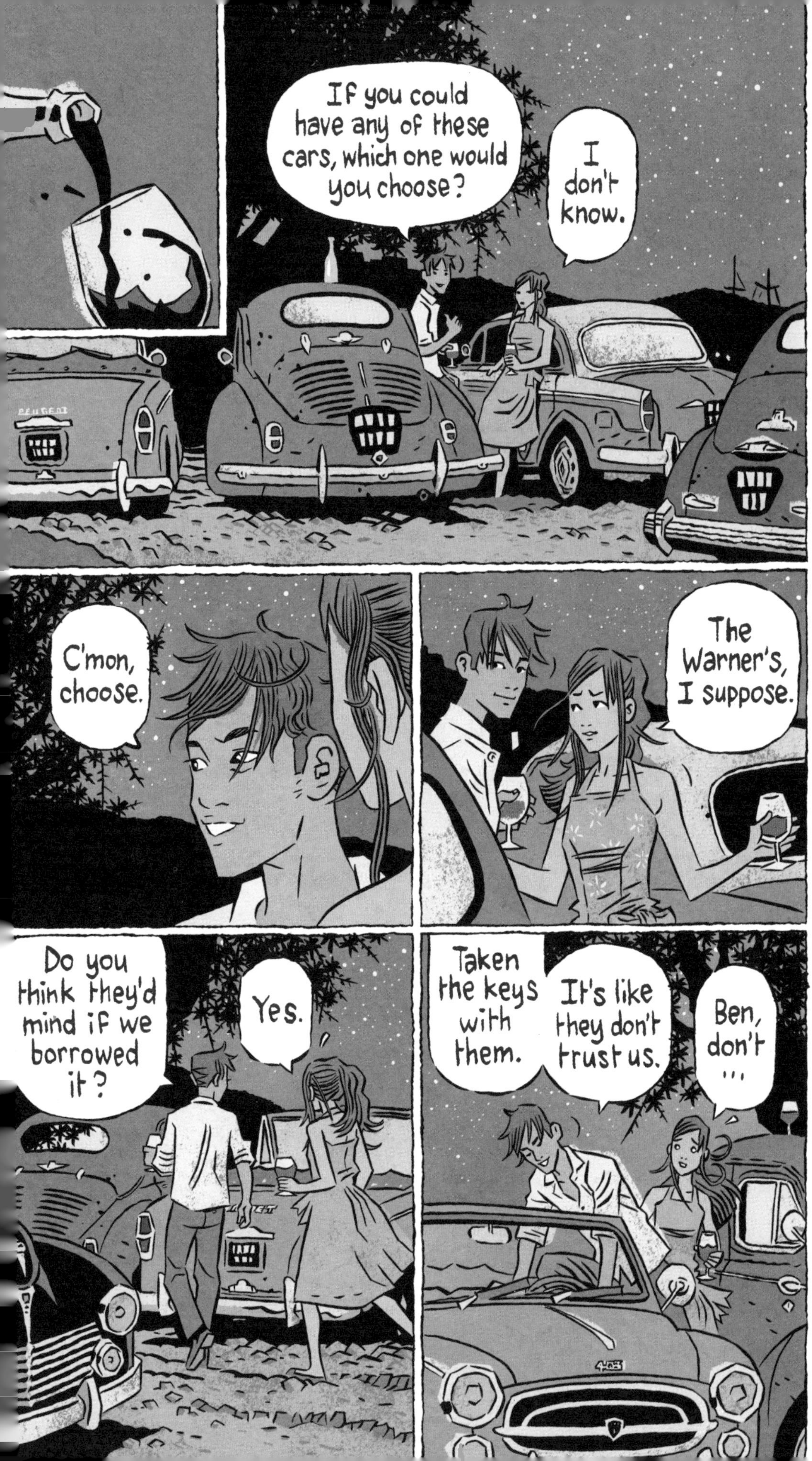
If you could have any of these cars, which one would you choose?
I don't know.
C'mon, choose.
The Warner's, I suppose.
Do you think they'd mind if we borrowed it?
Yes.
Taken the keys with them.
It's like they don't trust us.
Ben, don't ...

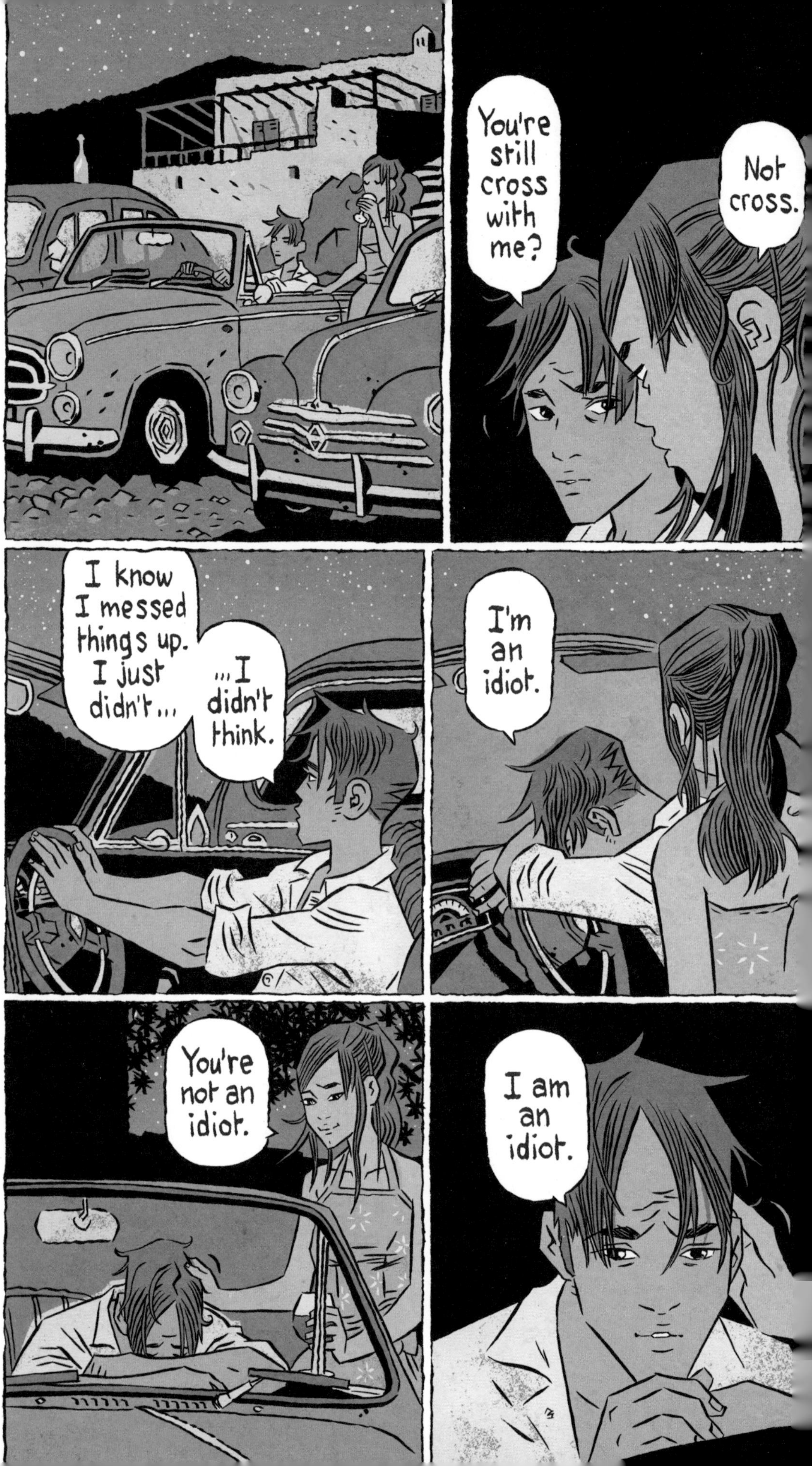
You're still cross with me?
Not cross.
I know I messed things up. I just didn't...
...I didn't think.
I'm an idiot.
You're not an idiot.
I am an idiot.

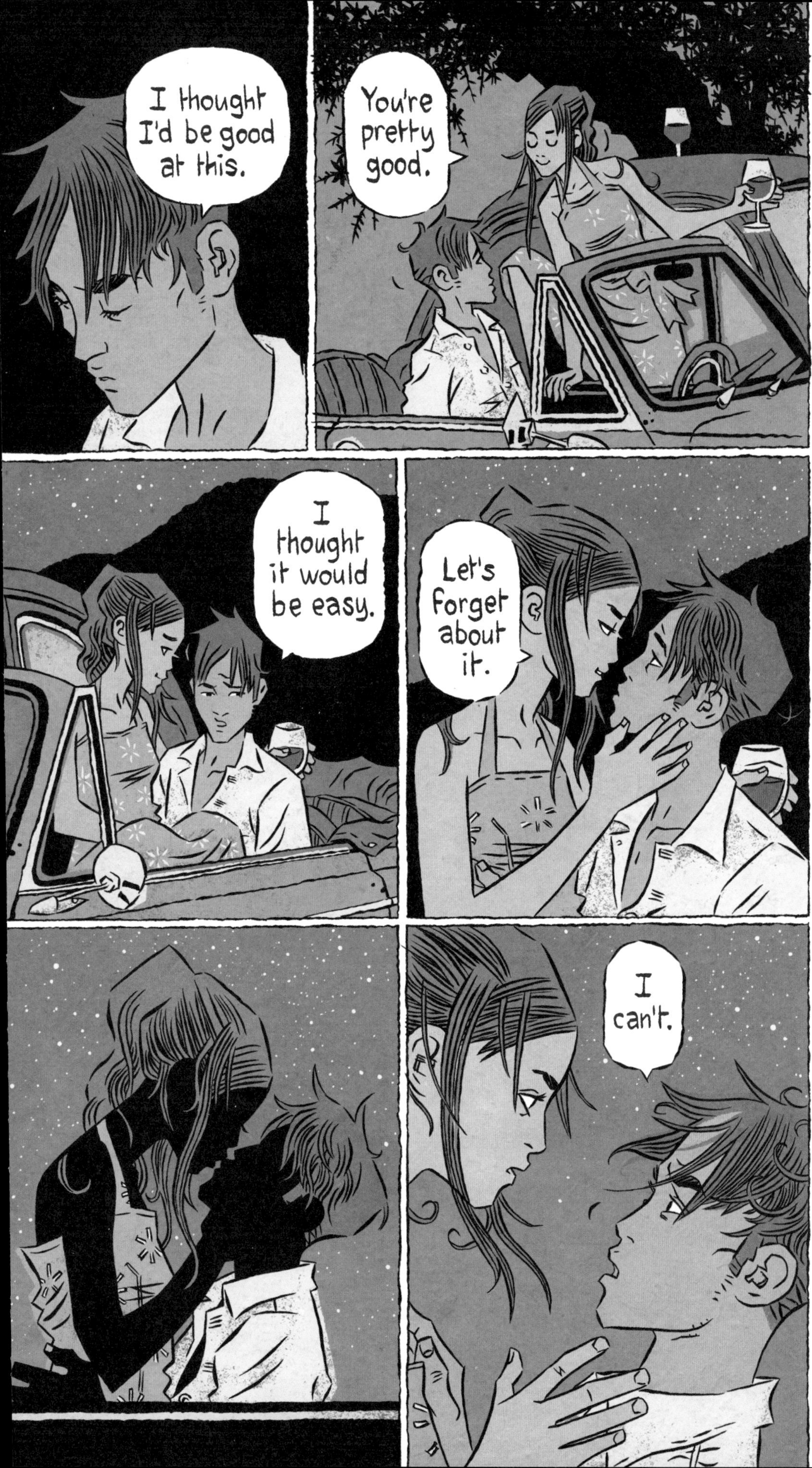
I thought I'd be good at this.
You're pretty good.
I thought it would be easy.
Let's forget about it.
I can't.

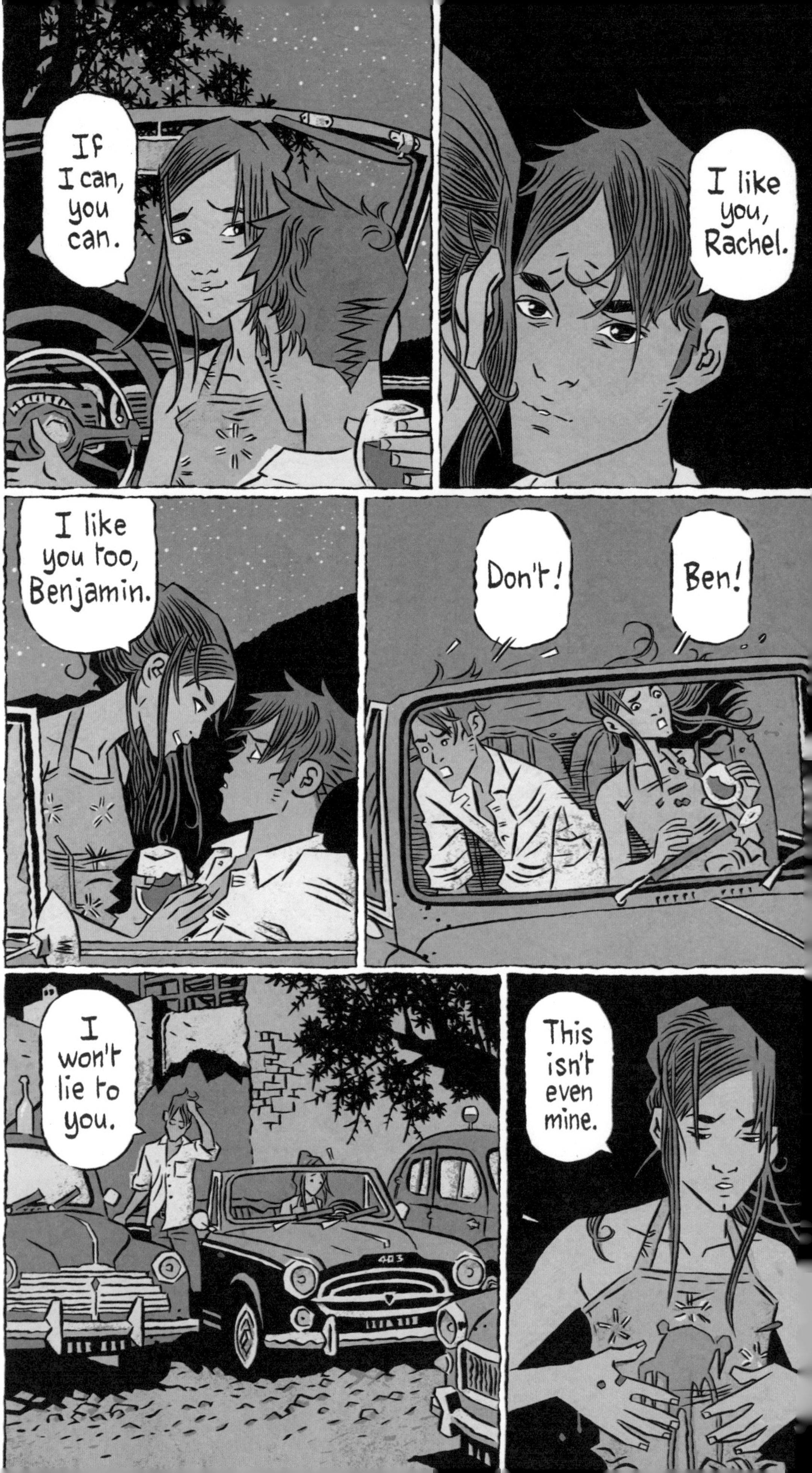
If I can, you can.
I like you, Rachel.
I like you too, Benjamin.
Don't!
Ben!
I won't lie to you.
This isn't even mine.

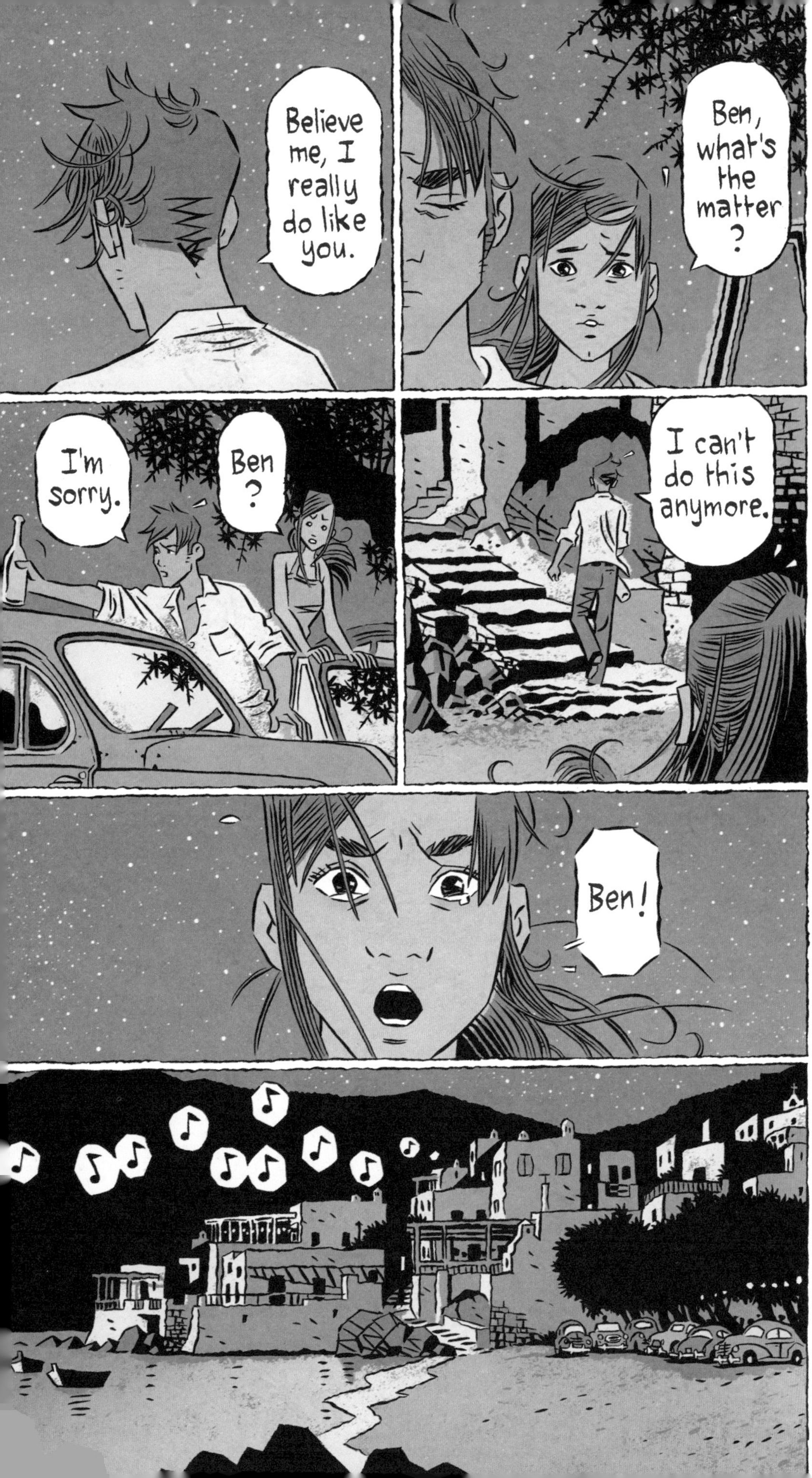
Believe me, I really do like you.
Ben, what's the matter?
I'm sorry.
Ben?
I can't do this anymore.
Ben!

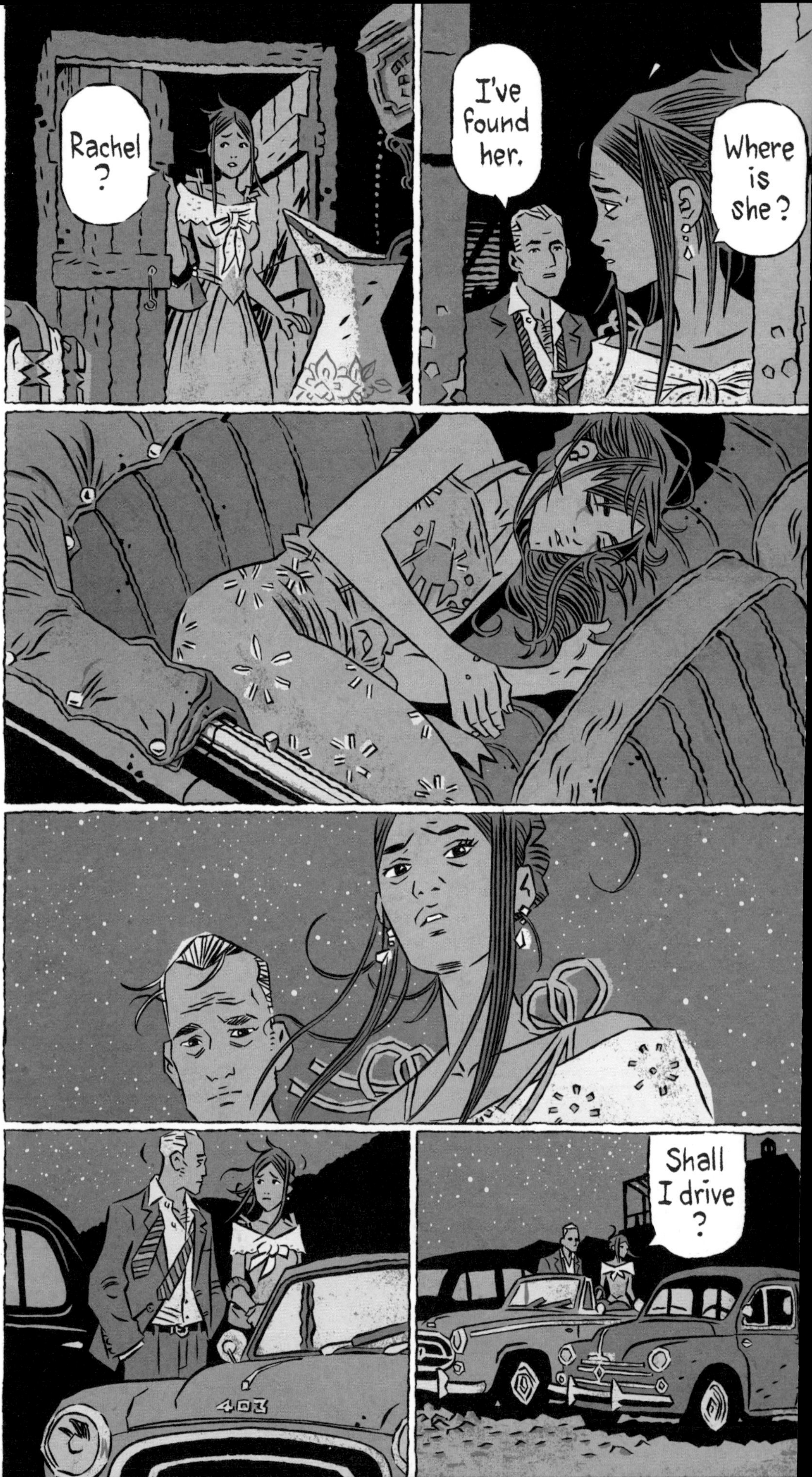
Rachel ?
I've found her.
Where is she ?
Shall I drive ?

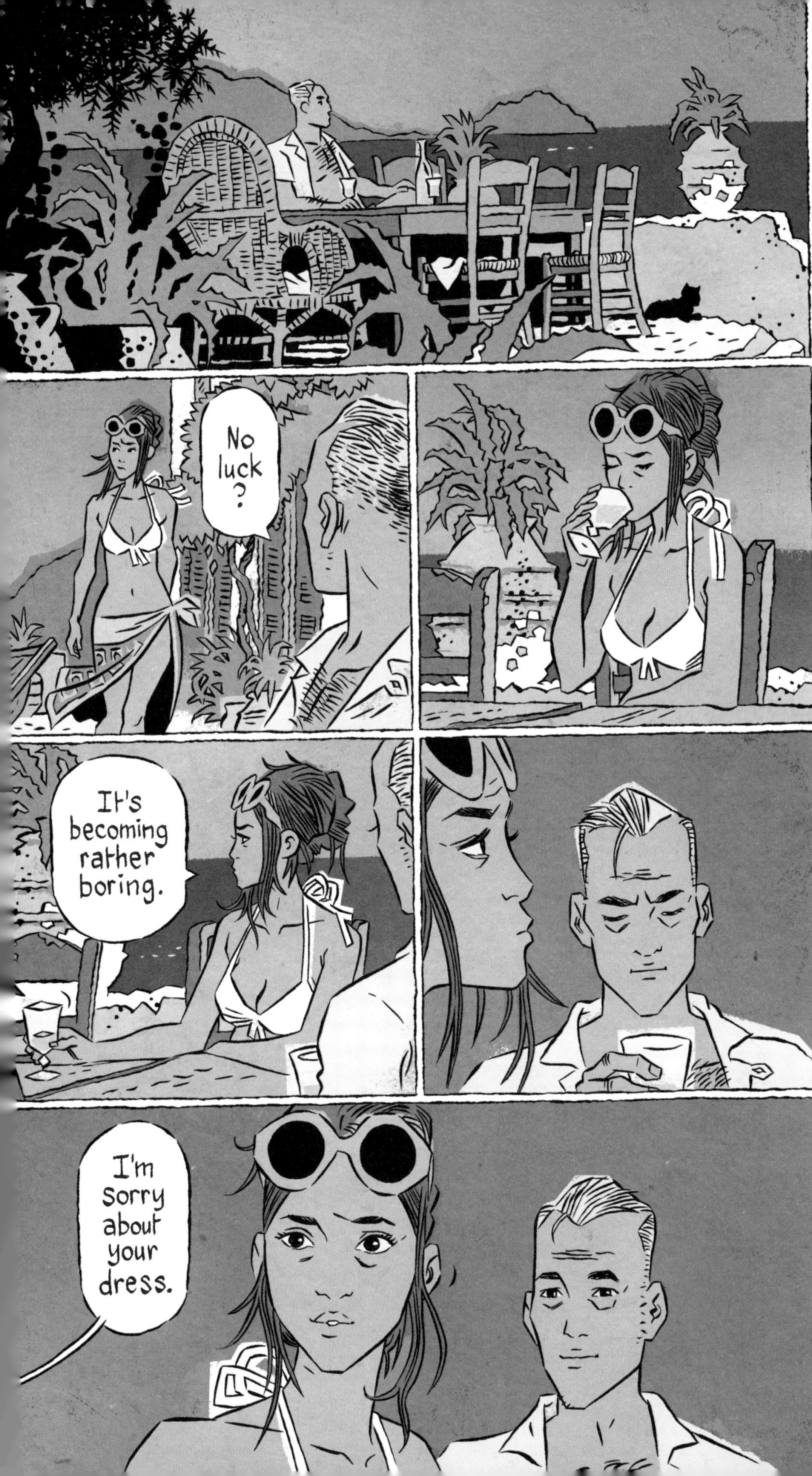
No luck?
It's becoming rather boring.
I'm sorry about your dress.

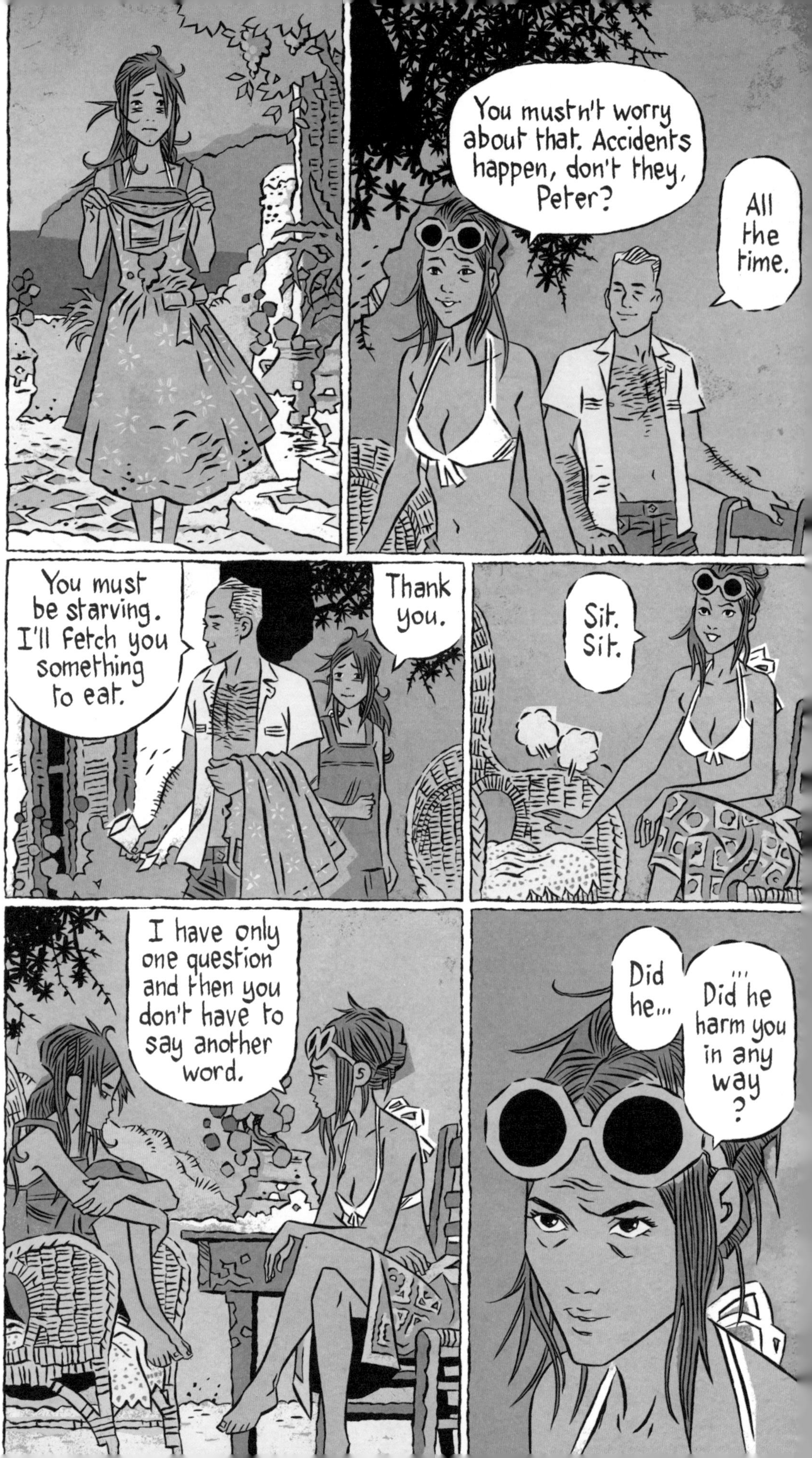
You mustn't worry about that. Accidents happen, don't they, Peter?
All the time.
You must be starving. I'll fetch you something to eat.
Thank you.
Sit. Sit.
I have only one question and then you don't have to say another word.
Did he...
... Did he harm you in any way?

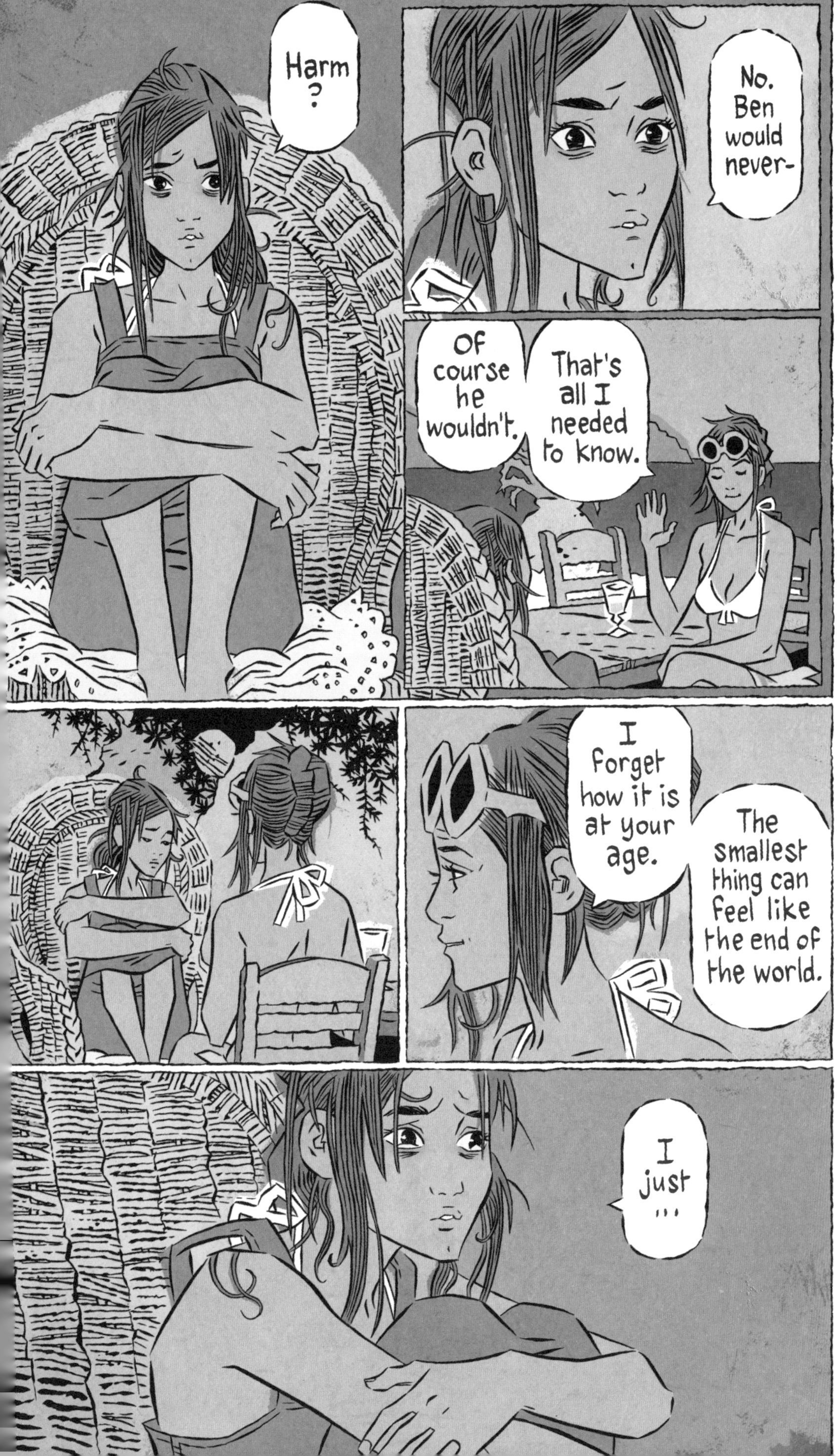
Harm?
No. Ben would never-
Of course he wouldn't.
That's all I needed to know.
I forget how it is at your age.
The smallest thing can feel like the end of the world.
I just ...

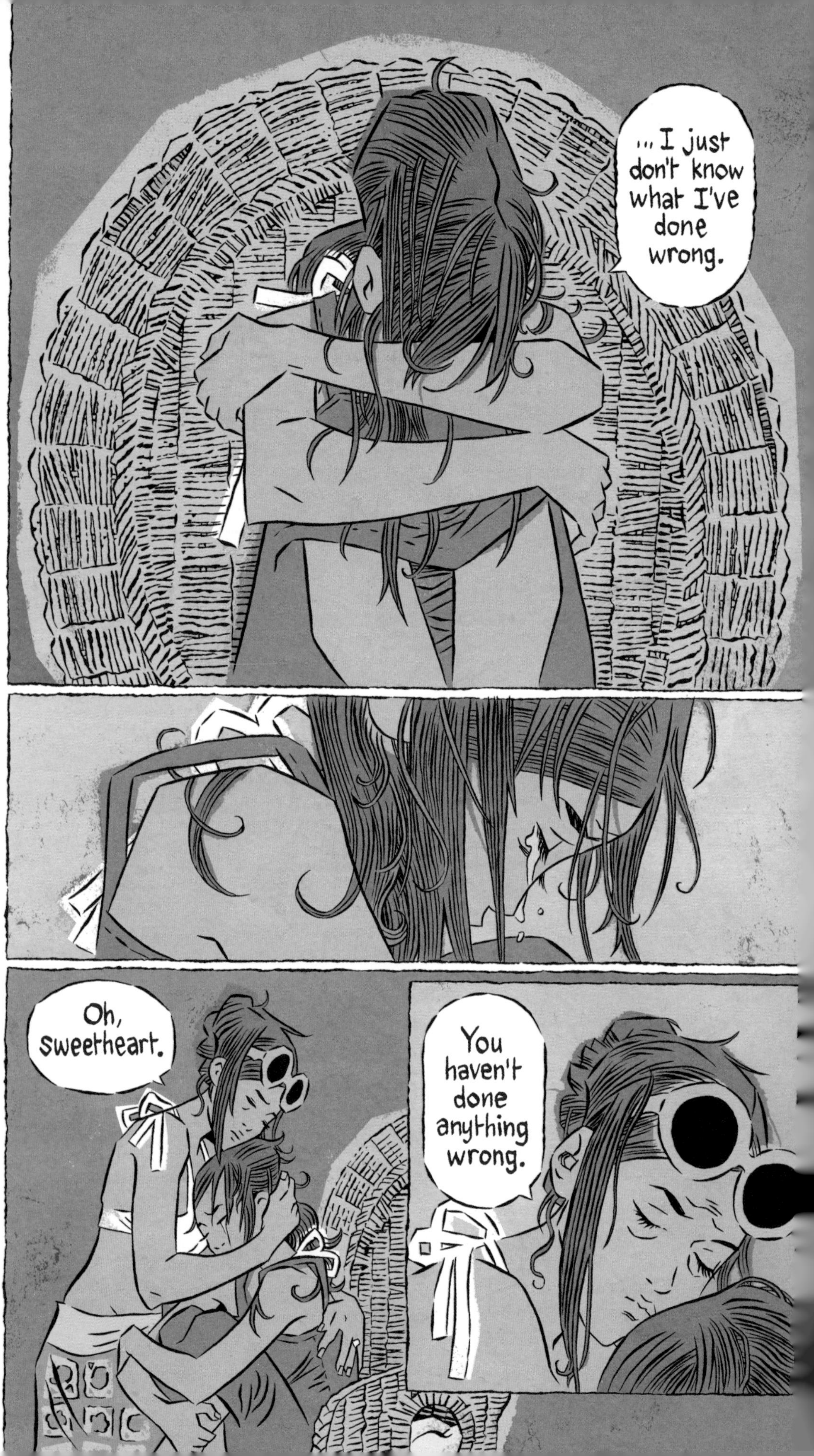
...I just don't know what I've done wrong.
Oh, sweetheart.
You haven't done anything wrong.

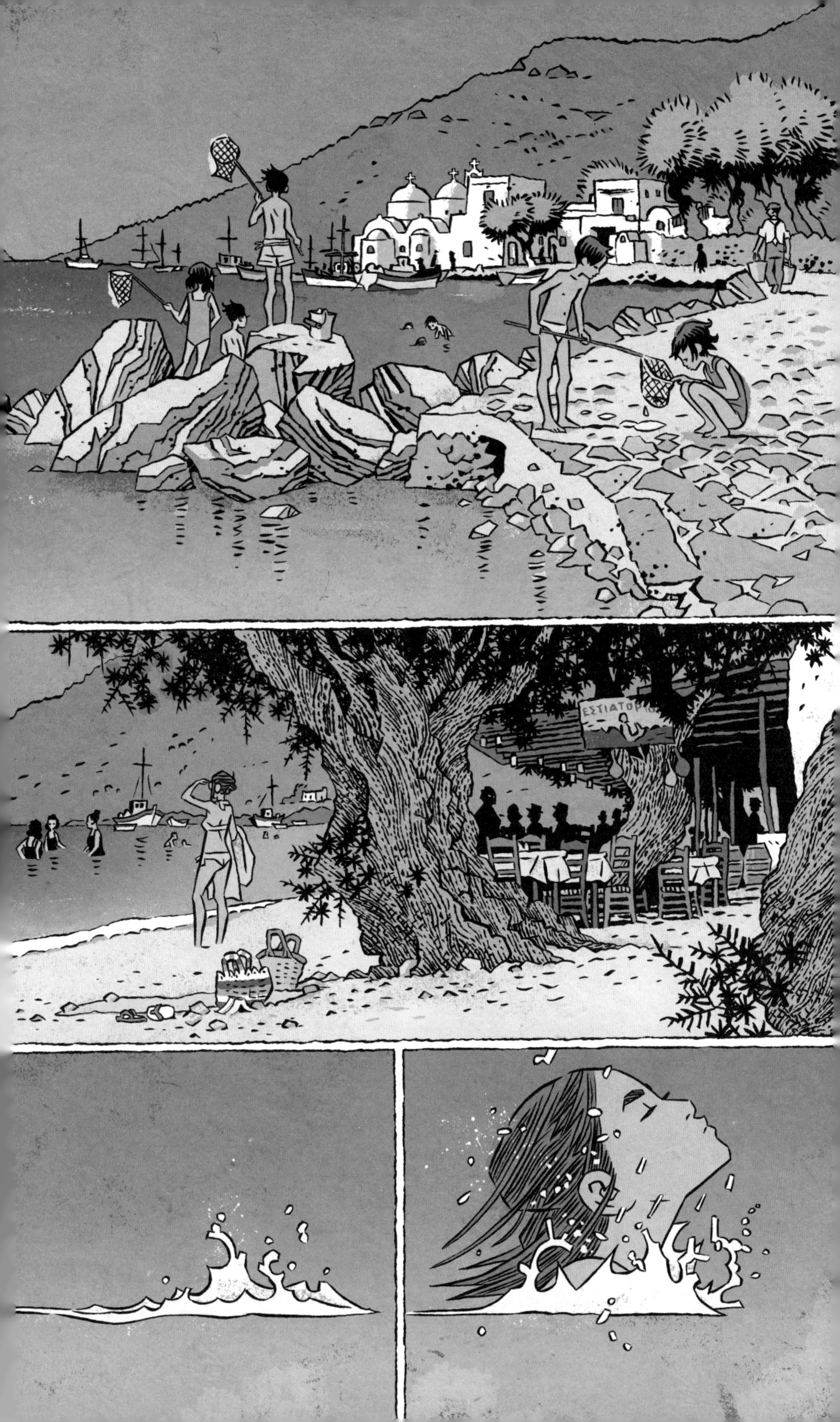
ΕΣΤΙΑΤΟΡ

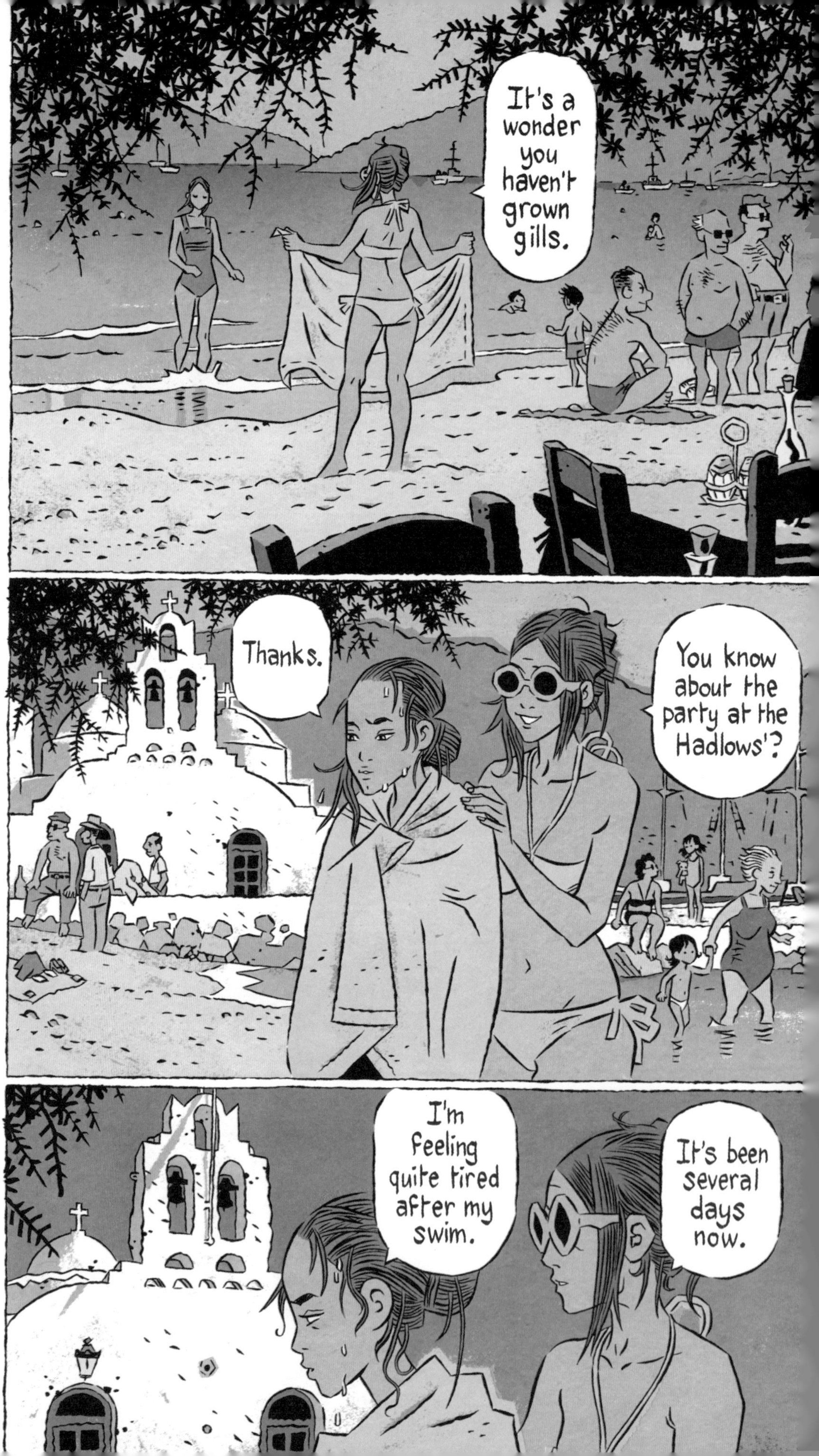
It's a wonder you haven't grown gills.
Thanks.
You know about the party at the Hadlows'?
I'm feeling quite tired after my swim.
It's been several days now.

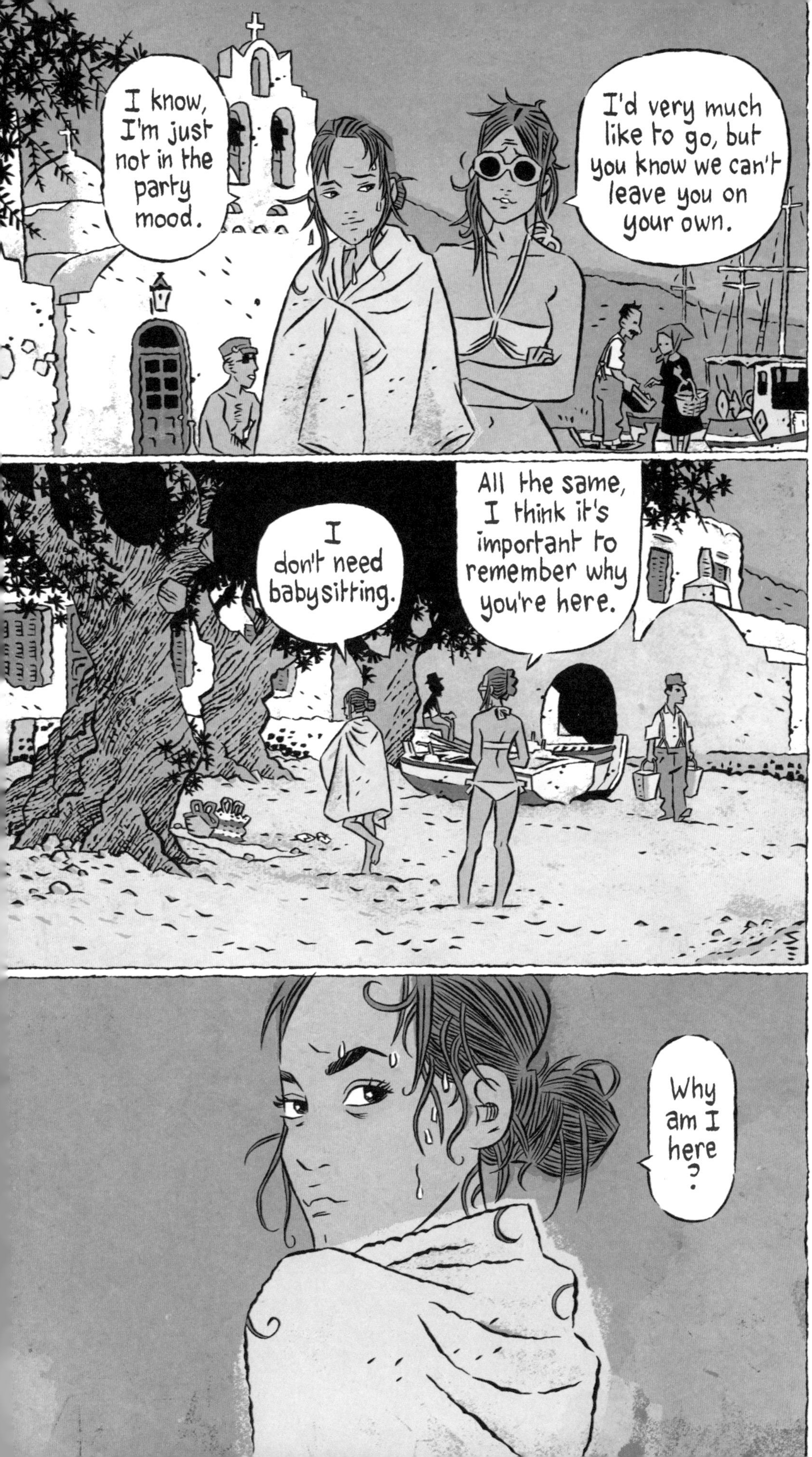
I know, I'm just not in the party mood.
I'd very much like to go, but you know we can't leave you on your own.
I don't need babysitting.
All the same, I think it's important to remember why you're here.
Why am I here?

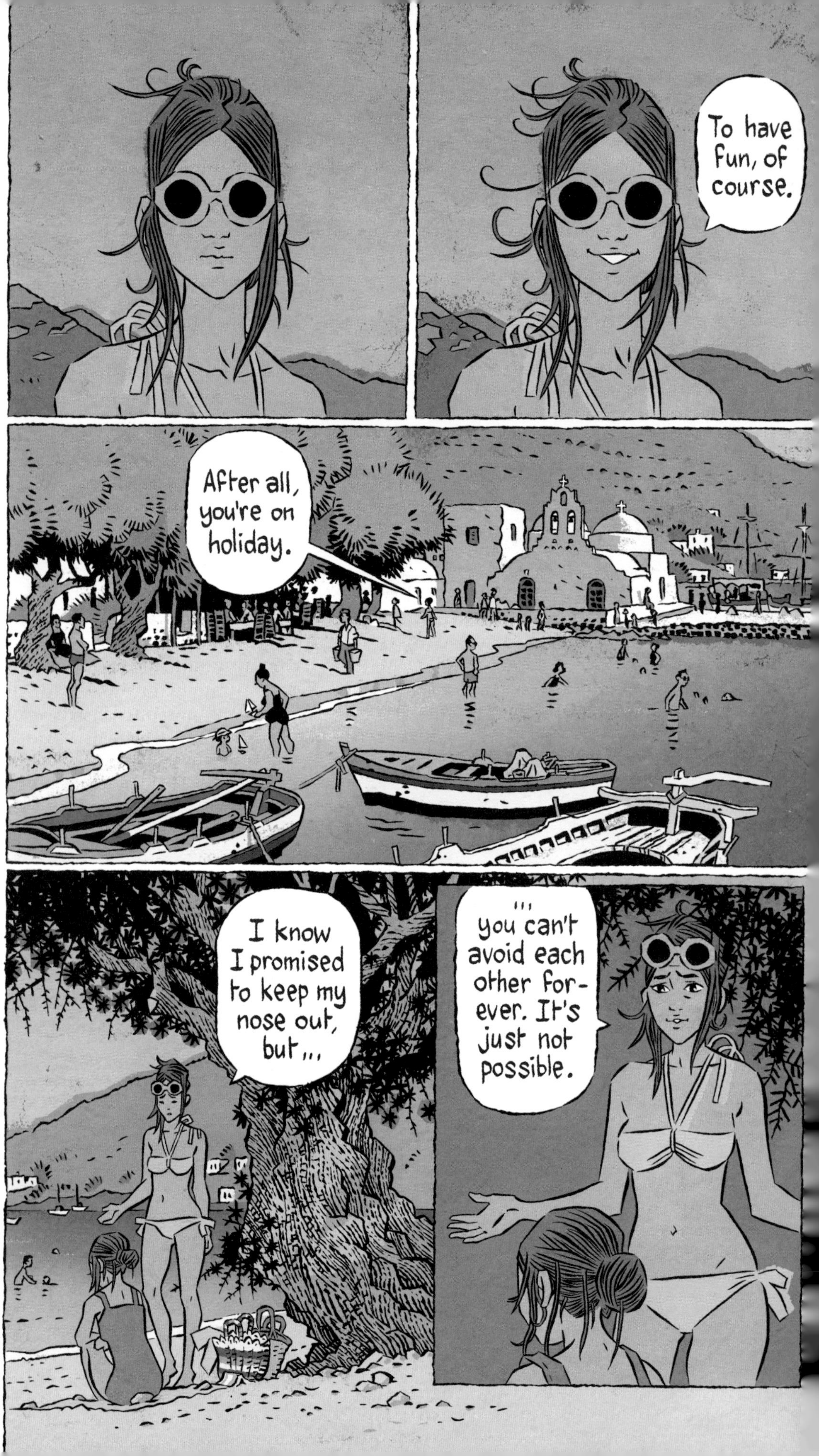
To have fun, of course.
After all, you're on holiday.
I know I promised to keep my nose out, but...
... you can't avoid each other for-ever. It's just not possible.

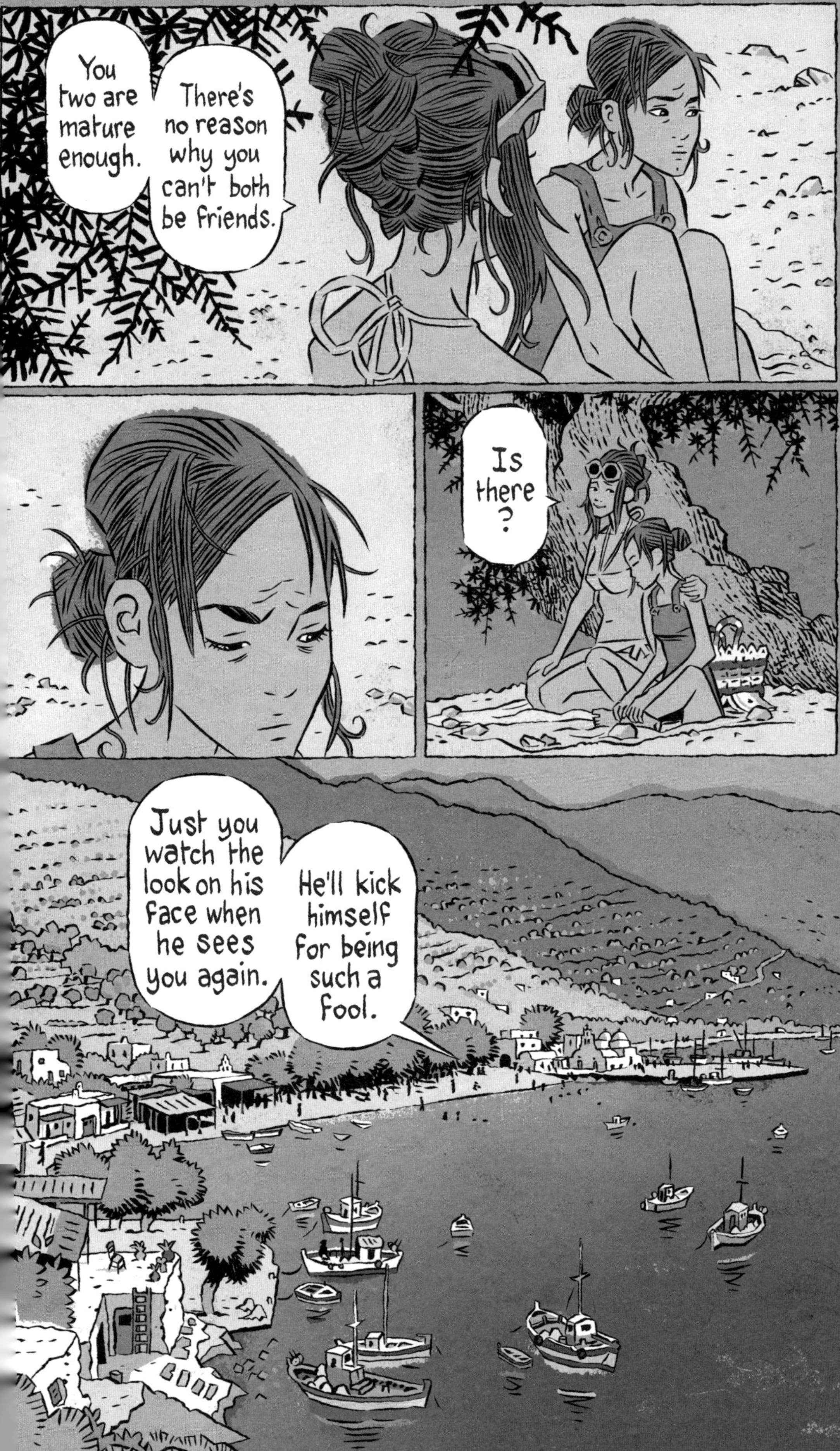
You two are mature enough.
There's no reason why you can't both be friends.
Is there?
Just you watch the look on his face when he sees you again.
He'll kick himself for being such a fool.

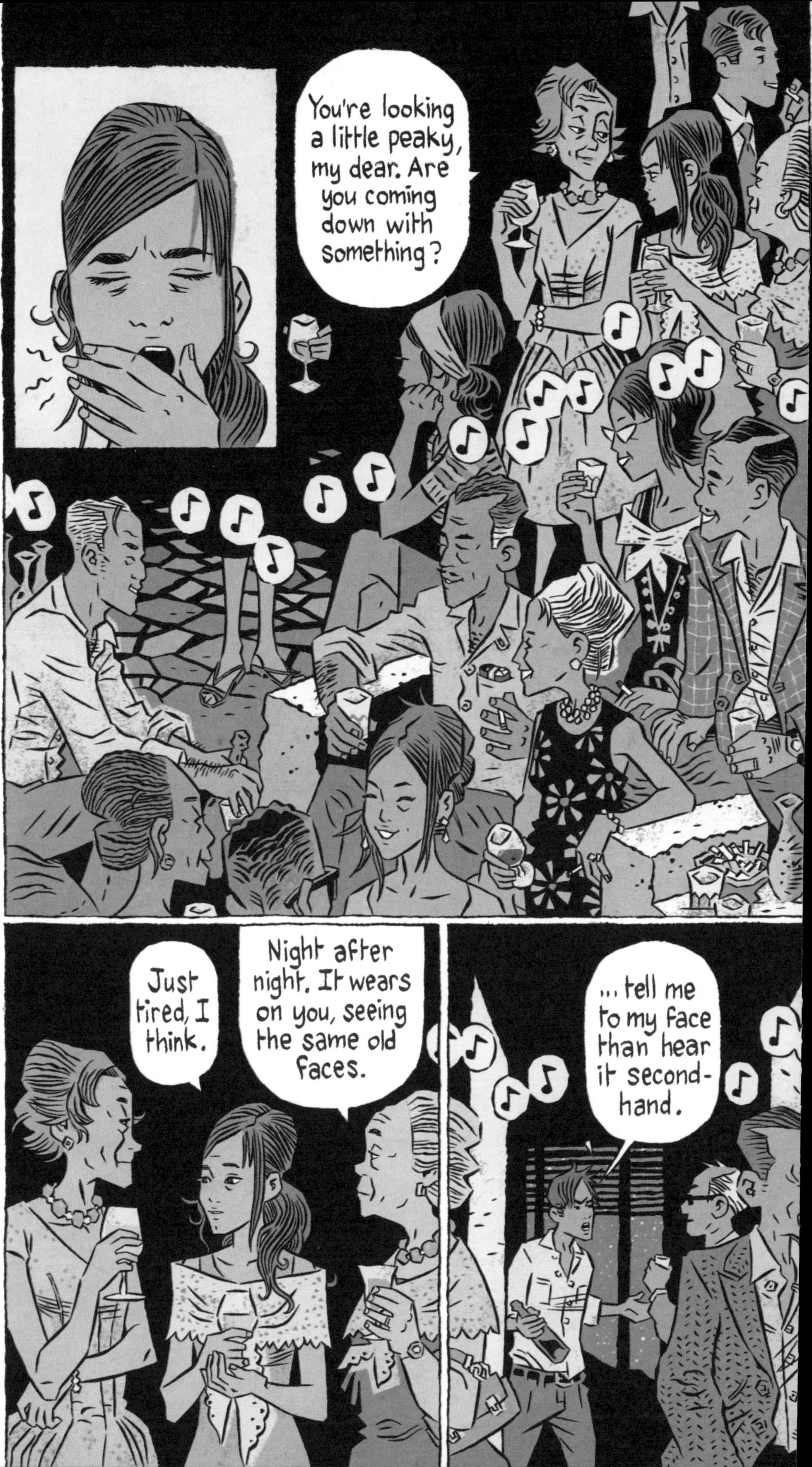
You're looking a little peaky, my dear. Are you coming down with something?
Just tired, I think.
Night after night. It wears on you, seeing the same old faces.
... tell me to my face than hear it second-hand.

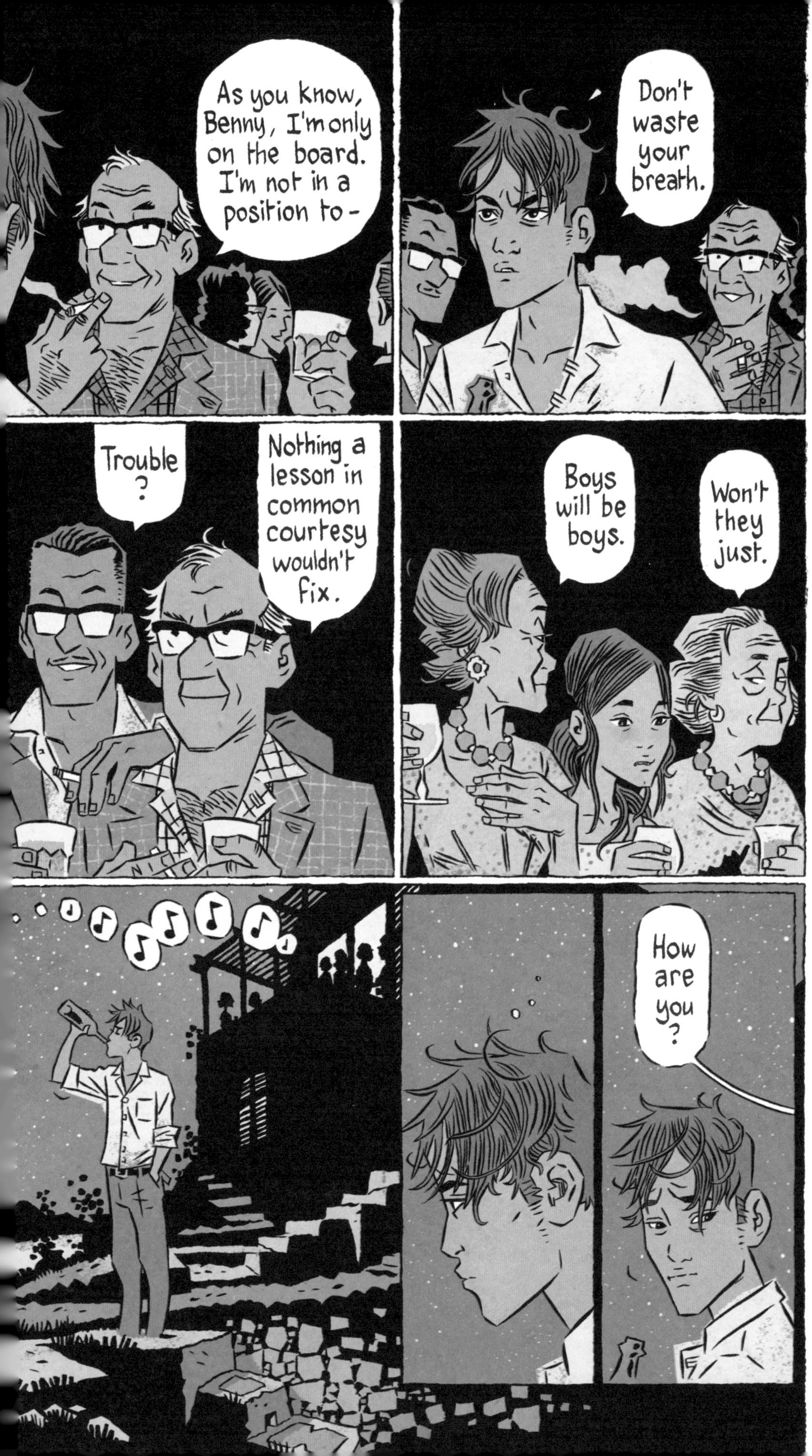
As you know, Benny, I'm only on the board. I'm not in a position to -
Don't waste your breath.
Trouble?
Nothing a lesson in common courtesy wouldn't fix.
Boys will be boys.
Won't they just.
How are you?

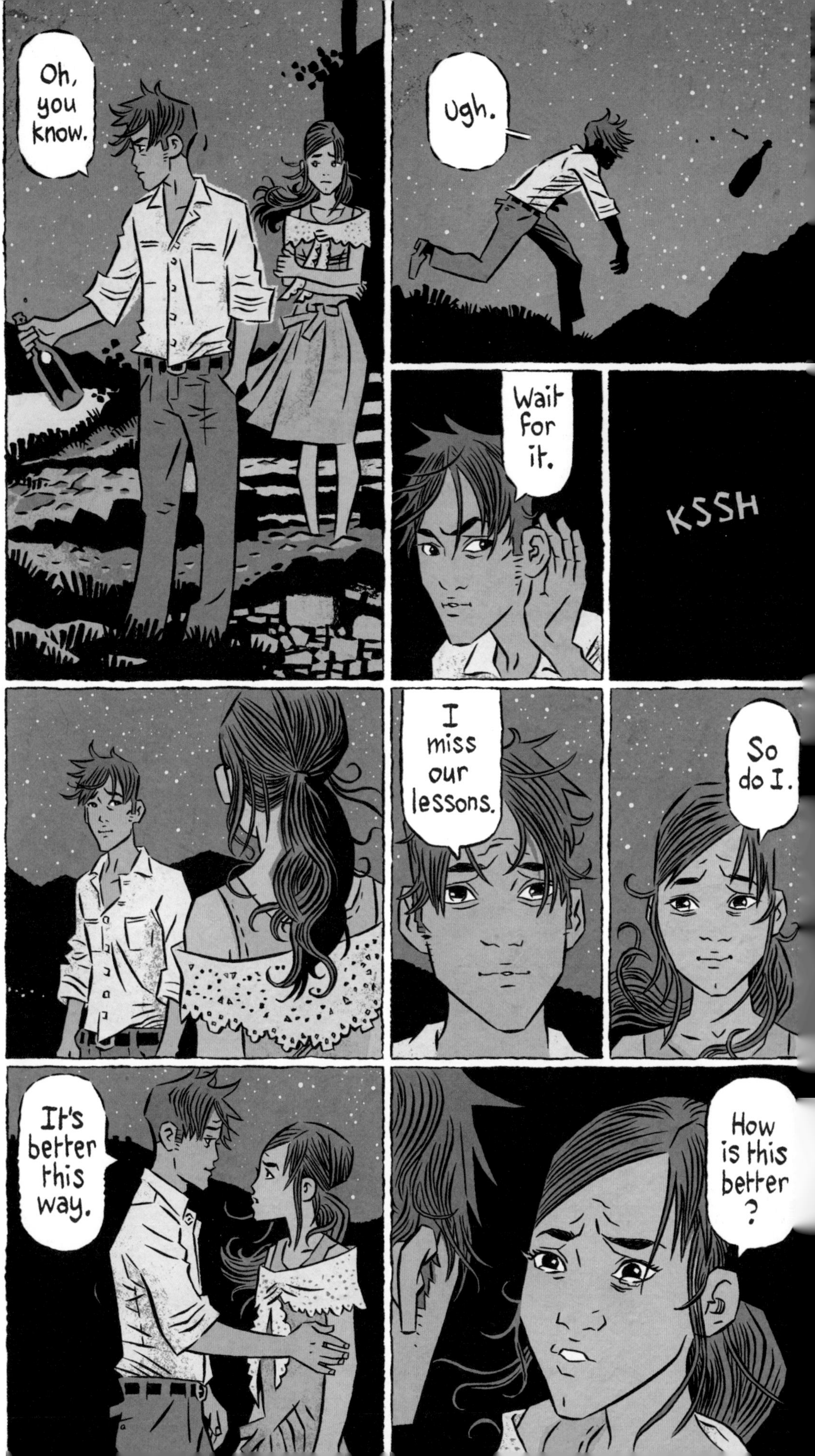
Oh, you know.
Ugh.
Wait for it.
KSSH
I miss our lessons.
So do I.
It's better this way.
How is this better?

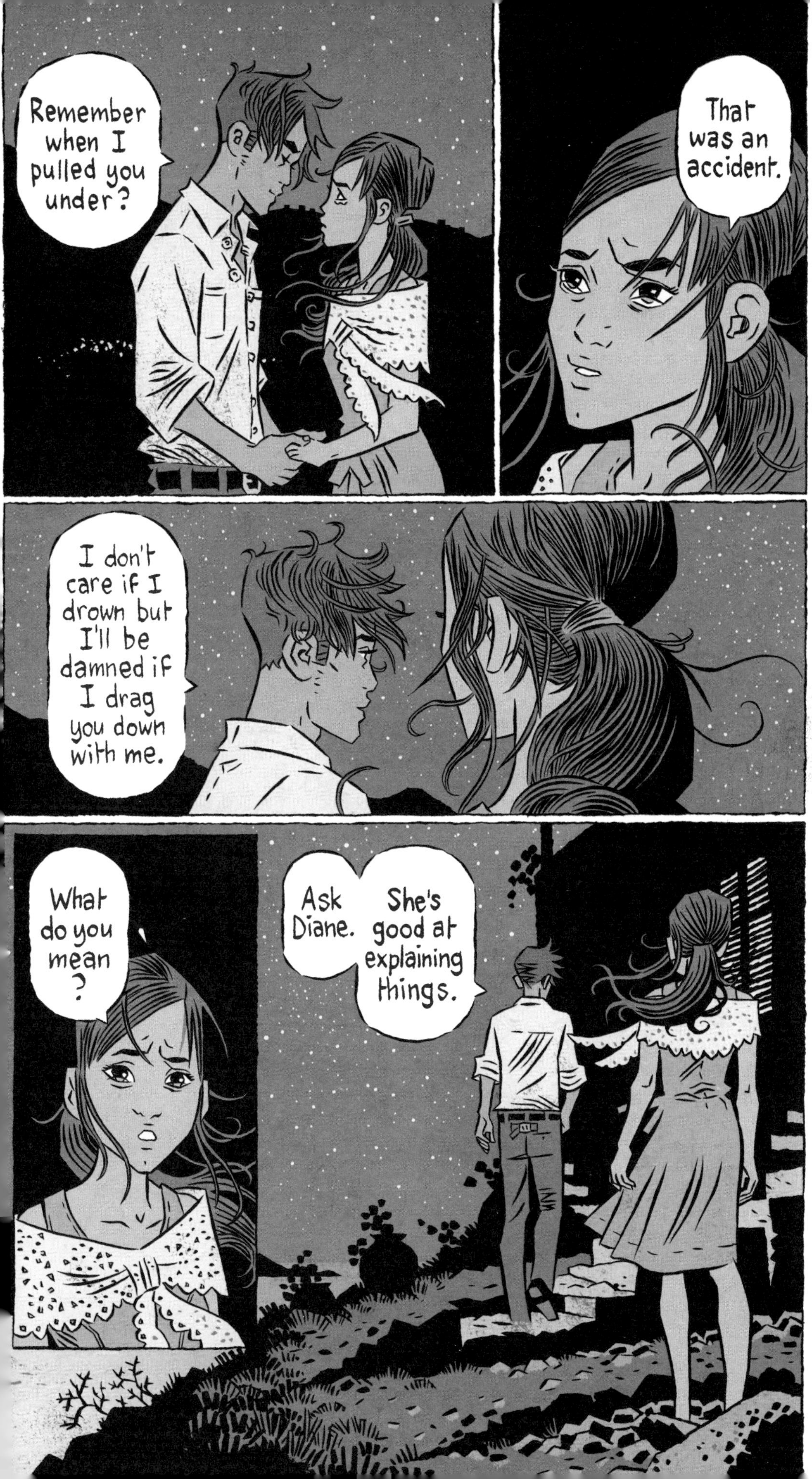
Remember when I pulled you under?
That was an accident.
I don't care if I drown but I'll be damned if I drag you down with me.
What do you mean?
Ask Diane.
She's good at explaining things.

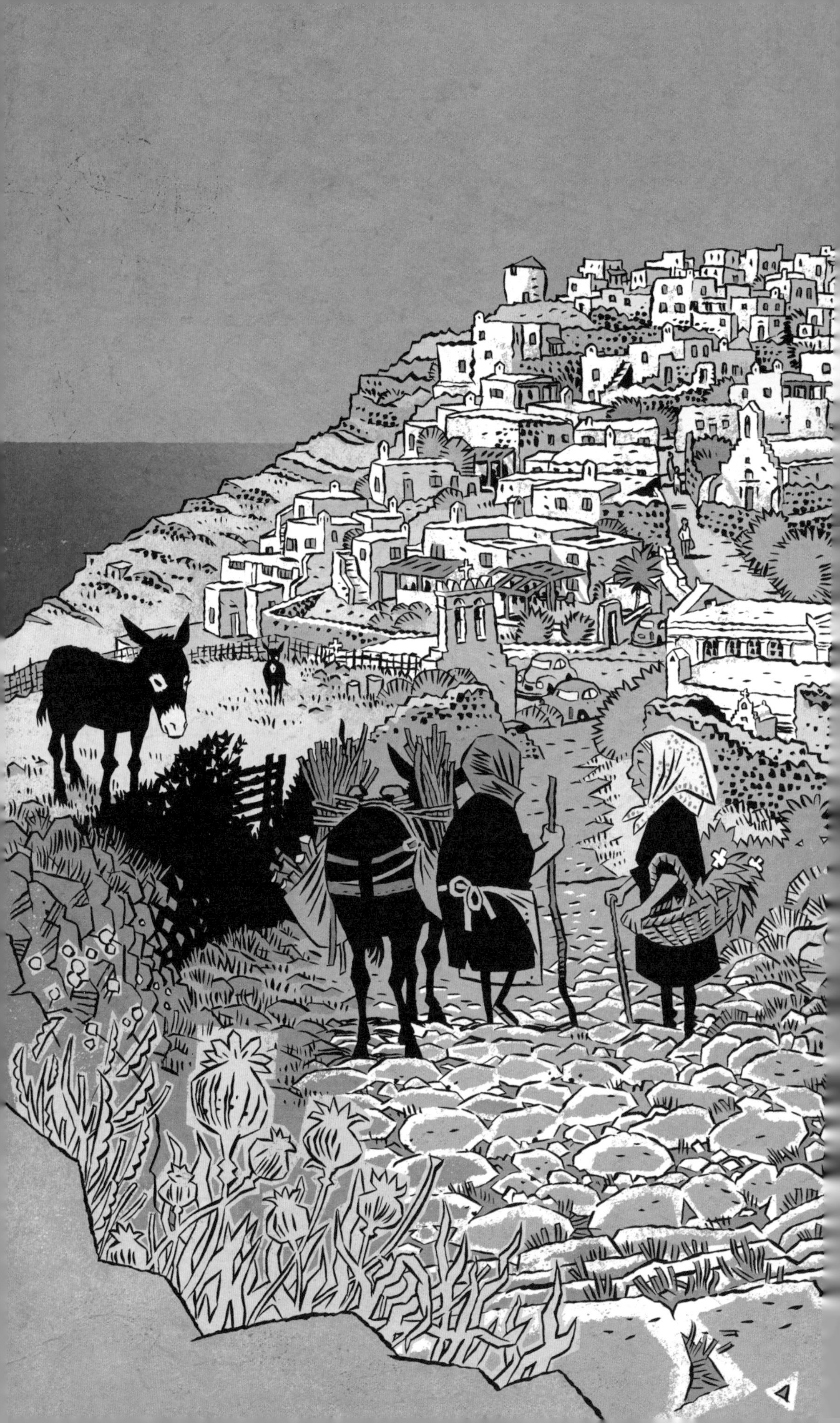

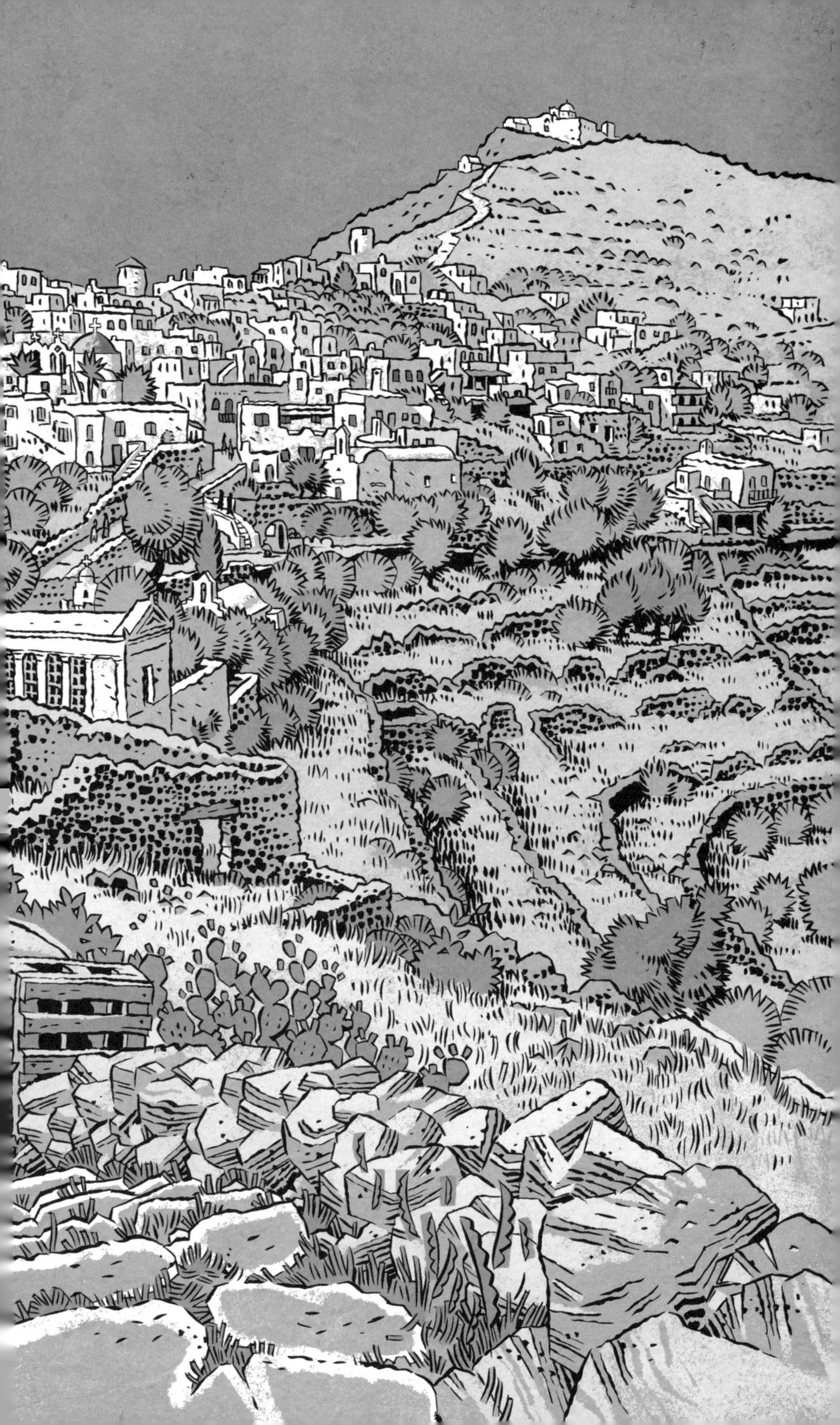

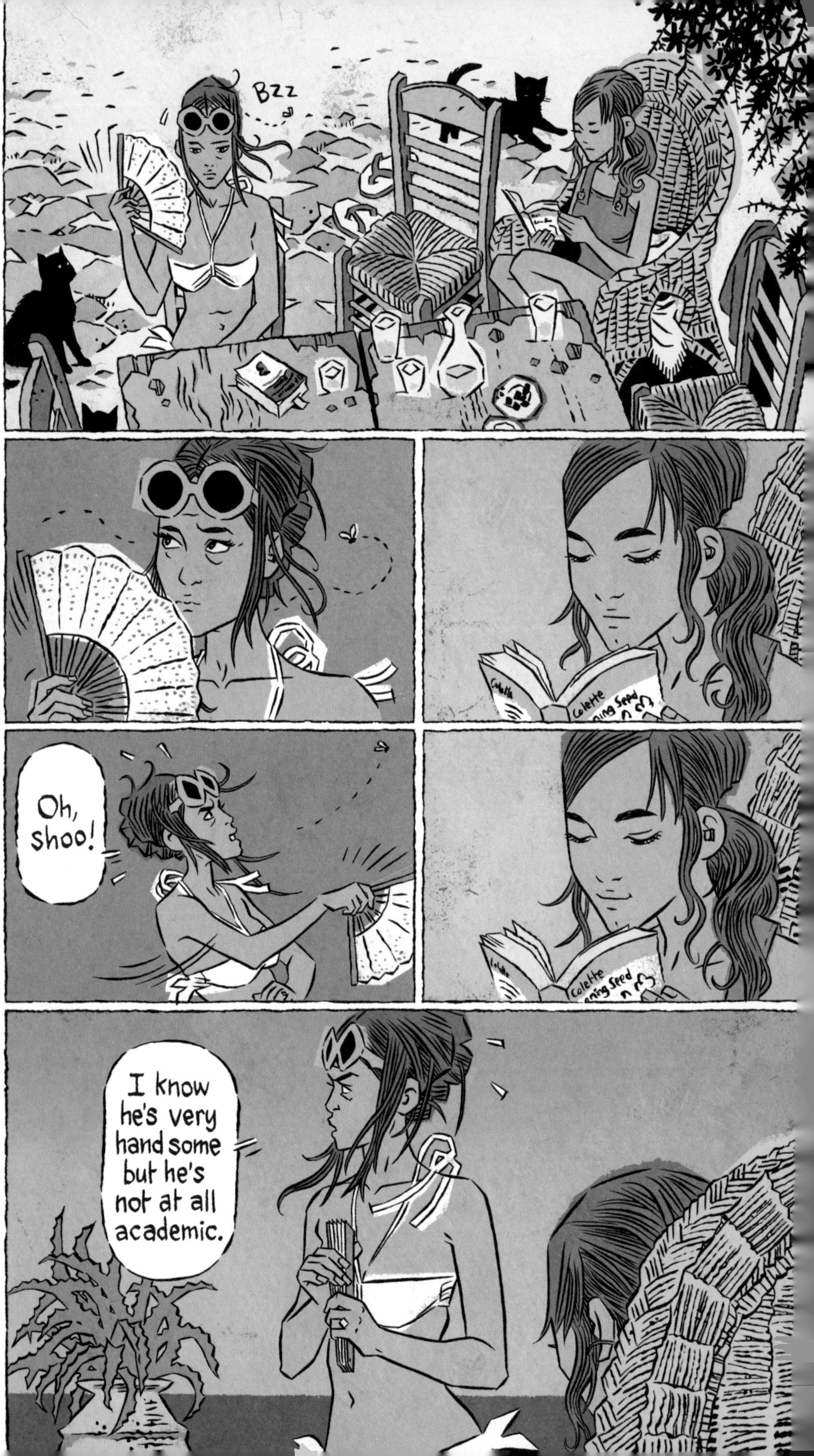
Bzz
Colette
Oh, shoo!
I know he's very hand some but he's not at all academic.

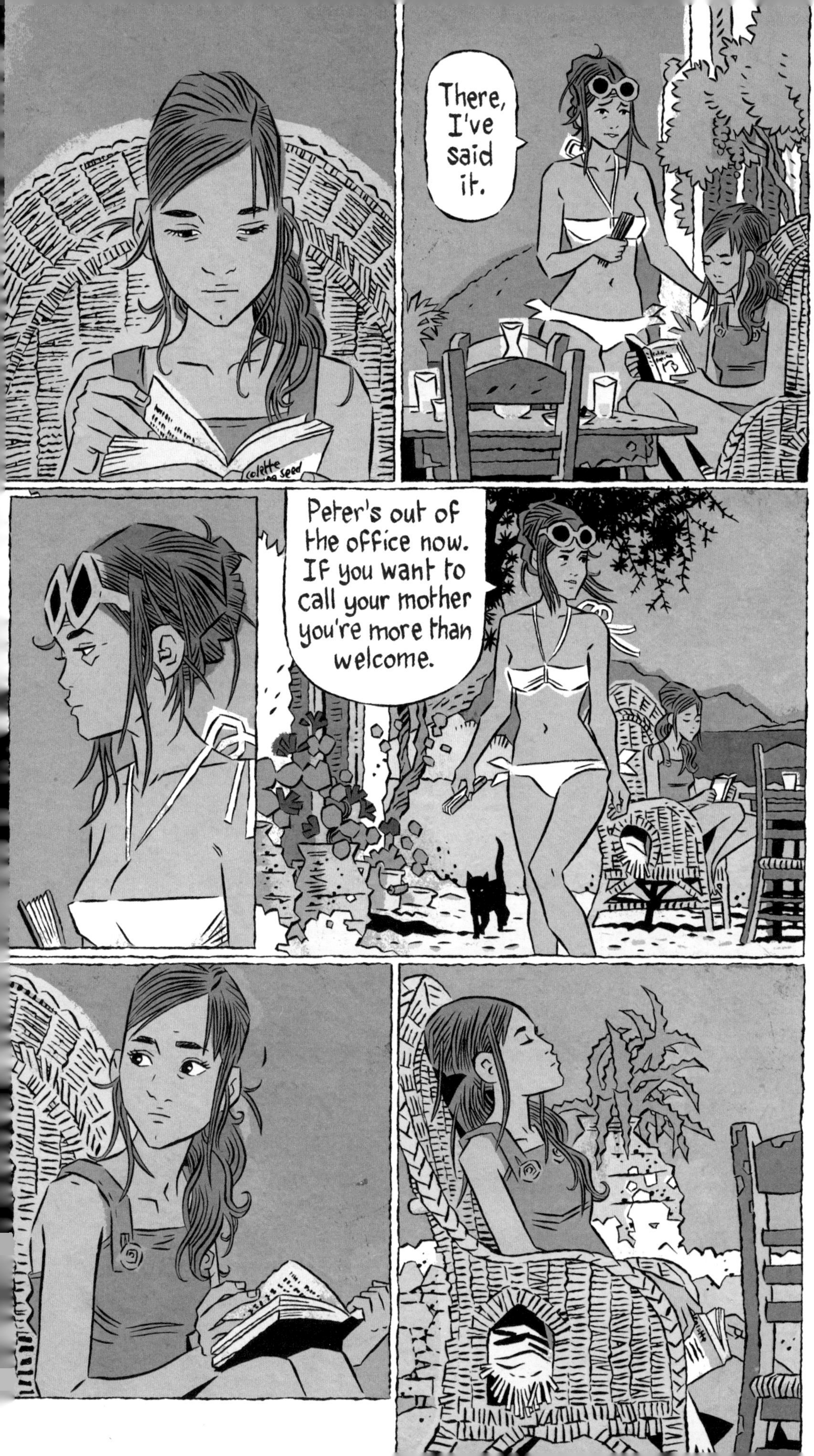
There, I've said it.
Peter's out of the office now. If you want to call your mother you're more than welcome.

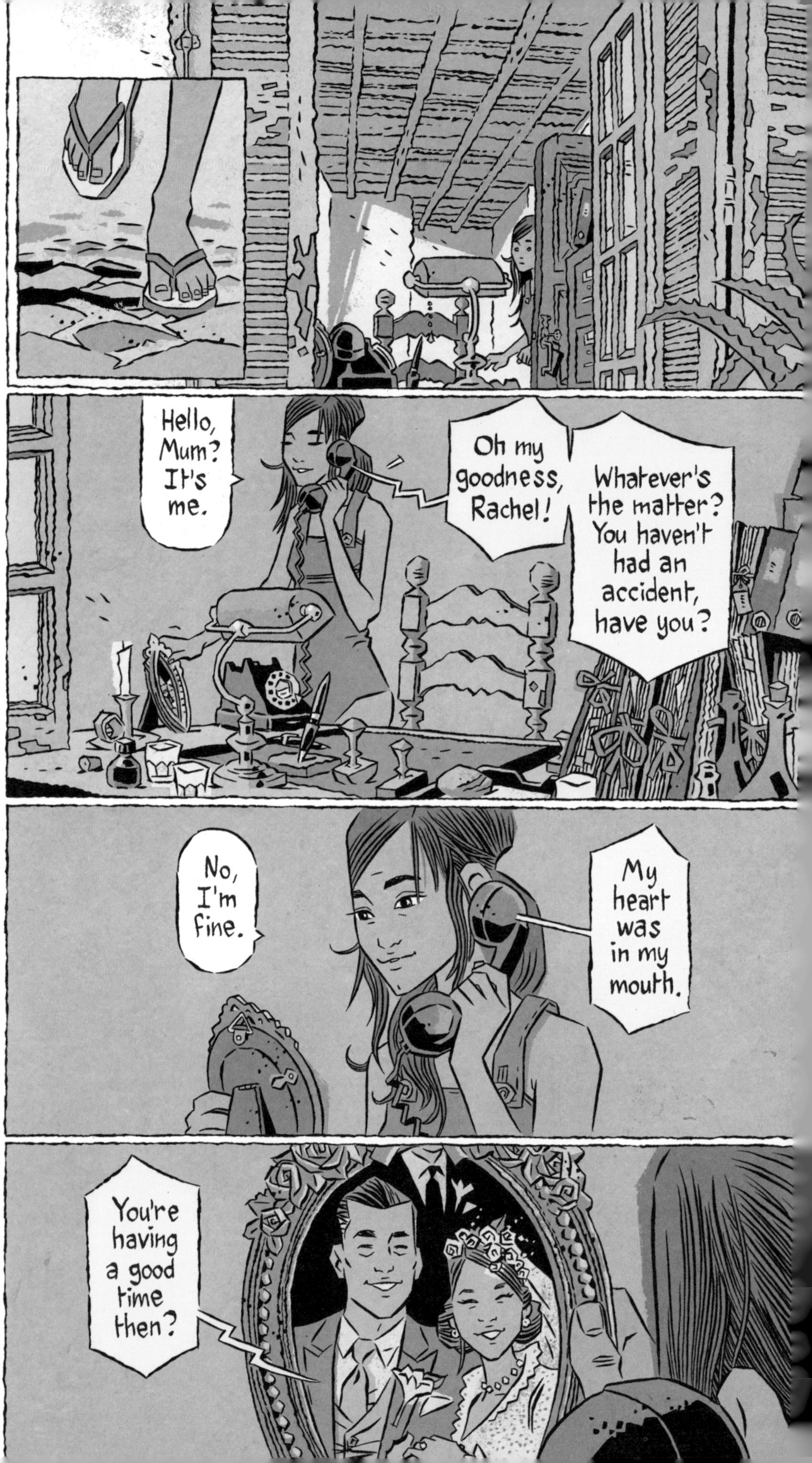
Hello, Mum? It's me.
Oh my goodness, Rachel!
Whatever's the matter? You haven't had an accident, have you?
No, I'm fine.
My heart was in my mouth.
You're having a good time then?

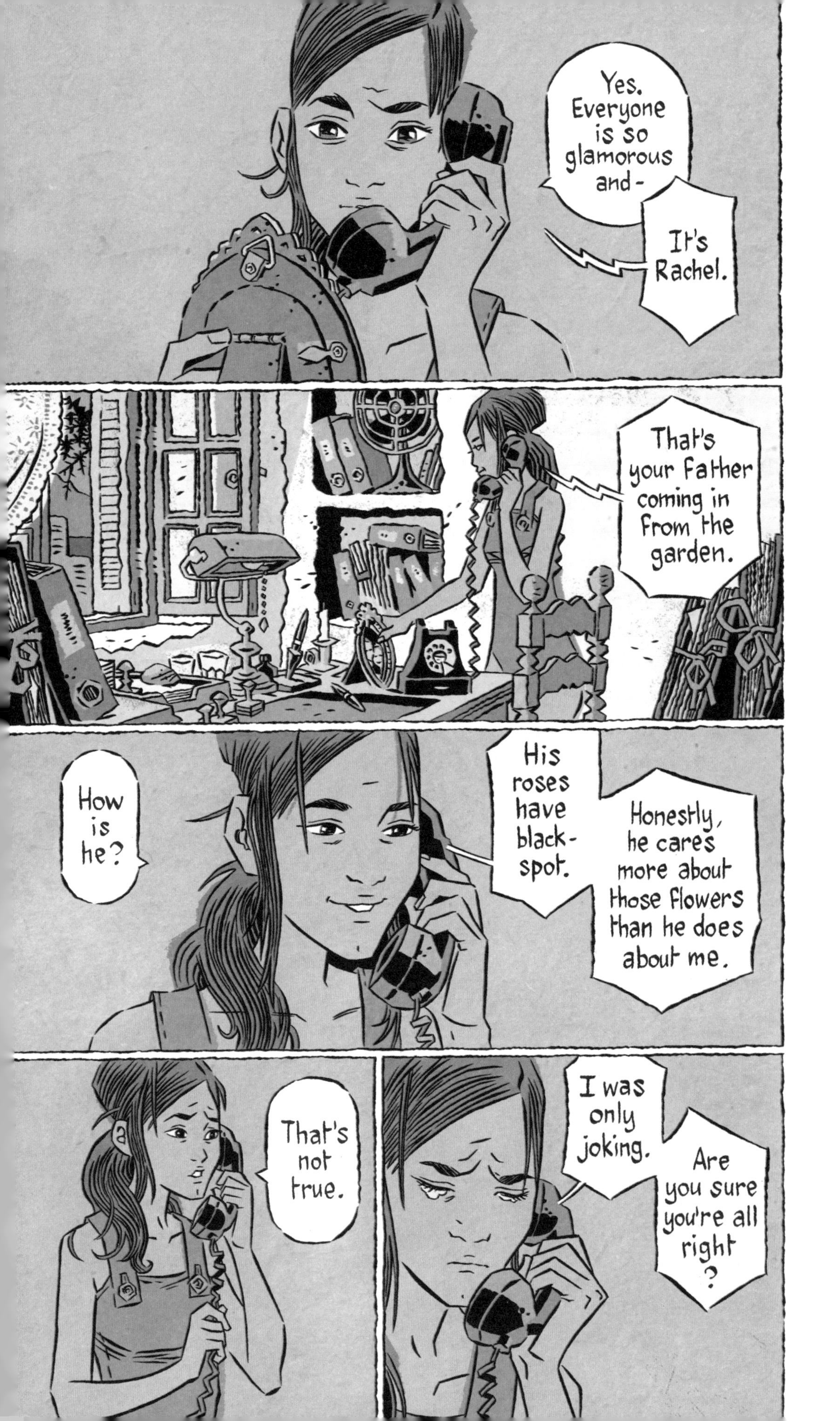
Yes. Everyone is so glamorous and -
It's Rachel.
That's your father coming in from the garden.
How is he?
His roses have black-spot.
Honestly, he cares more about those flowers than he does about me.
That's not true.
I was only joking.
Are you sure you're all right?

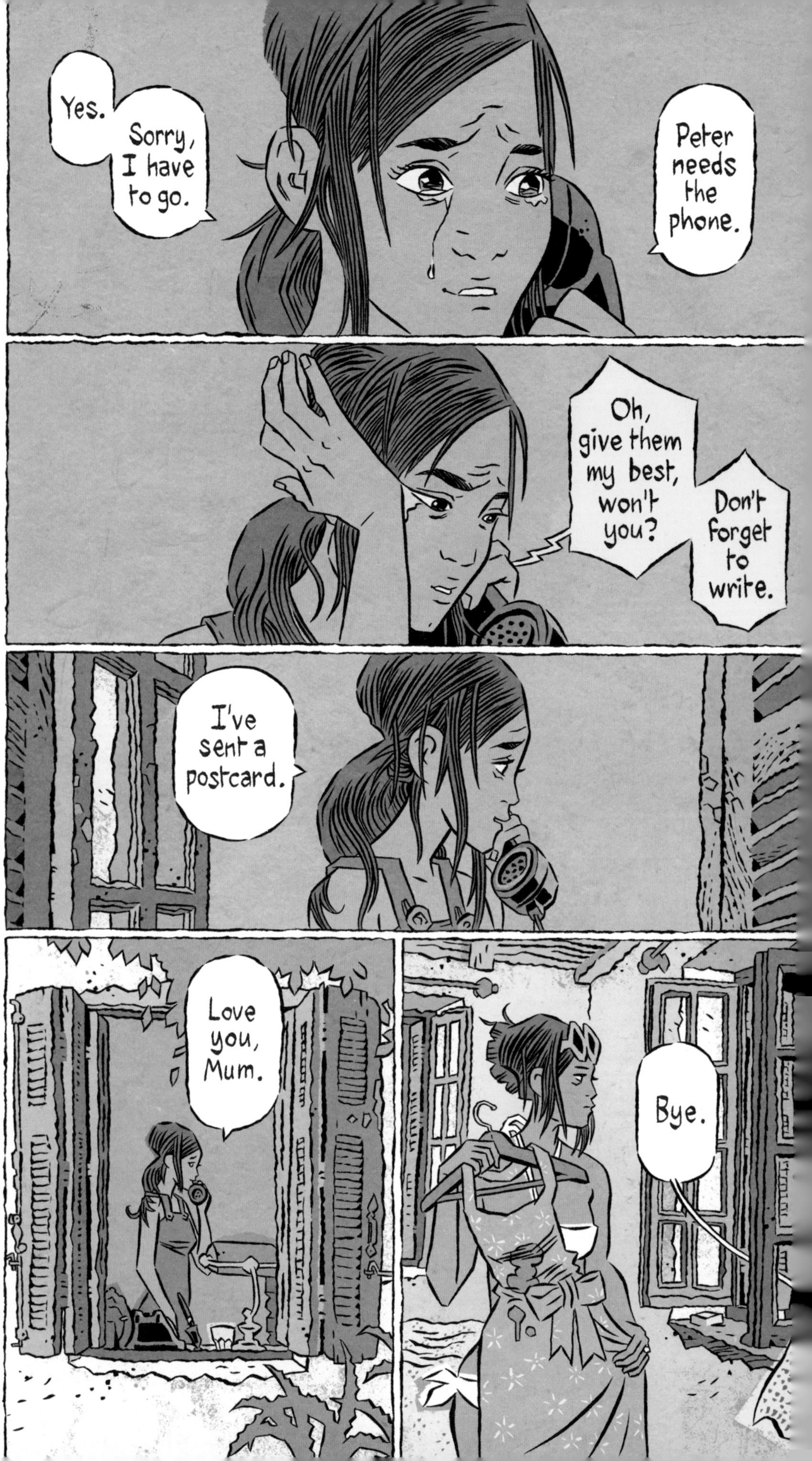
Yes.
Sorry, I have to go.
Peter needs the phone.
Oh, give them my best, won't you?
Don't forget to write.
I've sent a postcard.
Love you, Mum.
Bye.

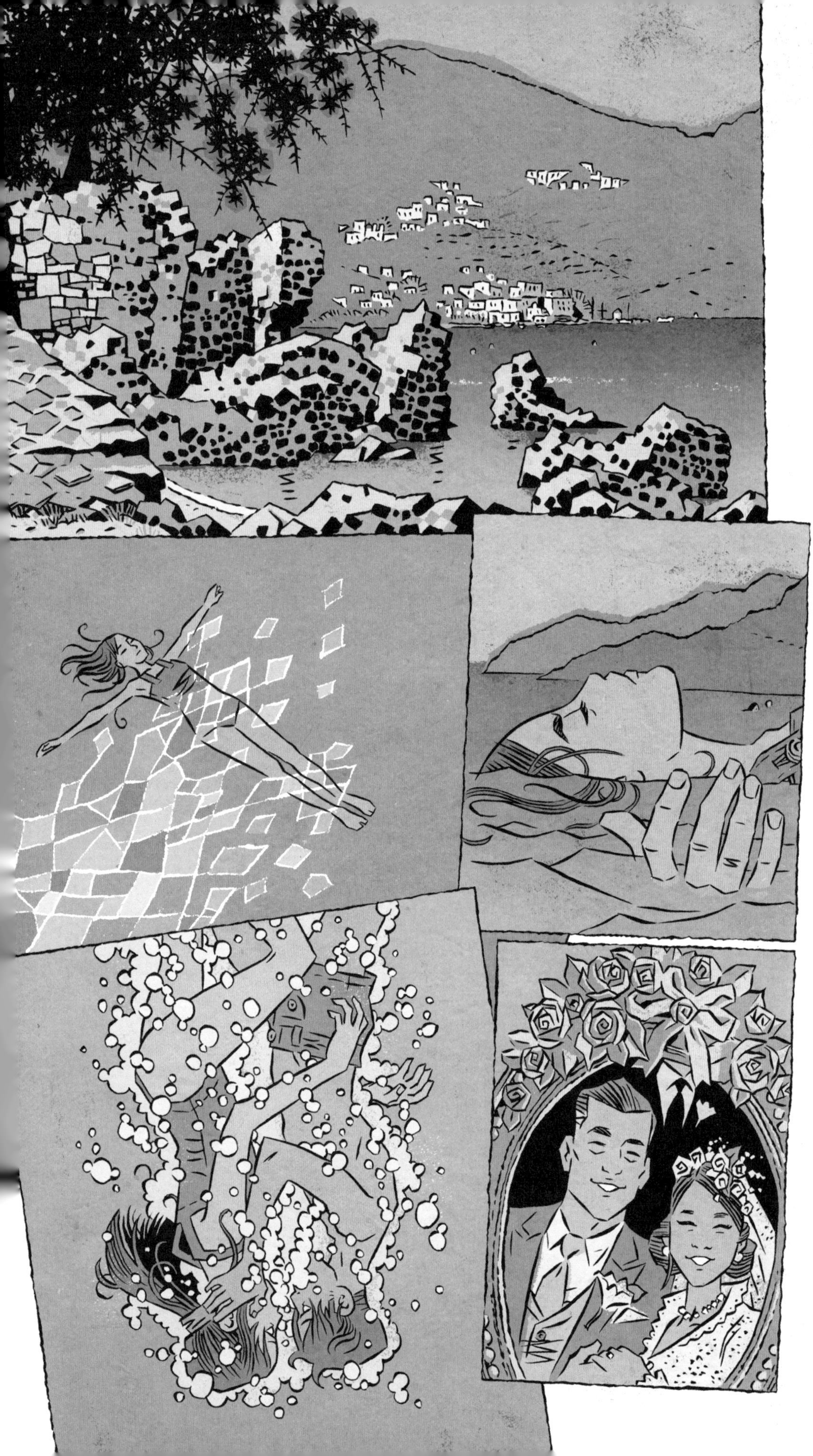

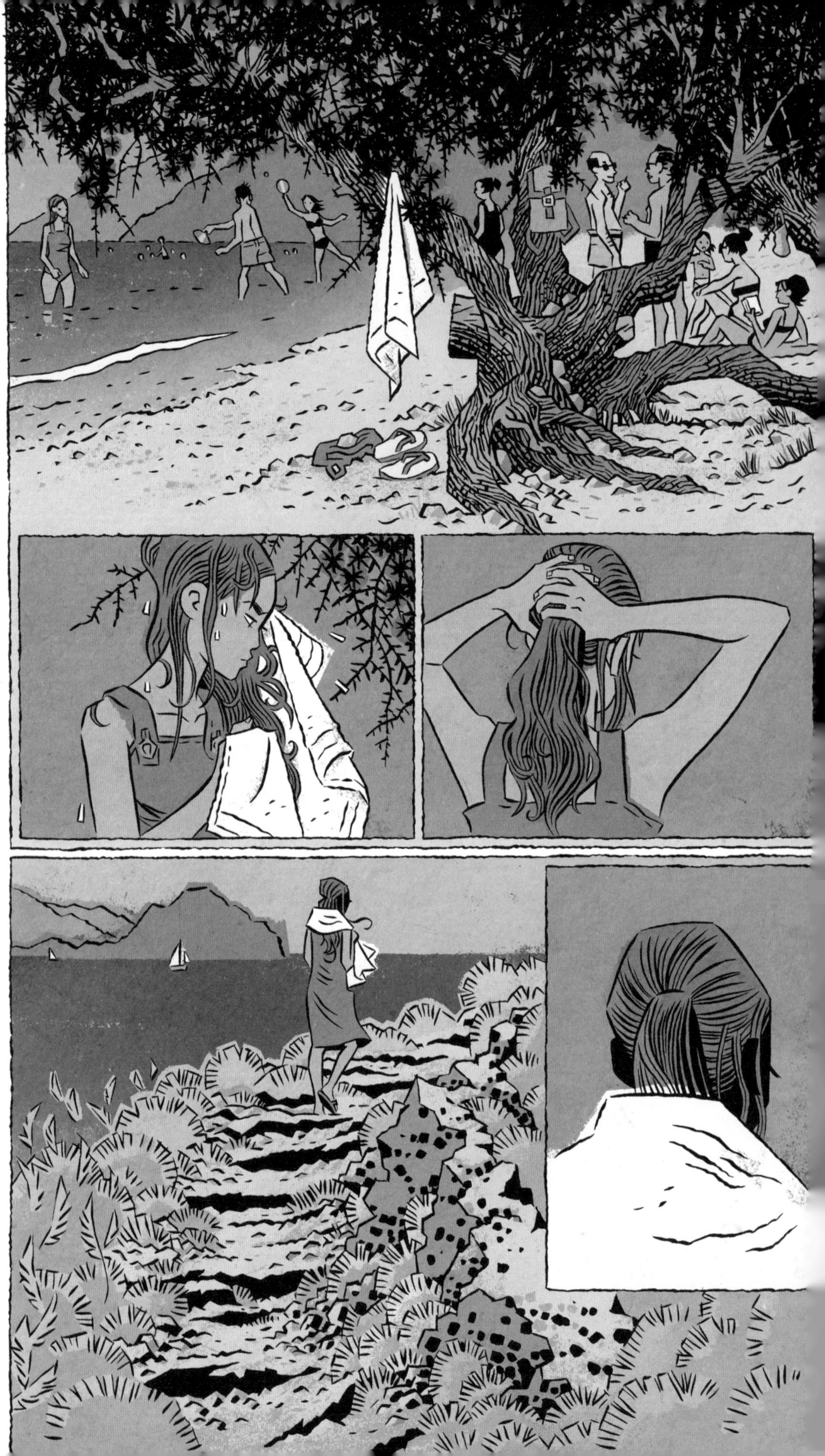

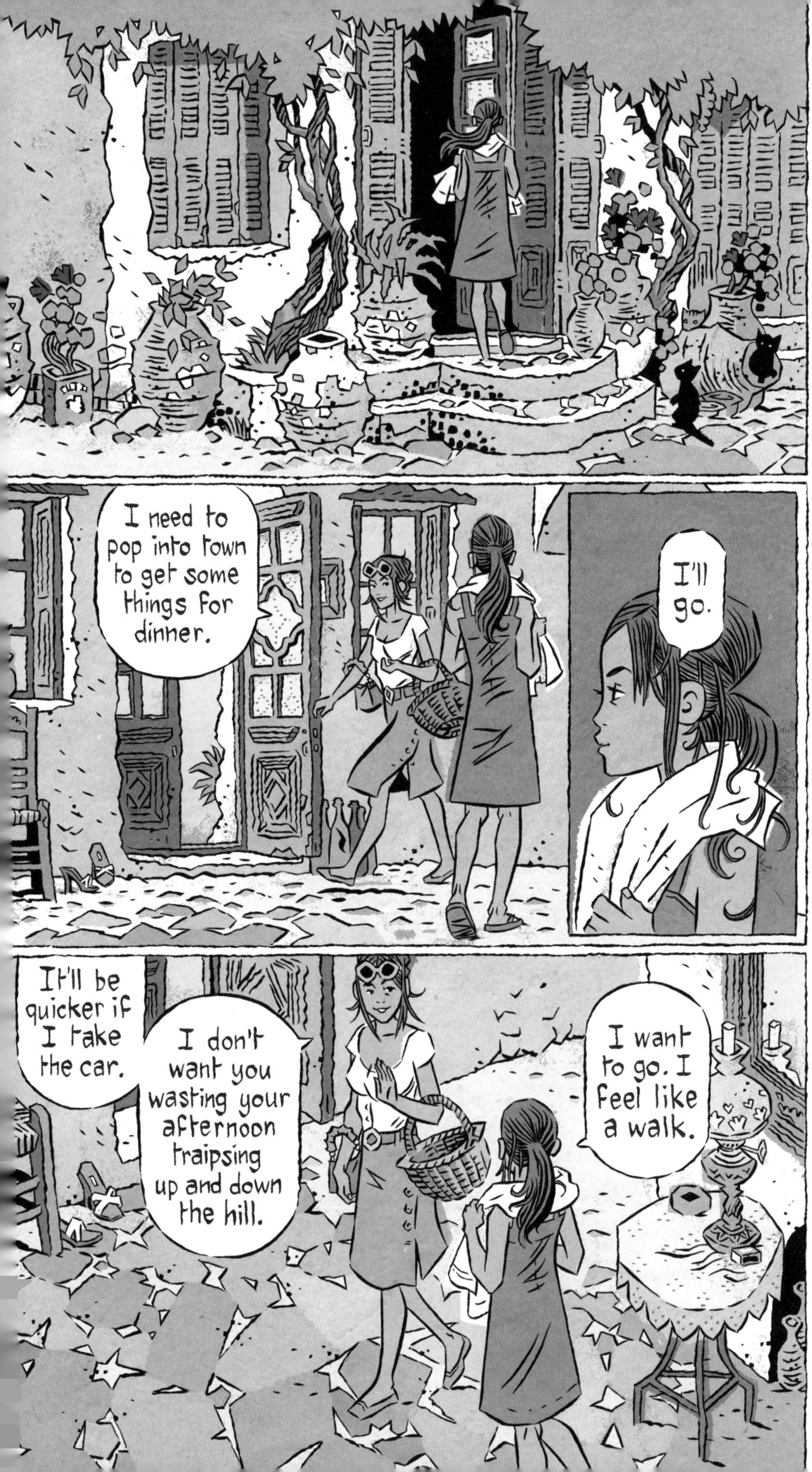
I need to pop into town to get some things for dinner.
I'll go.
It'll be quicker if I take the car.
I don't want you wasting your afternoon traipsing up and down the hill.
I want to go. I feel like a walk.

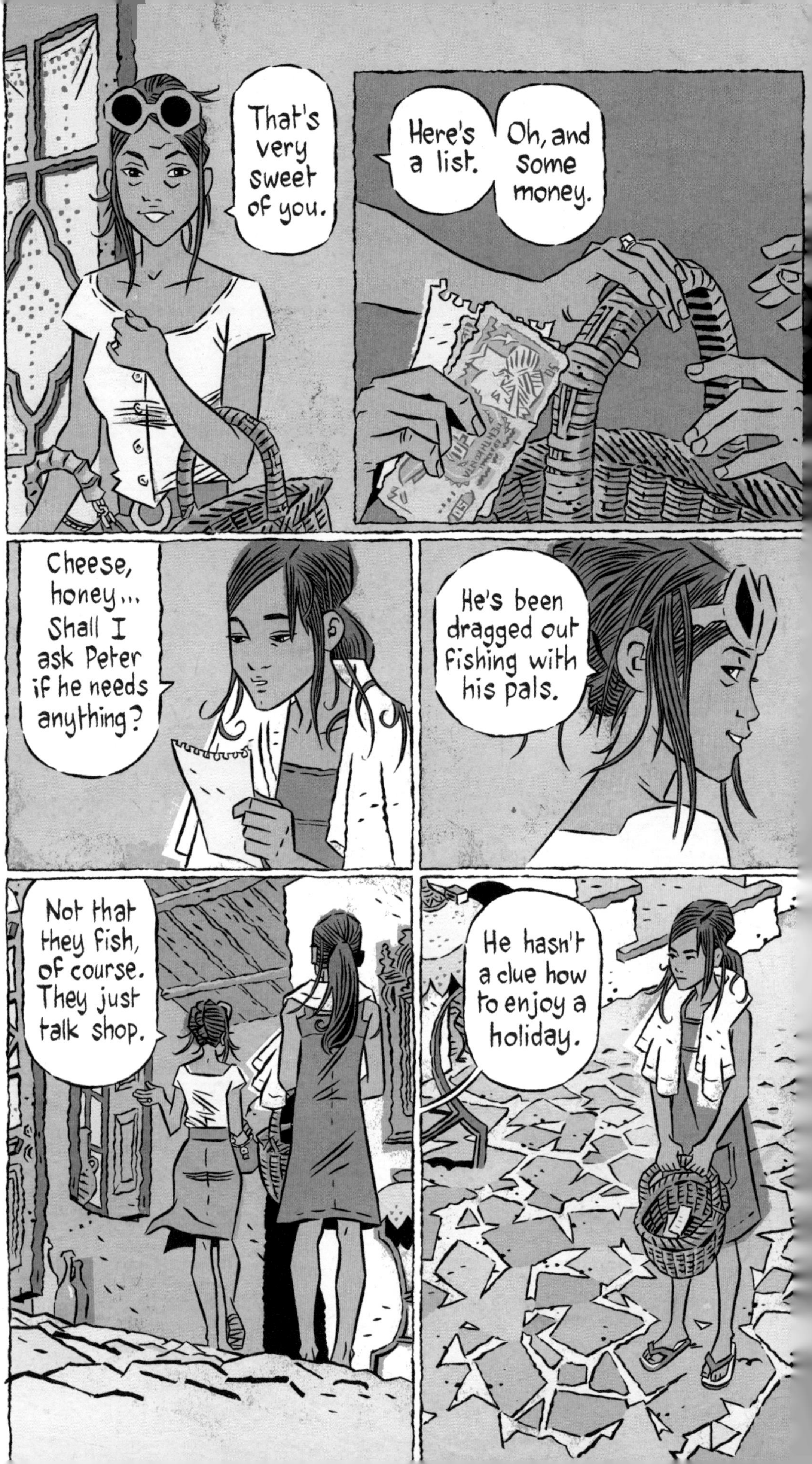
That's very sweet of you.
Here's a list.
Oh, and some money.
Cheese, honey... Shall I ask Peter if he needs anything?
He's been dragged out fishing with his pals.
Not that they fish, of course. They just talk shop.
He hasn't a clue how to enjoy a holiday.

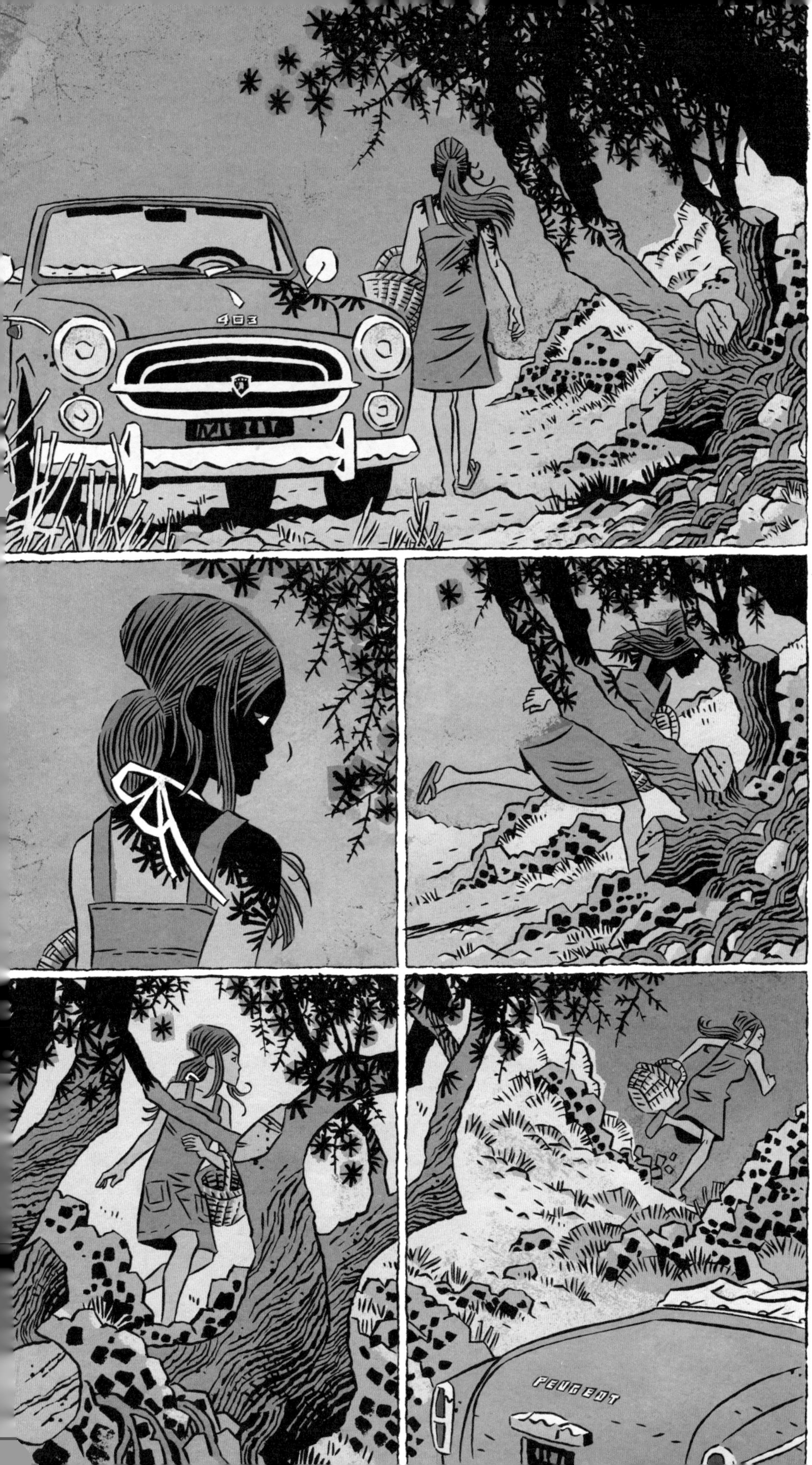
403
PEUGEOT

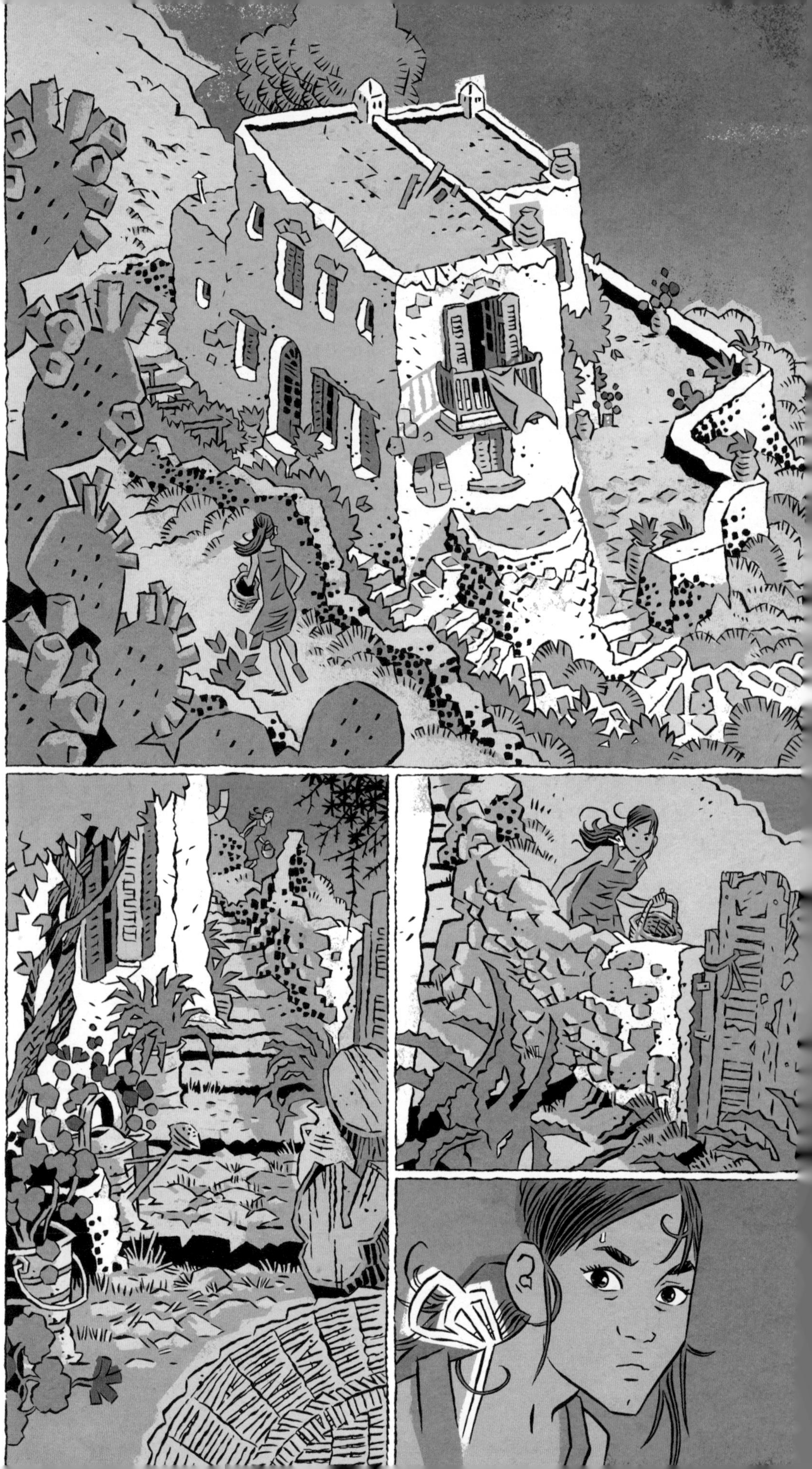

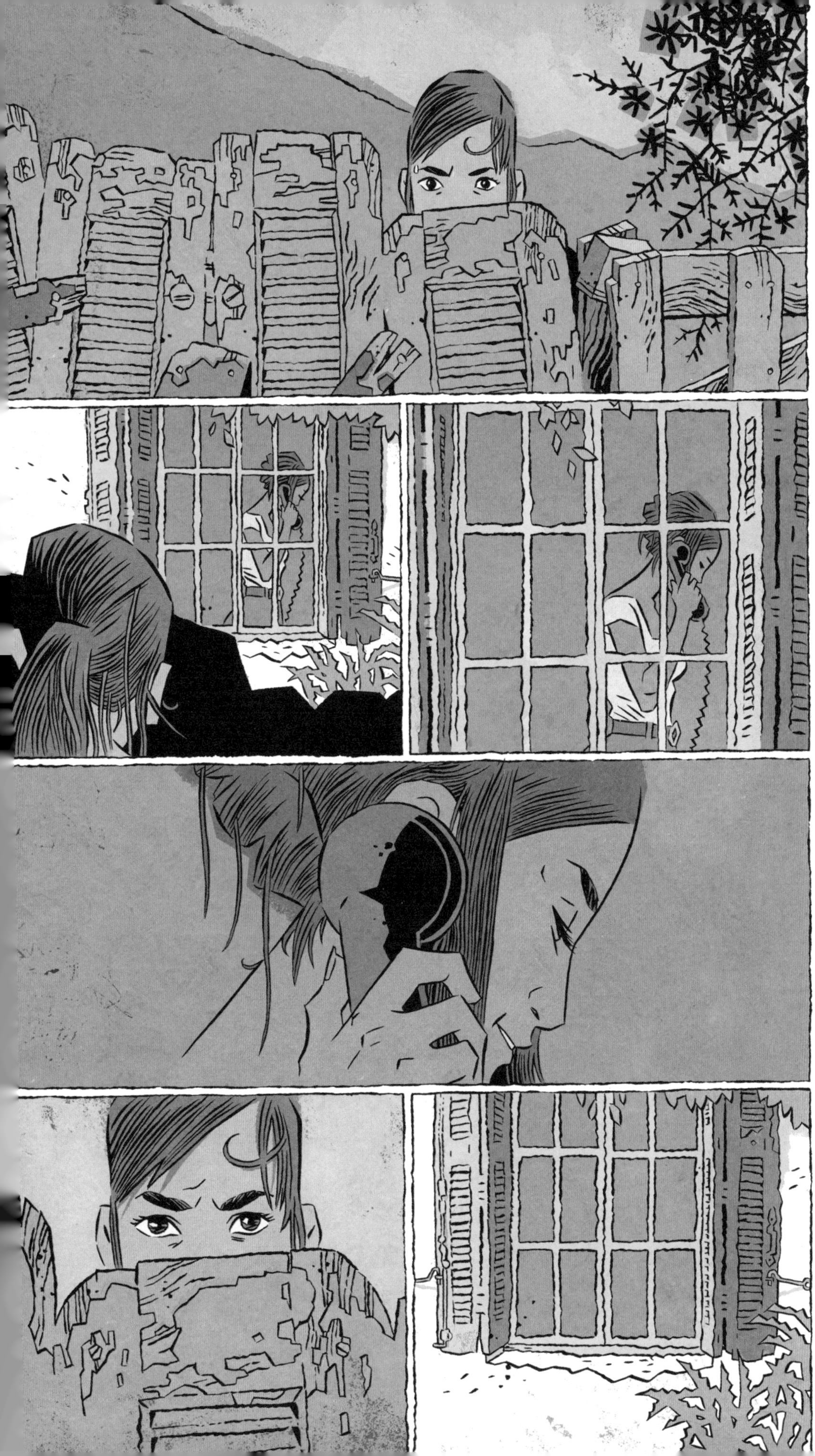

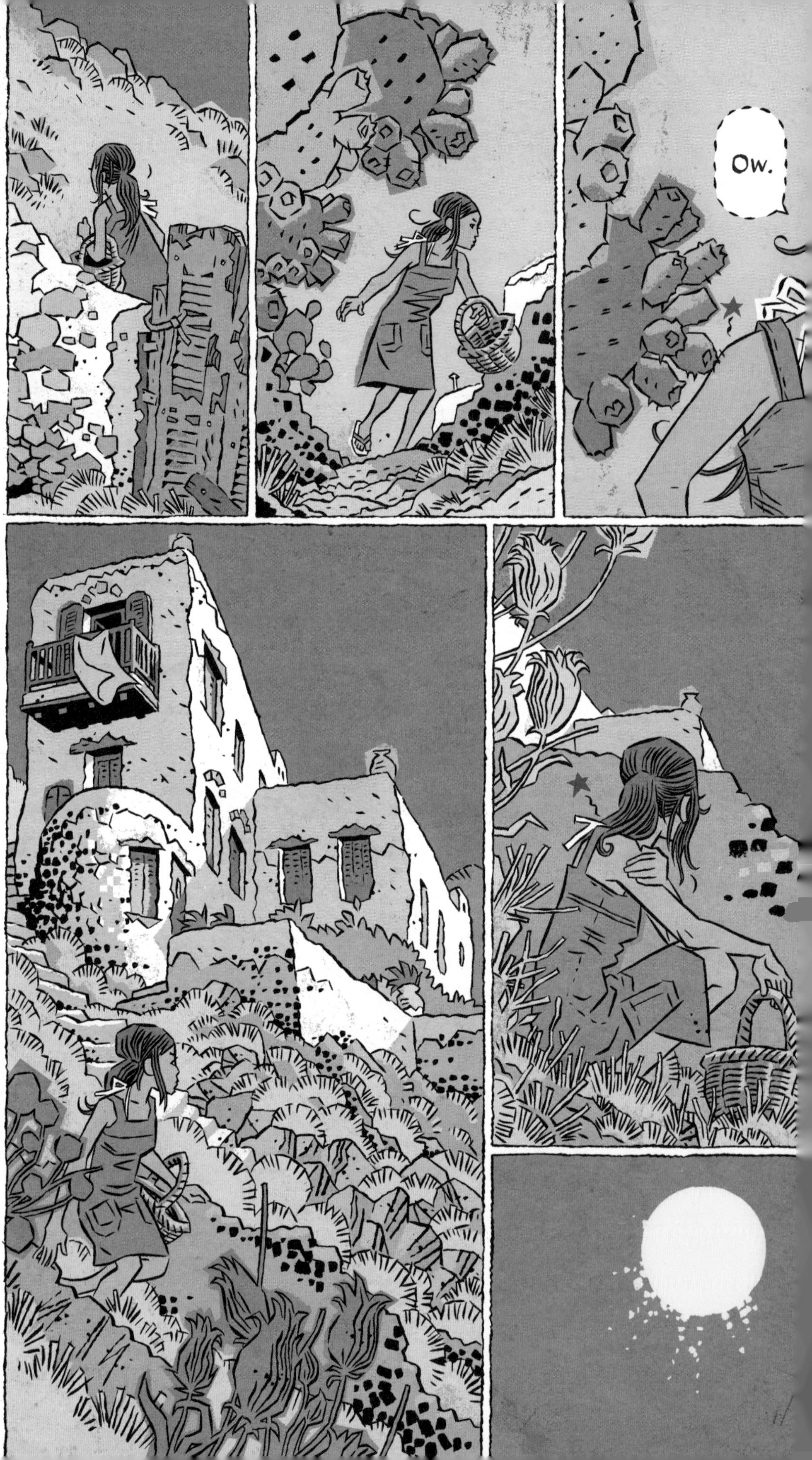
Ow.

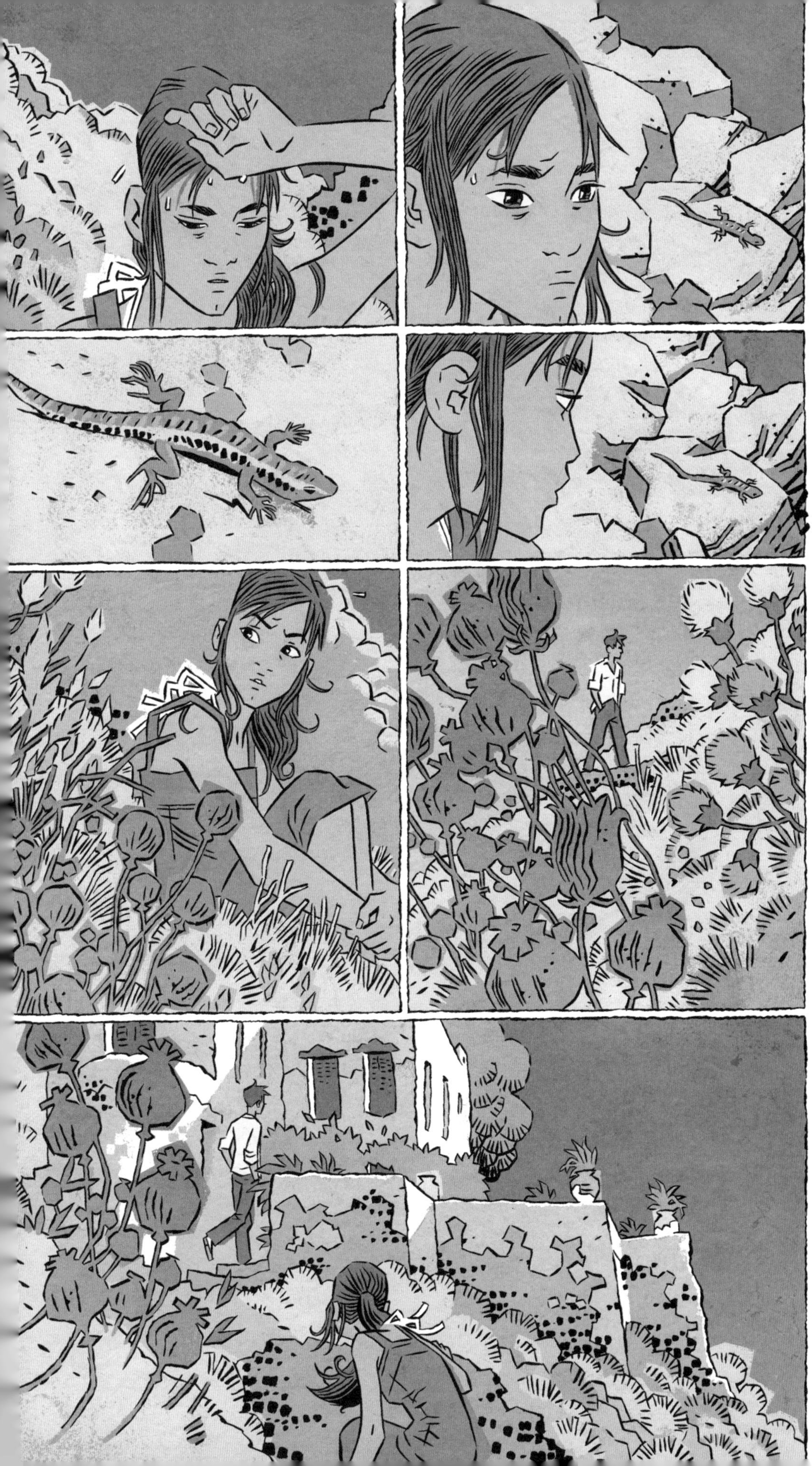

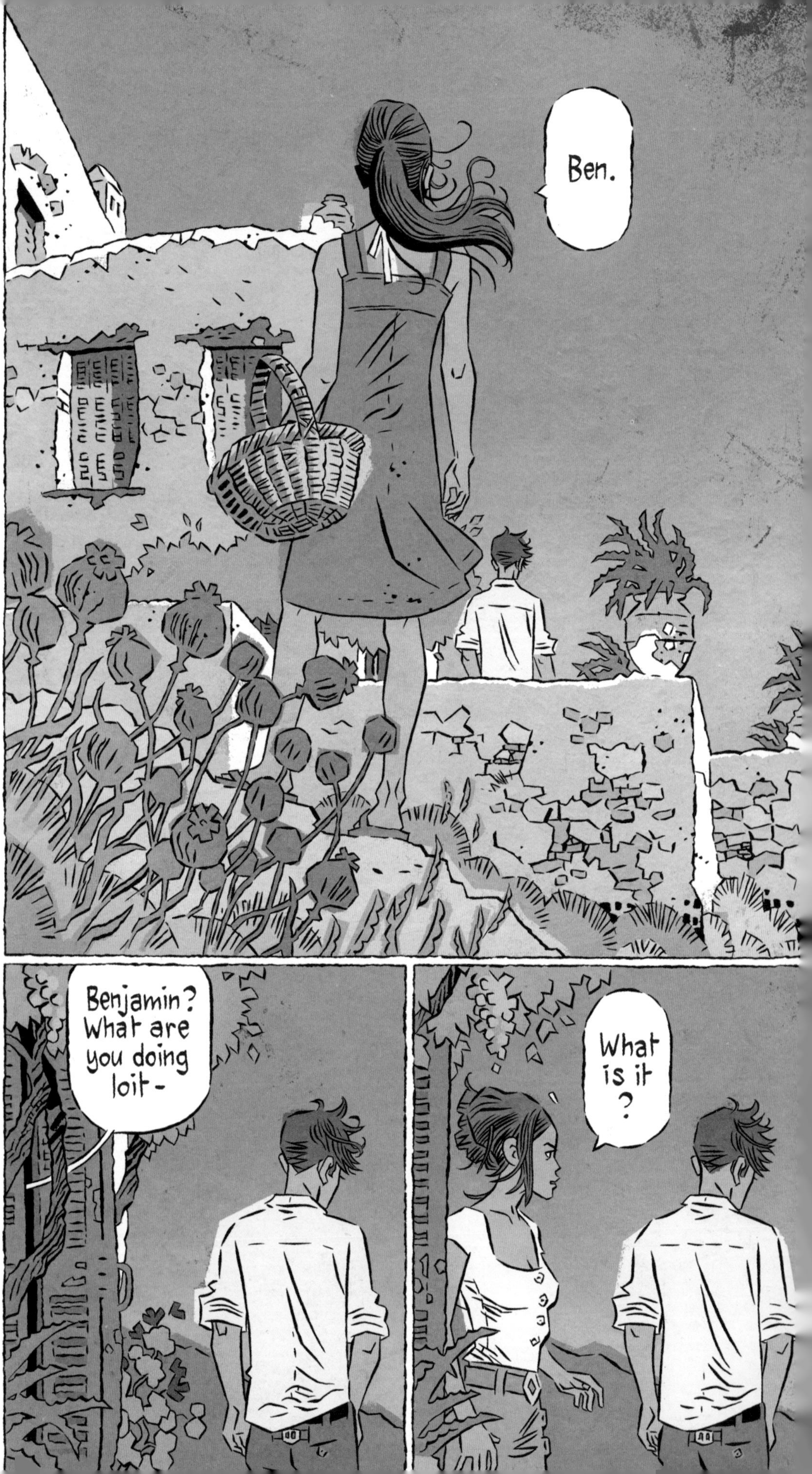
Ben.
Benjamin? What are you doing loit-
What is it ?

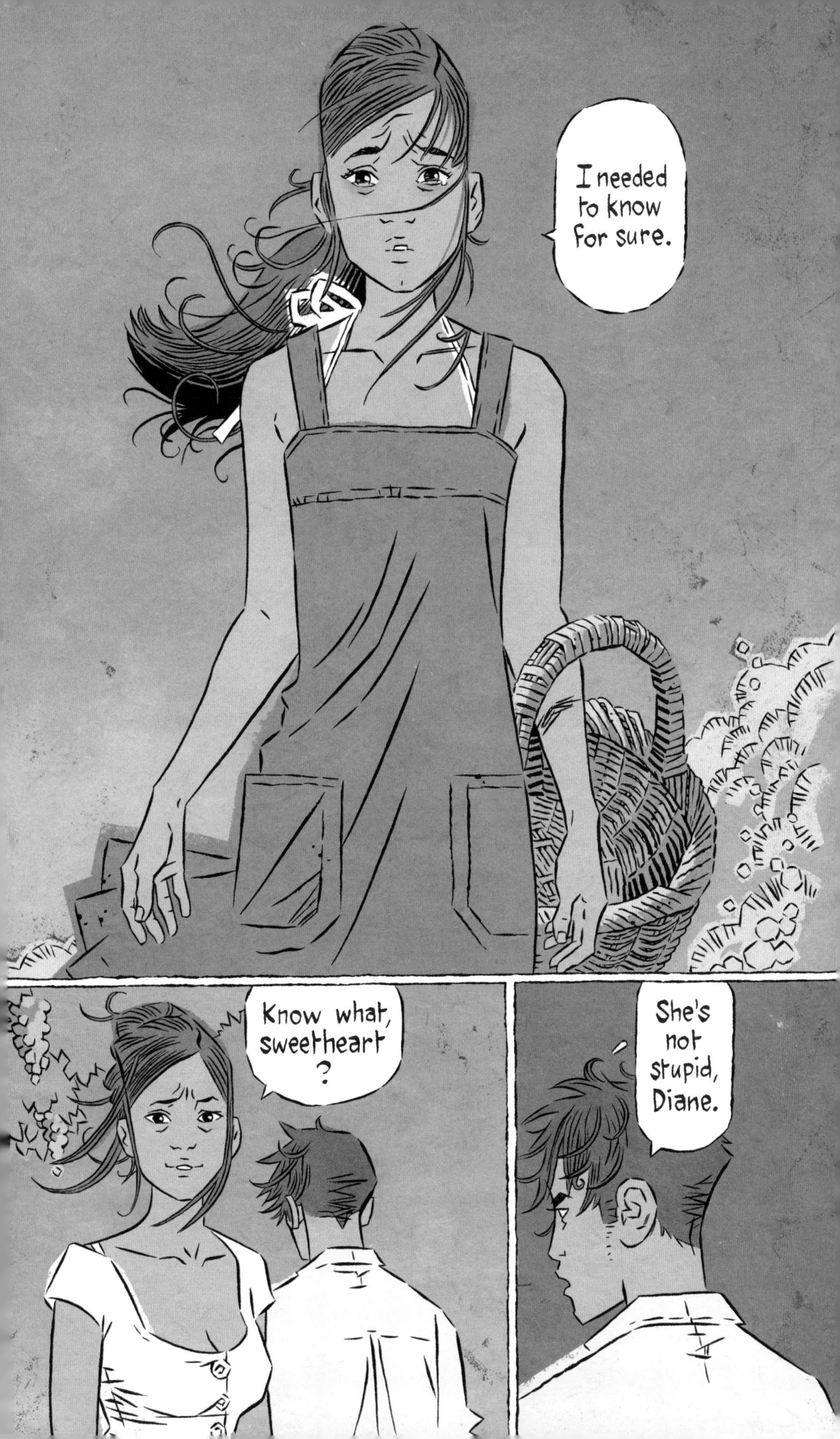
I needed to know for sure.
Know what, sweetheart?
She's not stupid, Diane.

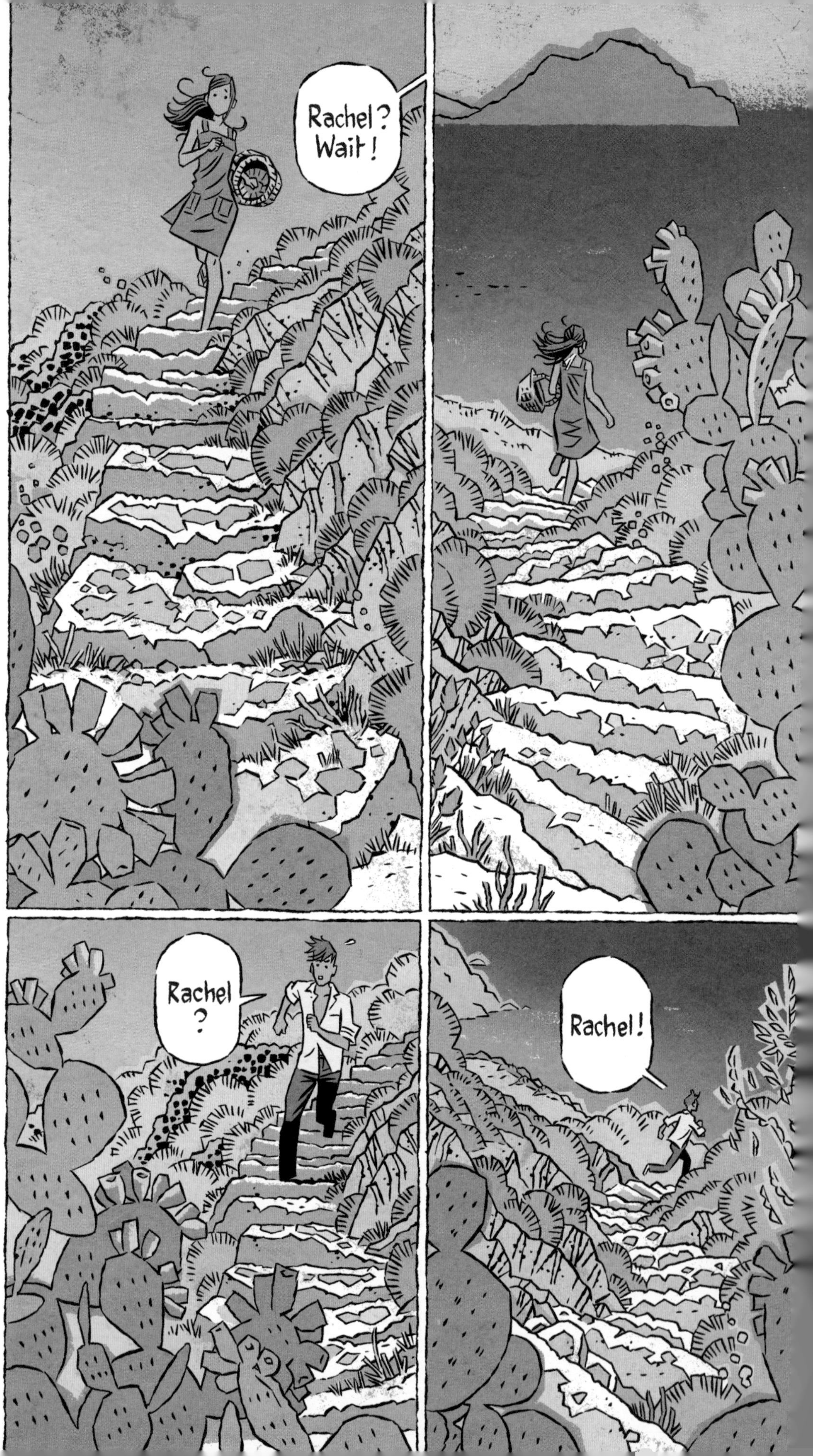
Rachel? Wait!
Rachel ?
Rachel!

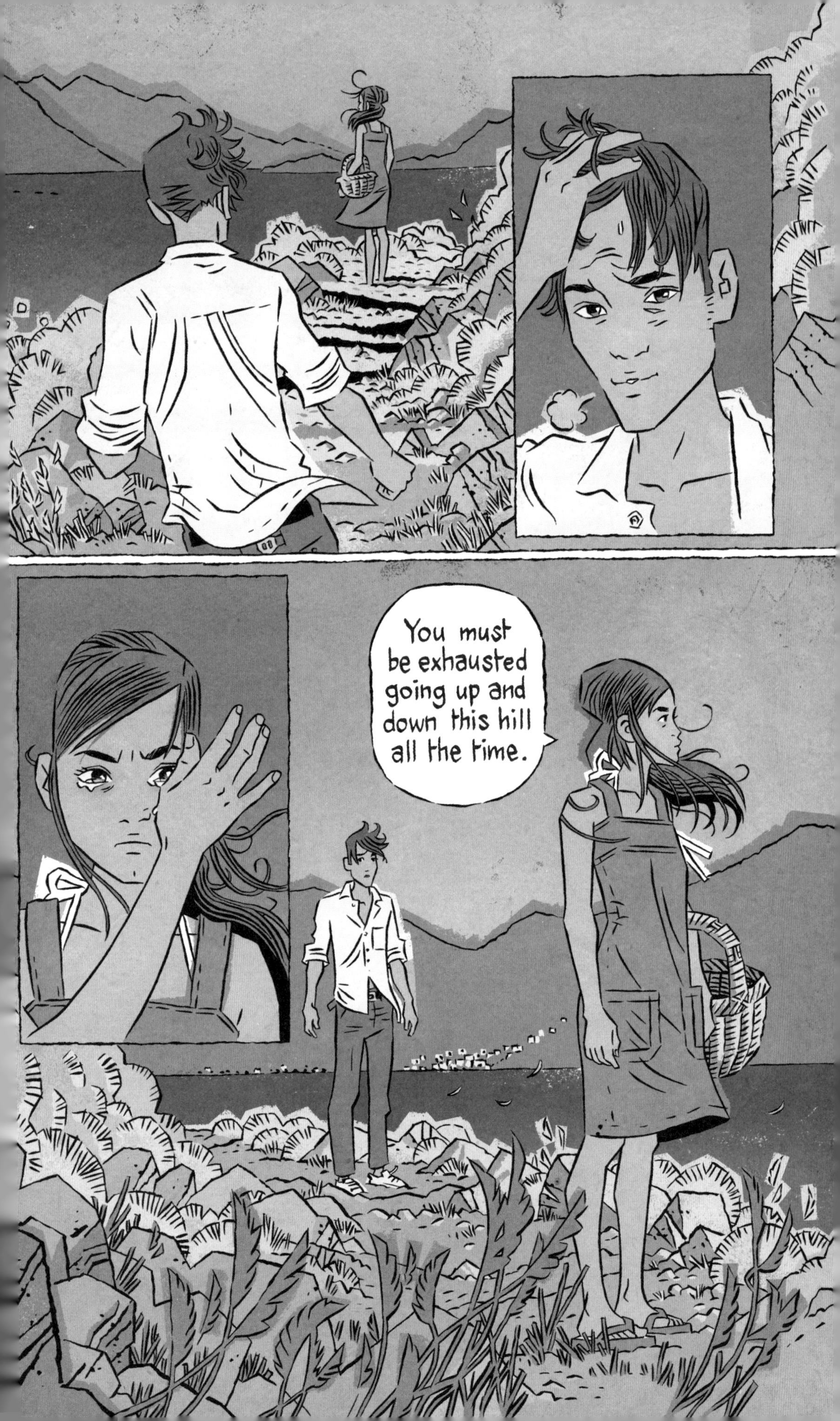
You must be exhausted going up and down this hill all the time.

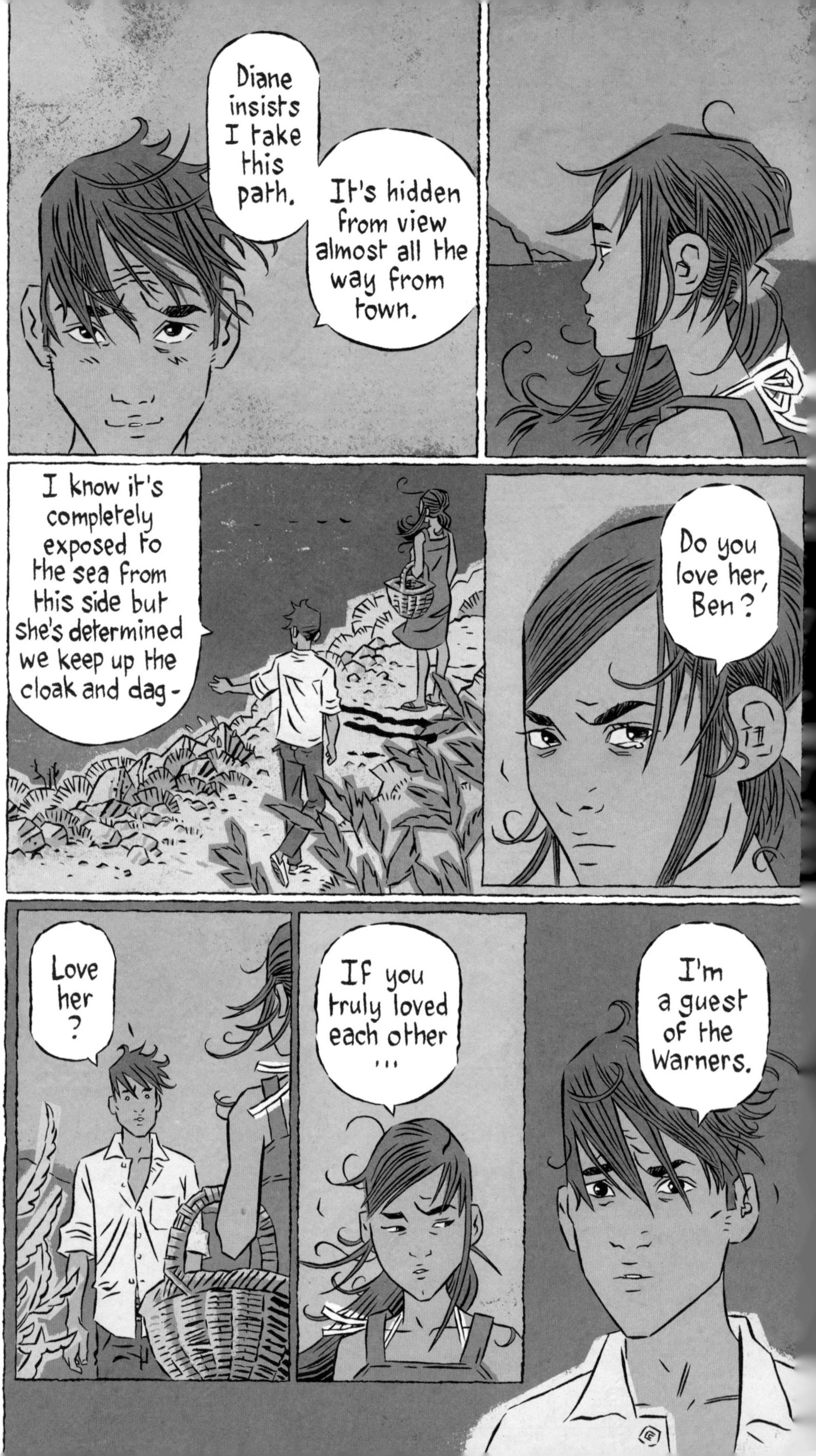
Diane insists I take this path.
It's hidden from view almost all the way from town.
I know it's completely exposed to the sea from this side but she's determined we keep up the cloak and dag-
Do you love her, Ben?
Love her?
If you truly loved each other ...
I'm a guest of the Warners.

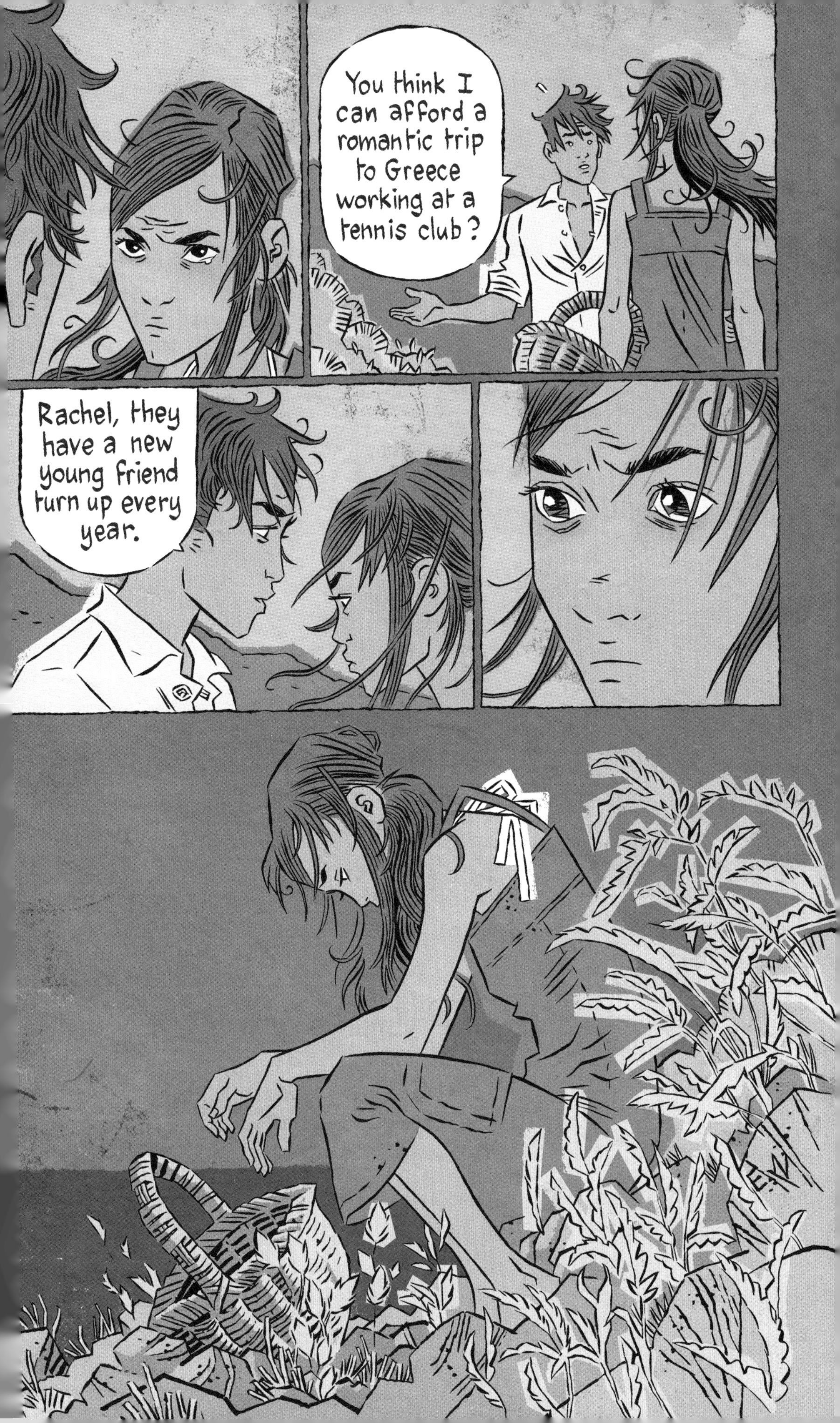
You think I can afford a romantic trip to Greece working at a tennis club?
Rachel, they have a new young friend turn up every year.

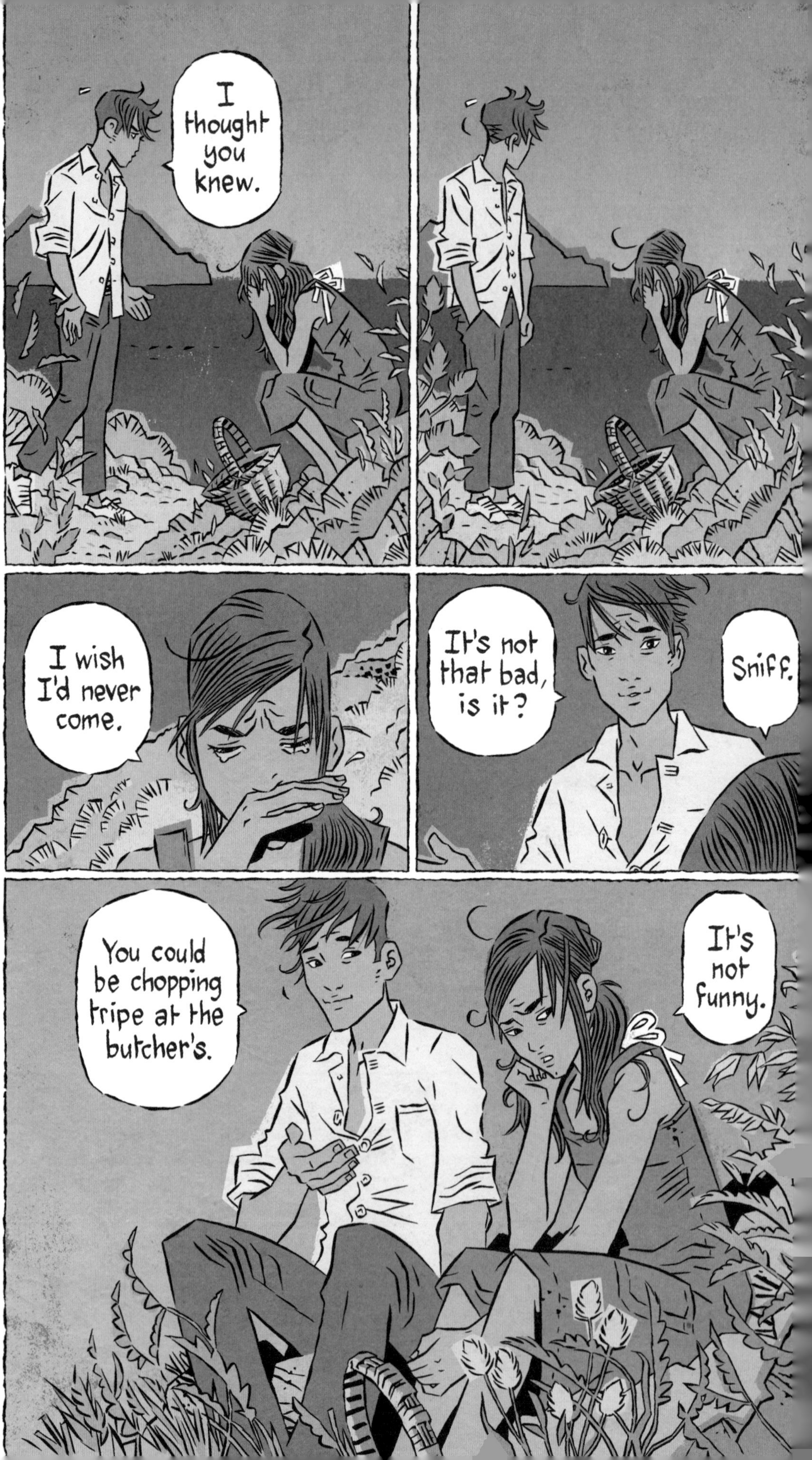
I thought you knew.
I wish I'd never come.
It's not that bad, is it?
Sniff.
You could be chopping tripe at the butcher's.
It's not funny.

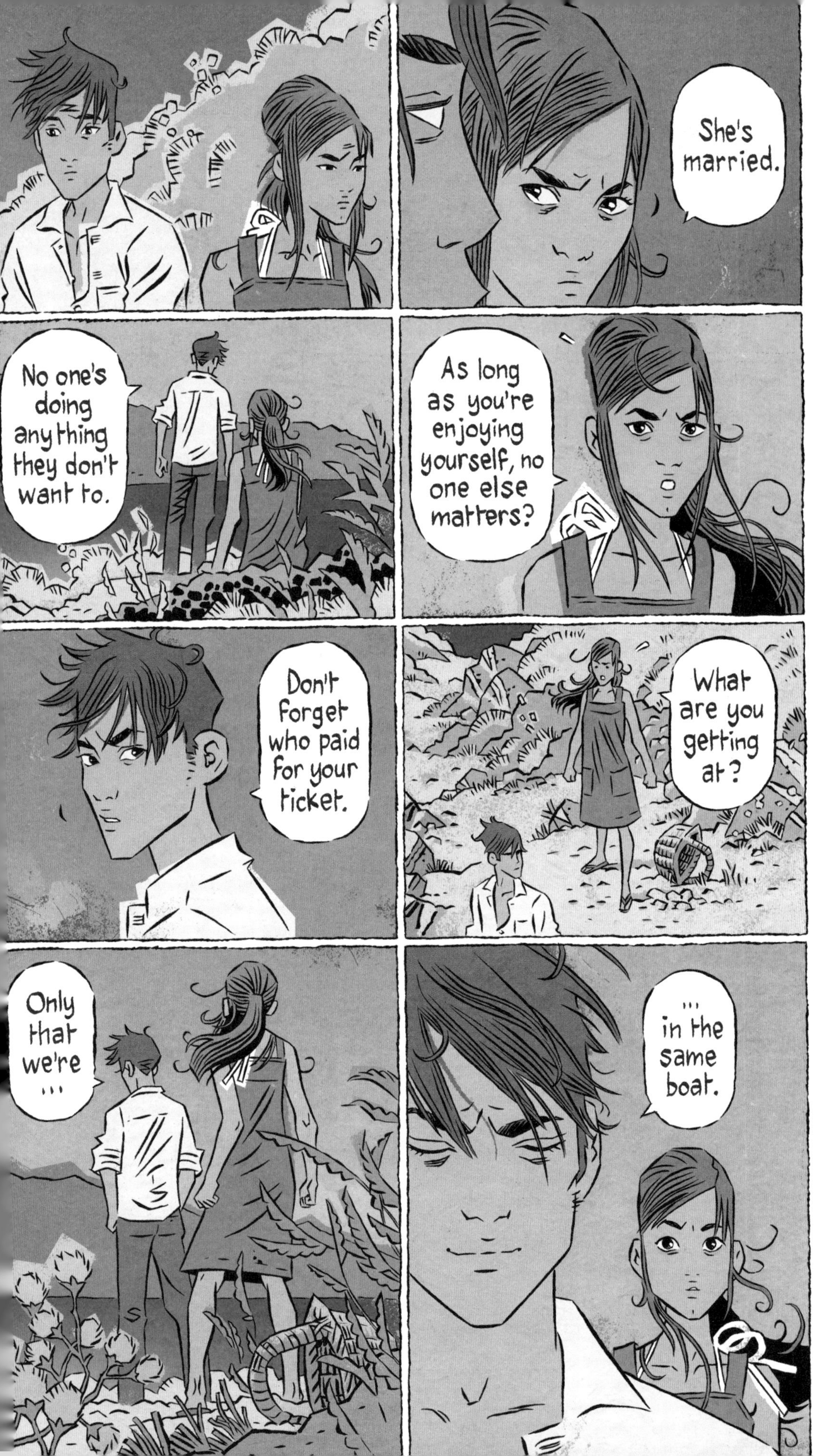
She's married.
No one's doing anything they don't want to.
As long as you're enjoying yourself, no one else matters?
Don't forget who paid for your ticket.
What are you getting at?
Only that we're ...
... in the same boat.

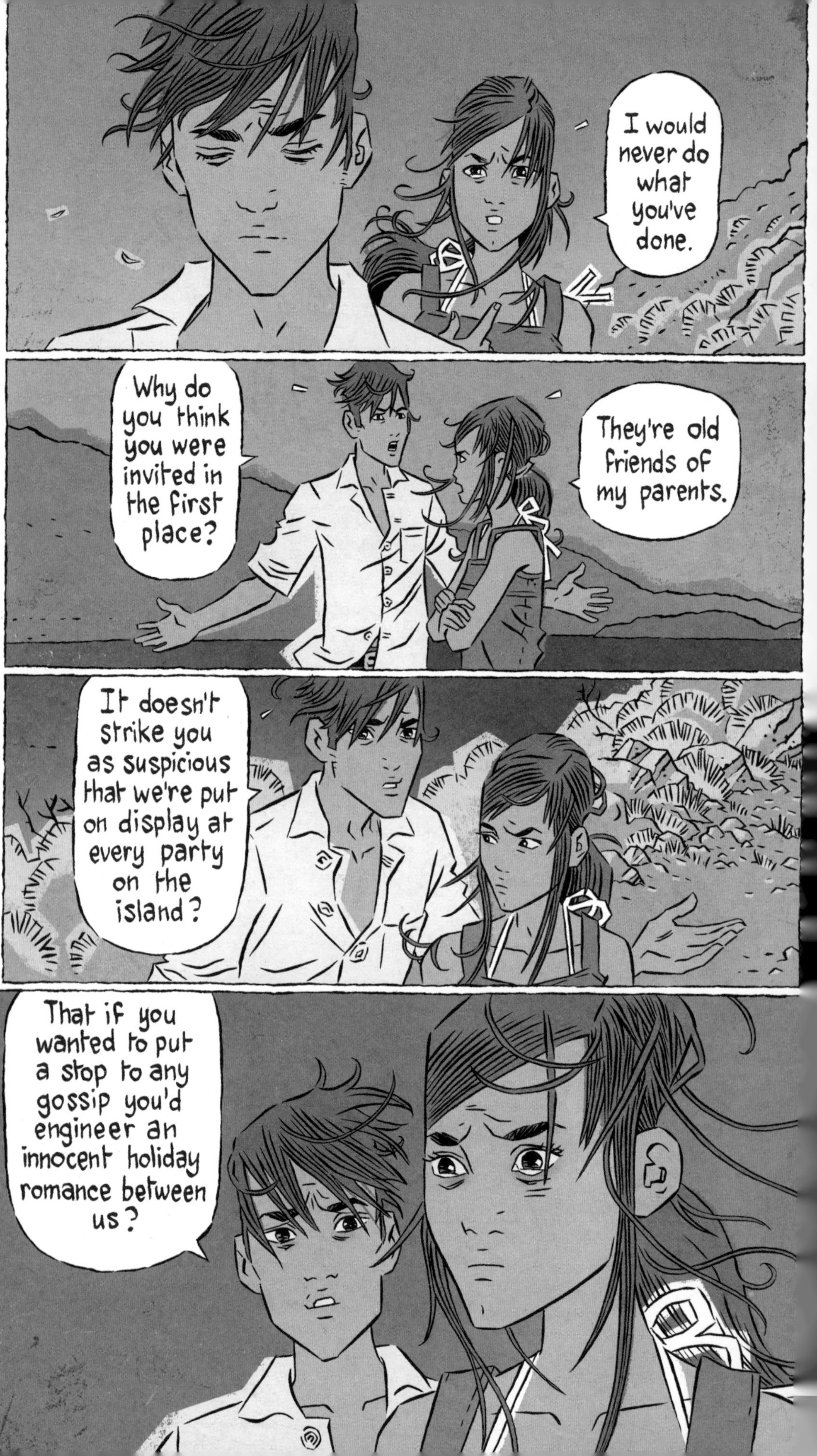
I would never do what you've done.
Why do you think you were invited in the first place?
They're old friends of my parents.
It doesn't strike you as suspicious that we're put on display at every party on the island?
That if you wanted to put a stop to any gossip you'd engineer an innocent holiday romance between us?

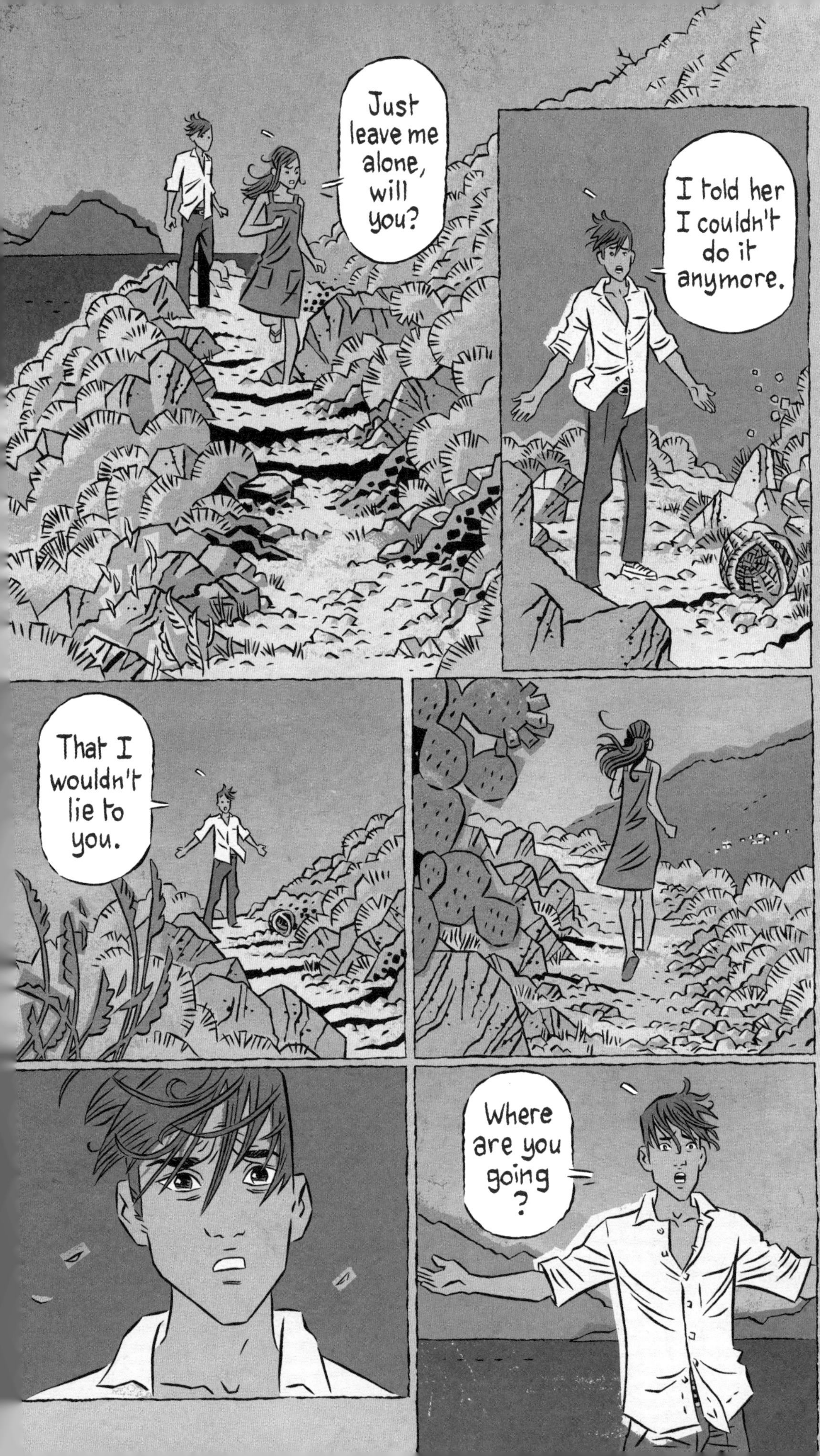
Just leave me alone, will you?
I told her I couldn't do it anymore.
That I wouldn't lie to you.
Where are you going ?

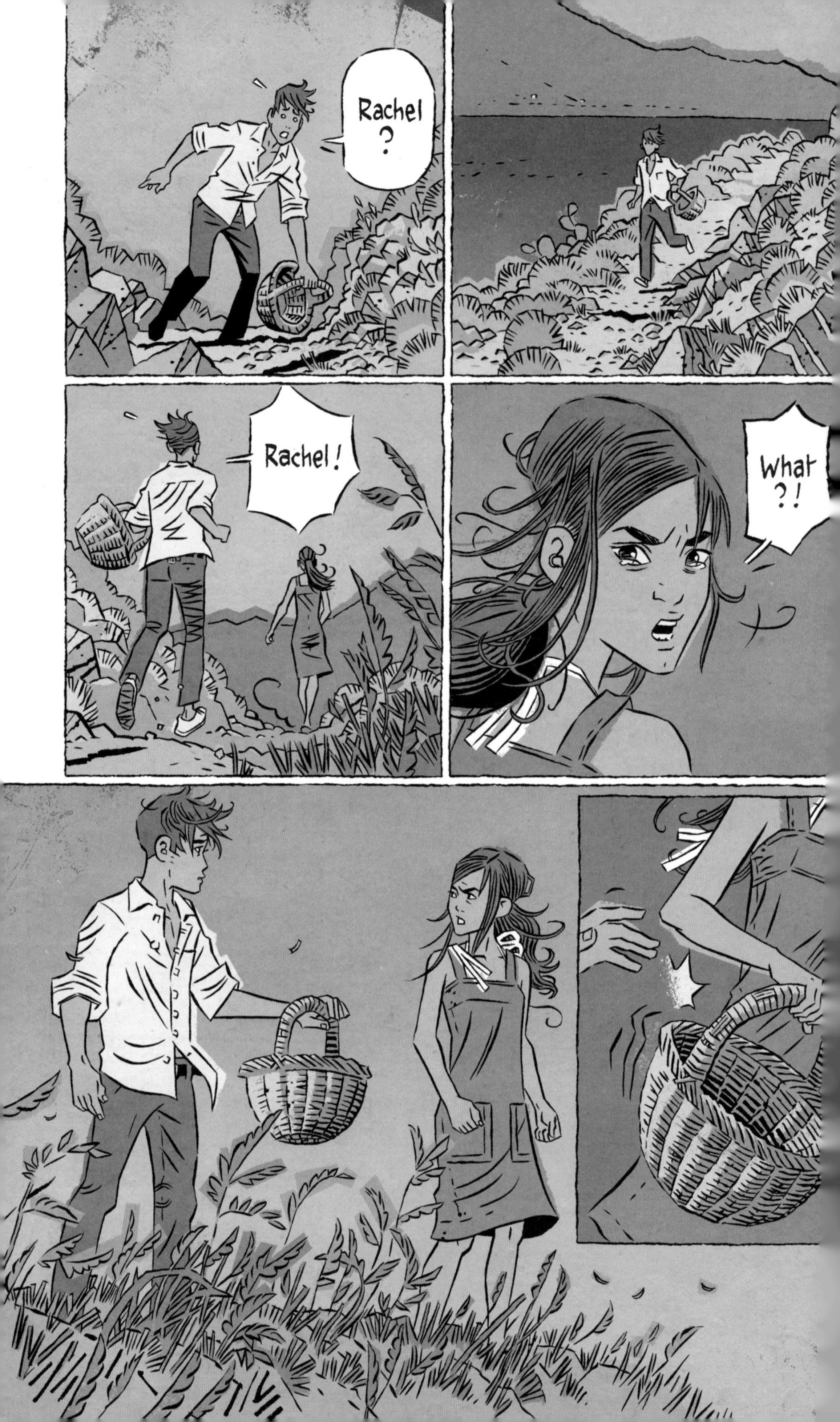
Rachel ?
Rachel !
What ?!

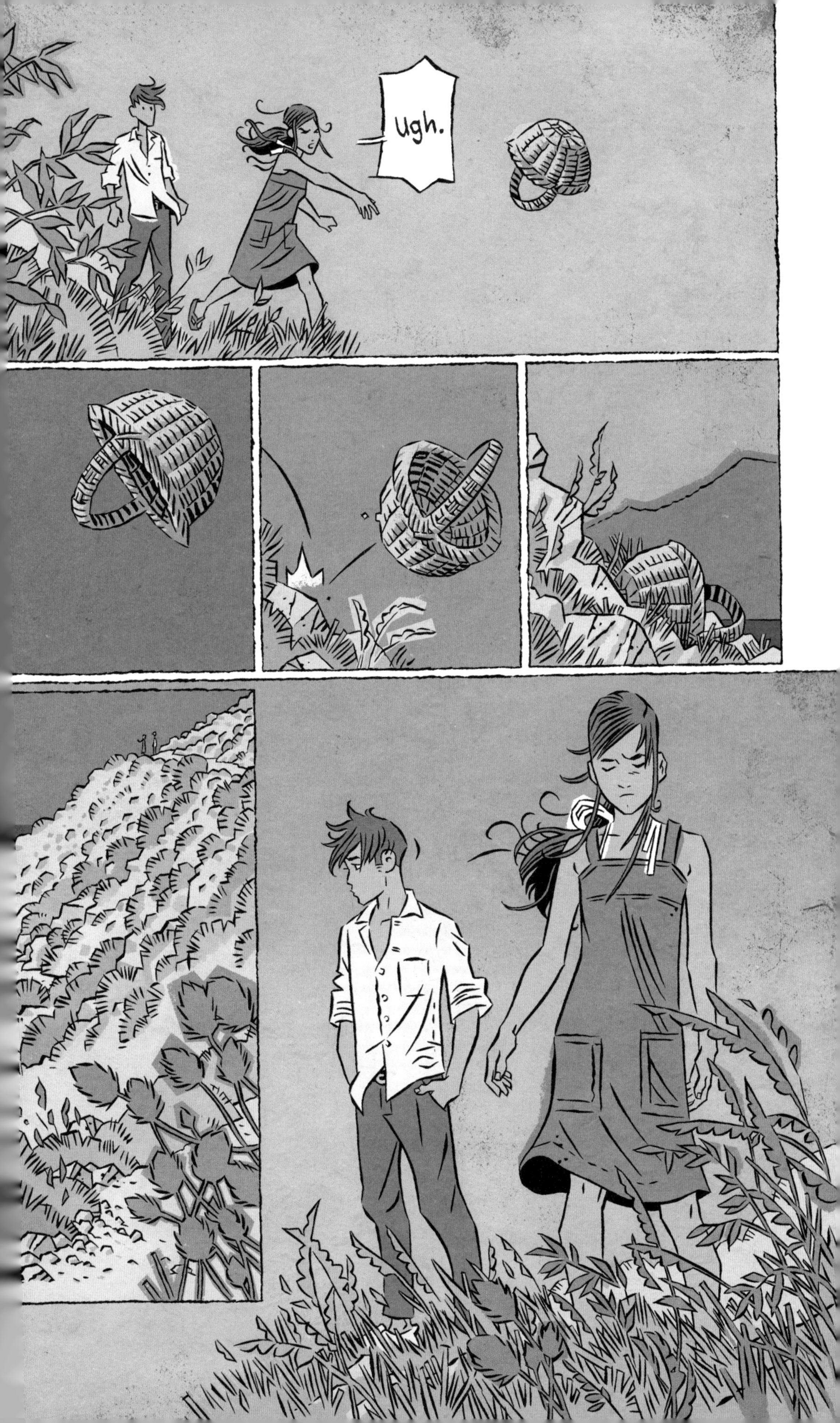
Ugh.

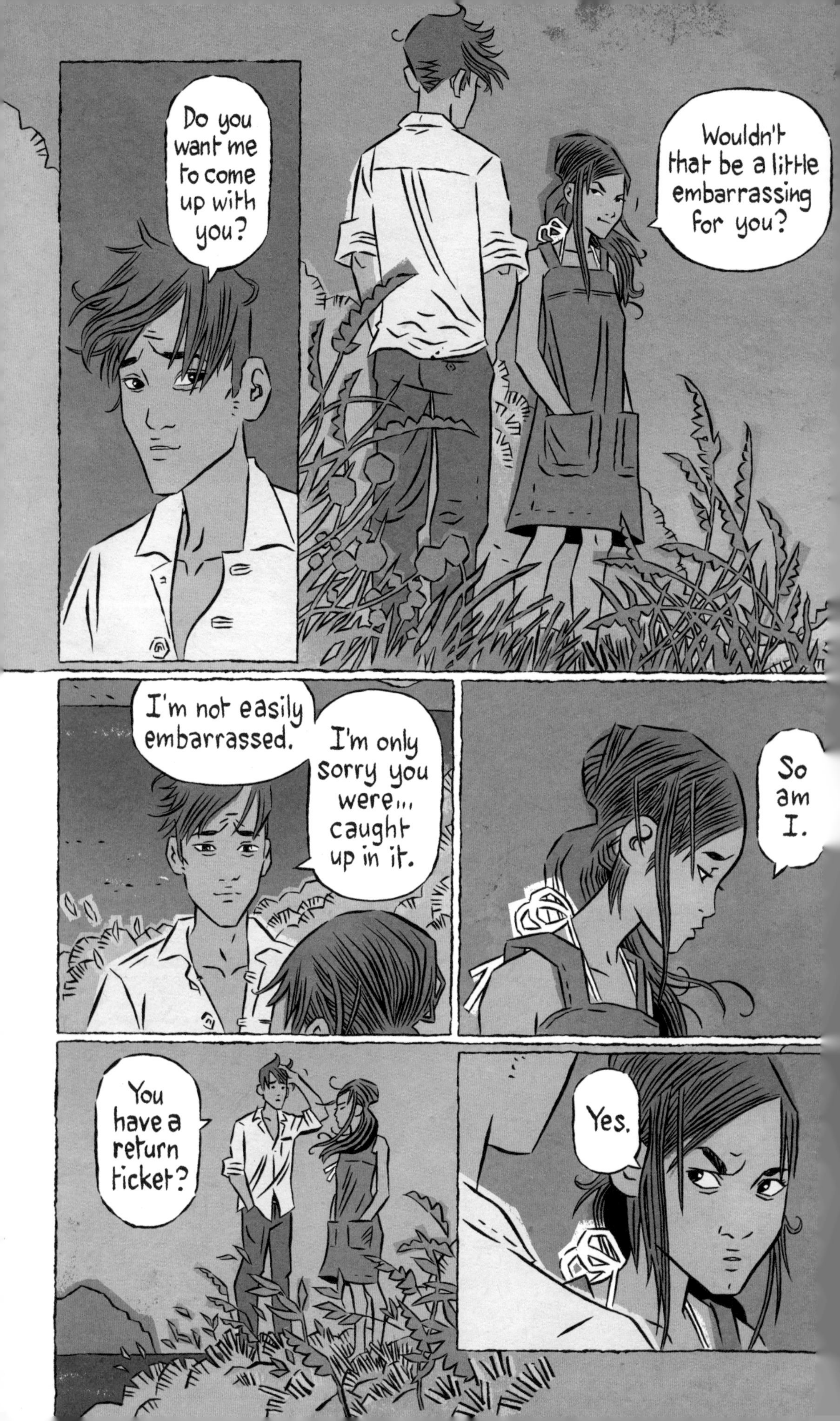
Do you want me to come up with you?
Wouldn't that be a little embarrassing for you?
I'm not easily embarrassed.
I'm only sorry you were... caught up in it.
So am I.
You have a return ticket?
Yes.

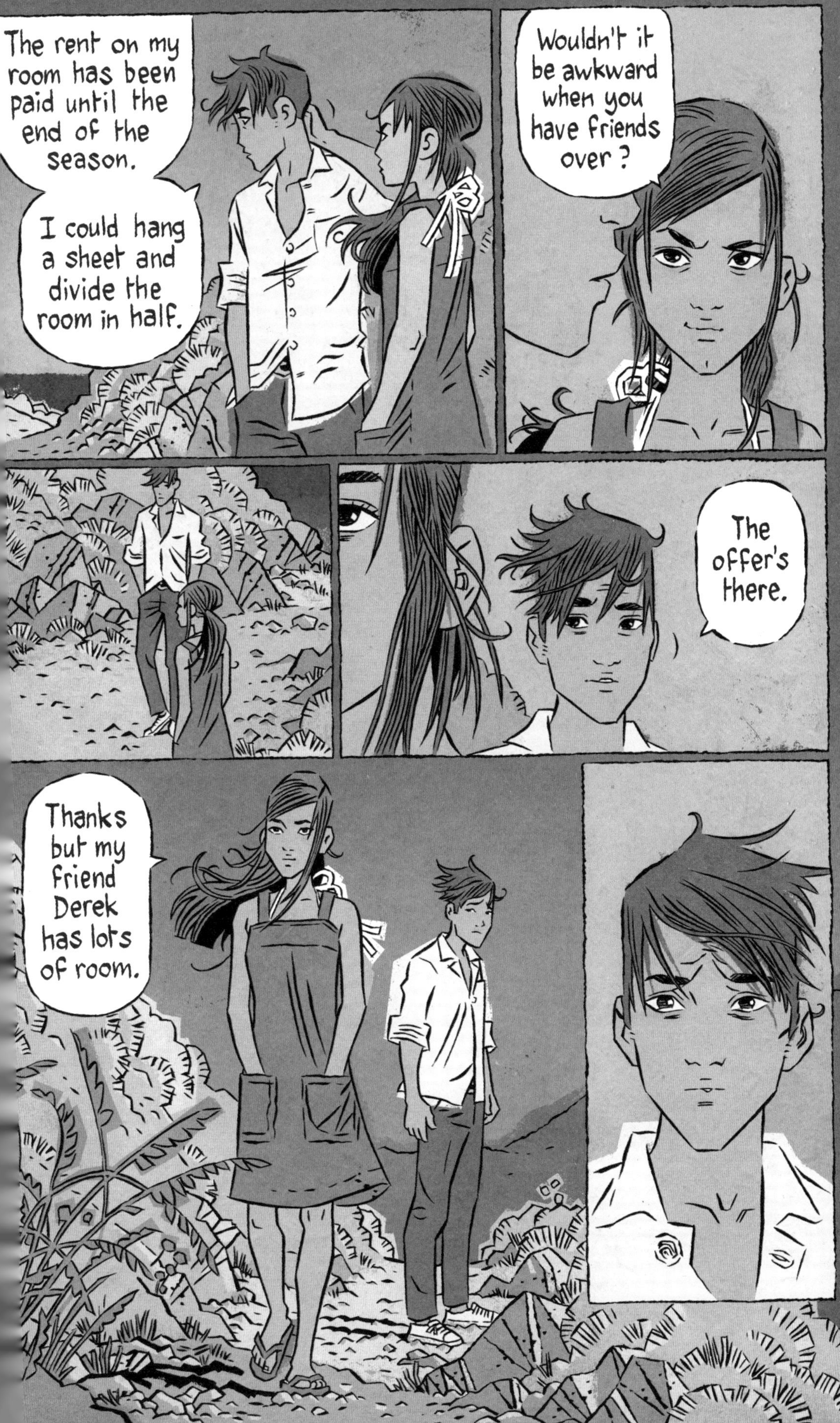
The rent on my room has been paid until the end of the season.
I could hang a sheet and divide the room in half.
Wouldn't it be awkward when you have friends over?
The offer's there.
Thanks but my friend Derek has lots of room.

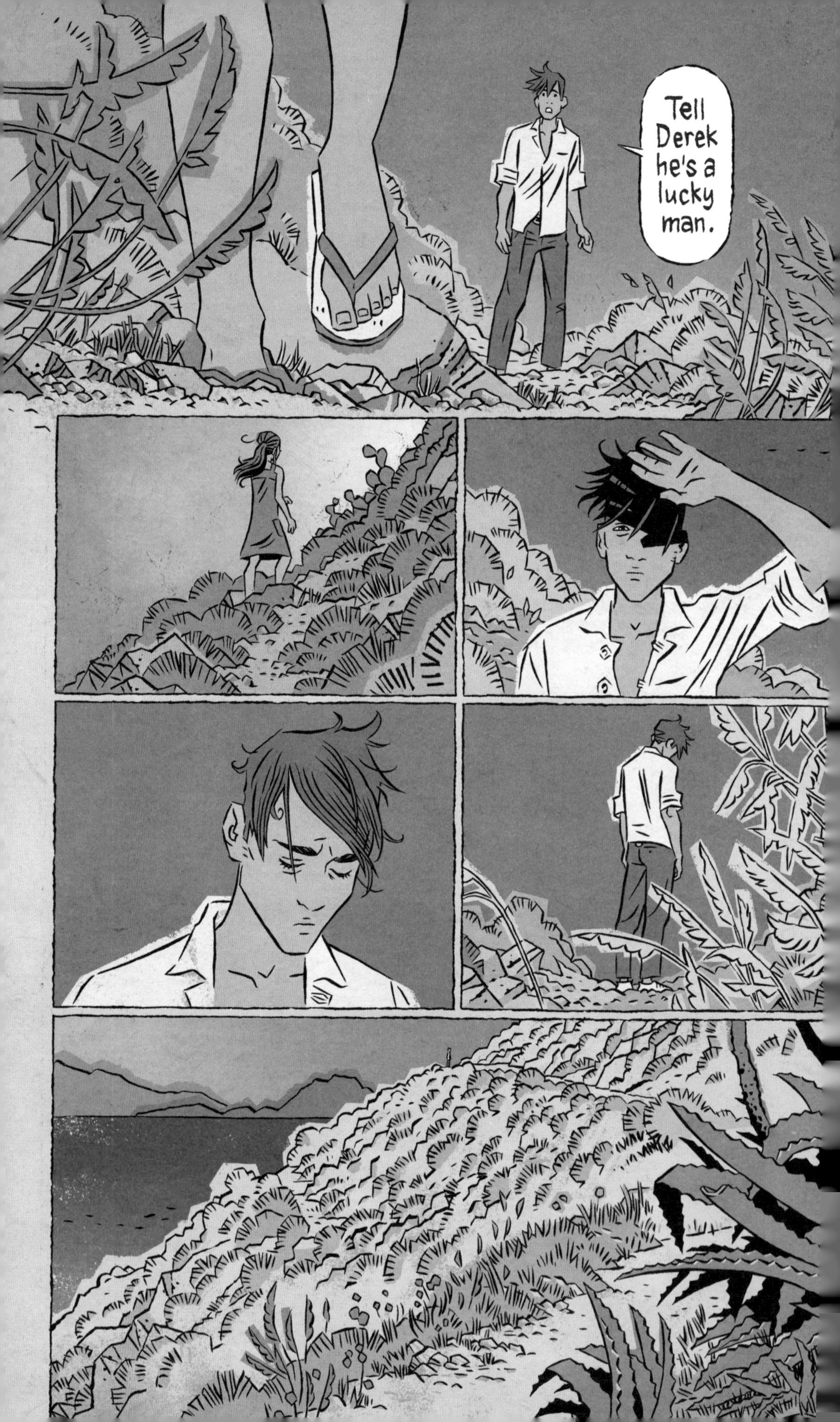
Tell Derek he's a lucky man.

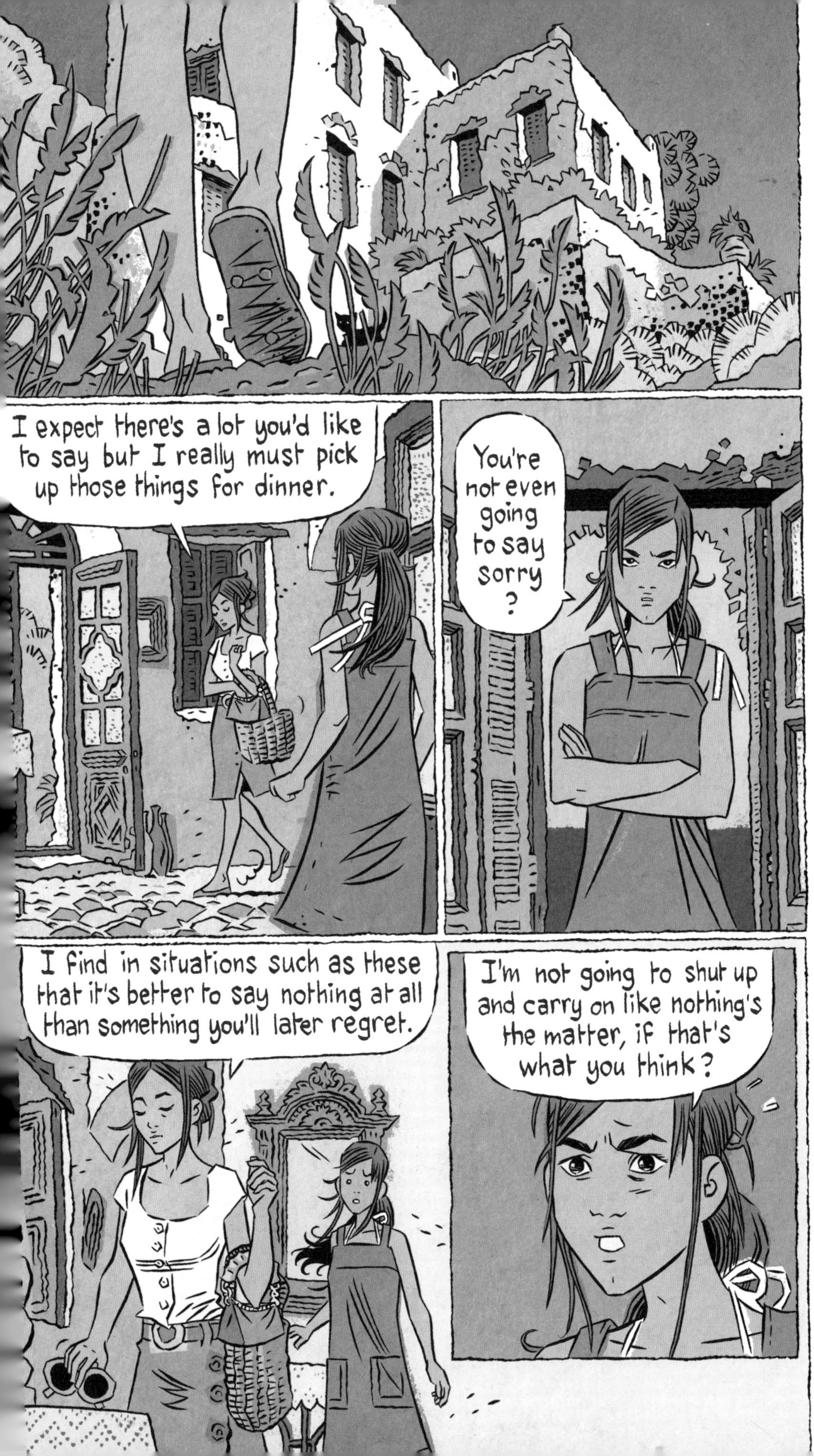
I expect there's a lot you'd like to say but I really must pick up those things for dinner.
You're not even going to say sorry ?
I find in situations such as these that it's better to say nothing at all than something you'll later regret.
I'm not going to shut up and carry on like nothing's the matter, if that's what you think ?

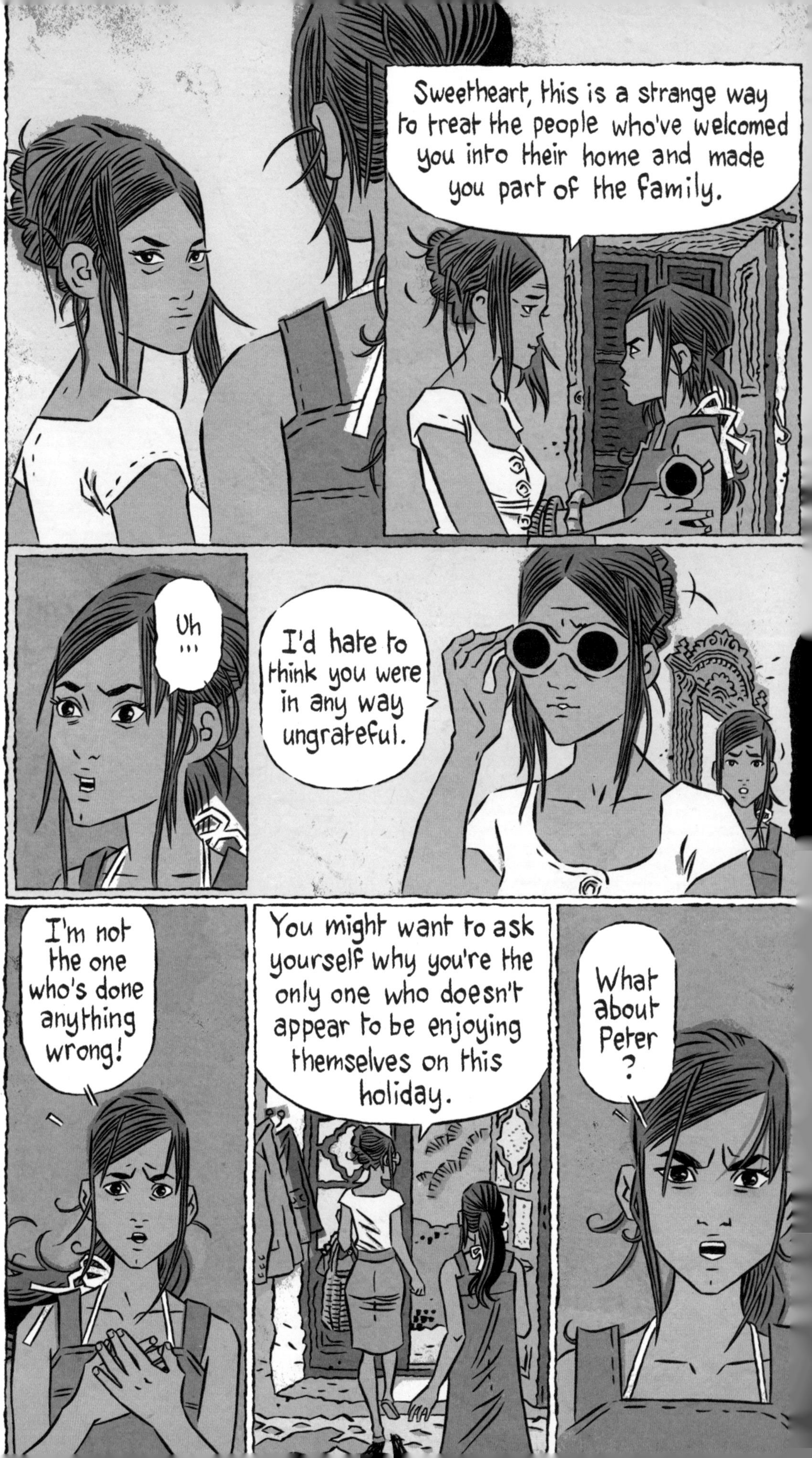
Sweetheart, this is a strange way to treat the people who've welcomed you into their home and made you part of the family.
Uh ...
I'd hate to think you were in any way ungrateful.
I'm not the one who's done anything wrong!
You might want to ask yourself why you're the only one who doesn't appear to be enjoying themselves on this holiday.
What about Peter ?

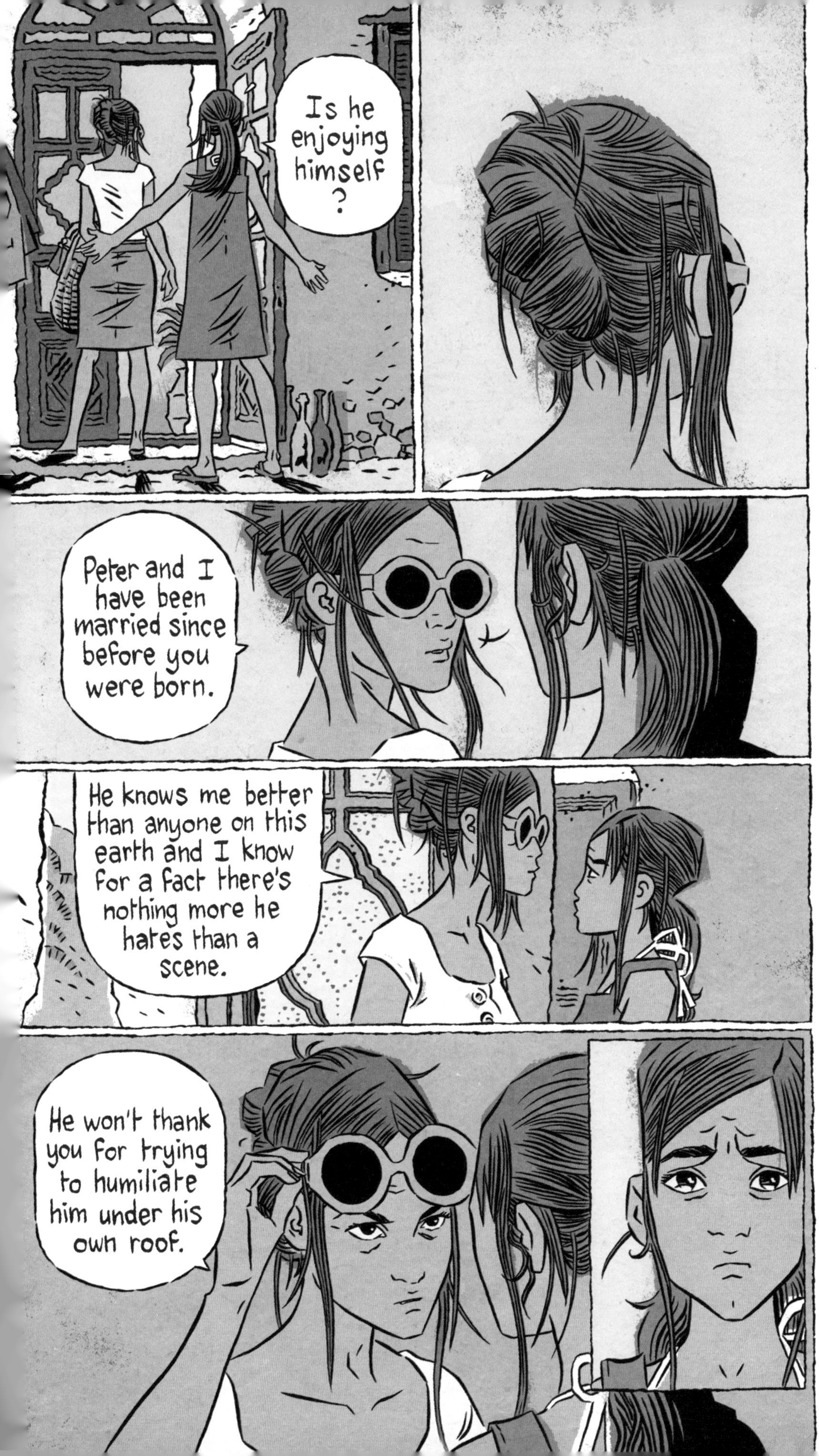
Is he enjoying himself ?
Peter and I have been married since before you were born.
He knows me better than anyone on this earth and I know for a fact there's nothing more he hates than a scene.
He won't thank you for trying to humiliate him under his own roof.

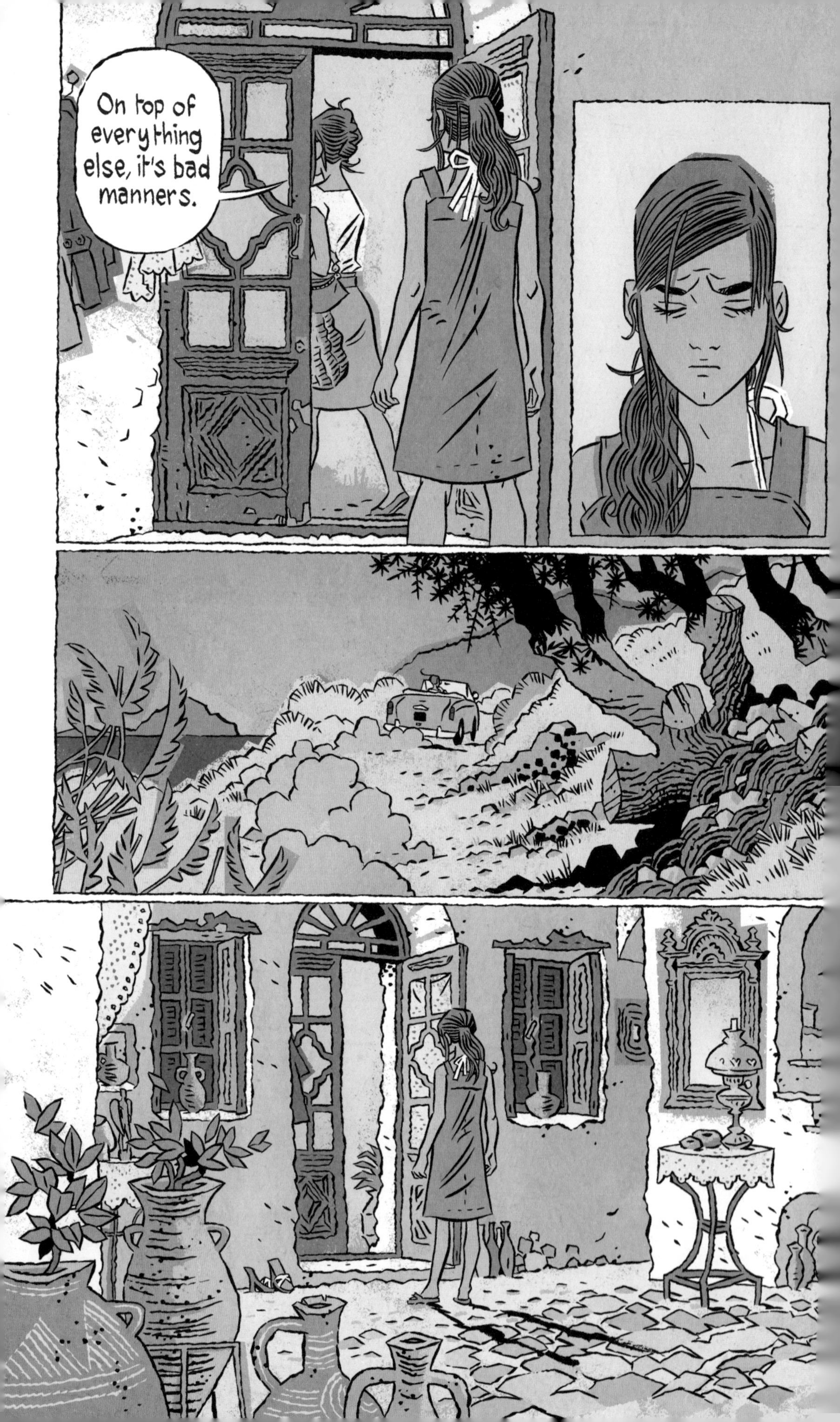
On top of everything else, it's bad manners.

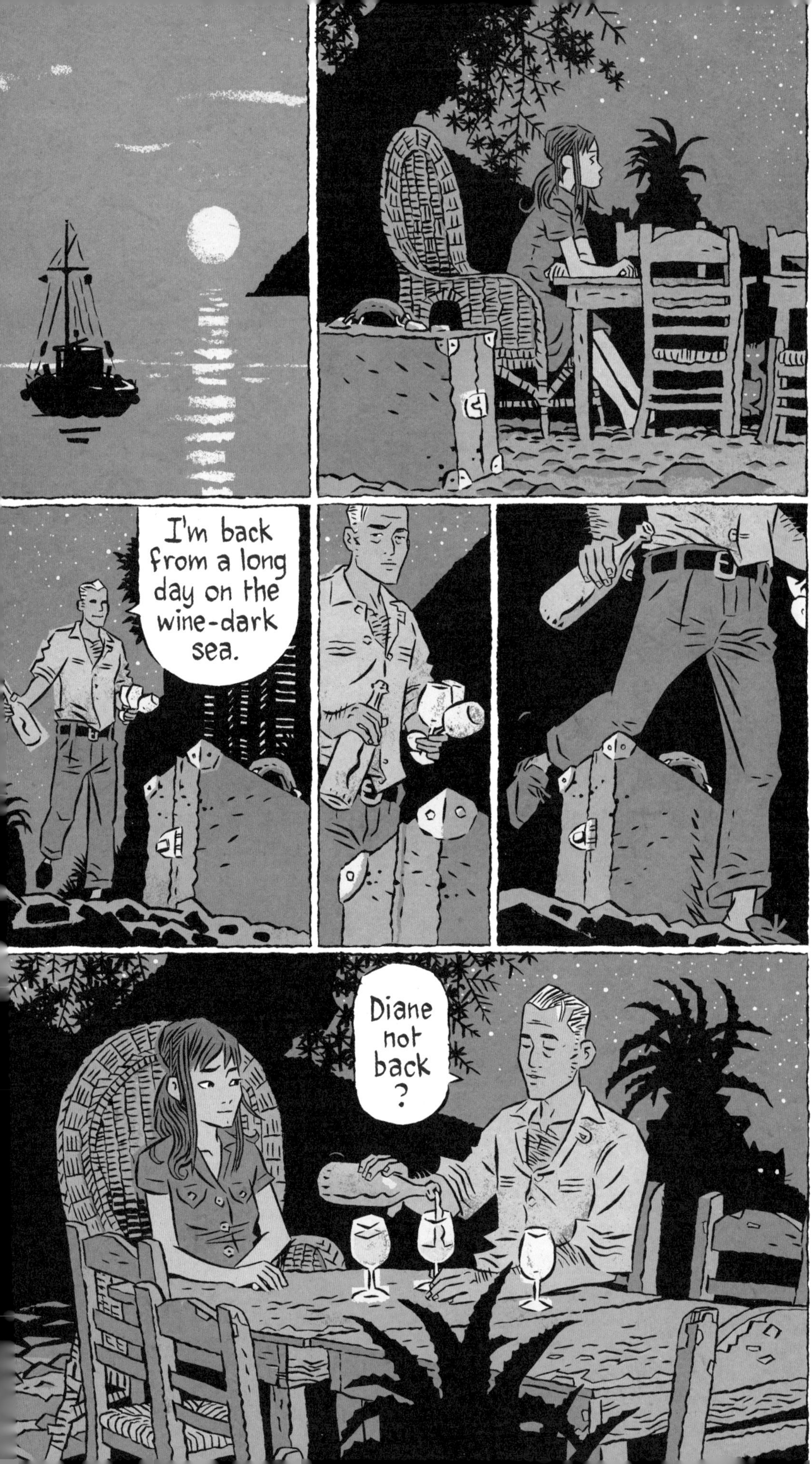
I'm back from a long day on the wine-dark sea.
Diane not back?

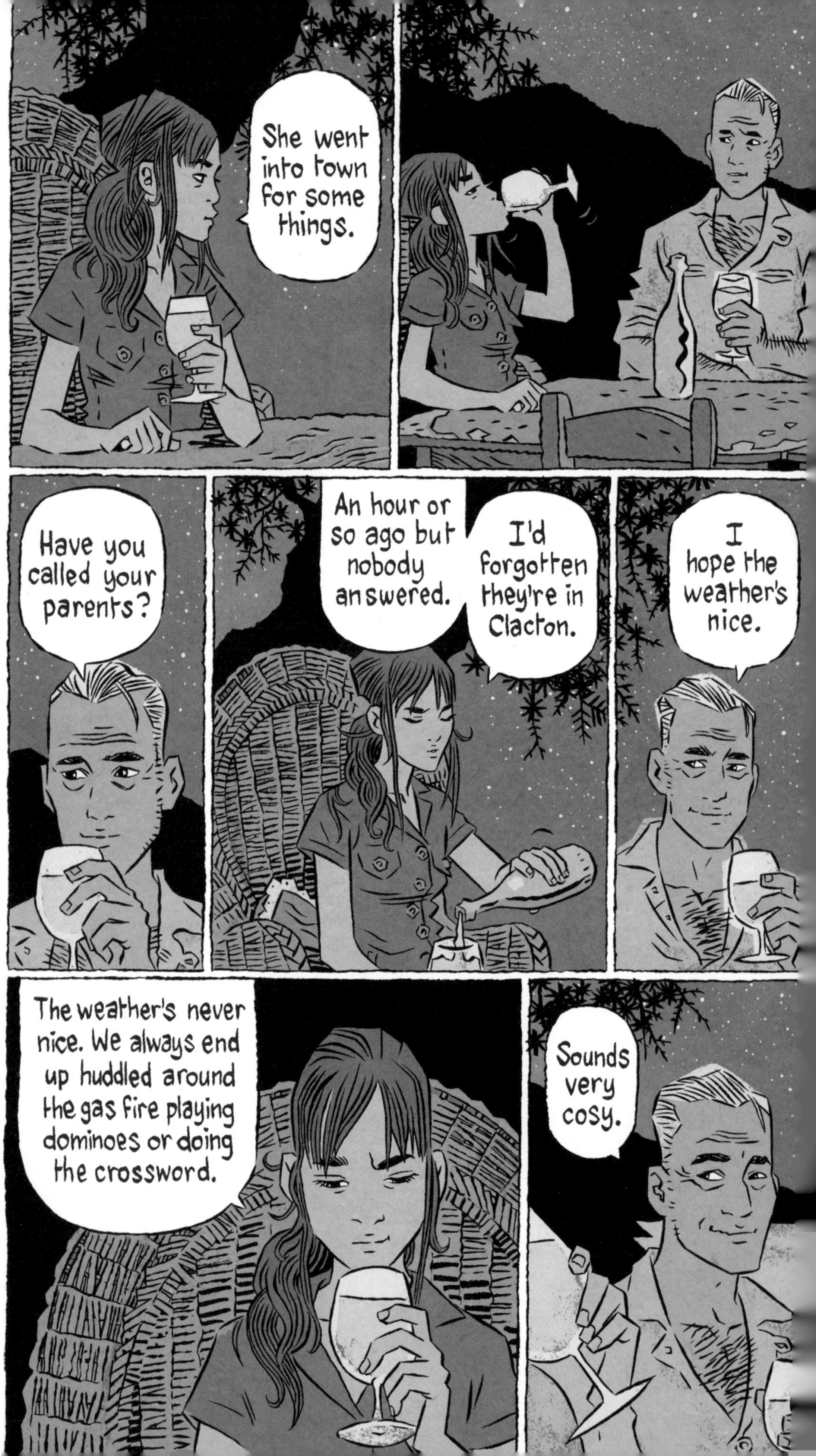
She went into town for some things.
Have you called your parents?
An hour or so ago but nobody answered.
I'd forgotten they're in Clacton.
I hope the weather's nice.
The weather's never nice. We always end up huddled around the gas fire playing dominoes or doing the crossword.
Sounds very cosy.

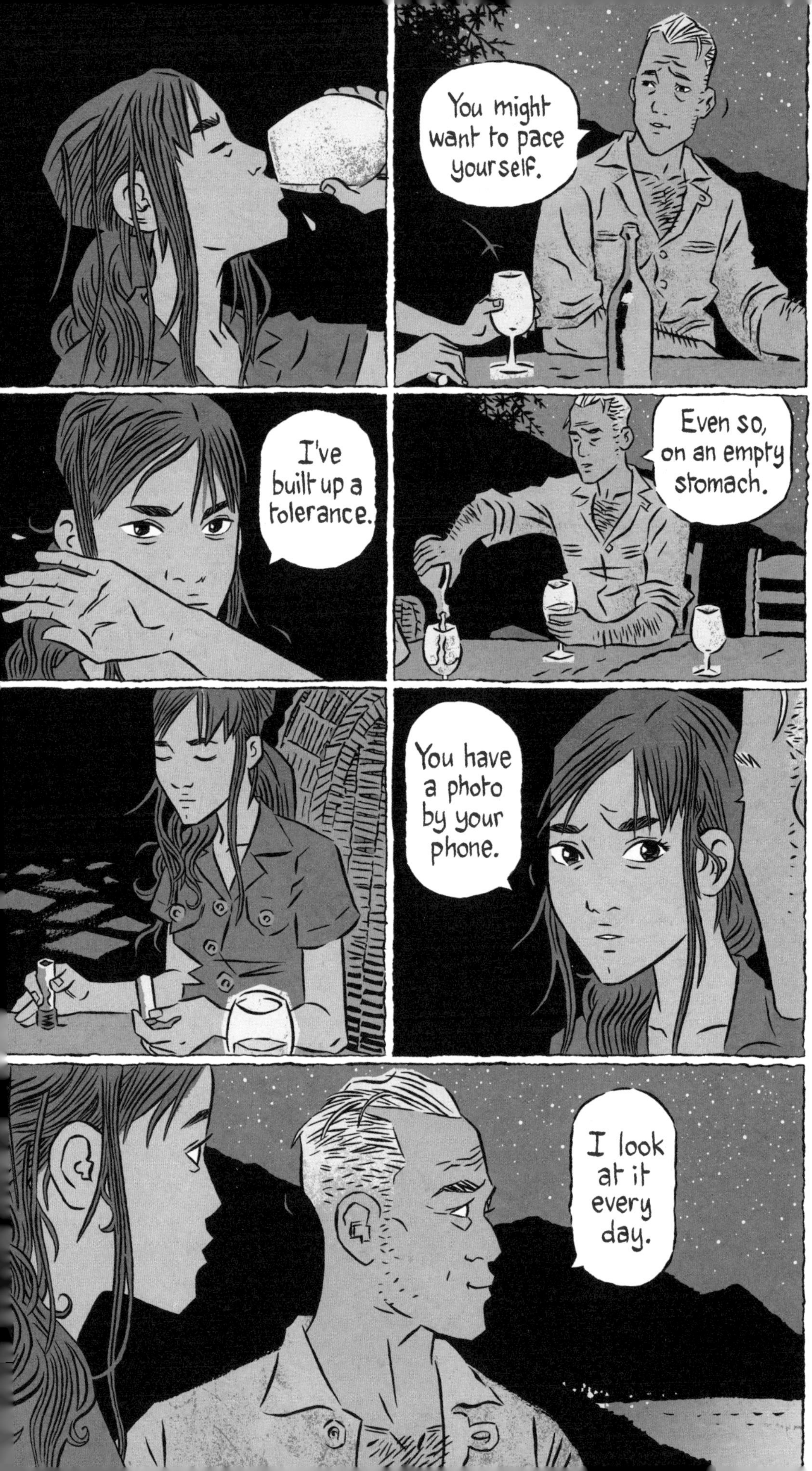
You might want to pace yourself.
I've built up a tolerance.
Even so, on an empty stomach.
You have a photo by your phone.
I look at it every day.

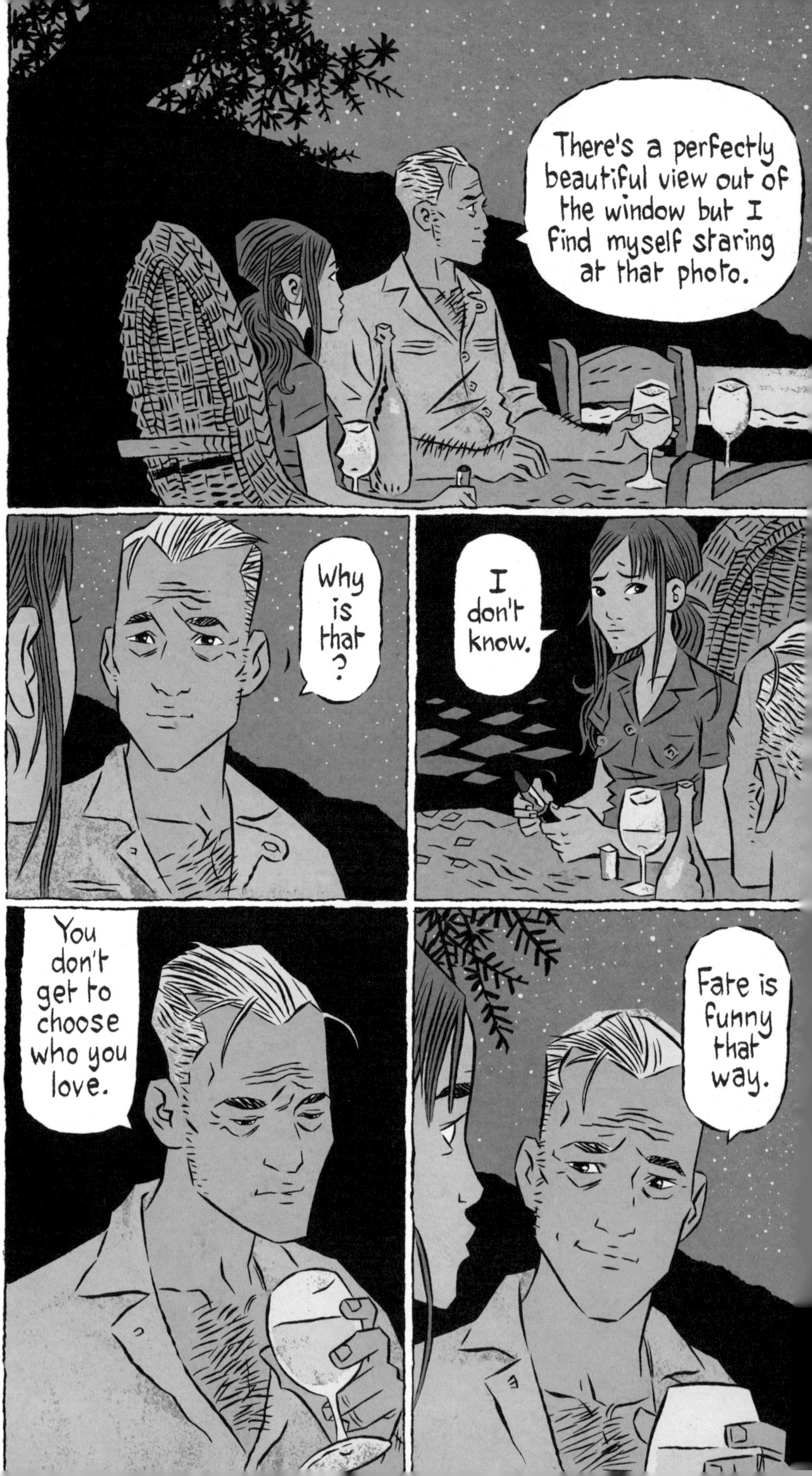
There's a perfectly beautiful view out of the window but I find myself staring at that photo.
Why is that?
I don't know.
You don't get to choose who you love.
Fate is funny that way.

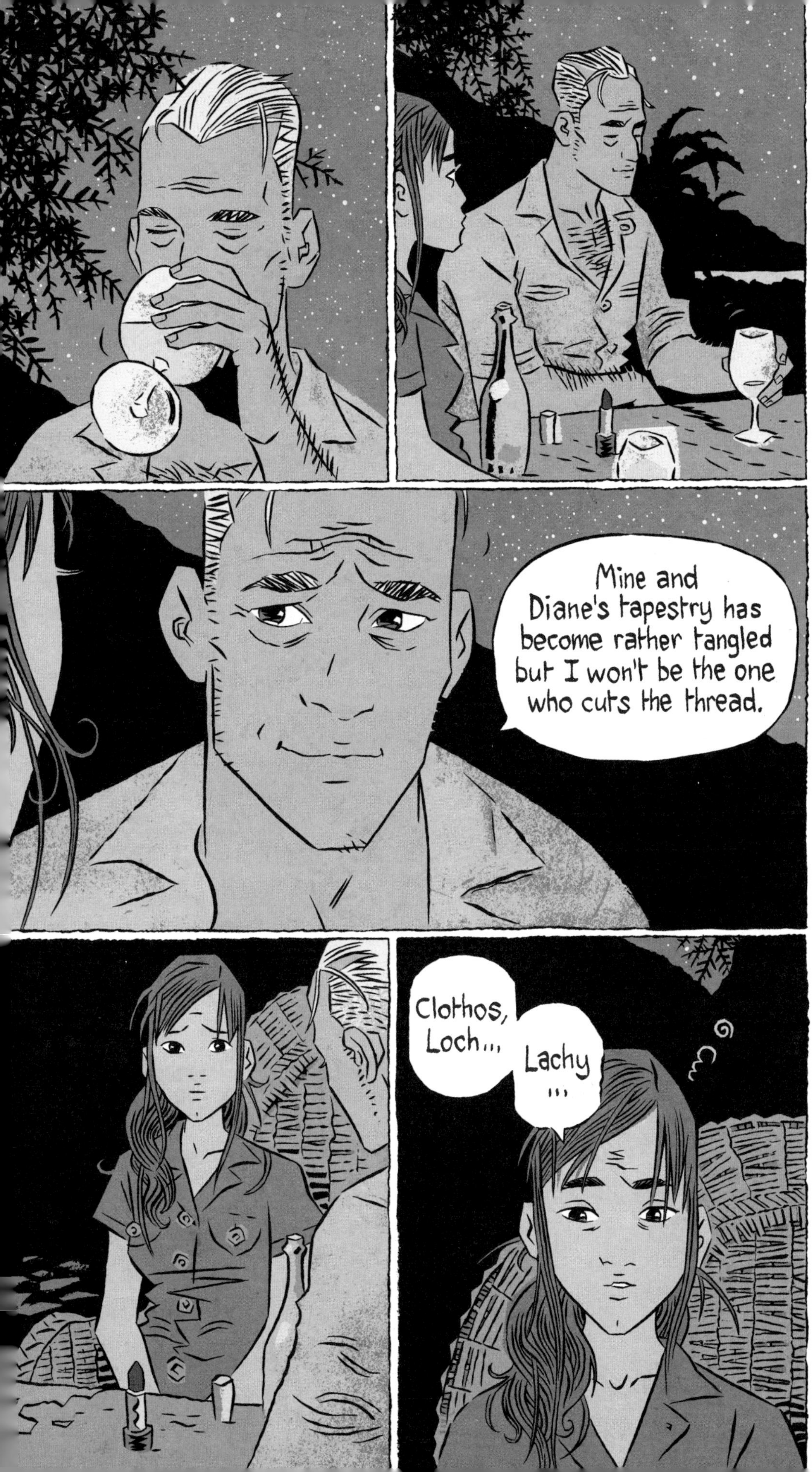
Mine and Diane's tapestry has become rather tangled but I won't be the one who cuts the thread.
Clothos, Loch...
Lachy ...

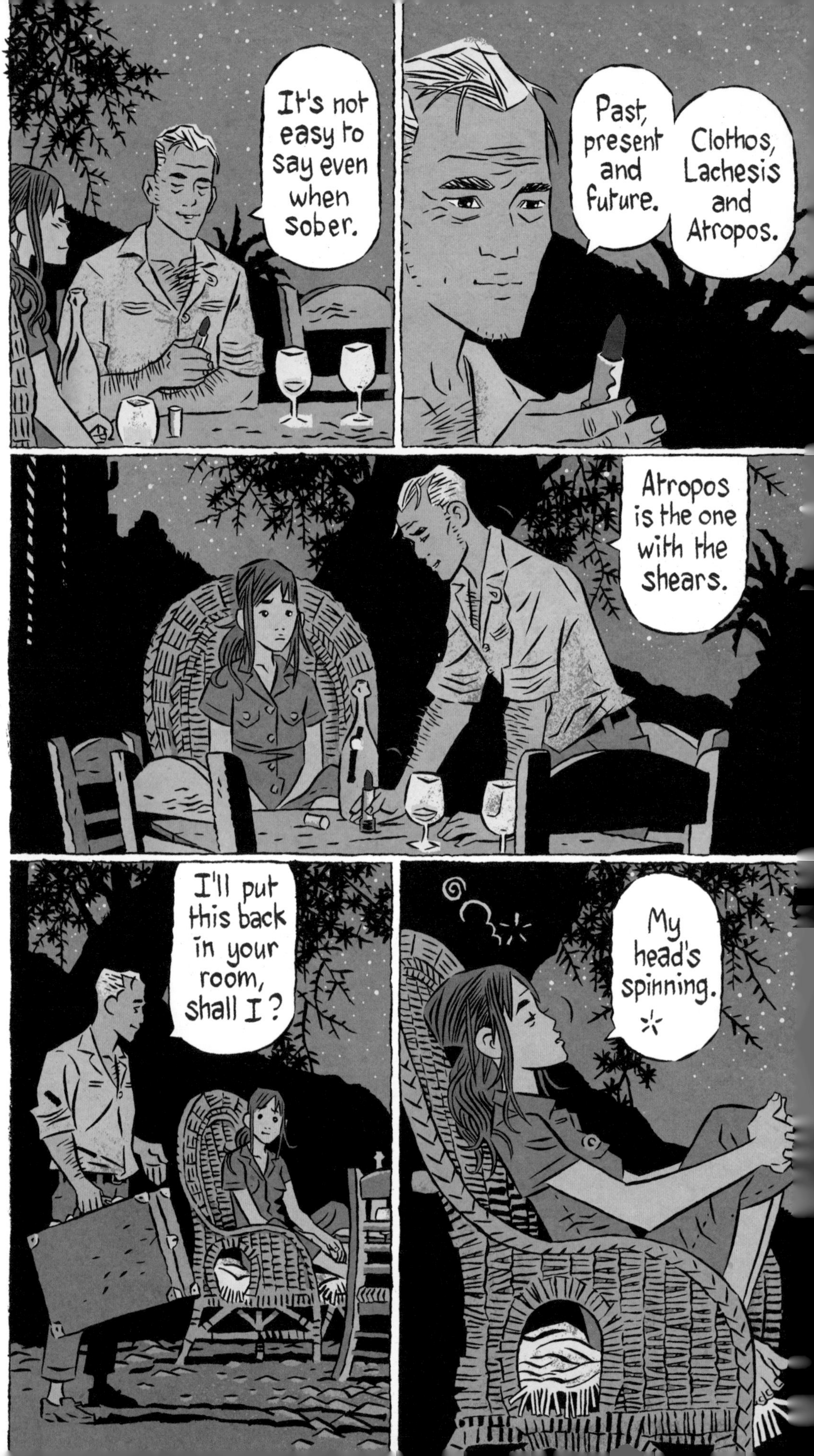
It's not easy to say even when sober.
Past, present and future.
Clothos, Lachesis and Atropos.
Atropos is the one with the shears.
I'll put this back in your room, shall I?
My head's spinning.

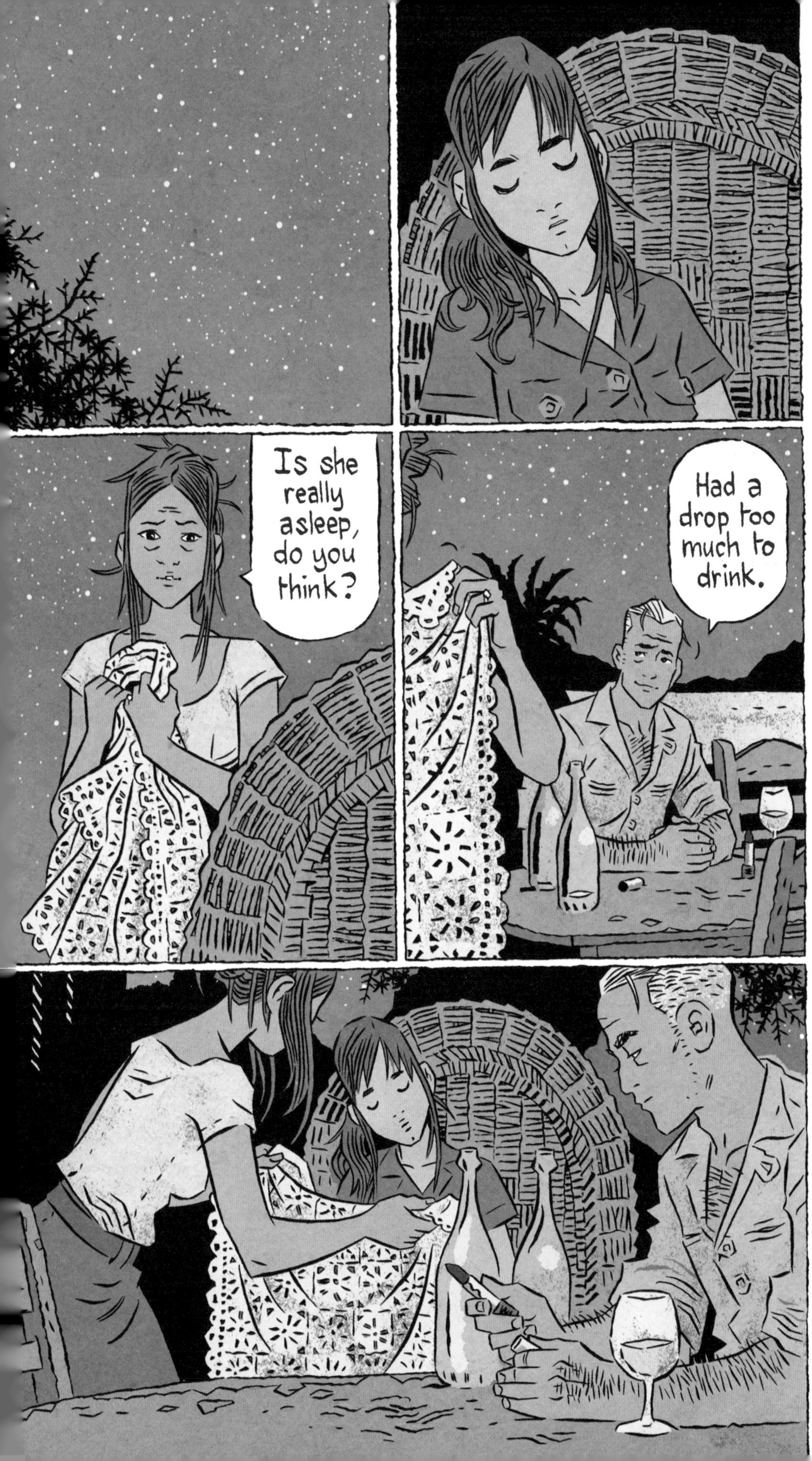
Is she really asleep, do you think?
Had a drop too much to drink.

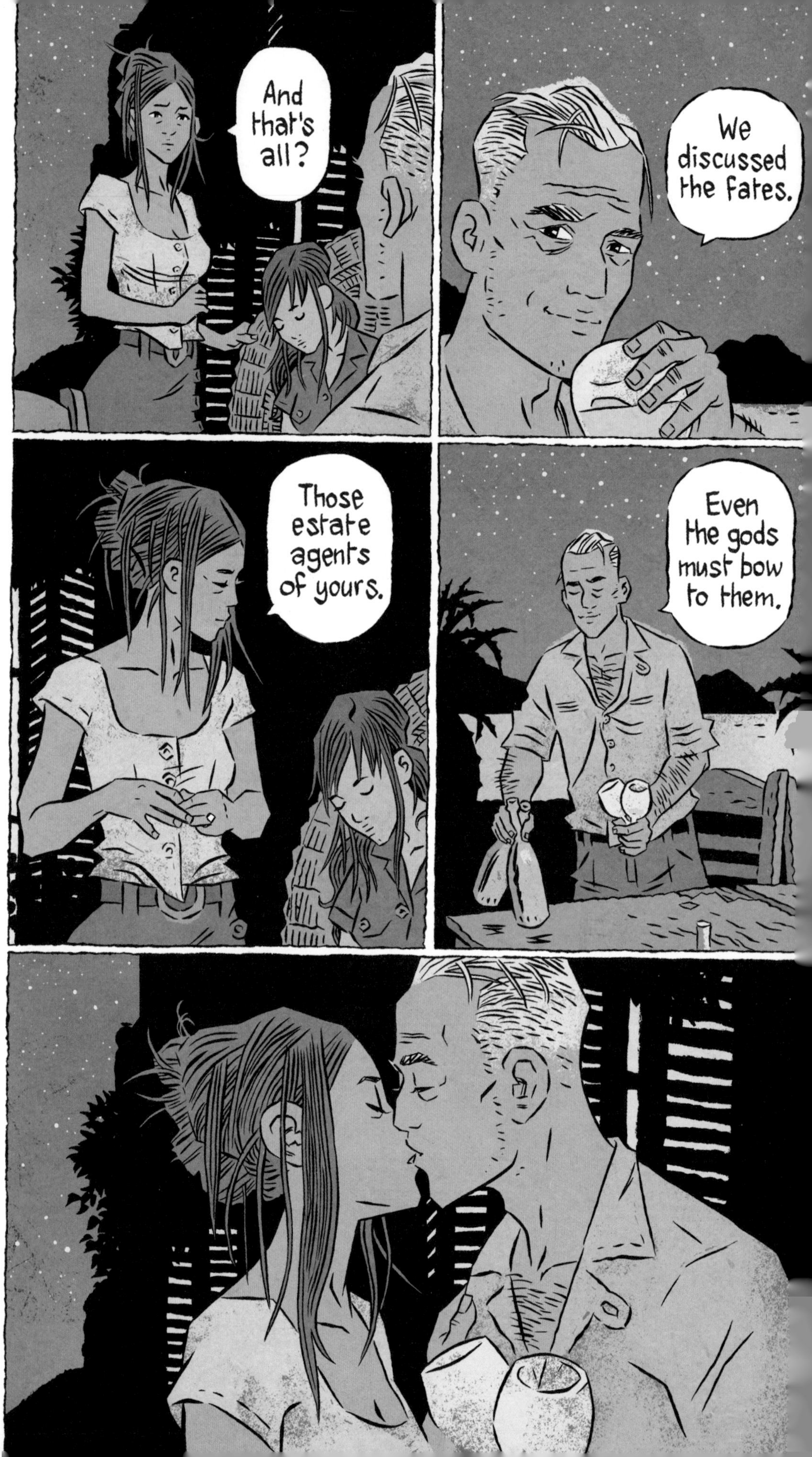
And that's all?
We discussed the fates.
Those estate agents of yours.
Even the gods must bow to them.

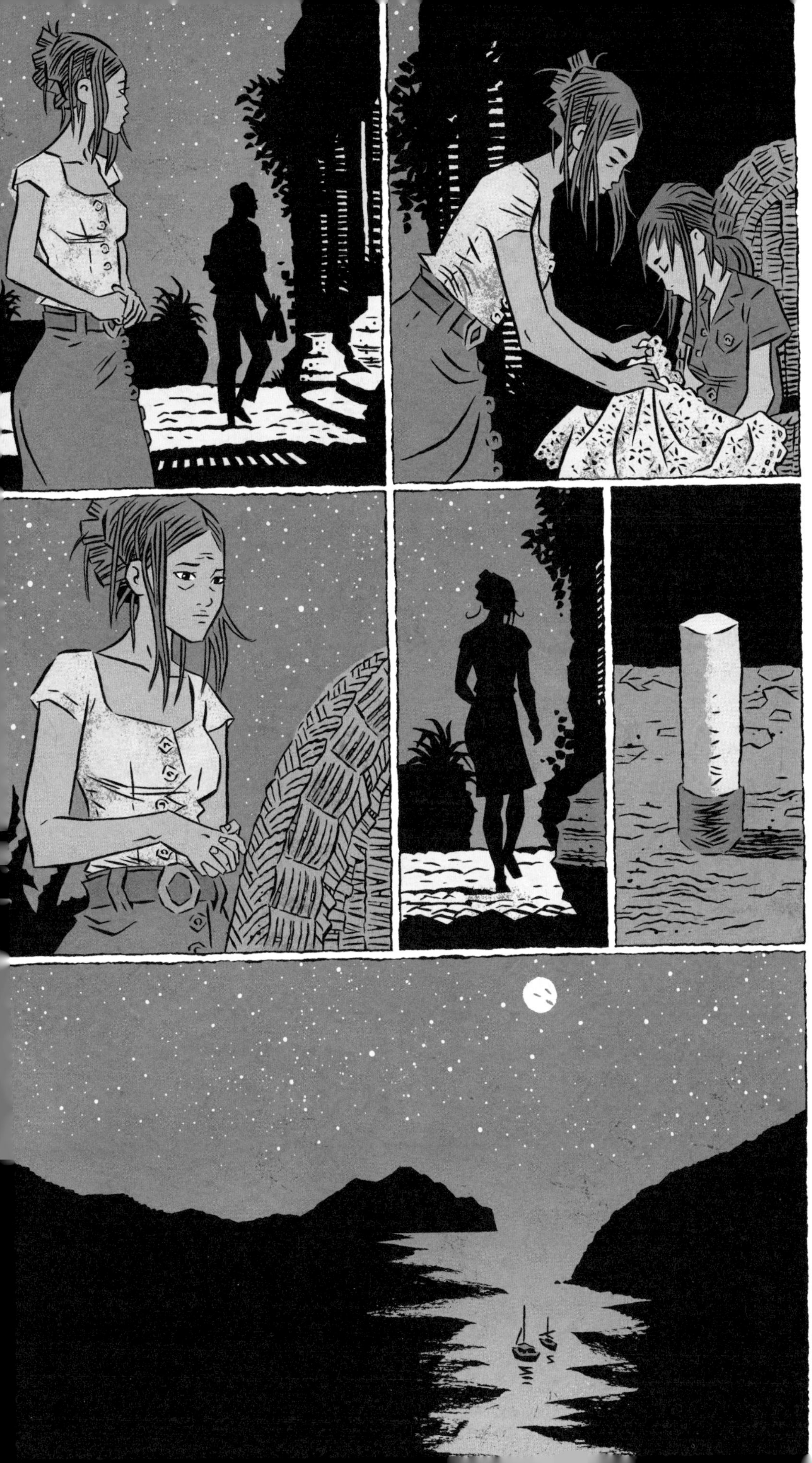

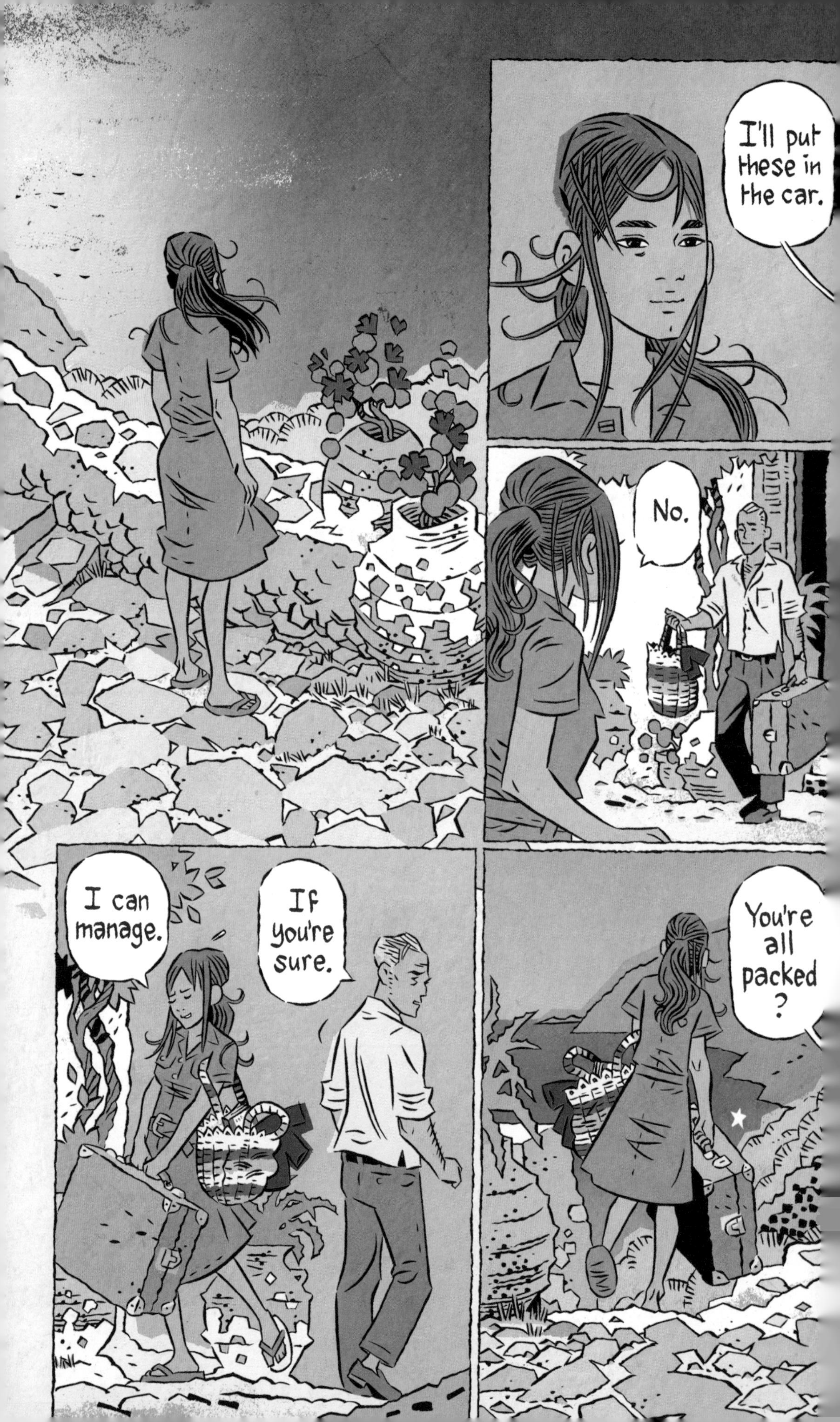
I'll put these in the car.
No.
I can manage.
If you're sure.
You're all packed ?

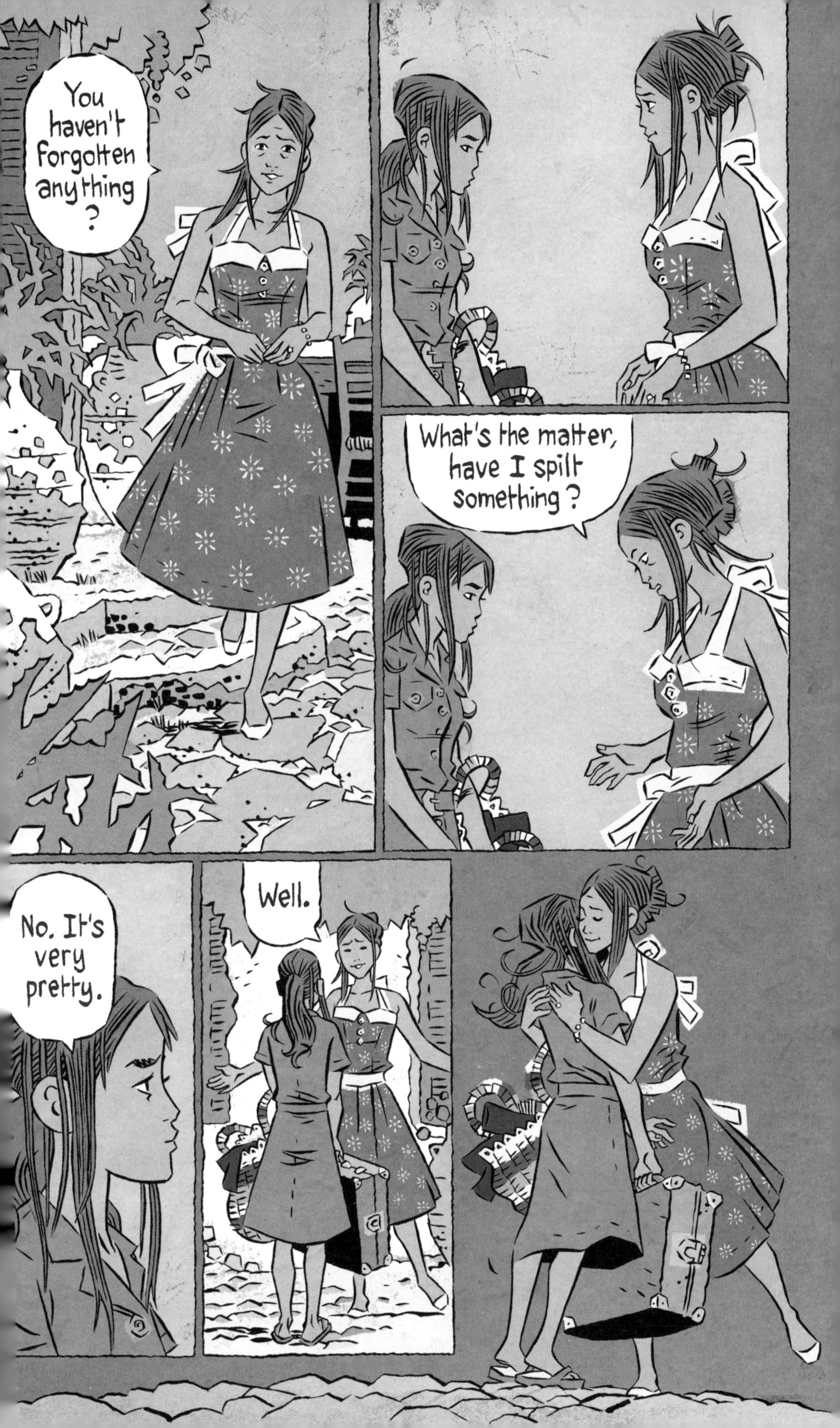
You haven't forgotten anything ?
What's the matter, have I spilt something ?
No. It's very pretty.
Well.

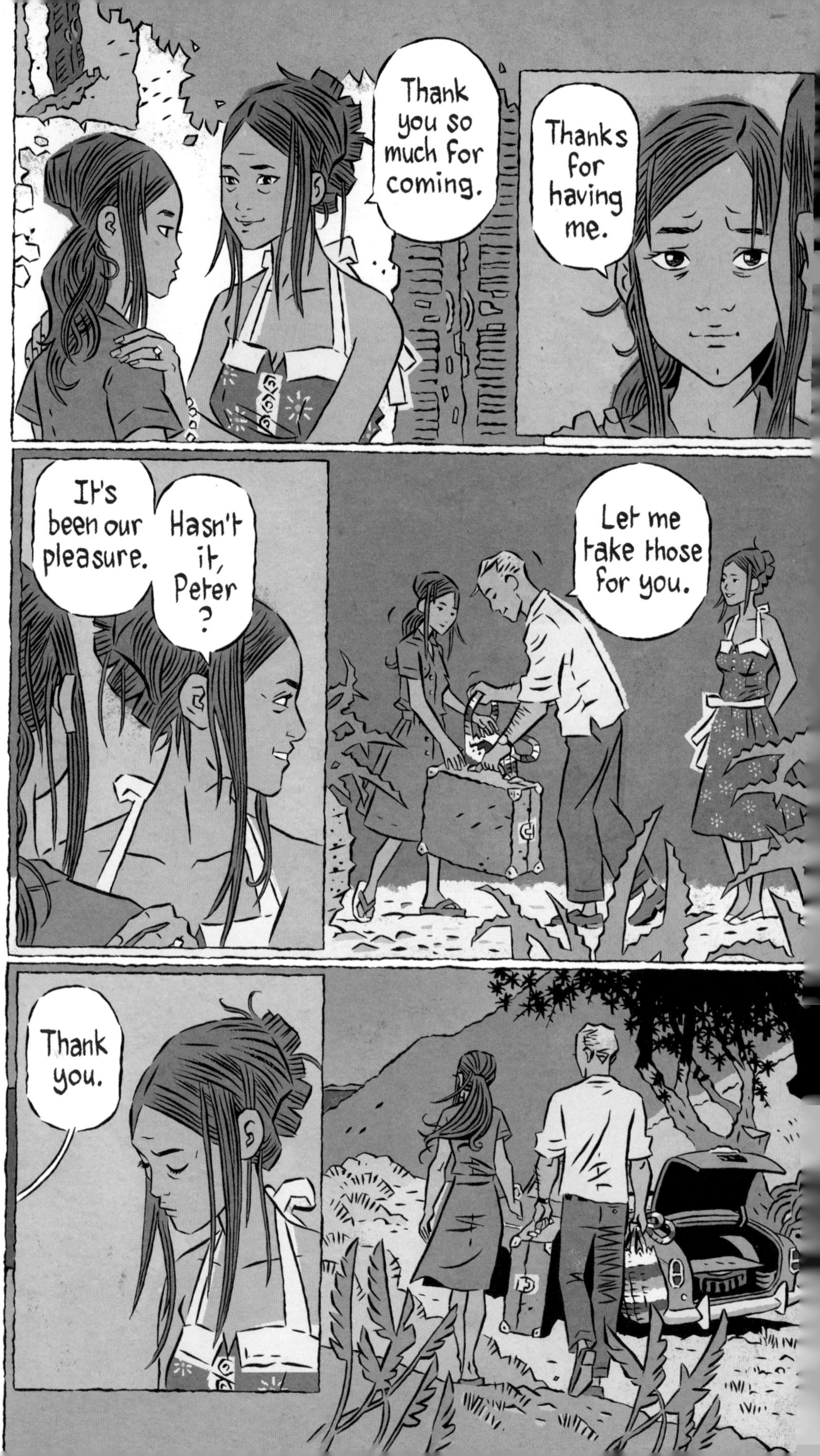
Thank you so much for coming.
Thanks for having me.
It's been our pleasure.
Hasn't it, Peter?
Let me take those for you.
Thank you.

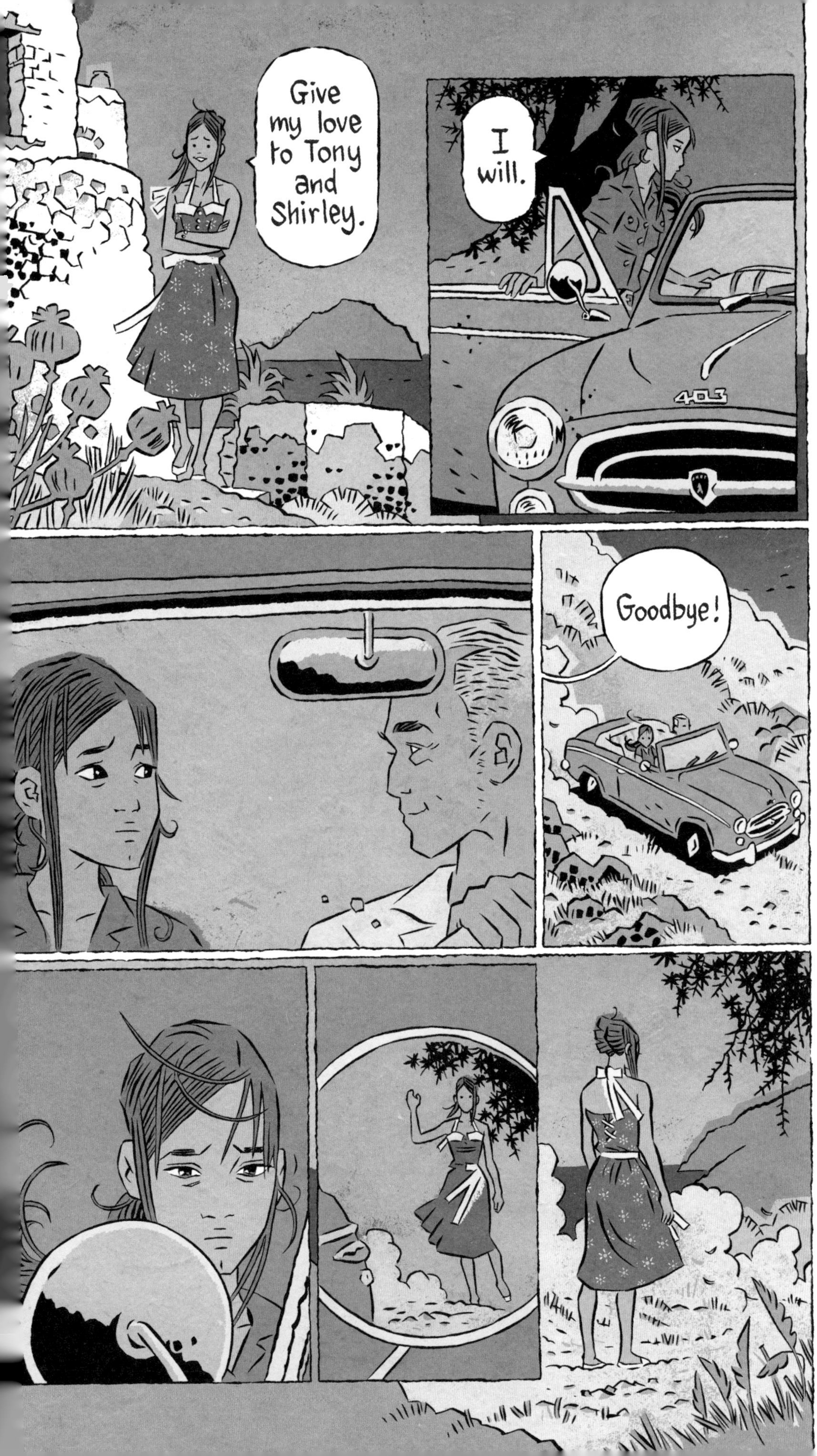
Give my love to Tony and Shirley.
I will.
403
Goodbye!

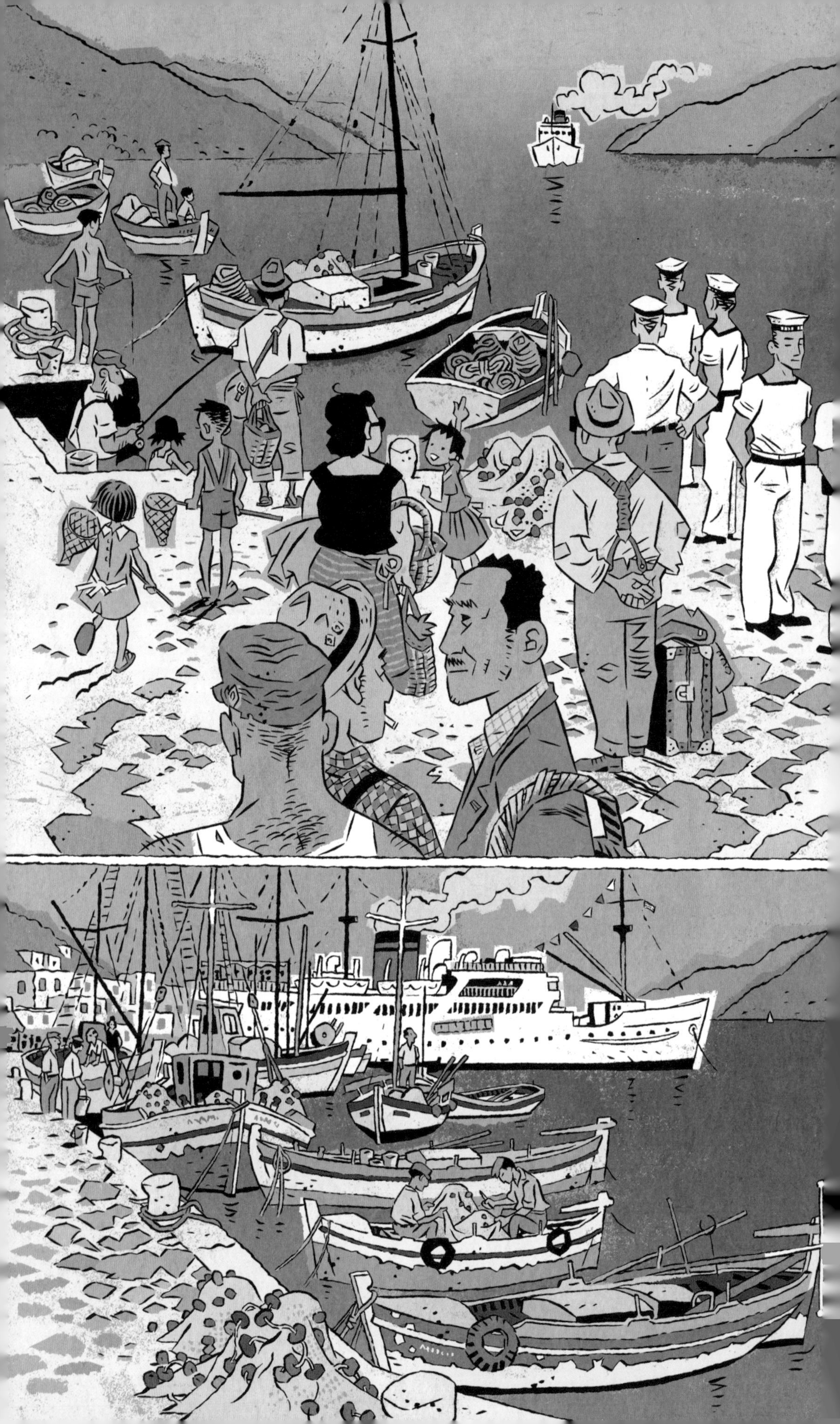

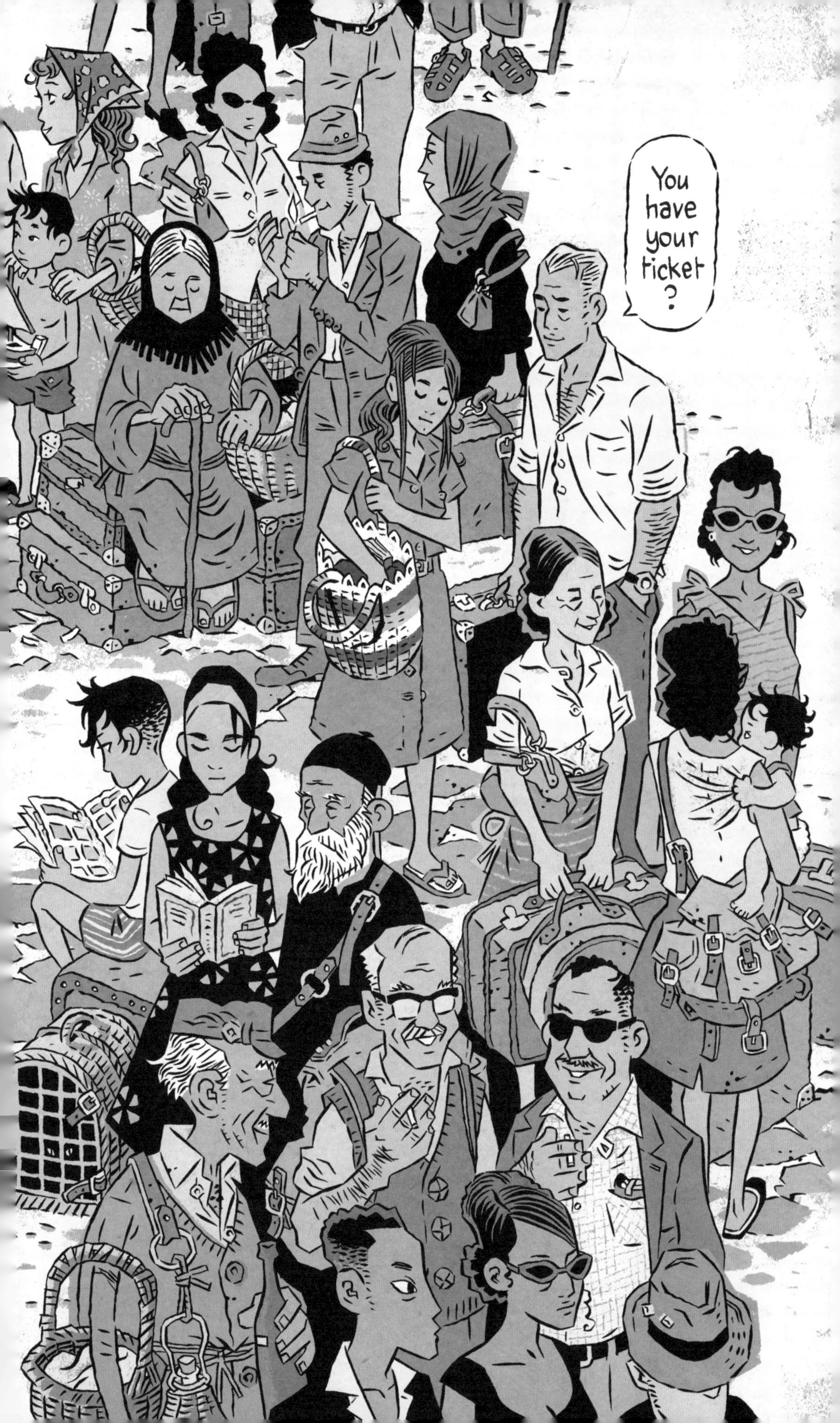
You have your ticket?

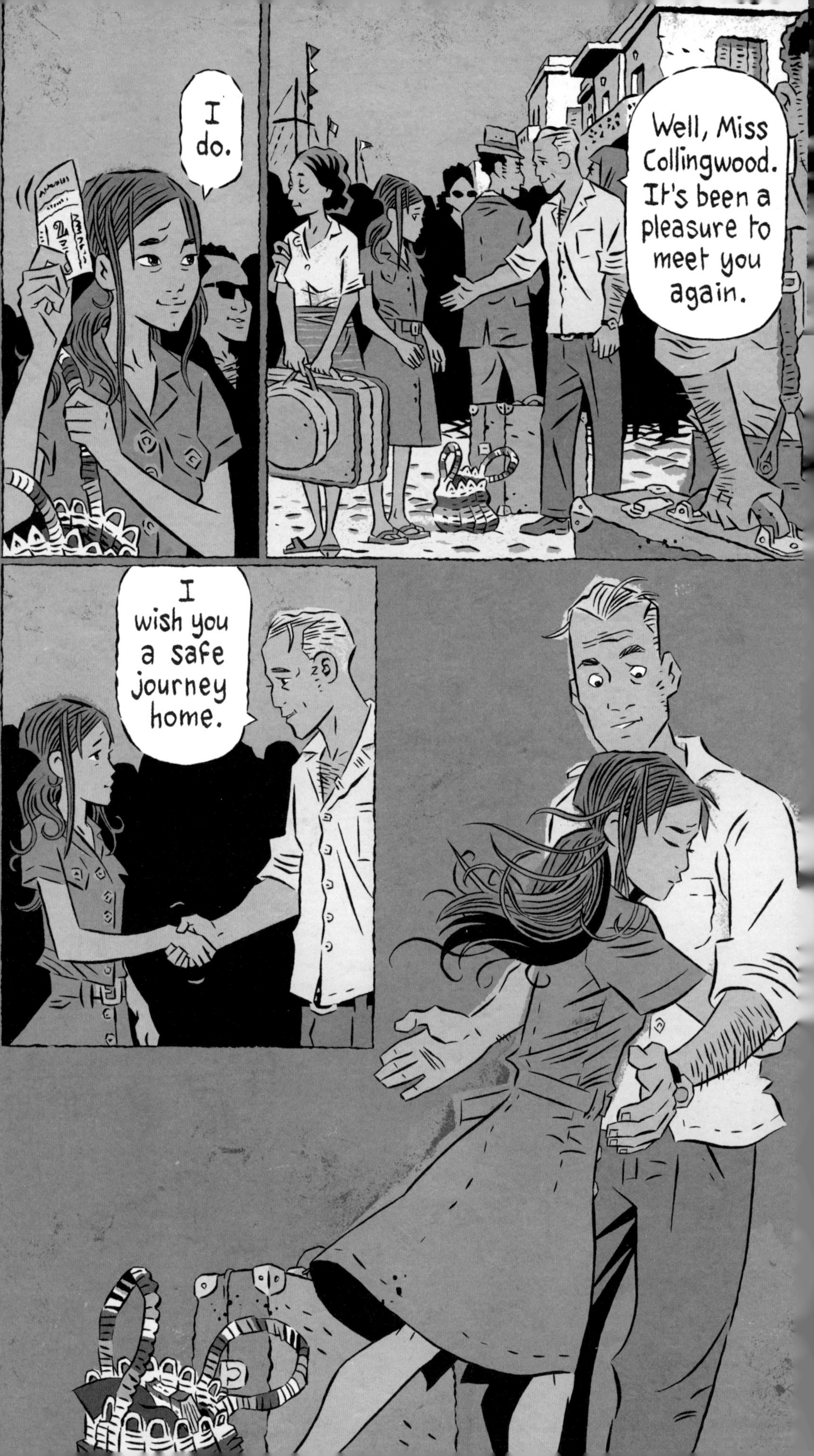
I do.
Well, Miss Collingwood. It's been a pleasure to meet you again.
I wish you a safe journey home.

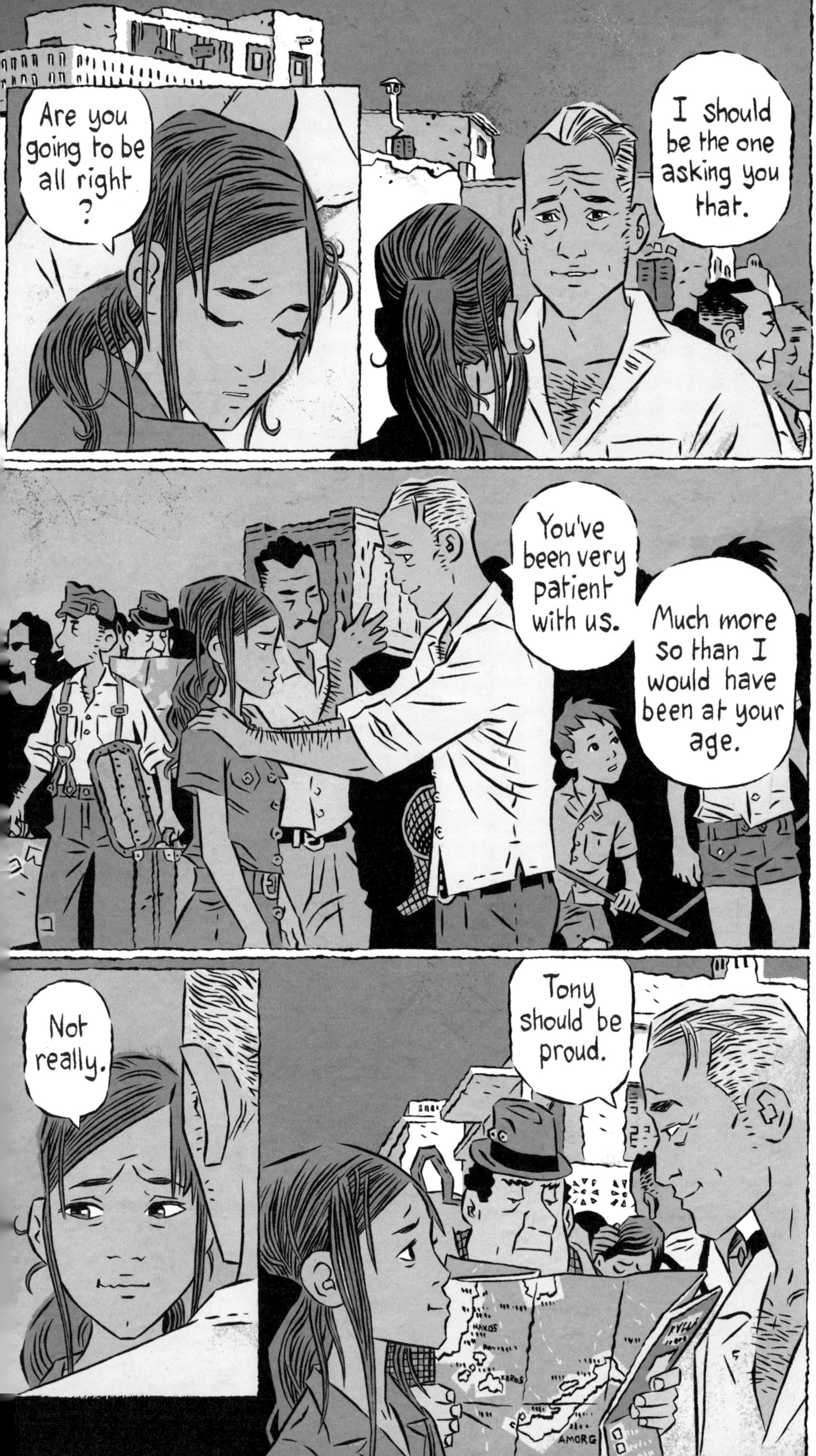
Are you going to be all right?
I should be the one asking you that.
You've been very patient with us.
Much more so than I would have been at your age.
Not really.
Tony should be proud.

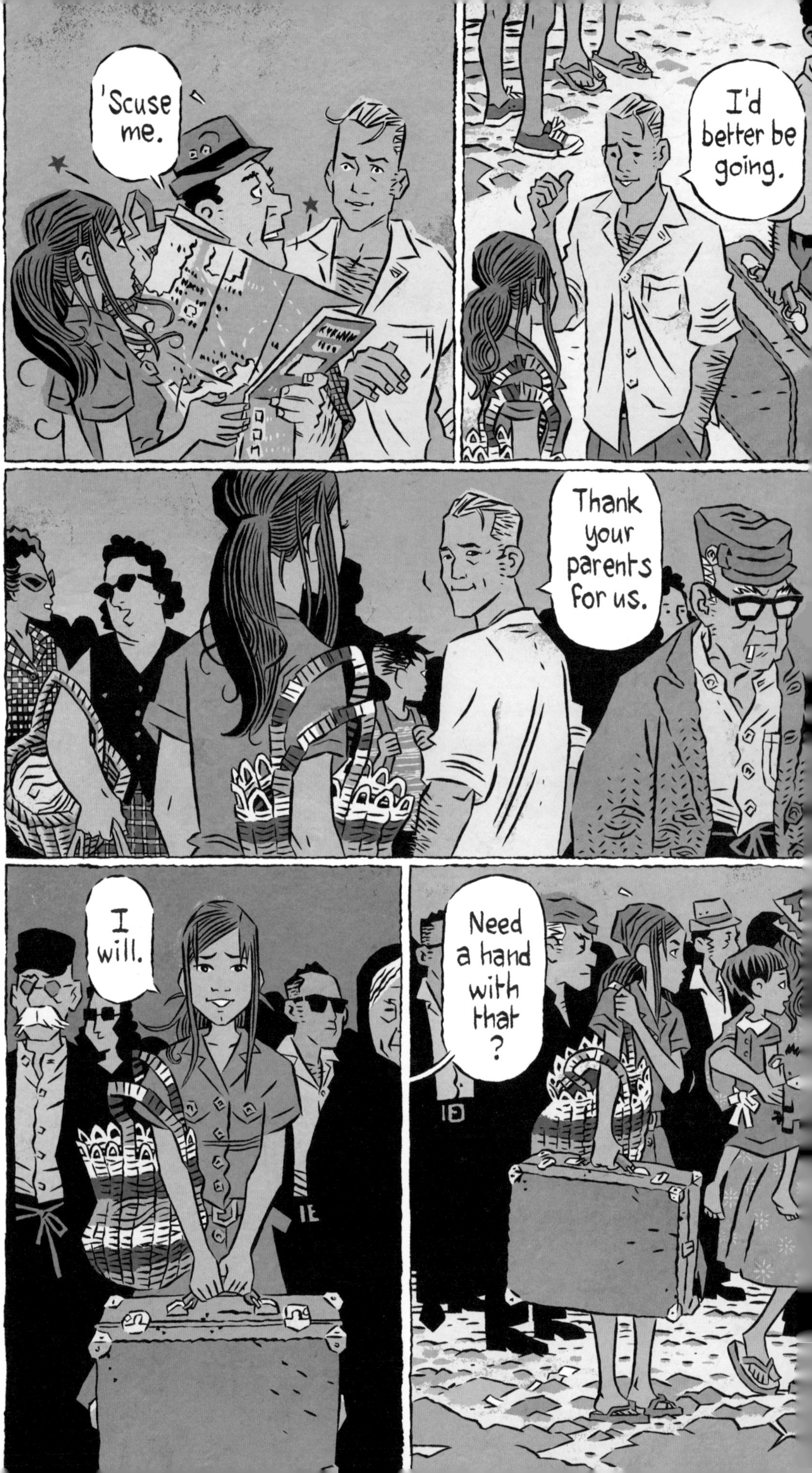
'Scuse me.
I'd better be going.
Thank your parents for us.
I will.
Need a hand with that?

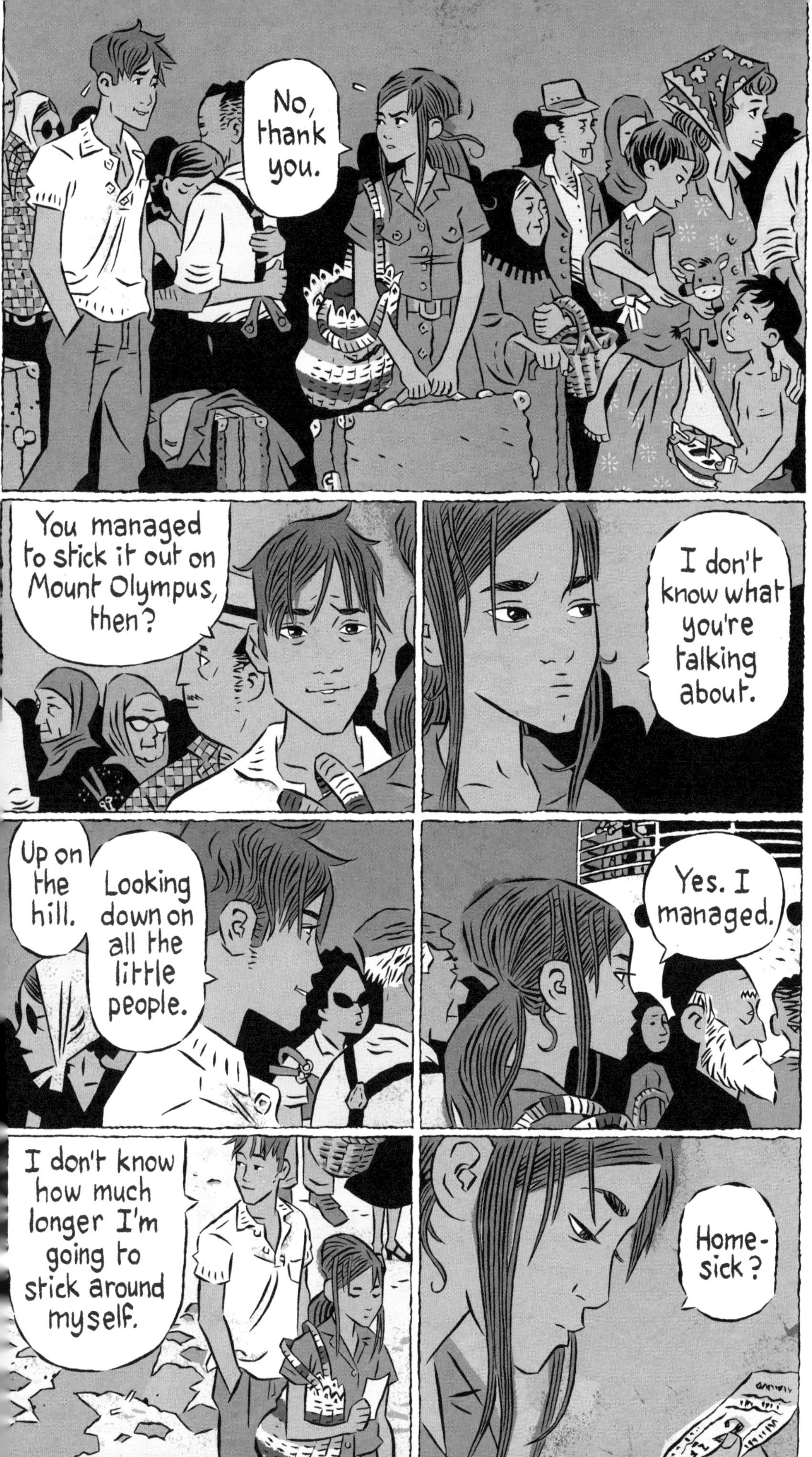
No, thank you.
You managed to stick it out on Mount Olympus, then?
I don't know what you're talking about.
Up on the hill.
Looking down on all the little people.
Yes. I managed.
I don't know how much longer I'm going to stick around myself.
Home-sick?

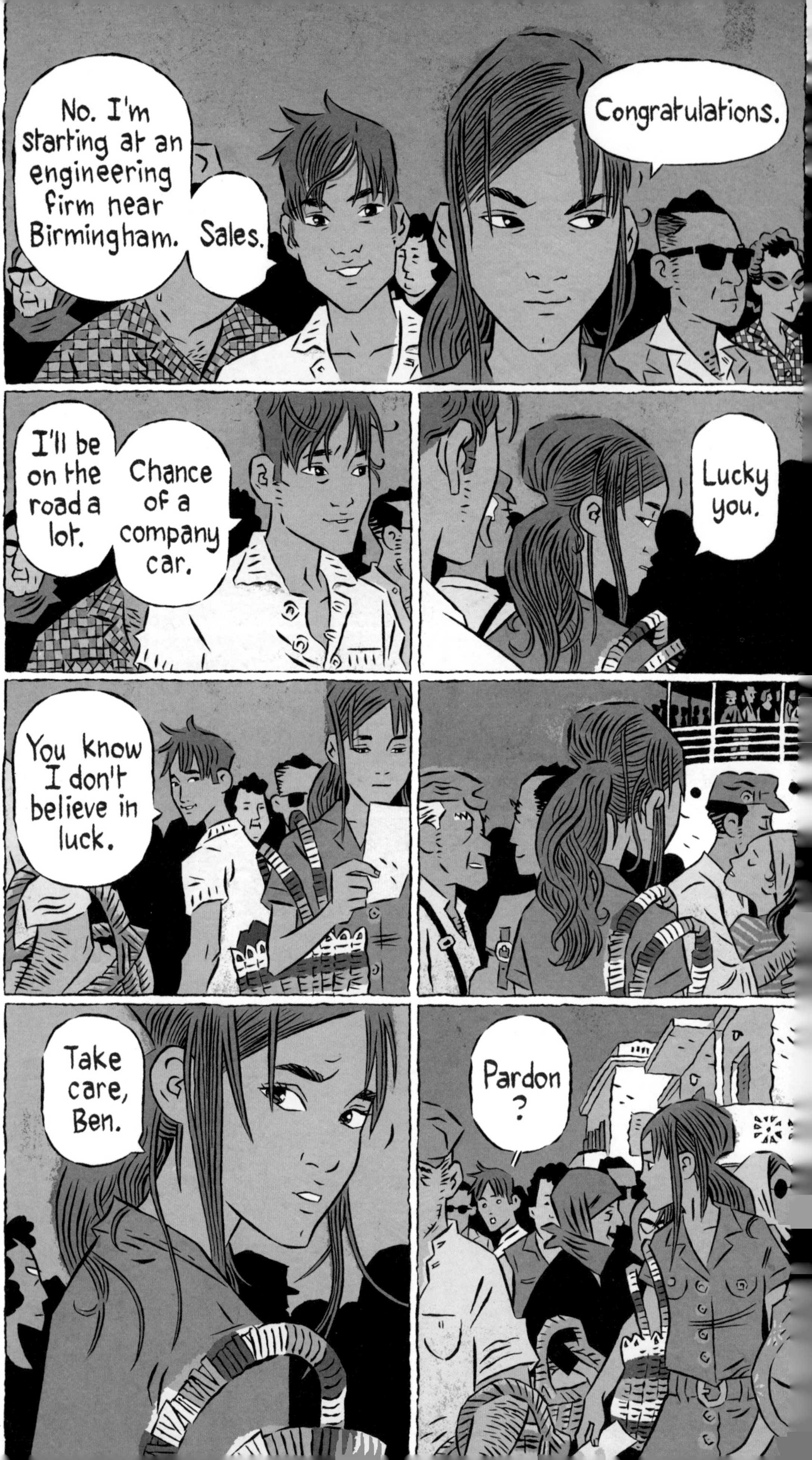
No. I'm starting at an engineering firm near Birmingham.
Sales.
Congratulations.
I'll be on the road a lot.
Chance of a company car.
Lucky you.
You know I don't believe in luck.
Take care, Ben.
Pardon?

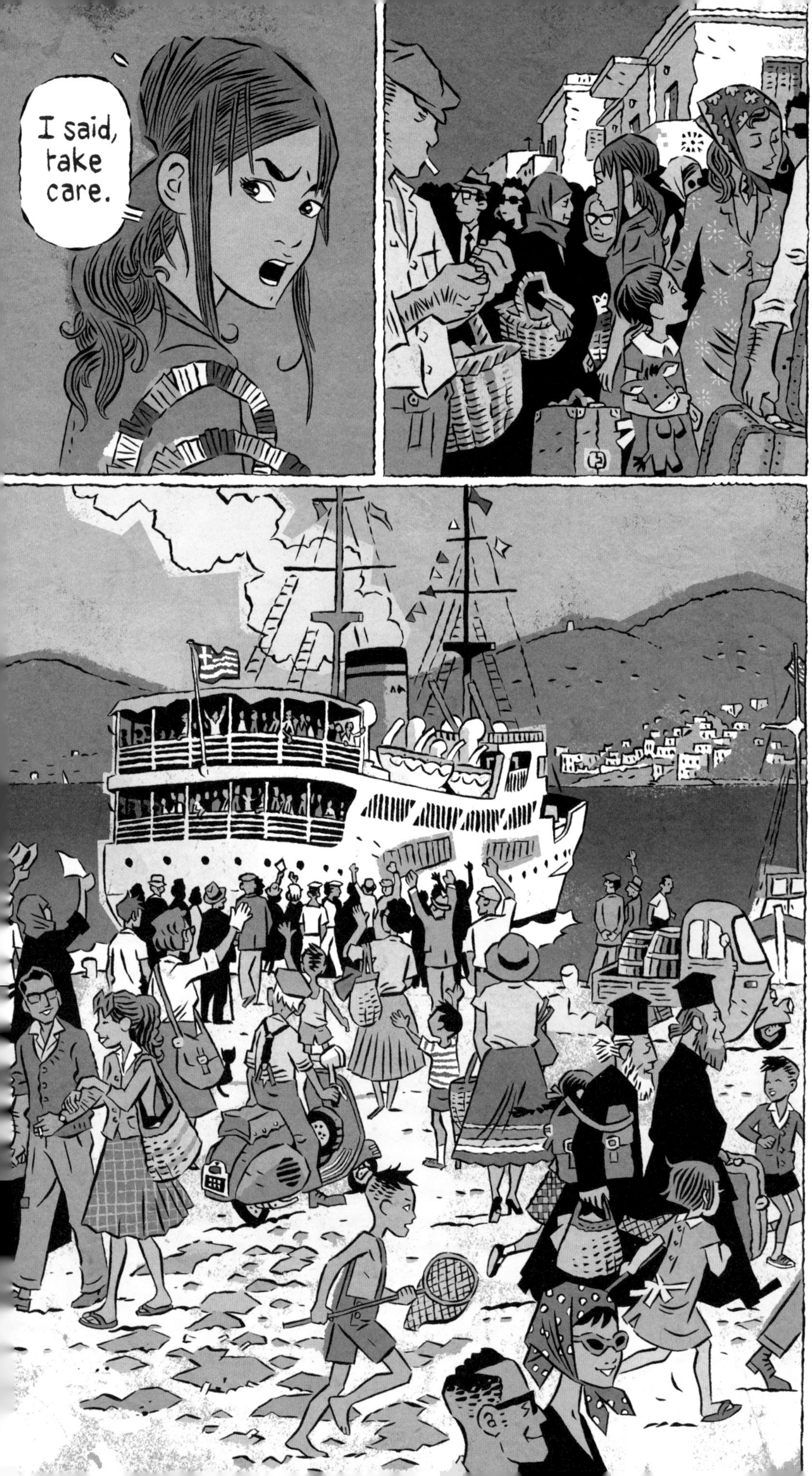
I said, take care.

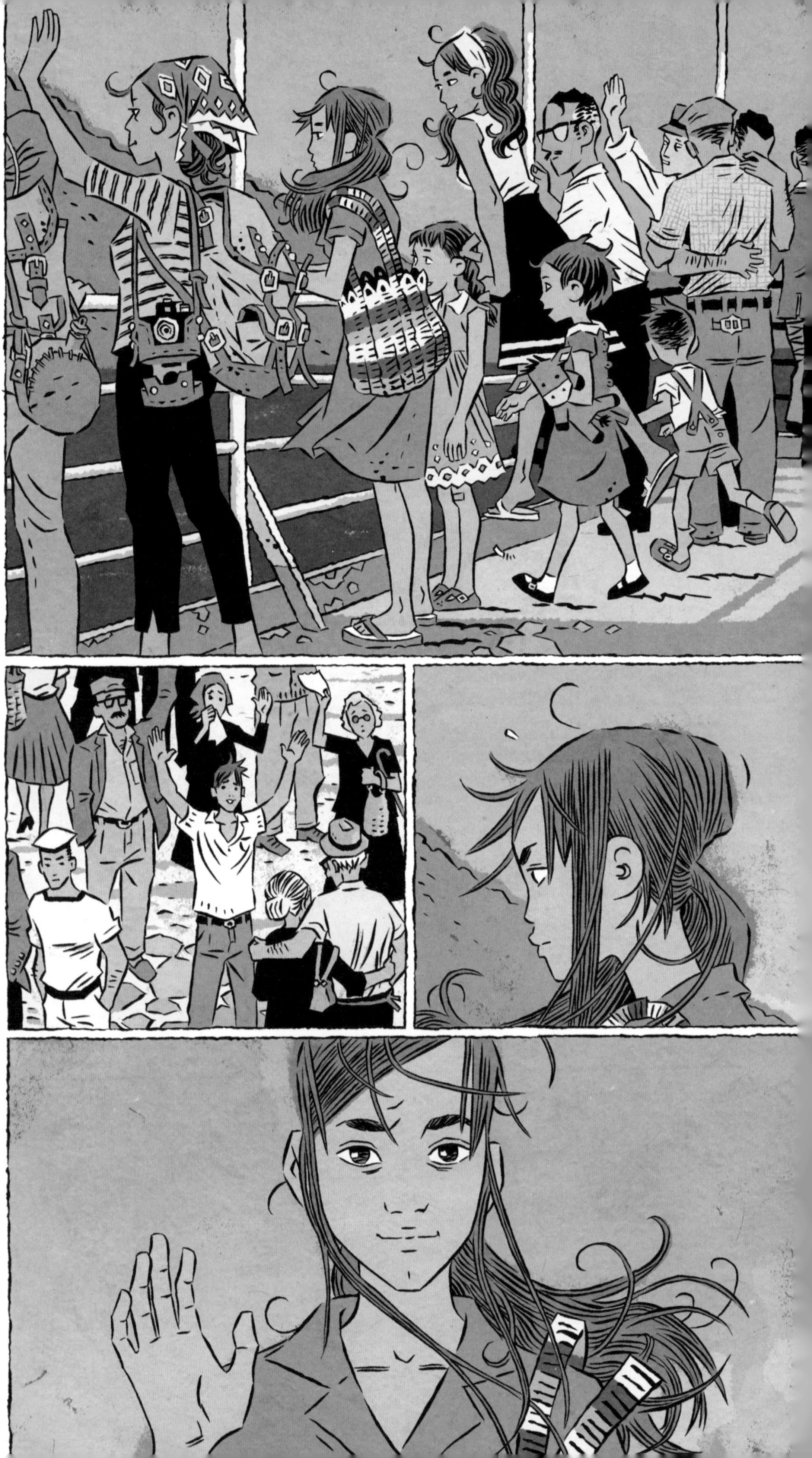

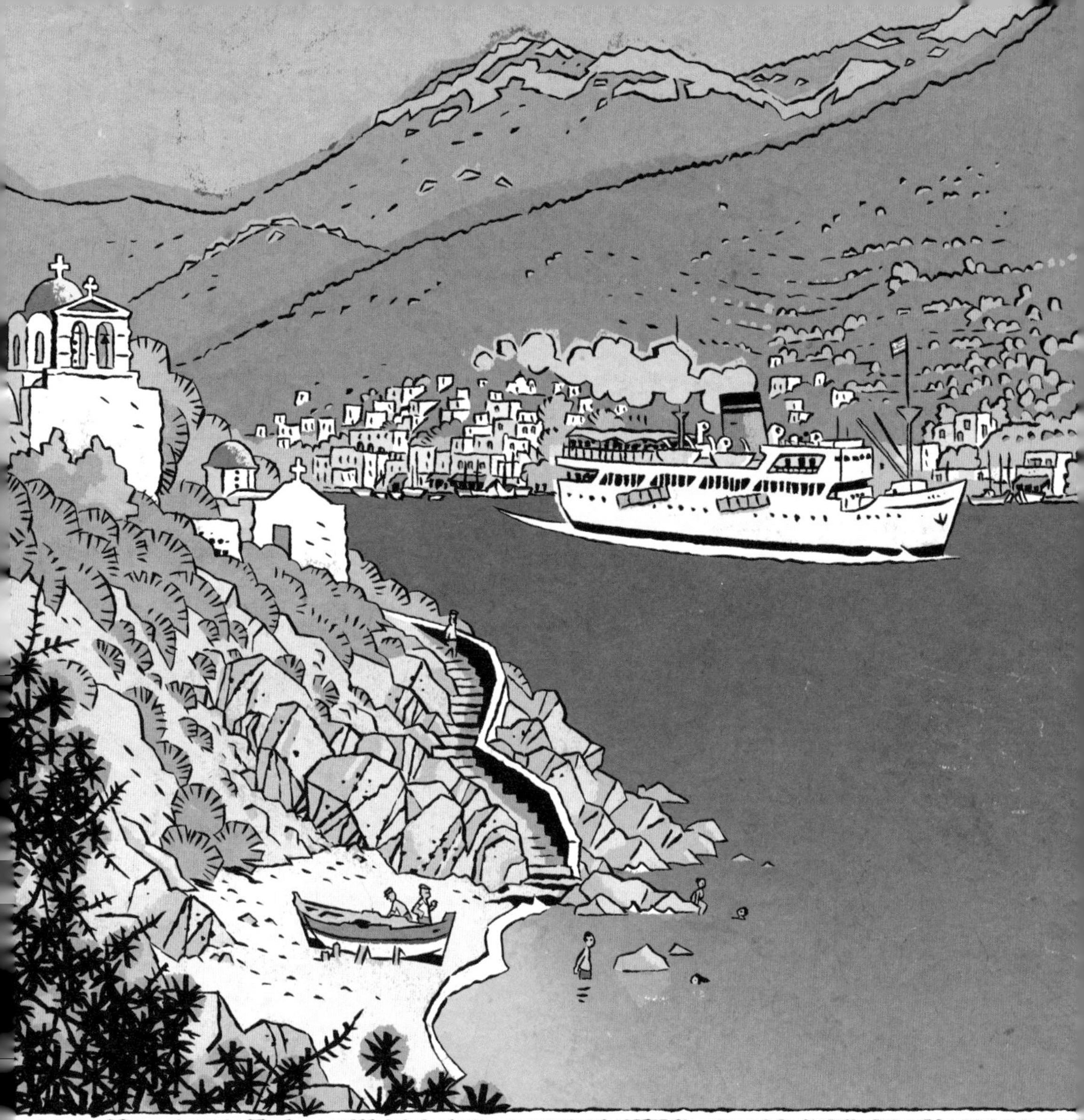
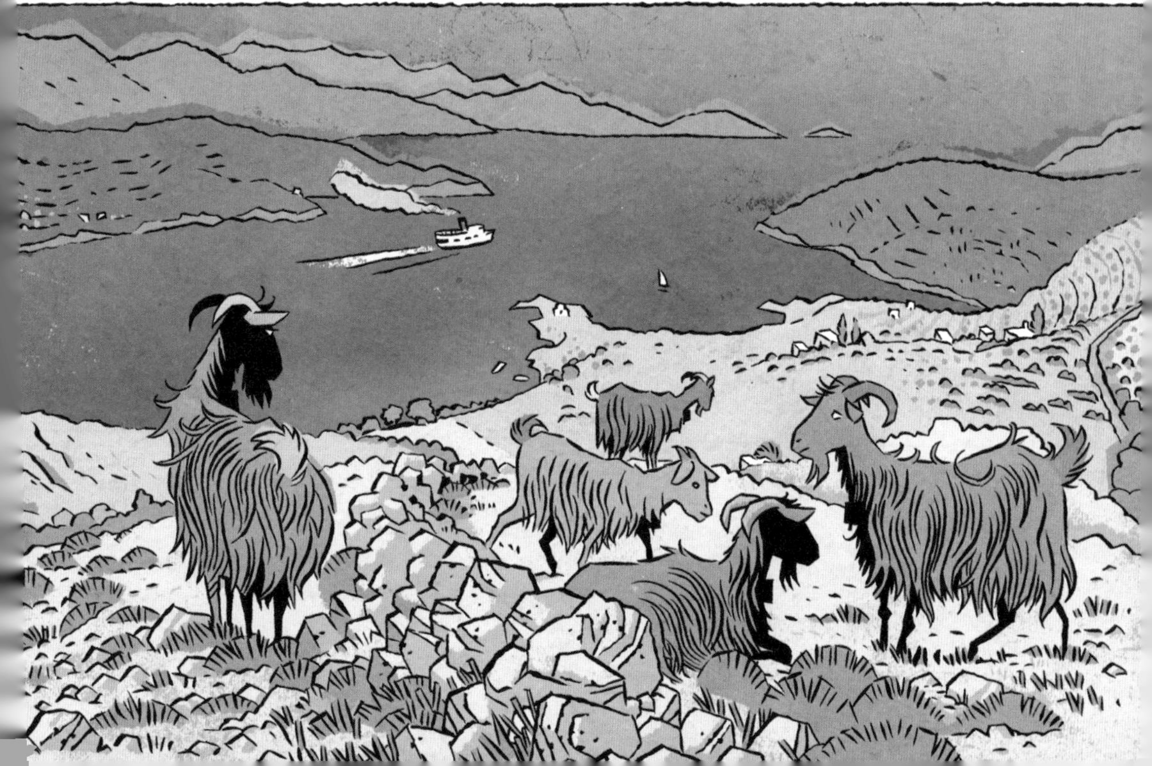

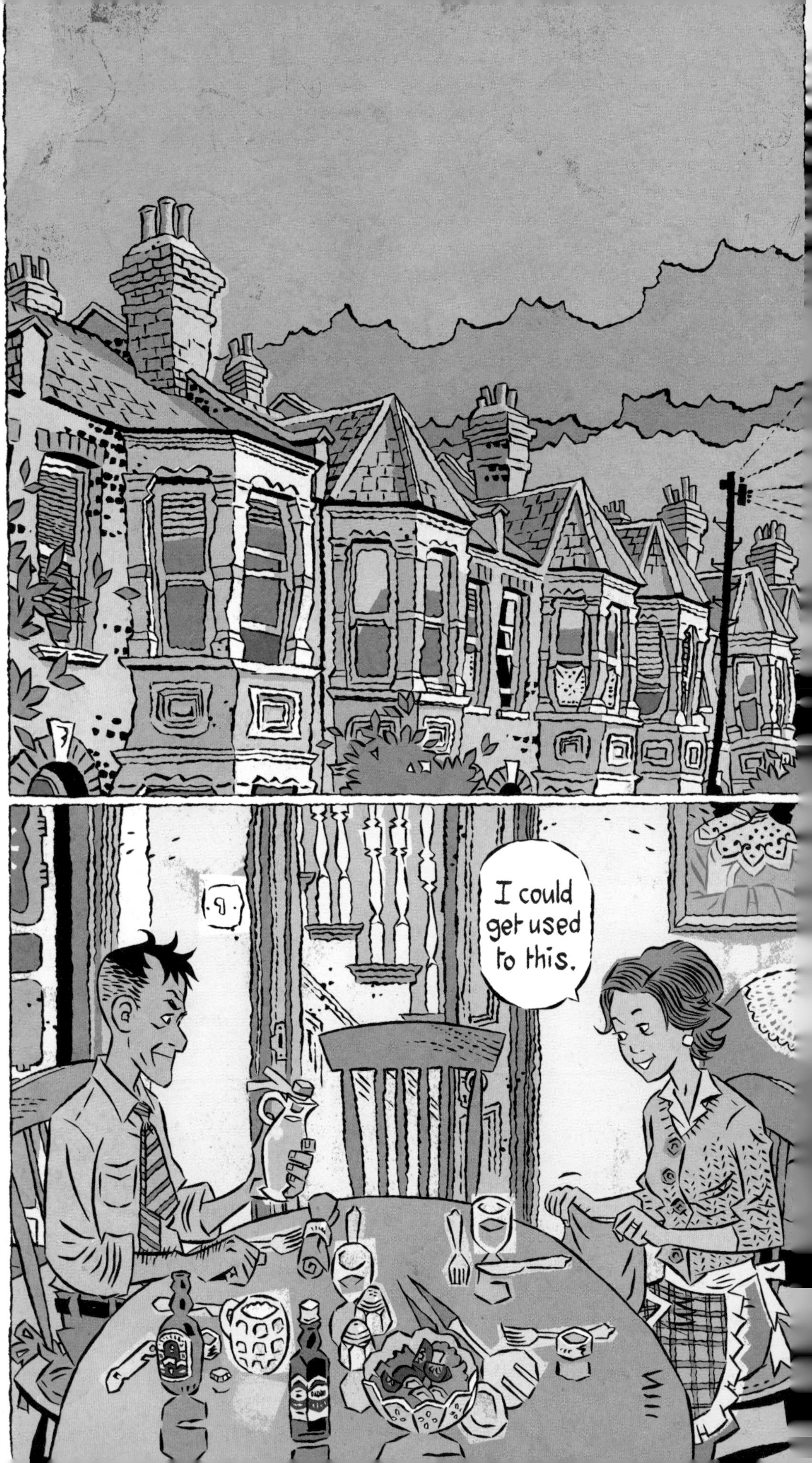
I could get used to this.

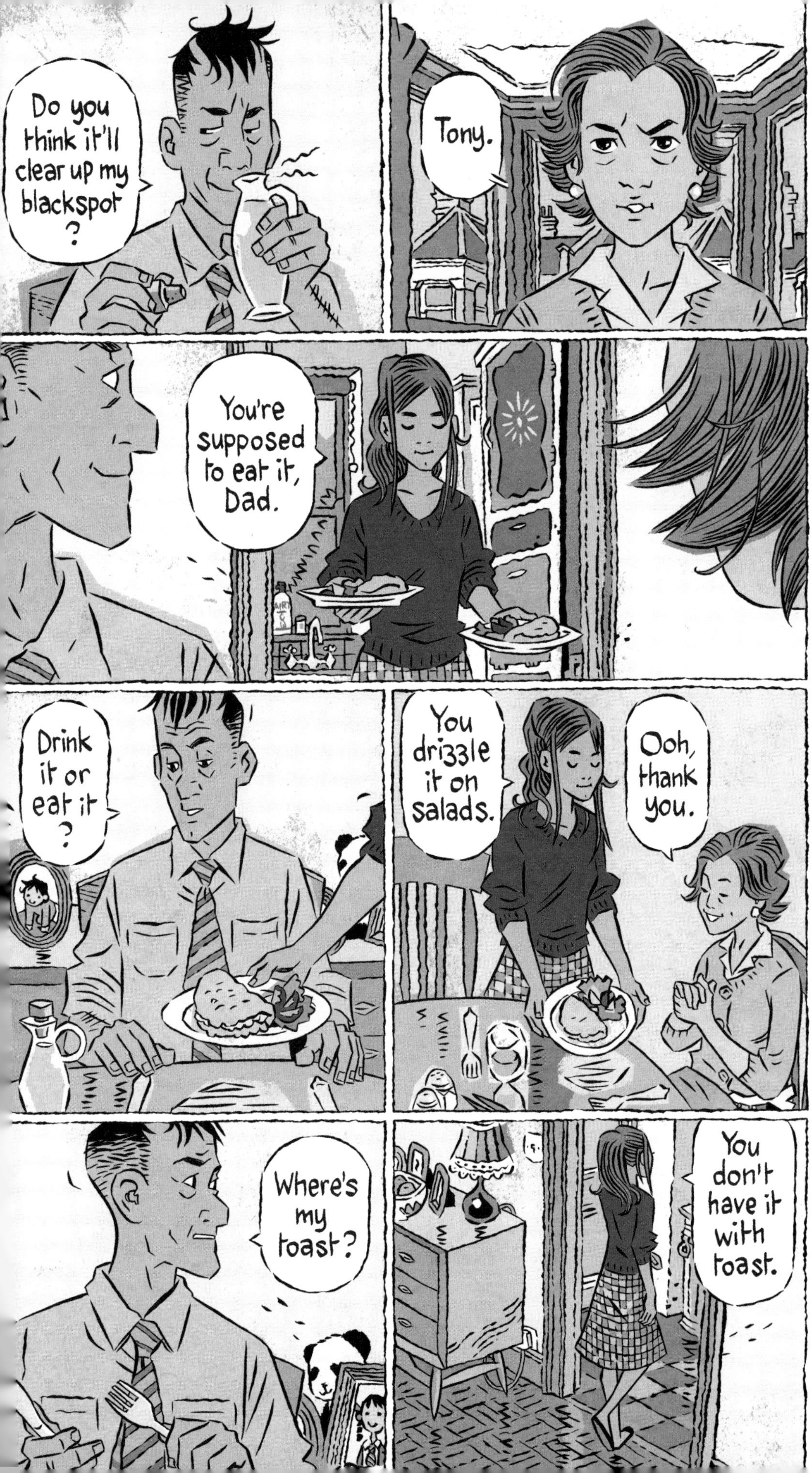
Do you think it'll clear up my blackspot?
Tony.
You're supposed to eat it, Dad.
Drink it or eat it?
You drizzle it on salads.
Ooh, thank you.
Where's my toast?
You don't have it with toast.

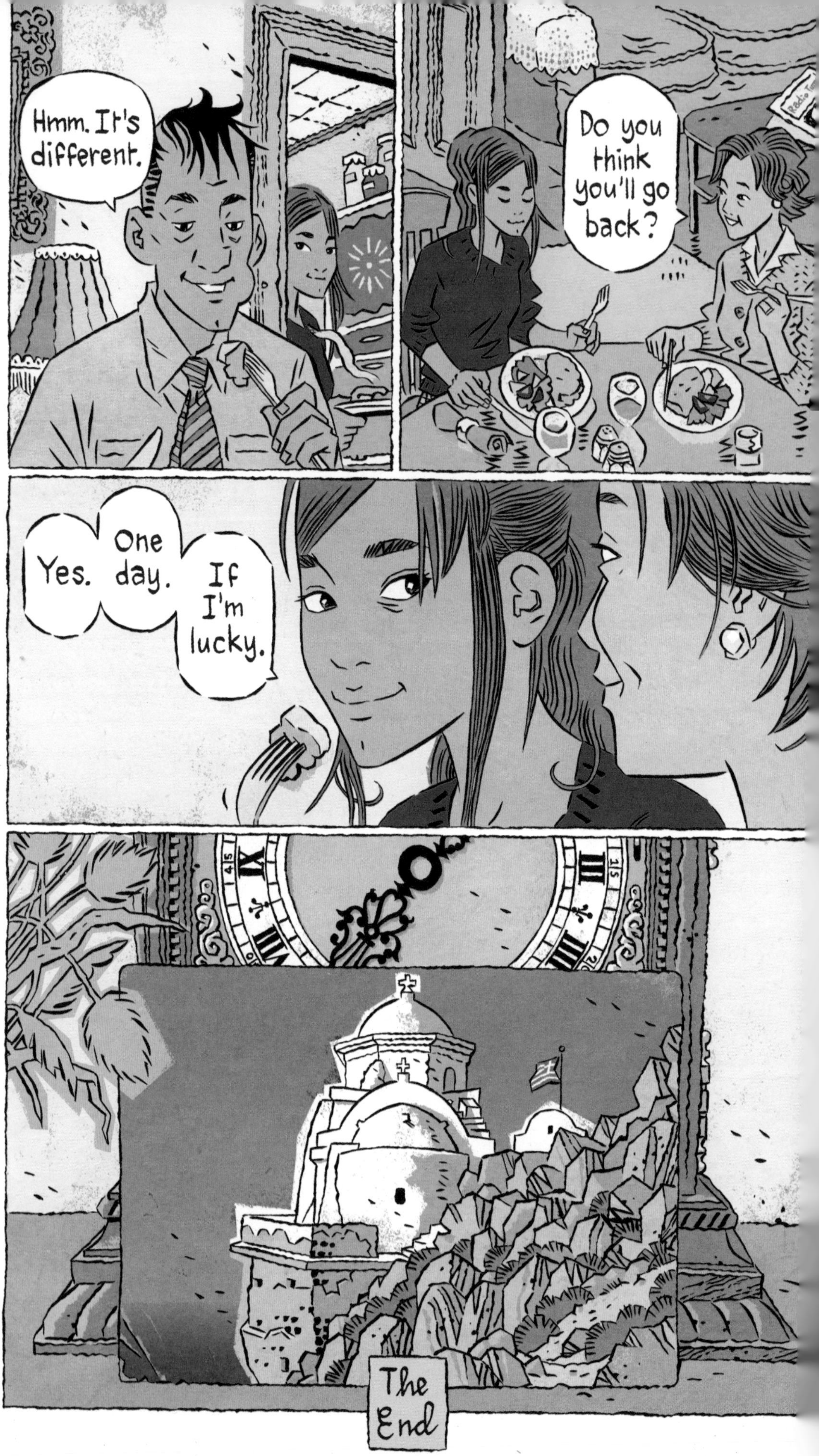
Hmm. It's different.
Do you think you'll go back?
Yes.
One day.
If I'm lucky.
The End

ANDI WATSON

Andi's other books include: *The Book Tour* from Top Shelf, *Kerry and the Knight of the Forest* from Random House Graphic, *Glister* from Dark Horse, the forthcoming *Punycorn* from Clarion and *Paris*, also in collaboration with Simon and published by Image Comics.
Site: andiwatson.info | Twitter/Instagram: @andicomics

SIMON GANE

Simon's other comics include: *They're Not Like Us, Godzilla, Ghost Tree* and *Paris*, also in collaboration with Andi and published by Image Comics.
Twitter: @simongane | Instagram: @simonjgane

LOCATIONS

This is not intended to be an accurate portrayal of a specific Greek island, or life on them, but rather to convey the beauty of the region, still very much in evidence today. The locations are based on the Cycladic islands of Amorgos, Serifos, Kythnos, Folegandros, Anafi, Kimolos, Sifnos and Sikinos and on Skyros in the Sporades (pictured here).

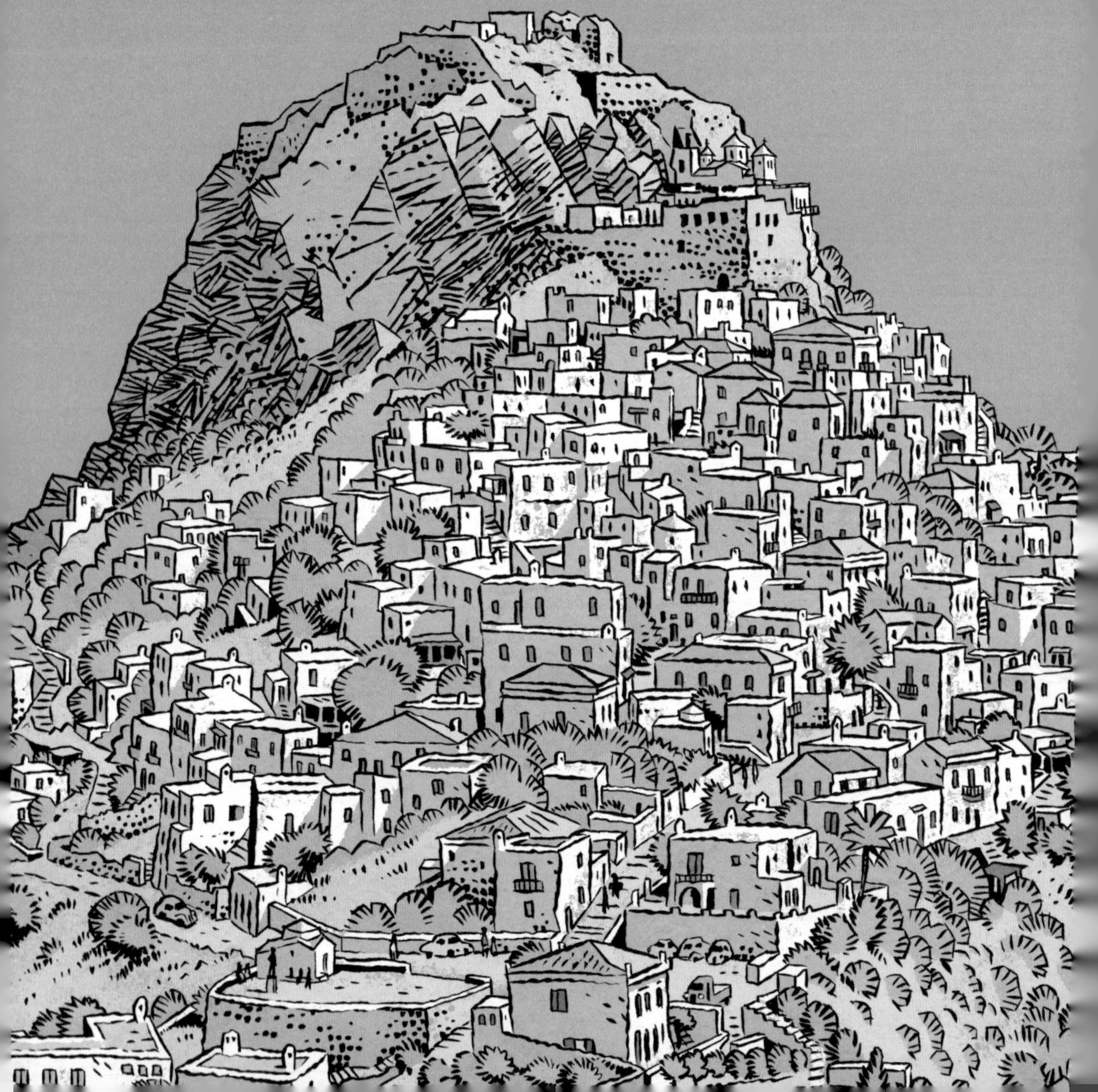